Dying Breath

LIZ MISTRY

ONE PLACE. MANY STORIES

HQ
An imprint of HarperCollins*Publishers* Ltd
1 London Bridge Street
London SE1 9GF

www.harpercollins.co.uk

HarperCollins*Publishers*
1st Floor, Watermarque Building, Ringsend Road
Dublin 4, Ireland

This paperback edition 2022

1
First published in Great Britain by
HQ, an imprint of HarperCollins*Publishers* Ltd 2022

ISBN: 9780008532499

To my family, as always, for all that you do and all that you are. And also, this time, to poor wee Winky, who died late last year.

When he saw the blood, it was as though he had drunk a deep draught of savage passion. He fixed his eyes upon the scene and took in all its frenzy ... He watched and cheered and grew hot with excitement.

St Augustine *Confessions* 6.8

January

Sunday

Prologue

With her heart hammering against her chest, her feet pounded the uneven ground. Snow fell in thick horizontal lines, drenching her as it soaked into her inadequate clothing. But she was thankful for it, as in this stark unfamiliar wilderness, it was only the snow and darkness that concealed her. Her jeans, heavy with moisture, wrapped her thighs like icy tentacles. Her hair dripped glacial droplets which unerringly found their way down the gap between her soaked scarf and the back of her sodden coat. Shivers rocked her body; still, she continued, slipping and sliding forwards over the rugged ground, aiming for a small grouping of trees in the distance that might offer cover. She muttered words of encouragement to herself under her breath as she ran. Whistles and whoops echoed eerily through the murky night as she tried to get her bearings, but with only the moon casting light over the unfamiliar terrain and her vision obscured by the sleet, she was lost. Erratic flashes of activity far in front of her and to the side drew her attention as she strained to make sense of them. Torches flickered, indistinguishable shadows flitted, restless shapes inexorably moved towards her, surrounding her – and not one of them was friendly. Deep in her gut she knew she was on her own, with her pursuers catching up. She glanced behind, seeking out the menacing looming figures drawing closer with every second. Then, the taunt pierced the night air.

'Little girl come out to play. Today's the day, I'll make you pay.'

Five Days Earlier

Tuesday

Chapter 1

'Get the bloody things in the cages, right now. I didn't spend all this time sorting out the gig for you lot to fuck it up last minute.'

Jacko watched as the boss yelled at Calhoun and Knox, the men he paid handsomely to transport the animals to the grounds. His yells prompted a chorus of frenzied barking from inside the outbuilding where they stood and the two young lads cast anxious glances towards the door. No wonder. Fugly's raised voice had roused the hounds of hell and now they'd be even more difficult to handle.

His gap-toothed grin betrayed how he revelled in the sounds from behind the men. The bastard knew full well what he'd done, and Jacko suspected *that* was his intention. What Fugly lacked in height, he made up for in meanness. Tanned and balding, he wouldn't win any beauty contests, but then again, the only contest the short-arse was interested in was making money and subjecting his employees to his own unique brand of pure nastiness. Jacko rolled his neck, trying to release the tension that gathered across his shoulders. He'd never had this bother before he began working for old Fugly here. He grinned. That was a term he'd picked up from his grand-sprog. Little minx thought she could get off with it because she didn't actually use the 'f' word. His granddaughter really did make him laugh. Not that Jacko would ever call him Fugly to his face.

His neck creaked and groaned as he manipulated it, hoping to offset the headache that throbbed almost continually in his temple. He was constantly fighting to keep on his boss's good side. *Suppose our similar ages helped with that one.* Still, some of the crap Jacko turned a blind eye on made him grumpy. Even the grandkid said so.

As Fugly moved away from the men, he failed to notice their angry eyes or the glares they sent him. No, Fugly was too damn arrogant to realise that his men despised him. Or more likely, the short-arse didn't care. It was only the promise of being paid well that guaranteed their loyalty. That and the fear factor of never knowing what the fucking psycho would do next.

Fugly marched over to Jacko, a wide sneering grin on his ugly face as he spoke, his voice loud so the lads would hear. 'Can't get decent fucking workers these days, eh, Jacko?'

'You're not wrong there, boss.' Inside, Jacko cringed at his arse-licking tone. When Fugly had continued past, Jacko shrugged, rolled his eyes at the men whose shoulders slumped like they'd been beaten, jerked his head at Fugly's back and mouthed the word 'tosser' in their direction, adding the universal hand gesture for emphasis. If the shit hit the fan, Jacko didn't want to be too closely aligned with Fugly. Not with his increasingly out-of-control behaviour. Grins broke out on their faces and the slump to their shoulders lessened. With a final smiling nod, Jacko took off after Fugly, glad he'd connected with the lads. It was harder for him to connect with the girls Fugly employed. They were too much like his own daughter for him to be comfortable that they'd become involved in this crap. Jacko wanted to keep a foot planted in each camp so that when the time came, when the boss's plans became progressively more flamboyant and risky, he'd have allies. It might be sooner than he thought.

Fugly turned and waited for him to catch up. His voice sounded out again, cold and hard. 'Come on! What you waiting for? It's time to rock and roll.'

As he strutted away from the lads, trusting them to get the job done, Jacko moderated his strides to Fugly's shorter ones. The boss's phone rang and he slowed, before pulling it from his jacket pocket. 'Give me the juice.'

A dutiful servant, Jacko paused beside him, pretending not to listen as the boss ranted on to his bookie, making sure he was racking up the bids. He'd already confided the finer details of his operation to Jacko over a few whiskies the other week. This would be a *big* money-earner. Fugly's contacts had worked hard to advertise it. They'd got bookies bidding against one another and each animal's condition report was circulated via the dark web. Fugly had even arranged paid online viewings as well as in-person spectators. Jacko didn't understand it. Some of these blokes seemed to get off on the smell of blood and animal testosterone and as long as there was dosh to be made, Fugly was all for that. Jacko found it distasteful, but he needed the job, so he kept his head down and did whatever Fugly ordered.

Tonight's fight was going to be not only the biggest Yorkshire had ever witnessed, but would also include the boss's little 'added bonus' to make it extra special. The very thought of it curdled Jacko's stomach. It was sick stuff indeed, but now he was in too deep with no escape plan – not without risking his life.

Fugly was determined to capitalise on the fight, and he didn't care who he hurt in the process. He was talking about the police now, and Jacko's ears pricked up. The last thing Jacko wanted was to be arrested, but that might be preferable to this mess. Maybe he should throw himself at the police's mercy. But that was a no-go. Fugly had a sixth sense about these things. If he got even a whiff that Jacko was wavering, he'd feed him to the fucking dogs.

'Course I know all about Operation Sandglass. Do you think I'm an idiot? I don't care if the pigs are on my tail, this fight's too big, too economically important to delay. It's all part of the bigger plan and there's no way we're deviating from that.'

He stopped and Jacko nearly bumped into him, but stopped himself in time, although he stood in a bloody puddle. Ended up with his new trainers soaked and still Fugly ranted on and on. The poor guy on the line must have been dying to slam the phone down, but he wouldn't dare, not with so much at stake. Besides, after what the boss did to that young lass the other night, it would take a brave – or foolish – man to challenge him. Jacko was unsure if the girl would walk again. The memory of the kneecapping, using that home-made cudgel, lurked like a foul smell at the back of his mind, no matter how hard he tried to shove the thoughts away. It was the girl's screams that were the worst. They were like an animal in pain and Jacko thought it would be a kindness to put her out of her misery. At least Fugly didn't let loose on the lad as much – reserved his fury for the lass, didn't he? Jacko didn't know why the girl got the brunt of Fugly's demented ire and there was no way he was going to ask him. Still, that other kid was still with them, chained up beside the dogs. Jacko had snuck the kid a blanket when he'd checked on him later because he wasn't sure he'd have survived the freezing temperatures otherwise.

When Fugly – overalls all blood splattered – went indoors to shower, Jacko and two other kids had wrapped the moaning, almost unconscious girl in cellophane and loaded her into the boot of a car before dumping her at Pinderfields Hospital, hoping that someone would find her before it was too late. Petrified of being found out, they'd told Fugly she'd copped it and that they'd torched the van with her inside near Sheffield. *No way can they trace it back to us. No way.* Jacko glanced at Fugly as if scared his boss could read his thoughts, but he was still yapping on the phone.

'We've got extra precautions in place. My men are on the ball and have every angle covered.'

Hmph, that was true. Fugly's security thugs could easily spot a trap a mile off. They'd alert the boss if anything looked off, but short-arse didn't expect that tonight, and neither did Jacko. They'd dropped too many misleading breadcrumbs, and Jacko was sure that the bribes the boss paid would have assisted in that. Moving away from him, Jacko lit up a cig. He could still hear him, but it was good to have a bit of space. As if sensing Jacko's need for a breather, Fugly turned. His lips formed the same snarling grin that made the younger kids shit themselves. Funnily enough, it was the girls who were the toughest. They barely gave Fugly an inch. Looked at him, all insolent and stuff. Maybe they were hiding behind their tattoos, dyed hair and piercings, Jacko didn't know. But whatever prompted their attitude, it pissed the boss off.

Jacko held the smoke in his lungs, ignoring the burning as he waited to see if the boss was going to explode. Had the bookie annoyed him? But then his shoulders relaxed, and he winked at Jacko before turning aside. The smoke drifted through Jacko's nostrils and, for a moment, he felt light-headed, but it wasn't from the nicotine. Shit, that was a close one. The boss was edgier than he'd been all week, and Jacko knew to keep his head down and just do what he was told. But sometimes those other idiots didn't seem to realise it. Sometimes those wankers thought that being on the other end of a phone, meant they could say what they liked, get away with a bit of cheek. *Fuck!* Didn't they understand that with tonight creeping up on them so quickly, everyone's principal aim should be to keep Fugly happy?

'The vet's assured me the animals are …'

Blah, blah, blah! On and on he went. Jacko was freezing. He wanted to be indoors next to the fire. Have a cup-a-soup to warm him up, but Fugly stood there, yapping on, kicking at little bits of ice with his wellies. He was right though. The boss *had* located some choice animals – well trained ones. He'd sourced some illegally bred American Pitbull terriers and the punters were wild for those. Jacko and the kids had each of them on the treadmill for two hours per day, along with time on tyre exercises, and they were in peak condition. The boss expected an exciting round of fights this evening and he'd done his best to make sure that would happen. Jacko wasn't happy about his job, but he had little option. Covid had put the kybosh on a lot of his usual money-making activities and he'd managed to spend most of his savings. Despite being resourceful, his finances were dwindling. Which was why, although not to his taste, Jacko had ended up here working for a short-arsed psycho.

He shivered and sniffed the air. More snow was coming, which was a damn pity. The weather had been crap for days now and that was the one thing nobody could control. However, the boss had contingency plans. The moors were a great place for this sort of stuff – especially in winter, and as long as Jacko did everything Fugly asked, they'd be able to transport the punters from the lower points right up to the fight site. Flicking his fag end away, Jacko did a last mental run through his responsibilities. Fugly insisted on heaters to make sure that despite the freezing temperatures, his 'clients' would be warm and Jacko had supervised their transportation yesterday, adding another generator. Fucking machine weighed a ton.

The booze was also already on site. Alcohol, warmth and plenty of tension would be enough to guarantee the boss's pleasure. This was why he and the boss had spent so much time on the damn wind- and snow-swept moors recently. The boss, when he was in one of his good moods, kept singing some stupid song about a bloke called Heathcliff and his bint, Cathy. Maybe if the old fascist had a Cathy to keep *him* warm, he wouldn't be such a bastard to everyone else. Jacko snorted. He doubted that a woman would calm Fugly's temper. Just as well he was single if his attitude to the lassies were anything to go on.

The deep laughter of the guy on the end of the line reached Jacko's ears as the boss set his phone on speaker and placed it on an old barrel to roll himself a ciggie. Jacko imagined the bookie rubbing his hands together, like some bloody old banker

– or should that be wanker? Either would suit the bill. Cringing, Jacko wished the caller was more deferential to Fugly, for all their sakes. 'The turnout's gonna be good. At least a hundred, a hundred-fifty and they're expecting a show. Hope you can give them what they want.'

The boss licked the paper to seal his rollie and his eyes narrowed, the snarling grin back on his lips. Jacko stood stock still, waiting for the explosion as he glanced at the barking dogs, straining and barrelling themselves against the metal bars of their cages, the lads rattling the bars with poles to keep them on their toes. It was only him and the boss that knew about 'the little added extra'. Something that the boss thought would go down well with some of the more, in his words, 'adventurous' clients. When he replied, his voice was frigid. 'Leave the show to me. *Your* job is to get the punters on board. Leave the rest to me and we'll be quid's in.'

The bookie, oblivious to the thinness of the ice on which he was walking, continued. 'You'll need …'

The boss tutted, his face flushed and shoulders tensed as he raised himself up to a combative posture. 'I'm in charge, and you need to bear that in mind.'

Eyes narrowed, he scowled and injected even more ice into his tone. 'Stick in your own lane, lad, or perhaps I'll put *you* in the ring with one of my best.'

For a moment, there was silence. Then an edgy half-laugh filtered down the line. 'Good one, boss. Yeah, you're the man. I'll stick to my job.'

The boss grinned and sent another wink in Jacko's direction. Message delivered. Swallowing the sick burning his throat, Jacko grinned back, thankful that, for now at least, the boss's temper was assuaged. 'You do that. Oh, and so we're clear, I expect tonight to be a success otherwise …' He laughed. 'Well, let's just say, that last threat won't be so idle after all, eh? Hate to see you lose a limb if we can avoid it.'

Chapter 2

The last thing DS Nikki Parekh needed when she got home was a family drama. It had been an early start followed by an emotional and exhausting day and she had the uneasy feeling that both Sajid, her reliable detective constable, and her boss, DCI Archie Hegley, were keeping something from her. Unfortunately, her daughter, Charlie, had other ideas.

'For God's sake, can't we just loosen up a bit now? I'm fed up with having Ali or Haris or one of their Neanderthal henchmen breathing down my neck all the time. I want some freedom. It's been *weeks* since you heard anything from your *dad*.' Charlie threw the word dad out as she flung herself onto the couch and glared at her parents.

Nikki's mouth went dry, and her earlier tiredness seemed to seep even further into her limbs, draining what little energy remained. *Not now Charlie! Please not now. Not when I'm so damn knackered.* With a desperate look at Marcus, she swallowed. Against Marcus's better judgement, Nikki, in an attempt not to frighten her family, had withheld the information that Downey's postcards continued to arrive every few days with regular monotony. Concealed in their oh-so-ordinary envelopes, sometimes he addressed them to her home and occasionally he sent them to Trafalgar House police station, where she worked, but they always contained a threatening message like: *I'm back. Your choice – who's next, you or your sister?* Or: *I'm back. Your choice – who's next, you or one of the kids?* Or: *I'm back. Your choice – who's next, you or your poofter partner?* Or: *I'm back. Your choice – who's next, you or your fuck buddy?*

As if that wasn't bad enough, each successive postmark suggested Downey was making his way closer to Bradford – nearer to those Nikki loved. They'd started off postmarked from Venezuela and then he appeared to have moved to Thailand, which was reassuringly distant from Yorkshire. Then, after Christmas, Downey seemed to have returned to Venezuela and had sent another with a Venezuelan postmark followed by others postmarked in Algeria, Italy and France. Downey was like a demon breathing down her neck, yet just out of sight, out of her reach.

The most recent and also the most chilling one was the postcard that arrived addressed to Isaac, at the Lazy Bites café only two weeks ago. Nikki's mum had kept an eye out for the lad after his mum died and now, because of his vulnerability, Nikki had welcomed him into her home. He was like a second son to Nikki and she was so proud of the way he lived life to the full, especially after he'd been so badly bullied because of his Downs Syndrome the previous year. Isaac had been ecstatic at its 'Thinking of you, see you soon' message, and Nikki hadn't been able to tell him it meant he was in danger. Instead, she'd made sure that there was an increased police patronage of the café and arranged for Isaac to be accompanied to and from work. His flat was secure, but because of Isaac's trusting nature, Nikki couldn't stop worrying about him. He was so easily convinced. All it took to gain his trust was a little bit of kindness. So, in the end, she and Isaac's care worker devised a convoluted story involving refurbishment of the flats and Isaac had moved in with Nikki. This proved beneficial for everybody because Sunni, her youngest child, and Isaac were in *Dr Who* Tardis heaven and Isaac's innate goodness helped ground Nikki.

However, it wasn't these thoughts that caused Nikki to glare open-mouthed at her eldest daughter, unable to summon even a single-word reply. Charlie's use of the term '*dad*' instead of Downey ... or 'that bastard' or 'hell's devil' or any other derogatory moniker had not only stunned her, it had pierced her like a dagger to the heart worsened because someone she loved administered it. It weighed on her mind that she'd not informed the kids of the subtle and some not-so-subtle communications from Downey. Nobody understood better than Nikki how restricting the precautions they'd put in place to protect everyone were, but she'd thought she was doing the right thing. She'd often wondered if they'd been wise to keep the kids, especially Charlie, Ruby and Haqib, out of the loop. In hindsight, the answer 'probably not' flashed neon bright in Nikki's mind. The complacency of not knowing that the most evil person Nikki had ever encountered was getting ever closer to them, lurking in the shadows, had made Charlie rebel. Her eldest daughter was angry and, of course, normal teenage hormones exacerbated everything. Still, they hadn't taken the decision lightly and the venom in Charlie's words made her wonder if they'd have been better upping sticks and moving – changing their identities, creating new lives for themselves elsewhere. That was one solution mooted by both Interpol and 'the powers that be'.

Deep down, though, she and Marcus realised that relocation wasn't an option. They couldn't spend their lives running and looking over their shoulders. It wouldn't be fair to them and it certainly wouldn't be fair to the kids. Their second choice had been for her three children, Isaac, her nephew Haqib and her sister Anika to move to Ramallah to live with Charlie's other grandma for a while. However, that was met with such resounding opposition from everyone, bar Sunni, that they'd caved. No one wanted the upheaval and emotional distress of moving away from everything they knew. So they'd dug their heels in and decided to face whatever was coming their way, albeit with Nikki pulling in any favour she could and putting in place every precaution possible to protect her extended family.

Nikki, Marcus, the kids and Anika had sat down with Nikki's team, including DCI Hegley, DI Zain Ahad, Ali and Haris. Between them, they'd thrashed out a series of precautions and protocols that Nikki and Marcus implemented. Zain Ahad had been crashing in a hotel since his transfer from Manchester to Bradford in November, so, much to Haqib's excitement, he'd moved into a spare room in Anika's spacious terraced home. The knowledge that Anika wasn't living alone and that her lodger was a capable and physically intimidating police officer reassured Nikki and left her to concentrate on protecting her own children.

This was where Ali and Haris had stepped in, with the occasional support of Nikki's team in the form of DC Williams, DC Anwar and her work partner Sajid. Stringent protocols about never being outside alone, always being accompanied by a 'minder', always being escorted to and from school or events were initially exciting for the kids. However, Charlie, and Ruby to a lesser extent, were now chafing against the restrictions.

It was difficult for everyone. Nikki was aware that her team enveloped her in a protective bubble at work, and adapting to having limited 'me' time had been hard. Yet Nikki knew she had to protect herself in order to protect her family. Still, that didn't give Charlie the right to behave like a bitch. *How bloody dare she?*

Thankfully, Marcus stepped into the breach. His new buzz-cut accentuated the wrinkles on his face and made his eyes appear bluer. It also revealed the additional lines and crevices that the last few months had carved into his handsome profile. His taut jaw showed how hard he was struggling to keep a lid on his anger, but somehow he managed, for when he responded, his tone, though cold, was calm. 'No need to be a bitch, Charlie.' He paused, his eyes fixed on Charlie's rebellious ones. 'And there's definitely *no* excuse for referring to that son of a bitch as your mum's dad.'

He stared her out, waiting for her to avert her gaze, before adding, 'He *killed* your grandma, he *abused* your mum, he *murdered* other people, he's a *racist*, a *rapist* and a *paedophile*. Do. Not. Ever. Not. *Ever.* Refer to him as your mum's dad!'

He moved his gaze to encompass Nikki and a small smile slid over his lips – one that made Nikki glow. Made her bask in the warmth of his love, the security and safety he provided as he ended his dressing-down with, '*He* doesn't deserve that honour.'

Charlie's lower lip trembled and her look skirted over Nikki. 'Sorry, Mum. That was mean, and I wanted to hurt you. I am *reeeeally* sorry, it's just …' She shrugged, her eyes filling up. 'It's *so* hard, Mum *and* it's scary. I can *never* forget that he's out there like some bogey man waiting to snatch me or Ruby or Sunni. I *hate* him, I really *fucking* hate him and I wish he was dead. *Dead* as fuck. Dead! Dead! Dead!'

In an instant, Nikki was beside her, gathering Charlie in a hug and rocking her as heart-wrenching tears tore down her eldest daughter's cheeks for what felt like hours. Nikki, her own heart breaking, turned her gaze to Marcus, whose blue eyes reflected her anger and frustration right back at her. Keeping her tone steady, Nikki hugged Charlie tight, relishing having her daughter here safe in her arms. 'I wish he was dead too, Charlie. I wish he was dead, too.'

Marcus nodded, an unspoken understanding passed between them that, until Freddie Downey was dead, they'd have no peace. When Charlie's distress ebbed, Nikki cupped her daughter's face in her hands and kissed her forehead. 'Charlie, I promise you this. I …' She glanced at Marcus and gave a half smile. '*We* will sort this. We *will* get this fixed, but in the meantime, we *need* to stick to the plan. I can't focus on catching him if I'm worried about whether you and the others are safe. *Your* job is to ensure your brother and sister are being careful and that means leading by example. I promise, we'll sort this.'

Despite her tear-stained cheeks, a ghost of a smile flashed

across Charlie's face as she extended her hand to her mum. 'Pinkie promise?'

Nikki grinned and looped her own little finger through her daughter's. 'No, brownie promise.'

When Charlie left the room, Nikki turned to Marcus, a frown marring her forehead. 'Are you convinced she's totally on board?'

Marcus exhaled, then shook his head. 'Not in the slightest. We must keep an eye on her. Charlie's recent behaviour is out of character.'

Nikki let Marcus's words sit with her for a moment before responding. 'Teenage hormones combined with mega-trauma and all these added security measures are enough to upset anyone.' Her gaze drifted to the ceiling as if she could see through her own bedroom and into Charlie's attic room. 'She's right though. We have to make a plan. We need to locate him and lure him out.' She shuddered. 'He won't be far away. We've got to find him and take the ball out of his court ... then we can bury him.'

Despite his twitching lips, Marcus's tone was firm. 'I hate your mixed metaphors, Nik, but I agree with your strategy. Downey has to go down soon ... and permanently.'

Chapter 3

Cowering in the corner of the shed, I shiver against the freezing gusts that infiltrate every damn gap in the corrugated shelter's structure. When they'd moved me earlier, I'd thought that would be the end of me. But here I am, in an even colder building. Freezing but alive. I try to twist my body into more of a ball, hoping to protect my skin from the piercing chill. Crippling numbness prickles up my spine and through my legs and arms. The fucking handcuffs nip my wrists like pincers and the chains they've put on me stretch only as far as the metal loop sunk into the floor, so I can hardly move. The cold will do for me … if the fecking dogs don't first, that is. I wonder if my fingers will turn blue then black from frostbite before falling off. At least I'd be free to move then – well, maybe not. I'm so damn stiff; I can scarcely feel my legs. The blanket the bastards gave me is too thin, yet I suspect it's only that meagre covering that's keeping me alive. That and the prickly straw underneath me. I edge right into the wall, grasping pieces of straw to stuff in the cracks that let the cold air through. My fingers, swollen and numb, will hardly bend, yet I keep going, knowing my life depends on keeping warm. Mind you, is it worth it?

The chill factor's the least of my worries at the moment. The damn dogs' barking and yelping does my head in. Makes my heart skip a beat every time they rattle their sodding chains. The cages are sooo close. Only a few feet away. Their bulky bodies, their slavering snarls, their fucking razor-sharp teeth, their raving feral eyes – all of it brings me out in a cold sweat. They are always moving … pacing … their eyes always on me, eyeing me up like I'm their next meal. Fuck's sake. I probably am their next meal – a damn dog's dinner.

They'd reeled me in too easily. Far too easily. I should have been on my guard – realised it was too good to be true. Instead, I placed my trust in someone I felt deep down was shifty. Everyone knew that Calhoun was a bad fucker. Everyone else gave him a wide berth, but I'd been desperate. Desperate and stupid. Too stupid to believe in my own mortality. Too fucking stupid to listen to advice. That's always been my problem. Ever since I was a nipper, I've done my own thing. Ignored the warnings of my family. No, *more* than that – I took delight in flouting their advice. Enjoyed seeing the worry on their faces as I took reckless risk after reckless risk. Celebrated my 'bad kid' image and laughed at their caution. The only problem was, this time, I didn't realise just *how* dodgy my so-called mate was or how deep he was embroiled in this crap or, in fact, how fragile his position in this gang actually was.

The bastard really stabbed me in the back, but in all honesty, I couldn't entirely blame Calhoun for introducing me to Jacko in the pub. I should've known that making a deal with a stranger when I was pissed was risky. That bastard in the mask was behind it all. I know he was. In truth, I'd been aware that it wasn't exactly legal. Nothing in that particular boozer ever was. But I was arrogant, and that, combined with the booze, clouded my judgement. I was desperate. Work was hard to come by and I was happy to do almost anything to earn a few quid. Besides, I was angry, and that anger had been with me for months. I was constantly looking for something, some way to purge the rage that consumed me. Now I've taken a risk too far and ended up in a position I can't escape from and it's *all* my own stupid fault.

A gurgling half-laugh erupts from my throat, only to morph into a strangled sob. There's nothing remotely funny about this. It's a dire situation. I'm here, in the arse-end of nowhere, freezing my balls off, with only rabid beasts for company and the threat of further beatings. At least the masked man hadn't kneecapped me, like that girl. I saw Jacko and the others wrapping her up and shoving her in the boot of a car. When they returned to check on the dogs, they stunk of petrol and I suspect they burned her. Maybe that's what they'll do to me. Might be better than being fed to the dogs. Neither Calhoun nor Jacko covered their faces, and I've watched enough police shows to know what *that* means. The only one who kept his face hidden was the guy who did the kneecapping. Fuck! He might be short, but he made up for that with sheer viciousness. Tears roll down my cheeks and the more I try to contain them the worse they get as they trickle, hot and salty, over cold cheeks, mingling with snot and stinging as they drift over my split lips and the other cuts on my face.

As if sensing my weakening state, the dog's barking intensifies as they strain to reach me through the bars of their cages. I don't know what would be worse – the dogs getting me or being tied in that chair again and beaten till the bruises that already cover most of my torso are revisited. Next time, the masked man will kneecap me too. Then, Jacko and Calhoun will roll me up in plastic and I'll disappear, never to be seen again. I tried to plead with the hooded man, but he just laughed at me as he struck me again and again, with his homemade cudgel. It looked like a thick sock and it felt like he'd filled it with rocks. Whatever was in the sock didn't only bruise, the sharp edges sliced through my skin, leaving a thousand mini cuts all over me. I suppose I should be thankful for the numbing cold, but even that isn't enough to anaesthetise my aches. I'm sure that besides my ribs, my nose is broken. Every breath splintered my chest into a million fragments. Awkwardly pulling the blanket round my shivering frame and up and over my head, I'll do anything to block out the feral yelps from the dogs. Perhaps it would be best if hypothermia put an end to my misery.

Wednesday

Chapter 4

The abattoir – for that's the only word Nikki could find to describe the hell she currently stood in – made her skin crawl. Huge cages were lined up around the periphery of the old barn. They were piled three-high on top of each other, their open doors signifying the rush in which their occupants had been taken. The air was pungent with the lingering stench of faeces, rotting flesh and gore. It was enough to make Nikki want to turn vegetarian. Despite her crime-scene mask and a liberal dollop of Vicks, the pervasive odour grabbed Nikki by the throat and clung on for dear life, like a supernatural presence sucking all joy from her. Oh, wait – wasn't that a Death Eater? Nikki had been reading Harry Potter to her youngest child, Sunni, the previous night and had scoffed at the idea of such a creature – *now* she got it. This stink was a Death Eater, leeching all happiness and humanity from the world – and this slaughterhouse was where they lived. One glance at her partner, the newly promoted Detective Sergeant Sajid Malik, told her he too was having trouble keeping his breakfast down. His usual ebullient manner deserted him as he cast anxious eyes around the massive outbuilding.

'Why are we here, Saj?'

He raised an ineffectual hand in the air, before dropping it to his side as if realising that the gesture did not encompass the horror of the scene. 'No idea. This is fucking dire. Never seen owt like it.'

Nikki agreed. The scene was dire, and she too had witnessed nothing remotely similar. Nor did she want to ever again. Still, that didn't explain their presence here. She left the barn and began prowling the perimeter using the carefully situated treads placed by the CSIs. Thankful for the breeze, she ripped off her mask and inhaled huge gusts of fresh country air, hoping it would dislodge the Death Eater aura that gripped her throat. The barn, constructed from rusting corrugated metal and tiles, was leaky. The wind blowing through the gaps sounded like an asthmatic pig snorting and as the sound was carried away over the moors, sleet stung Nikki's face.

As she strode round the desolate area, she pulled her coat tight around her and yanked the hood over her head. It was a Christmas gift from Marcus and had replaced her leather jacket. Despite her moans about it being the sort of coat her mum would've worn, Nikki welcomed its warmth and protection from the icy weather. Although the derelict farm stood in the arse-end of nowhere, someone had taken the time to create a bumpy, yet serviceable route from a minor B-road to the barn. The track-rutted quagmire to the side, spoke to the number of vehicles that had parked there recently. Judging by the depth of the tracks, some had difficulty leaving the site. The CSIs, oblivious to the freezing temperature, worked to retrieve car treads from the moist ground. Aware that they were working against the elements, they kept their heads down and focused on their work. Nikki didn't care. Conversation wasn't on her mind right now. Instead, she observed two CSIs struggling to erect a shelter, hoping to preserve the tyre marks from the threatened snowstorm that was about to land on them.

Puzzled by Archie's cryptic message earlier – *go to the scene, observe and then decide* – Nikki allowed her gaze to drift into the distance as she scanned the landscape. What had he meant? She'd come to the scene with Saj, glad of the comfort of his car's heated seats, which more than made up for his continual moaning about the effect of the rustic track on his Jaguar's suspension. She'd not come up with a conclusive reason for their presence there. The scene was clearly an illegal dog fighting arena. Vile though that was, Nikki wasn't sure why Archie had directed her here. Apart from there being more than enough officers around and a distinct lack of witnesses, this was definitely the remit of the animal abuse team, so why had Archie requested her presence? Nobody seemed concerned that she and Saj were there. None of the officers had suggested she was stepping on their toes. In fact, they'd all ignored her. If Nikki was to succumb to paranoia, she might assume that they had heard rumours of her breakdown at a crime scene last year and were avoiding her because of it. However, she was no longer in 'that' place. This Nikki didn't give a flying monkey's toss if they thought she was loopy, she'd been sent here with instructions from her DCI and she was going to carry them out. She shivered and turned her gaze back to the barn. Two of Archie's three requests were complete. She'd come to the scene and she'd observed, which left only the last task before they could be on their way.

The only problem was, she had no idea what she was to 'decide'. *Bloody Archie!* Hell, with her current brain freeze, she was incapable of making a decision. Miles and miles of undulating marshy land spread before her, no other buildings in sight, not another human in shouting distance, bar the ones working the scene. With a frown she realised she'd given little thought to who had called the crime scene in. Unlikely it had been a passer-by, yet the call had come in early this morning. She pulled her mask back over her mouth, took another glance at the pinkish sky and wondered if a shepherd might have stumbled across the destruction inside.

On her return to the bloodbath, she went over to Sajid and repeated her earlier question. 'Why are we here, Saj?'

Before he could answer, Gracie Fells, the CSI Manager,

approached. Nikki tensed, waiting for a snarky comment from her. Since they'd had a very personal falling out before Christmas, Nikki made it her mission to avoid the woman. Now, she had little option but to engage with her on a professional level. She hoped Fells could get over herself enough to do the same. Fells inclined her head, first to Nikki and then Saj. Her mask covered most of her face, making it difficult to judge her thoughts, so Nikki returned the nod, but remained silent.

'The answer to your question might be there.' She gestured beyond Nikki's shoulder. 'We've found an arm.'

'An arm? You mean one that's not attached to a body? A human arm?'

If the situation wasn't so dire, Nikki would have laughed out loud at the disgust that pulled Sajid's eyebrows down as he pursed his lips in distaste. Instead, she waited till Fell's nod confirmed that indeed they'd discovered a human arm, minus its body, at the crime site. With a million questions about the whys and wherefores of an arm turning up near an illegal dog fight, Nikki restricted herself to one. 'Where is it?'

Nikki hoped that her neutral expression was reflected in her tone. She had no desire to be at cross-swords with Fells. Gracie was an excellent CSI, and although her attitude to Nikki's break-down had both angered and hurt her, Nikki preferred to move on. She'd bigger worries than Gracie Fells. Besides, if this crime scene was going to be part of her investigation, Nikki wanted the best CSI working on it.

Seemingly of a similar mind to Nikki, Fells shrugged and angled her body away from them in order to point. When she spoke, her manner was polite and professional. 'In the back of one of the indoor crates – that one over there. You can look if you want. We've documented it and taken all the samples we need from there without moving it. Dr Campbell's on his way. We thought it best he sees it in situ, in case he's got tests or things he needs to do.'

Now Nikki realised why Archie had sent them. The human

body part made this not only an investigation into illegal dog fighting but also a possible murder investigation. With Saj by her side, she moved over to the stacked-up cages. There were two pens, one on top of the other. Why had the dog fight organisers not removed their equipment? Surely that was asking for trouble. Any of those cages could harbour a fingerprint that could lead them right to their door, so why take such a risk? Almost as if she could read Nikki's thoughts, Gracie pointed at the metal bars. 'We'd hoped to get fingerprints from these, but not a bloody one. Either the dog trainers always wore gloves – which bearing in mind the weather, isn't a huge stretch – or they wiped everything down before they left. Still doesn't explain why they left their equipment behind. If they'd time to take forensic counter-measures, then they'd time to pack up their cages.

That puzzled Nikki too. 'If the dogs aren't in the cages, then where are they?'

Fells shrugged. 'When we've processed other scenes like these, they've taken their equipment and doused the entire area with bleach – that's what they tend to do, so I've no idea why this was different, unless ...'

'Whatever happened to the person who lost their arm spooked them and they split in a rush,' offered Saj, peering through the open gate.

Nikki nodded and joined him by the cage where the dismembered body part lay. 'Or they wanted us to find it. It looks fresh to me – not that I'm an expert. Langley will be able to give us more. She sniffed and scrunched up her nose, wishing she could feel it, but the icy air had numbed it. 'Unless they just decided that these cages were past their sell-by date and not worth the effort of removing them. They look rickety to me and rusty.'

She cast her eyes over the door that hung by only one hinge. 'These might not even have belonged to the dog owners.' As another shiver rolled through her body, she sniffed again. 'Whatever the scenario, it's strange that a dismembered arm ended up here. With no sign of the rest of the body.'

With her head as close to the arm as possible, her eyes were drawn first to an intricately detailed yet faded Celtic knot tattoo in greens, blacks and blues, stretching from the incision point beneath the shoulder down to just below the elbow. The mastery of the tattooist was amazing. Nikki's initial thought was that until they found the rest of the body, this might serve as a means of identification. She frowned. Although the tattoo sleeve remained intact, the fingers were missing. The absence of fingers made it even more suspicious. There was generally only one reason for the removal of digits, and that was to confound identification of a corpse. Still, Nikki couldn't rule out that their absence was due to some accident or other. Odd though – no body *and* no fingers? There seemed little evidence of decomposition, so Nikki was fairly sure this was a recent amputation, but she'd leave that to Langley to confirm. Many details would contribute to ascertaining approximate time of death, including ambient temperature, which over the past week had been close to or below freezing. Could it have been left here recently? She glanced towards the still fresh blood spatter, in the middle of the huge building. Was this body part-dismembered as recently as the previous night? Was the arm related to a dog fight event?

Her eyes trailed up to the ragged wound at the top and she shuddered. To her inexperienced eye, it looked like the arm had been ripped from the shoulder – perhaps it was some sort of accident. She'd noticed rusting farmyard machinery outside and wondered if that might have caused the dismemberment or was it something altogether more ominous? 'Might be worth checking the farm equipment for blood stains.'

Only vaguely aware of Fells issuing instructions to check that out, Nikki's gaze moved downwards, taking in a series of bloody injuries on the lower arm. 'Those might be defensive wounds. They look deep and could be the source of some forensic evidence.'

'I thought that,' said Fells.

Despite detecting the extra effort Fells was making, Nikki couldn't bring herself to reciprocate fully. Fells had been out of order and Nikki wasn't quite ready to forget yet. Leaving Sajid to tie up the conversation, Nikki focused on the two metal cages. As they'd approached this area, the stink of animal faeces and ammonia got stronger. And although only two crates remained inside the barn, the CSIs had placed number tags near where rectangular marks stood out against the dust floor. A quick calculation and Nikki reckoned there must have been at least four cages on the ground and if, like the one containing the human arm they had been stacked two high that meant a possible eight cages. Eight dogs and that didn't take into account the empty cages outside. Nikki looked at the remaining cages for a moment. They were small, so the occupants must have been cramped and uncomfortable. Nikki's hackles rose. How dare anyone keep animals in such conditions?

She turned round, her eyes pulled to the blood-spattered concrete ground and the makeshift arena that was sectioned off in large rectangles by sturdy wire panels, each about six feet high with reinforced steel bars extending horizontally across the centre of each panel. Nikki's stomach churned as she observed the way some panels bulged outwards and images of scared and testosterone-driven dogs landing against them played out before her as she imagined the scene. Gaps between the metal strips allowed unobstructed views of the arena, but were small enough to restrict the animal's snouts from causing damage to the spectators. The word 'unfortunately' sprung to her mind. Those who watched were the real animals, not those confined to the cages or the arena. Her voice snapped. 'Check those fences for prints and DNA. I bet the sweaty bastards watching this weren't as circumspect as the organisers when it comes to forensic counter-measures.'

Seats made from hay bales were positioned around the area offering prime viewing of the slaughter. It reminded Nikki of a boxing ring. The only difference was that these participants had no choice. Not for the first time, Nikki wondered just how humans could stoop so low to achieve vicarious thrills. As usual, she was aware that money was the driving force behind such illegal activities. Now, though, a human body part was in the mix, and Nikki wondered what the story behind that was. Was the person to whom the body part belonged dead? And if so, was it an accident, or had they been killed. ? And where was the rest of the body? Judging by the musculature and the well-formed biceps, the arm belonged to a male, however, Langley, the pathologist, would confirm that. It seemed Nikki had made her decision. This case was hers. 'Right Saj, I've seen enough for now. Let's head back to Trafalgar House. Looks like we have a body minus an arm to find. Whether it's dead or alive remains to be seen, maybe Langley will clarify that point.'

Chapter 5

Long lens camera to his eyes, Jacko looked down on the scene before him. As instructed by Fugly, he'd placed the anonymous call only a couple of hours ago, yet the police were out in full force with two CSI teams, plus all their paraphernalia. He recognised a few of the Operation Sandglass team from the photos Fugly had insisted they all studied. He didn't want any of the police task force infiltrating his little set-up and Jacko couldn't blame him. Though where he got his intel from was a mystery. Fugly had contacts in high places, it seemed. People able to dive into the dark web and what not. Not that Jacko understood such things. He couldn't even turn his grandkid's laptop on, never mind surf the net or whatever the youngsters called it.

Jacko was still reeling from the events of the previous evening. Things had gone way beyond illegal dog fights and though he wouldn't admit it to the others, he was shitting himself big time. He hadn't signed up for this – not the torture, not the killings and not that bloody trick Fugly pulled last night. Sick, totally sick and the thought of it churned his stomach which threatened to release its contents onto the snow-covered moorland. He took a deep breath, cursing himself for being so stupid. So naive as to think he was in control. It was almost laughable that only yesterday he'd hoped he might be able to extricate himself from this mess. Today, after everything that had happened, and with worse to come, Jacko could barely focus on the task at hand. Yet he knew that to fuck up now would mean the end of him and there was no way he was going to let that happen. His wife wouldn't be able to manage on her own. Not with their drug-addicted daughter turning up whenever she fancied, trying to gain access to his granddaughter. No, he couldn't leave her to cope with that alone. He had to find a way out. He just had to. His thoughts turned back to the man who paid his wages. Fugly was becoming increasingly erratic. As if he was on a mission to prove himself the cruelest, nastiest piece of shit ever to walk the earth. He had his secrets, Jacko knew that. He'd heard him mumbling in his sleep after he'd downed a few. Seen him salivating over something on that laptop of his – porn, more than likely … then, when he saw Jacko watching him, he'd slammed the lid down and growled at Jacko, telling him to knock next time. Sweat beaded Jacko's forehead. That had been a close one, and he'd got away with only a tongue-lashing because he'd apologised, swearing he hadn't seen a thing – which he hadn't and then, thank the Lord, a delivery arrived and Fugly was out of his seat, locking the laptop up and heading out to check on the product.

Despite the snowstorm, Jacko was feverish. His coat stuck to his back, but it wasn't the snow that caused it, it was fear and anxiety. No matter how shivery he was, acrid sweat drenched his body. Knowing better than to take his eye off the ball, Jacko studied the people moving about below him. Every so often, as instructed, he zoomed in on a face and took a few snaps. Although he couldn't put names to most of them, he recognised their faces. DI Jewkes, the head of the Bradford side of the investigation, hadn't appeared yet, but Jacko suspected he wouldn't be far behind the rest of his team. No doubt he'd be cursing himself for following the false trail laid by Fugly's cyber contacts. That piece of trickery had directed the task force well off course, towards Rotherham.

He wished he'd been a fly on the wall inside the spacious airy barn. Fugly would have liked that too. Jacko knew *exactly* why he'd been ordered to hang about freezing his balls off. Fugly wanted everything documented. Fugly wanted proof that his little offering had been found, but was too much of a fucking diva to wait here himself. Instead, he'd sent his gopher. Despite the acid burning in his gut, Jacko too was fascinated to find out what the pigs' reactions would be, not only to discover they'd been duped, but also that a 'gift' had been left for them. Jacko had questioned the wisdom of taunting the police, but Fugly had laughed in his face.

'You don't have the full picture, Jacko, my man. I'm the brains of this operation and I know exactly what I'm doing. Now, you do pre*cisely* what I've requested and you'll be well rewarded.'

Which was why he was here, freezing his arse off and not able to stop thinking about the disgusting scene he'd witnessed the previous night. What did soldiers call it when they had flashbacks to the terrible things they've seen? Post trauma or something. *Maybe I'll have that now … if I survive this …* Still, it piqued his curiosity. What would the police make of it all? Hell, he didn't know what *he* made of it, never mind the pigs. Still, he couldn't shake the feeling that he was living on borrowed time and that Fugly might turn on him at a moment's notice.

Jacko, confident that he was out of sight of the officers below, watched with interest as the very posh, very 'unsuitable for the terrain' Jaguar jerked and jolted along the pot-holed path. Unable to contain his smile when he homed in on the driver, he allowed himself a single snort. He didn't recognise this face from the ones Fugly had made them memorise. So, this was his chance to gain some brownie points from Fugly. He directed the camera onto the driver's face and snapped a few images. If his tight lips and the way he hugged the steering wheel were anything to go by, the driver was *not* amused and Jacko couldn't blame the lad. If he owned a beauty like that one, he'd not be driving over the moors. In this weather, they'd have been better off using another car. Still, it provided Jacko with a welcome distraction from the monotony of watching the CSIs' business, and he knew that Fugly would be interested in the new faces.

The car's occupants got out, huddled in warm jackets, and Jacko smiled as he focused on the passenger. A small lass, huddled up in a bright red puffy coat, with a matching bobble hat and scarf. The sight of her warm clothing made him shiver. He was stiff and cold from hanging around out here for the past few hours, but fear of what might befall him if he failed to carry out his instructions made him stay in position. Everything from the way she raised her chin to the way she glared round at her surroundings indicated that she was pissed off.

Jacko frowned. Did she look familiar? Had he seen her somewhere recently? As his unease built, he pointed the camera to her face and zoomed in closer before taking more snaps, and then settled in to watch her as she raised her gloved hand and briefly stroked the faint scar that marred her cheek before thrusting both hands back into her pockets. She was familiar, yet Jacko was convinced he'd never spoken to her before. He exhaled a puff of white steam and shuddered. If he dwelt on it, he'd never remember where he'd seen her. He'd just let it lie and no doubt he'd be watching TV or downing a pint and it would come back to him.

Still hidden behind the snow-covered outcrop long enough to watch her enter the barn and then, only a short time later, come back out. A tight, humourless smile formed on his lips as he observed her gulping down gasps of fresh air. He knew the cause of her anguish. He knew how bad it smelled inside the barn and he sympathised with her. Between the stench and the little gift, the poor lass must be reeling. She walked around the yard, her eyes flitting over the property, but when she stopped, her gaze moving across the countryside and scanning the moorland, he dropped back, crouched and remained completely still. He doubted she'd be able to spot him from this distance, but he was damned if he would tempt fate.

Chapter 6

Even after so long, it was strange being in Bradford, but Freddie Downey was pleased to be back. This time, at last, he could focus on bringing about the one thing he craved above all else – the end of his bitch of a daughter, Nikki Parekh. Although this had been his driving force for so long, he hadn't expected to return so soon, but hey, you gotta roll with the punches. Thailand and Venezuela had been grand – until they hadn't. He'd spent his money and despite his best efforts to cash in on some of the schemes going on in the Far East, he'd run out of luck. Nobody wanted to share their illegal enterprises with an aging Scotsman with little clout. In effect, Downey had been a minnow in a pond full of sharks, and that made him uncomfortable.

Of course, he'd made the best of it. Took his pleasures where he could. Cashed in the odd job for cash in hand, did a few low-level dodgy deals and undercut a few of the kingpins, but then the pressure built up. He'd run a couple of girls – picked them up in the slums – and everything had been great for a while. How was he supposed to know that stupid American punter would be too rough with one of them? Bastard went too far and ended up strangling her to death. Shame really. At twelve, she still had a good few years left in her.

After that, he'd tried to lure others, but surprisingly, for girls so young, they were already owned by the younger pimps, who had beaten him up for his efforts. He knew that the next time would be his last – his final grand hurrah to the world. Last thing he wanted was to end up in some filthy Asian gutter when he still had unfinished business at home to deal with. Then Lady Luck cast her mystical magic over him. He'd received a message from the UK that made his heart ignite with joy. The brat, Nikki Parekh, had suffered a breakdown – *aw diddums, poor wee mite, grieving for her mum, blaming herself, poor wee soul was too damaged to hack the guilt and just gave in*. Receiving those recordings from his crappy little sprog's psychiatrist, Dr Mallory, had given him the jolt he needed – a wake-up call, complete with an escape plan and hours of in-house entertainment – what more could a man want?

Fortunately, Lady Luck was still on his side, for before her downfall, Mallory set him up with a substantial sum of money and access to some of her not insubstantial resources. Judging by the extent of Mallory's anger, his annoying little bint of a whorish daughter made friends and influenced people wherever she went. He laughed at that.

Shame the Nikita whore wasn't more like her mum. Lalita Parekh had been pliable and needy, easily manipulated and even easier to control, and he'd made sure she was in thrall to him – until she wasn't. His frown was momentary, soon to be replaced with a smile when he remembered that ultimately *he'd* won their battle of wills. Lalita Parekh may have tried to cut him out of her life, but in the end, he'd snuffed her out like the piece of shit she was. Still, the nagging image of her in her last throws, staring him down, stuck in his craw. The bitch had sacrificed herself for her worthless brats and that pissed him off. Now, he was dead set on making sure he got even. All he had to do was slaughter her eldest daughter. Killing Nikki Parekh would give him the greatest pleasure. However, making her suffer *first* would sustain his thirst for revenge and allow him the bonus of tying up loose ends along the way. He'd wait till she was the last woman standing before he favoured *her* with death.

In the recordings sent by Mallory, he'd revelled in seeing his eldest daughter broken and raw over the death of her whore of a mother. He'd cradled the knowledge that *his* actions had resulted in this wraith of a woman, snotty and snivelling in a psychiatrist's chair, revealing her guilt and fears to a perfect stranger. He'd got off on her pain. Often, he paused the recording and zoomed in on her face. Her dark eyes wide and glassy, like a stuffed animal whose soul died on the forest floor after being shot. Her cheeks were sunken, her chin had wobbled as she spoke and when he hit play again, her fingers twanged that damn elastic band again and again and again. Twang! Twang! Twang!

Some of the later recordings showed her feeble frame filling out again. Her eyes had lost their robotic look and her skin wasn't so pale. She resorted to the band twanging less frequently, and it pleased Downey to realise that her psychiatrist had built her up for her own ends, only to splinter her into a trillion pieces by enlisting Downey's help. It seemed Lalita's eldest daughter made enemies with the same frequency and intensity as he inflicted pain and trauma on people.

It was easy to re-enter the UK without being detected; he'd built up enough contacts over the years and he'd got a good business idea to capitalise on too. So, with his contacts he'd built up his own money-making outfit in Yorkshire. Overnight, his investor had made him a man of independent means with the staff and know-how to direct business away from his competitors and towards his own enterprise. Once more, he was the king of his own little illegal piece of the pie, enabling him to set up the torture rack and tighten the screws bit by bit and turn by turn. Nikki Parekh wouldn't come out of this one so easily. He'd seen the effect her bitch of a mother's death had on her, so let's see how she'd enjoy seeing her family decimated one by one. There

41

was nothing she could do about it. Not a single sodding thing. He would torture and taunt Nikki Parekh for as long as he wanted. He'd make sure she paid for every single inconvenience she'd ever caused him from when she was a tadpole in her tramp of a mother's belly, to the day she'd stopped him pimping her out, to the day she'd bitten him on the wrist and told her slut of a sister to run so he wouldn't give her one, to the day she convinced Lalita to leave him.

Even with the death of her mother, she hadn't paid *nearly* enough for her existence. He craved to splinter her, to crumble her into a multitude of miniscule pieces, and so help him God, that's exactly what he planned to do. Just a shame that Mallory was no longer so easily contactable – never mind, she'd given him everything he needed to do it on his own. She was just one more slut who'd served her purpose.

He picked up the postcard he'd selected: Bradford Mirror Pool. He had fond memories of sitting on the bench there the previous summer. Sun beating down, he'd watched the world go by, keeping an eye on Lalita as she went about her business oblivious to the threat he represented. It was fitting that he use this card. He smiled, his tongue jutting between his lips, as he penned his message. The last postcards had been a mere prelude; *this* was the start of the actual concerto. He lifted it and studied his handiwork. This one was different from the others:

Blame Nikki Parekh.

Satisfied, he nodded and put the postcard into its pre-addressed envelope. Things were hotting up big time, and he couldn't wait for the fireworks to go off. His single-minded focus on destroying Nikki Parekh and everything she loved and stood for was about to pay off.

Chapter 7

'I don't get why Archie was so melodramatic and cryptic about it. Why didn't he just tell me he wanted us to investigate the body part? Not like we've got anything else pressing to focus on right now, is it?' Nikki, huddled into the passenger seat, had kept up a continual rant since they'd left the deserted moorland farmhouse. Eventually, the warmth of the heated seats took the edge off her tension and she relaxed.

Nikki and Sajid were driving over the moor tops towards Bradford and, because of the heavy snowfall that had started before they left the dog fight site, Sajid focused on the road ahead. As he drove, he'd merely nodded along to Nikki's gripes about DCI Archie Hegley's lack of clarity, and her partner's lack of attention hadn't escaped Nikki's notice. The odd sympathetic 'hm' or 'you're not wrong there' was unlike him. Normally, Nikki's behaviour would have had him teasing her and pulling her out of her mood. But not this time. Nikki's brow puckered, and she swivelled round to see his face as he drove. 'You even listening to me, Saj?'

When her partner's response was an absent-minded, 'No idea, Nik.' She prodded his arm. 'For God's sake! Have you heard anything I've said for the last ten minutes?'

Sajid jerked his arm away from her and tutted. 'Will you stop *doing* that, Nik? It bloody hurts, you know!'

Snuggling deeper into the heated seat and savouring its warmth, Nikki smirked. 'Serves you right for not paying attention. I was just saying ...'

Interrupting her, Sajid rolled his eyes. 'Do you blame me? Your monotonous drone was getting on my nerves. You know as well as I do that Archie sent us there because this'll be a simple, not *too* dangerous investigation to get your teeth into and to take your mind off Downey and Mallory. *That's* why he sent us.' He indicated and pulled out towards Shipley before continuing, 'Not damn well rocket science, is it? Besides, I've got other stuff to think about.'

Nikki folded her arms across her chest and reflected on Sajid's words. He'd been preoccupied all morning, since before they even left Trafalgar House. 'You and Langley had a row?

'Eh?' Sajid darted a frowning glance in her direction.

'Lovers' tiff?'

Saj snorted and his face broke into a grin. 'Don't be daft. Langley and I seldom argue. I just go with the flow and he keeps me organised.' He winked at her. 'It works for us. No drama, no big emotional traumas, no danger.' His grin widened. 'After all, I get enough of that working with you.'

The smile faded, and he tapped the steering wheel. 'That said, Nik, I have to talk to you about something.'

Nikki snapped her fingers. 'You're getting a dog. Langley's finally convinced you. You're going to buy one of those yappy little designer ones you carry about in a bag. I *knew* he'd wear you down.'

'What?' Sajid glanced at her, swerving a little as he did so. 'No, course we're *not* getting a dog. Where did that come from?'

Nikki thought about it. She was sure she'd heard that Saj and Langley were considering adopting a canine friend. Then it clicked. Sunni! Little shit had set her up going on about them getting a dog and using a fictional tale about Saj and Langley getting one to back up his case. 'Sunni told me that. Little shit wants a dog, hasn't quite forgiven us for not getting him one for Christmas.'

'Aah! Sunni the master manipulator strikes again.' Sajid laughed. 'Surely a dog would be an improvement on a hamster ... or those white mice he was on about in the summer ... or a gerb—'

Nikki shuddered. 'Just stop it.' Then she grinned. 'That was another one of his better arguments for getting a dog, and I must say that one nearly convinced me. If we got a dog, it would *definitely* put the kybosh on bringing home those damn rodents from school, wouldn't it?'

Saj rolled his eyes. Neither of them spoke for a couple of minutes, then Nikki said, 'So?'

Sajid frowned. 'Eh?'

'So, what's on your mind? It's *not* a row with Langley and it's *not* about a dog, so what is it?

'Ah, well.'

A worm wriggled in Nikki's stomach as she observed the stress lines around Saj's compressed lips. 'That bad, huh?'

She slowed her breathing and prepared herself for whatever bombshell her partner was about to lay on her.

'Look, I was going to refuse.' Sajid's words left his mouth in a rush, making them hard to decipher. Then he added. 'Didn't want to leave *you*. Especially not right now. Wanted to be here for you, but, well ...'

Realisation dawned. 'You've been offered a permanent DS position?' She swallowed hard and forced her lips into a smile. 'That's great news, Saj! You deserve it. Course you can't put a promotion on hold on my behalf. I'm glad you took it. Where is it and when do you start?'

'That's just it, Nik. I've been allocated to Cybercrimes, based in Lawcroft House. Handy for me, as that's just opposite the flat. I'll be able to roll out of bed and shimmy over the road.' He paused, sneaked a glance at Nikki and added, 'I'm supposed to be starting next week. It's all been a bit rushed.'

Next week? Nikki wasn't sure how she kept the smile on her face. She'd expected more than a few days to get used to Saj's inevitable departure from her team, but she had to put her personal feelings aside. Saj deserved this, and she'd support him every step of the way. He'd never know how vulnerable the thought of him not being there made her feel. 'Well, this calls for a celebration, but don't think you can slack off. I expect your full attention on identifying the owner of our amputated arm until you go.'

Chapter 8

The stench is as unbearable as last night's memories. I'm back in the place they first kept me. I can smell my own shit and piss over the dog crap and the testosterone-fused sweat that wafts off the fecking animals. I've grown used to their company, but now I sense a change in them. Although still yelping, their cries are quieter, more resigned, as if they too are affected by the previous night's activities.

Two of them lie, head on paws, their eyes following every slight move I make, their tongues licking their lips. I can't bear to look them in the eye … I know exactly what they could do. I both pity them and fear them, but I can't unsee what they did to my one-time friend. God, the way he screamed! They treated his body like a tug-of-war until, with a final wrench of their powerful jaws, they'd wrenched Calhoun's arm from his shoulder. I'll never forget the unholy cry that rent the air; high and eerie, it lingered before dropping into a sudden and deep silence, broken only by snuffling dogs and subdued growls.

I couldn't unsee that scene and closing my eyes hadn't been an option. My masked tormentor, with Jacko shuffling his feet by his side as if he'd rather be anywhere else than there, had prodded me every time I did so. 'Watch, you little fucker. You need to see what we're capable of.'

The masked man's eyes had flashed like a maniac's, whilst Jacko, his face all pale and washed out, looked like he were going to throw up. When I saw what the dogs had done to Calhoun, I shat myself without warning and then my gut clenched and I was spewing vomit all over the floor. The masked man had merely laughed and signalled for one of his lackeys to drag me away, which was a welcome reprieve from the nightmare I'd just witnessed. It wasn't only the agonised screams of my friend that gave me nightmares, though. It was the whoops of excitement from the bloody crowd. What a bunch of sick fuckers they were. This was *their* sport and I had no doubt that men who could provide such entertainment and enjoy it so gustily would be more than happy to repeat the performance at the right price. As I lie here, defeated, I suspect it will be me who will provide the entertainment before too long.

Chapter 9

Back in Trafalgar House, about to bring her team up to date, Nikki thrust all thoughts of Saj's departure away and focused on the task at hand. She'd had the crime scene photos of the severed arm with its distinctive tattoo blown up and, whilst Saj pinned them to the crime board, she addressed the rest of her officers. DC Liam Williams, serious as ever, had his tablet poised to take notes whilst next to him, DC Farah Anwar nurtured a frown as she studied the photographs taken from different angles. Head tilted as she attempted to get a better look, she drooled over the design, but restricted herself to a quick observation: 'Nice tatt.'

'These images are available on your tablets now, along with the other crime scene photos and as we speak, the body part is en route to the mortuary where Dr Campbell will begin a post-mortem shortly. Sajid and I will attend.'

As Nikki waited for everyone to open their tablets and flick through the crime scene photos, DI Zain Ahad entered the room and signalled his intention to sit and observe from the rear. Ahad was new to their team, and Nikki was still getting used to working with him. Sajid called him the Dark Knight and, although Ahad had mellowed over the last few weeks and seemed less on edge, Sajid moaned about his infrequent abruptness, which sometimes bordered on cruelty. Aware of his tragic past, how he'd lost his wife and child and was grieving, Nikki tried to make allowances for his occasional abrasiveness, but unable to betray Ahad's confidence, she had to let Sajid's moans wash over her without comment. Besides, who was she to judge? Nobody knew better than her how life's momentous challenges could affect a person. Still, she cursed the fact that Ahad had chosen this moment to drop in. *Doesn't he have a meeting to go to?* Now, not only did she have Saj's recent bombshell niggling her, she also had her boss's brooding presence at the back of the room.

'As you can see, we discovered the body part at what we presume to be an illegal dog fighting site. By all appearances, it was used as recently as last night, judging by the blood on site and the fact that a lot of the foot and vehicle prints were still visible. The lab will either confirm or refute that in due course, but at least we have some forensic evidence Apparently, there's been an increase in dog-related crime in Yorkshire over the past few months. And not just illegal dog fighting – stealing pedigree dogs for breeding is another nasty little money-earner for unscrupulous villains. According to the Canine Abuse Unit, officers who investigate canine-related crime, this is of national *and* international concern.' She paused to let the enormity of this sink in. None of Nikki's team had investigated animal-related crimes before and she was sure this would take as much toll on her officers as crimes against children did.

'Whilst our team is tasked with identifying the owner of the severed arm and ascertaining whether foul play was involved, we will liaise with the Canine Abuse Unit. Over the past few months, the CAU has been involved in Operation Sandglass, a cross-regional and multi-disciplinary investigation into the increase in organised dog fighting rings. These illicit dog fights are often used to finance other serious and organised crime such as modern-day slavery, county-lines drug trafficking and the illegal firearms trade, hence the cooperative nature of the task force. After the post-mortem, DC Malik and I will liaise with the DI in charge of the Bradford branch of Operation Sandglass. They will work the dog fighting angle, whilst we're focusing on identifying the owner of the arm. We'll update the files after that.'

All red-faced and flashing eyes, Williams burst out with, 'Bastards! That's what they are. It's not the dogs who're the animals, it's the men doing this to them. We'd better catch them. It's barbaric.'

Nikki sympathised with his sentiments. Williams wasn't one to express his emotions, so Nikki cut him some slack. Normally she would have admonished him for swearing, but Nikki believed that releasing your emotions was beneficial, although she found it hard to do so herself. She met Ahad's gaze from the back of the room, his raised eyebrow and frown indicating that he wouldn't have been so lenient, which irked her. Chin jutting out, she stared him out, daring him to speak, but after a few seconds, he shrugged and smiled. Good job too, or she'd have had some choice words to say. This was her investigation, *her* team, and she knew how to handle them.

The stench from the scene lingered in her nostrils and she was glad that she hadn't witnessed the horror of an actual fight because the aftermath was horrific enough. Still, disgusting though the actions of those who brutalised animals in this way were, her focus was on identifying the owner of the arm. The officers involved in Operation Sandglass were experienced in their field and she had faith that the crime scene and their collaboration would throw up some useful evidence to take their investigation forward. Williams slumped in his seat, and as the colour faded from his face, he cast his eyes downwards to his tablet, embarrassed by his outburst.

Moving her attention back to the briefing, she nodded and in a quiet voice said, 'I agree, wholeheartedly. But our job is to focus on identifying the owner of this arm.' She frowned. 'That seems weird, right? Identifying the owner of this arm is a proper strange turn of phrase, isn't it?'

Despite his pallor, Williams's lips twitched, and he glanced at Nikki, swallowed hard then cleared his throat before saying, "Are we certain it's a male arm?"

Nikki exchanged glances with Sajid. 'I suppose it's the musculature that makes me think that. The biceps are well developed and the forearm is hairier than even Marcus's and he's quite hairy.' She scrunched up her nose. 'The post mortem will confirm either way, but for now is everyone happy to go on the assumption that the severed arm belongs to a male victim?'

As everyone nodded, William's piped up. 'Well, we could do a Voldemort on it.'

Nikki frowned and shook her head. 'Sorry …?'

'You know, Voldemort? He who must not be named? From Harry Potter?'

'Eh, yeees, I know that Voldemort's from Harry Potter, but …?'

Williams, a flush replacing his earlier gaunt expression, grinned. 'He Who Owns The Arm. Get it? Instead of "the arm's owner" or "whoever the arm belongs to" or "the identity of the severed arm", we could all refer to him as "He Who Owns The Arm."'

As a stunned silence grew around him, Williams sunk into his chair, the flush draining from his cheeks, his eyes flashing round at his colleagues, aware for the first time that his suggestion might appear insensitive. 'I mean. I'm not trying to sort of like, em, minimise the horror of losing an arm. That's not what I meant.' He shrugged, slumping even more. 'I just meant, well. It's gruesome, innit? Really gruesome and I thought it might … you know, lighten things up a bit. Not for He Who Owns The Arm, like? Nothing could lighten things up for *him*.'

Sajid was the first to react as he burst out laughing. Then Nikki joined in and Anwar. Although aware of the disapproving frown across DI Ahad's forehead at the back of the room, Nikki didn't care. The crime scene was awful and the idea of a person minus their arm was awful and she got that maybe they needed to lighten things up just a little if they were to cope with the horror of what might have happened to 'He Who Owns The Arm'.

She slapped a hand on William's shoulder making him jump. 'You're right, Liam. Sometimes a bit of dark humour brings light into an awful situation. I think we'll all use "He Who Owns The Arm", moving forwards. Now how shall we proceed?'

Williams flicked through the images and stopped when he had the ones of the severed arm on screen. 'I suppose we'll have to wait for the PM results to find out if he was alive or dead when he lost his arm?'

Saj nodded. 'Yeah. The wound at the top of the arm looks rough, not a clean incision. It couldn't have been pleasant, but perhaps we should avoid speculating on *how* he lost his arm till we have more information and focus on identifying him.'

'No other body parts discovered at the site, then?' Farah, sitting straight-backed in her chair, her brown eyes alert and engaged, was also studying the various angled images of the arm.

'Not so far, but they are still processing the scene. Seems unlikely though, as the CSIs had already processed the main scene before we left. Of course, the outlying areas could throw up something.' With a glance out the window, where the snow was now falling hard and fast, she added, 'The chances of the CSIs being able to continue in this weather are slim. We might not get any more information from them until this snowstorm passes. So, how do we identify the owner of the arm? Thoughts, anybody?'

Nikki knew that in her absence before Christmas, DS Springer, who was on sick leave due to complications with her pregnancy, had failed to train the two DCs. Saj tried, but now she was back in charge, she was determined to prioritise it. Williams and Anwar were too good to fall through the cracks, and Nikki would do all she could to make up for the blip in their training.

Williams, earlier embarrassment forgotten, straightened and thrust his hand in the air, like a schoolboy desperate to be teacher's pet. Nikki's lips twitched as she shared an amused glance with

Sajid. 'No need to raise your hand, Williams, just spit it out.'

'Can we cross-reference the tattoos with those on file from convicted criminals? I know our amputee may not *be* a criminal, but it's a starting point, isn't it?'

Not to be outdone, Farah added, 'We could use our Twitter account – put out an appeal for anyone recognising the tattoo to get in touch. We needn't mention it's from a body part. At the moment, we've no idea if the arm belongs to someone local.'

Nikki was pleased with their responses and, with a glance at her watch, headed over to grab her coat from where she'd dumped it on her seat when she came in. 'Both great ideas. You two get those actions in motion. Farah, make sure to crop the image you choose for Twitter so it doesn't show that the arm's not attached to the body. Also, get a couple of uniforms to check missing persons reports. Hopefully there'll be a PM report that matches our arm. Also, contact all hospitals and morgues throughout Yorkshire. We're looking for either hospital admissions of arm amputees or bodies minus an arm. That should keep you busy for now. Come on, Saj. We've the weirdest ever PM to attend.'

However, as she and Sajid headed out of the incident room, Ahad approached. 'The PM can wait a few minutes. Archie needs a word. It's important, so get a wriggle on.'

Saj glared at Ahad's retreating figure and mumbled, 'Tosser!'

He made to follow the other man, ignoring Nikki's giggles as she fell in place beside him. She said, 'Wonder what Archie wants. Any ideas?'

Saj shook his head. 'Don't know. Maybe he's got an ID on the arm or …'

Nikki's face blanched. She knew what Saj's hesitation meant. He'd been about to say that Archie might have received some intel about Downey. Nikki was well aware she was Downey's target and that he was making his way home. Whether he was actually in the country was unproven, but Nikki's copper's instincts told her he was. Although she wouldn't share her feelings with anyone but Marcus, her gut told her he was nearby. Maybe that was what Archie wanted to talk with them about. Bracing herself, she twanged her wrist a couple of times, then allowed her fingers to trace the scar that crossed her throat. If Downey was closing in on her, he'd better watch out, for Nikki was going to put an end to him one way or another. But when they reached Archie's office, the door was closed and DCS Clarke was inside. Judging by way Archie glared at Clarke and the raised voices emanating from within, this was an acrimonious discussion. Nikki looked at her watch again. She'd no time to wait for Archie's meeting to be over, so she turned, gesturing for Saj to follow her, and said over her shoulder to Ahad, 'Tell the boss we had to get to the PM. Whatever he needs to talk to us about can wait till tomorrow.'

Ahad looked about to object, but then he shrugged and nodded. 'Okay, first thing. It is important.'

With the words 'it's important' ringing in her ears and her mind foraging through the multitude of likely reasons for Archie demanding a meeting so abruptly in the middle of an investigation he had landed them in, Nikki felt the familiar tightening in her chest. Opting to run down the stairs rather than take the lift, she gave the band on her wrist a few desperate twangs and set off at a fast pace.

Chapter 10

The sights and sounds of the post-mortem suite rarely bothered Nikki too much anymore. However, despite still being preoccupied with whatever bombshell Archie had to drop, seeing the arm detached from its body and lying on the slab with Langley hovering over it struck her as surreal and decidedly nauseating. Sajid, sitting beside her in the observation area, focused on his mobile rather than looking at the strange post-mortem that his partner Langley was carrying out below.

Desperate to get the post-mortem over with so she could return to the station, Nikki shifted in her seat. 'Don't see why he's *so* excited about this.'

Without lifting his gaze from his phone, Saj shrugged. 'It's a challenge. Not every day you have to identify a person from their right arm alone, is it?'

Nikki conceded the point with a shrug. 'Still, you'd think he'd be able to rattle through the PM. After all, he's only got, what an eighth, even less, of the body, to work on? No need for all that dissecting carry-on, or the gloopy stuff when he weighs the organs. He should've been done by now.'

'You an expert in pathology now, Parekh? Dr P, the pathology expert? Dr P, the it'll only take a minute to PM the arm, expert?

Dr P, the PM speed queen?'

With an inelegant tut, Nikki jammed her elbow into his side. 'At least I'm *observing* the proceedings, unlike you, who can't even look at it. Not like there's loads of gory stuff. It's only an arm – no livers or spleens or lungs or bowels or …'

'Yeah, yeah, yeah. I get it Nik. But *only* an arm? What are you on about? It's creepy. It's like something from *The Walking Dead*.'

'Walking Dead? What the hell are you on about? I wonder about you. It's a clue. That's what it is – the arm's a clue. If we want to uncover the identity of its owner, then we need your beau to crack on with the PM, not just stand there admiring the damn body part.' She frowned and glanced from Langley to Sajid and back. 'It's not the tattoo, is it? He's not thinking of getting one, is he? Please tell me he's not, Saj. It's just not …'

Sajid glared at her. 'No.' The single word came out as a high-pitched squeak that had Nikki staring at him open-mouthed. He cleared his throat and started again. '*No.* Course, he's not thinking of getting a tattoo.' Then, despite his dislike of post-mortems and all things gory, he looked down at Langley, who was circling the table, bending down, studying areas of the severed limb at close quarters. 'Shit, Nik. He's not *really* thinking of getting one, is he?'

Hiding her grin, Nikki sighed. 'Well, it looks that way to me.' She nudged Sajid. 'You could get matching ones. That'd be nice. A shared experience and all that …'

All colour drained from Sajid's face and his mouth fell open. Nikki couldn't keep up her pretence any longer. Sajid was petrified of needles and had practically needed a sedative to get his Covid jab. 'Don't be an idiot! Of course, he's not looking at the damn arm for its aesthetic value. He's a scientist. You even said it yourself. He's intrigued in a geeky, sciencey sort of way. God, you're so easy to wind up.'

Eyes narrowed, Sajid turned his body away from her and, apart from a disapproving tut, refused to engage with her.

After a few moments, Nikki sighed and mumbled, so her voice

wouldn't carry. 'Oh, come on, Langley. There's only so many angles you can observe a tattooed arm from and you've used all of them. Hurry up, can't you? Some of us have work to get on with.'

Sajid gave another tut. 'For God's sake, don't say that aloud, Nik. He'll be pissed off if he hears you. Let him do his job, eh?'

Huffing an overly loud sigh and tapping her toe on the floor, Nikki resigned herself to a long wait and began playing a game of I Spy with herself. It was one of the strategies she employed to defog her mind. A challenge to make her focus – I spy with my little eye ten things beginning with S: stethoscope, Sajid, syringe, scales, silver … silly fu—

The crackle of static interrupted her thoughts, and she looked at Langley, aware that Sajid had sat up straight, phone nowhere to be seen. *Goodie two shoes. I'm-riveted-by-the-entire-PM-experience Malik!* The way Langley wafted his gloved hands in the air and bounced on his toes told Nikki that he was still in overexcited mode. Above his mask, his eyes gleamed and the crinkles at their sides showed the extent of his good humour. Nikki wanted to throttle him, but resigned herself to a muttered, 'Come on, spill the damn beans, Langley.'

'I've got a series of tests to run, but I'm quite excited by this one.'

'You *don't* say.' Sajid's nudge told Nikki she'd uttered the words too loudly, and a glance at Langley confirmed that. A frown tugged his eyebrows together and Nikki pulled her mask down and smiled. 'Sorry Langley. Not had my caffeine quota yet. Carry on.'

Langley's chin jutted forward in an 'I've got my eye on you,' sort of way, but thankfully, he continued. 'You're probably unaware of this, but there is a lot of forensic and identification information to be gained from a body part – even one without phalanges.'

'You what?'

'Fingers, Nikki, fingers.' Langley's tone moved from 'academic' to *Dumbo* in a second. 'Without fingers, we don't have …?' His voice went higher on the word 'have' and the pause afterwards placed him in 'teacher' mode.

Sajid's barely concealed laugh riled her. Okay, so she'd been too impatient, and yes, she needed stuff dumbed down, but Langley was taking the – as Archie would say – 'proverbials'. Ignoring the pause, Nikki folded her arms over her chest and remained silent. However, when the silence lengthened, she realised that Langley was expecting a response. With an exaggerated eye roll, she tutted and said, 'Fingerprints.'

'Exactly, DS Parekh. We don't have fingerprints. However …' His toe-bouncing increased in tempo and Nikki half expected a troupe of *Riverdance* dancers to join him. 'What we have is,' he pointed to the tattoo, 'ink identifiers from his body art which will help in matching the limb to a body, should you find one. Of course, and this is where your keen investigative skills come into play …'

'Patronising much?' Nikki's mumbled complaint elicited another nudge from Saj whilst Langley continued, oblivious.

' … the tattoo is so detailed that even with the obvious injuries to the forearm and the shoulder area, you should manage to find a match in a database, assuming the arm was once attached to a criminal.' Head to one side, he clicked his fingers, which, with his gloves on, made a strange poofing sound, 'Of course, a tattoo artist might be able to help too and certainly releasing an image to—'

Sajid cleared his throat. 'Erm, Langley, we're on that. Perhaps if you just give us your findings, eh? Could the owner of the arm be alive still?'

Langley exhaled. 'Well, of course it's possible. If they stopped the blood loss before he went into haemorrhagic shock and if he was tended to, then there is a chance he's still alive. However, that all relies on him being pumped full of antibiotics and given proper medical care. I'd expect him to need hospitalisation in order to survive.'

Sajid turned to Nikki. 'Good call on checking the hospitals, Nik. Let's hope we find him in a hospital rather than a morgue. He could give us valuable information on what happened at that dog fight and maybe he'll have some names too.' He turned back to Langley. 'Anything else?'

'Of course, of course. The arm belongs to a white male. Further tests may ascertain age and should we be unable to find the owner soon, we could use DNA phenotyping to pinpoint the geographic and ethnic origin of the victim.' Langley was on a roll and Nikki was loath to interrupt.

'Basically, the arm was ripped from the shoulder and I'm awaiting test results to find out whether this injury was pre- or post-mortem. Of course, depending on the treatment given to stop bleeding, the arm's owner could, at a pinch, still be alive … Unlikely I'd say, but not definite. The wounds you can see here …' He pointed to the forearm. 'These are canine bite marks. I'm hoping to get some DNA from the dog saliva. If it's not degraded, then you could match it to a dog, providing you find the dog. The positioning of the bite marks indicates the victim put his arm up like this.' Langley raised his arm to cover his face. 'That's assuming the arm was attached when it was bitten. If that's the case, then they are defensive wounds. I'll send you a more detailed report later on today.'

Stepping away from the post-mortem table, Langley pulled his mask down and grinned, all trace of the mad scientist or the school teacher gone. 'You okay, Nikki? Why don't you and Marcus come for tea this weekend? I've got a new recipe to try out.'

The thought of food after Langley's descriptions, combined with lingering memories of the remote dog fighting site, was unappealing. Still, Nikki mustered a smile. 'That'd be great, Langley. I'll tell Marcus.'

Chapter 11

'Boss. A call's just come in from Wakefield police. I think you should hear this. Could be relevant to our case.'

Nikki had just walked into the incident room when Williams hijacked her. His eager face told Nikki that something good had just landed in their laps. 'Spill, Liam. No time for dancing.'

Whereas before, Nikki's abrupt response would have made Williams flush, nowadays, he'd toughened up a bit and instead of shrinking before her eyes, he grinned at her and punched the air. 'Pinderfields Hospital called Wakefield police two nights ago. A young lass was dropped off in their car park, badly beaten and wrapped in cellophane. She's in a critical but stable condition ...'

Williams paused, waiting for his ta-dah moment ... 'They found dog bites on her limbs.'

'She missing an arm?' Langley had specified their arm was male, but the presence of dog bites was too coincidental for her not to ask the question. Langley was rarely wrong, but there was a first time for everything.

'No, she's got both arms, but it's too much ...'

Nikki had already spun on her heel and with Sajid in tow was out the door yelling. 'Text me the ward details and tell them to expect us and find out who attended from Wakefield CID – see

61

if they'll meet us there.'

Pinderfields Hospital was the main trauma centre for Wakefield and after entering the hospital at Gate 30 and making their way up to Level C where critical care was situated, Nikki was keen to discover whether the woman dumped at the hospital with dog bites on her limbs could be related to their arm. She'd hoped to be able to speak to the girl, who as yet, remained unidentified, but the doctor in charge had vetoed that immediately. 'She's intubated and although no longer critical, she has a long way to go.'

Instead, the doctor had allowed them to view the girl from the window of her room. 'She was severely beaten. Various broken ribs, one of which punctured her lung. She'd been kneecapped and even if she does recover, she'll never walk unaided again, so severe was the damage to her lower limbs. She was lucky to survive. If she hadn't been dropped off right outside, I doubt she'd still be with us.'

The black-haired girl, lying so peacefully in the room was still. The only sound was that of the ventilator and the only movement, the slight lift and fall of her chest as the machines keeping her alive did their job. Her skin looked so pale, Nikki imagined she could see the blood moving through her veins. Bandages and dressings covered her bare arms and Nikki knew they covered the bite marks that had drawn their attention to this unnamed girl's plight. A thought occurred to her and she turned to the bespectacled doctor by her side. 'Do you know if swabs were taken of the canine bite marks?'

The doctor flicked through the girl's chart and then smiled. 'Yes, the officer who responded to our call requested them. Seems he was on the ball. We sent the swabs straight to Wakefield forensics labs.

Nikki winked at Saj. 'I hope you'll tell Langley that I listened to his lecture at the PM. Maybe the swabs will link whatever happened to this poor girl with our arm.'

A tall man with a beer belly and a pockmarked face ambled

down the corridor towards them. 'Ah, here's the detective in charge of this investigation, DS Letts. He'll know more than I do.'

Nikki and Sajid turned to greet the detective and by mutual agreement headed down to the café. Once seated with coffees in front of them, DS Letts talked them through what he'd discovered so far. 'This was a bad one. Really bad. The poor girl was unconscious and they thought they'd lost her twice.' He slurped his coffee and wiggled on his chair, making Nikki concerned about whether the chair could hold his weight. 'A couple of witnesses saw three men dumping her from the back of a white transit. No ID on the men – they wore hats and were masked. Bloody Covid makes it easier for the baddies, dun't it?'

Sajid shrugged. 'You get the chance to check out the CCTV yet?'

Letts exhaled, sending wafts of pickled onion crisps over the table. Nikki risked a glance at Sajid, who had an aversion to pickled onion crisps, but to his credit, he didn't flinch as more oniony wafts drifted over. 'Yeah, checked CCTV. Got the plates – stolen.' He slurped some more coffee. 'As you'd expect. But we did find the vehicle torched near Sheffield. Whoever dropped our girl off was savvy enough to get rid of the van. We checked Missing Persons to see if we got a match, but nothing came up. She might not even be from this area. Our best bet on getting an ID on her is if she wakes up.'

'Did you backtrack the van's movements via CCTV to see where it came from?'

'Yeah, but again they were smart. Only caught them on CCTV around the hospital area but before that they must have taken the back roads with no cameras. Same on the route to Sheffield. Saw them briefly, but there were no cameras near where they torched the van and nothing to show who picked them up from there either.'

This was frustrating, but Nikki was used to dead ends. Still, she'd get her team to retrace Letts's investigative steps. He might have missed something and they could do with a lead. 'Can you send copies of your files to me and also the lab results for the canine bite swabs? Good call on that by the way. It might just provide a link to our detached arm investigation. Also, give us a heads-up if she regains consciousness. I've a feeling this girl could answer a lot of questions for us.'

Chapter 12

Jacko was frozen to the bone when he returned to base. With one hand grasping the small crucifix he wore round his neck, he prayed that the photos he'd got from his lookout position would mollify Fugly. His first concern when he pulled into the pot-holed farmyard was for the lad held captive beside the dogs. He'd looked in a bad way the previous evening and seeing what had happened to his mate must have shocked him. Jacko doubted any of the other kids would have had the guts to check on him. No, they'd learned their lesson after the kneecapping the other night and after last night's atrocity, no way would they do anything to rile Fugly. Although tempted to check on the lad before bracing himself to face Fugly, he decided to wait. A few hours wouldn't affect the lad's condition much and it might be the difference between Jacko keeping on the right side of short-arse Fugly and ending up as pig feed. So, he took a deep breath before leaving the jeep, wondering if the snatched call to his wife earlier would be the last time he told her he loved her.

With the familiar trickles of sweat soaking his jumper, he jumped down from the driver's seat and hesitated, before pulling his shoulders back, pasting his usual half smile on his lips and heading towards the building. It amazed him that such a picturesque vision of homeliness – a snow-covered sandstone farmhouse with smoke drifting from the chimney – could house such evil.

Even before he opened the kitchen door, he heard Fugly's voice from within. He paused, trying to work out who his boss was talking to. A few seconds of eavesdropping told him Fugly was on the phone, to either his bookie or one of his mysterious supporters. Thankfully, he seemed to be in a buoyant mood as he laughed and joked with the person on the other end of the line.

'Who'd have thought that little side show I planned would have gone down so well with the punters? Worked a fucking gem, it did. You should've seen it. They looooved it, absolutely, fucking loved it.'

There was a moment of near silence where the only sounds Jacko could hear were those of his boss moving round the kitchen. Then …

'Yeah, I know. I wasn't sure how to dispose of Calhoun, either. The irksome little irritant was getting to be a liability. You can always tell when they're going to turn, can't you? It's something about the way they don't quite meet your eyes when they talk to you. The way they're always a bit too keen to get away from you. But no, I don't think it was excessive. He deserved it.'

Again, a momentary silence, before Fugly spoke. 'Yeah, you're right. There's a thin line between them being nervous but under control and them being edgy and about to land you in the shit. Calhoun was ready to run. No doubt about it, the coward didn't have the stomach for it, so his little matey got a reprieve and Calhoun got it instead.'

Fugly's laugh bore traces of the previous night's testosterone-fueled adrenalin high and Jacko's heart sank into his boots. In this mood, Fugly was unpredictable and to top that, he still had blood lust running through his veins. Jacko was tempted to spin on his heel and leave, but where the hell could he go? Fugly knew where his wife and grandchild lived and his junkie daughter would be easy enough to find. Although Jacko couldn't abide to see her, she was his kin. Still his daughter. He was in an impossible position and there was little he could do about it, except keep his head down and pray. His fingers drifted to his crucifix once more, tapping sharply on the door.

'Hold on, someone's here. Give me a sec.' Fugly yanked the door open, mobile still held close to his ear and seeing it was Jacko, he moved the phone to his chest and peering right into his underling's soul, his eyes revealing nothing, he uttered a single word. 'Well?'

With Fugly's words to the anonymous caller ringing in his ears, Jacko met his boss's eyes and allowed a slow smile to spread across his lips. Was it his imagination or did Fugly's shoulders relax a bit as he stepped away to allow Jacko entry? Keen to push home this small advantage, Jacko willed the smile to make it up to his eyes. 'We hit the jackpot, boss. They were crawling all over the site in under two hours and …' He slapped his hand on his thigh, hoping he wasn't overdoing it. 'I got images of some pigs we've not seen before. It looks like we've got the CAU on the run. I waited till I saw them place the arm in a vehicle, then headed back. By then the snow put the kybosh on the CSIs' work and they packed up too, leaving only a couple of officers behind.'

There was a definite thaw in Fugly's posture as he grinned at Jacko. 'Well done, Jacko. Knew I could count on you. Make us both a cuppa, will you, whilst I finish this call, and then you can show me everything you've got.'

Heart pounding, relief surged through Jacko as he shrugged his coat off and draped it over a kitchen chair before heading over to the kettle. With his back to Fugly and under cover of filling the kettle, he exhaled a long breath. He wasn't out of the woods yet, but if he could convince Fugly that he was on his side for a while longer, he could work out a plan to extricate himself from this mess.

Behind him, Fugly's conversation with the unknown caller

continued. Jacko strained to hear every word in the hope he'd learn a nugget of information that might help him out of this situation.

'Those sick fuckers lapped it up. I think adding the human element to proceedings added that certain *je ne sais quoi*. Good job I have the captive in place. He'll be the next one to entertain the crowds.'

As he dumped a tea bag in two mugs, Jacko observed the slight frown on Fugly's forehead. Clearly his listener wasn't responding with the same amount of enthusiasm as Fugly expected, for his next words backtracked a little. 'No. No. You're right. They're definitely sick fuckers. Yes, it was barbaric. A bit too gory for me, but what the hell, it drew in the money. More than all the dog-on-dog fights put together.'

Fugly's frown deepened and his tone went up an octave as if he was trying to convince his caller of something. 'Look. From what I'm hearing, the demand for a repeat performance is high and I've got just the candidate in mind. You don't have to worry about that. You just keep being responsible for your end and let me handle this side of operations. I'm going on the principle of killing two birds with one stone. And the beauty is that there are so many of these isolated buildings in the heart of the moors that it's easy to find a secluded spot that's not *too* accessible for the public to become curious, but accessible enough for our purposes. Everything's on track. You've no need to worry. Anyway. I've something to deal with here. Speak again soon. Bye.'

Fugly threw the phone on the table, then stood for a moment, tapping his index finger on his pursed lips, the frown across his brow deeper than ever. Jacko poured boiling water into the mugs and placed them beside the phone. Was the fact that Fugly hadn't told his mysterious caller about the severed arm left behind at the site something he could use? Maybe not right now, but he'd store this titbit away with all the other little bits of information he'd gleaned over the weeks, and maybe one day he'd be able to use his knowledge to escape. 'Want me to tell you all about the pigs, boss?'

Fugly's frown disappeared as he smiled and held his hand out for the camera. 'Images first Jacko, I want to see if I recognise any of the police officers at the scene. Then you can tell me all about it.'

Jacko spent half an hour regaling Fugly about the officers whilst Fugly flicked back and forth through the images. He didn't comment, which set Jacko on edge wondering if he'd forgotten some crucial part of the plan, but then Fugly placed the camera on the table, pulled a bottle of whisky towards them and filled both their mugs with the amber liquid. 'You did good, Jacko. At least I can rely on you, even if the likes of Calhoun bottle it.'

Forcing a derisive snort from his lips, Jacko raised his mug to Fugly's. 'Calhoun. Hmph. Stupid little fucker got what he deserved. Here's to the next one, eh?'

Fugly clanged his mug against Jacko's and, gesturing for him to follow, he drifted over to the comfy seats beside the fireplace and slouched comfortably in the largest before slipping his slippers off and plonking his feet on the coffee table before him. The sight of Fugly's blackened big toe poking out from a hole in his sock sickened Jacko, but somehow he swallowed his distaste down and sat opposite him, allowing the warmth from the fire to soothe him as it dried his sweat and warmed his bones.

The two men stared into the licking flames for a few minutes, then Fugly stirred. 'You know Jacko, leaving the little taster behind was inspired. Bit of a distraction for the plods. Of course, I needn't have led them to it, but it seemed like too good an opportunity to miss.'

The only response Fugly needed to keep talking was a nod or a grunt from Jacko, which suited him for he didn't think he could manage much more than that.

'God knows I'll need a sound financial retirement plan for when I'm ready to hand in the towel … Planning, that's the way forward … Got to put yourself first …' All his words merged into a long spiel in Jacko's ears.

Fugly rose, snatched the half empty bottle from the table and refilled their mugs before tossing a couple of logs onto the fire and sitting down. 'I wonder what they make of all this. Thing is, they'll be focused on all their regular trainers … them who're too stupid to fly under the police radar, but I've been smart. I pay my boys well thus ensuring their loyalty and if it's in doubt, then I deal with it.'

Jacko grunted and raised his mug in a silent 'cheers' gesture, hoping that Fugly would continue his musings.

'And I've kept my face out of the spotlight. None of the other ringmasters will be able to land me in it. *They* can't identify me and neither can the punters. So, they'll be the ones landing in bother from the plods, not me. And whilst they're chasing their tails, I'll be swiping their bread and butter right out from under their noses.'

Fugly straightened in his armchair and stared straight into Jacko's eyes. 'The only folk who can land me in any shit are you lot, the ones I'm in direct contact with, but I can count on you, can't I, Jacko?'

Fearing that the sound of his pounding heart might reach Fugly's ears, Jacko leaned forward, scratching his chair across the flagstone floor. 'I'm your man, boss. Course you can count on me.' He considered pleading his case more, itemising all the things he'd done for Fugly, but bearing in mind Fugly's earlier comments about overkill, he left it at that.

Fugly held his gaze for a few seconds, then laughed out loud, a hard laugh that sent chills up Jacko's back. 'Course I can count on you.' He swigged a mouthful of whisky and ended with. 'I know I can, for I know where your family is if you try to fuck me over.' Then he burst into laughter again as if he'd just cracked the best joke ever, and once more clanged his mug against Jacko's. 'I've got your balls and all those other lads' balls in my hand. One hint of betrayal and my grip will tighten.' He held his free hand up and pulled it into a tight fist, holding it like that till his hand turned white and every sinew stood out, then he released it and chortled some more.

Chapter 13

Nikki and Sajid entered Lawcroft House and were directed to the Operation Sandglass incident room on the top floor. Curious to see the inside of the building she only ever saw from the outside when she visited Sajid and Langley in their flat, Nikki peered around her. It was mainly an administrative office as it didn't have any custody cells and was carpeted in muted grey tones, with magnolia walls decorated with local artists' paintings of the City Park Mirror Pool, Lister Park and Haworth Moor. The Operation Sandglass investigation was region-wide, with Sheffield police coordinating the entire operation, so the Bradford team had opted to use the larger facilities here because any arrests made during the investigation would be by Sheffield police.

As they entered the room, Nikki's eyes moved to the array of mugshots pinned up all over the walls and crime boards. The back wall was dedicated to evidence photos presumably taken at sites of illegal dog fights or the premises of fake breeders and dog abductors. Taking a few steps closer to the desk, which sported a range of computer equipment and partially hid the man stationed there, Nikki extended her hand. 'DS Nikki Parekh and DS Malik here to see DI Colin Jewkes.'

The man behind the screens unfolded his torso and limbs for

what seemed like an eternity until he reached an upright position and, towering over both Nikki and Sajid, he grinned and engulfed Nikki's hand with his own large one. At well over six-foot-three tall, the Operation Sandglass detective dwarfed them and Nikki was unsure how he'd been able to fold his long legs behind his desk. 'I recognise you from earlier, DS Parekh. Welcome to Bradford's Operation Sandglass HQ. You can call me Colin or Jewksy if you'd prefer.'

Nikki frowned. If this tall man had been at this morning's scene on the moors, she would have remembered him. Seeing her confusion, Jewksy laughed. 'You were getting into your car as I arrived. Not going to forget someone so short in a hurry, am I?' He winked at Nikki.

Ignoring Sajid's amused snort, Nikki rolled her eyes, but didn't rise to the bait. 'Nikki and Saj.'

Jewksy's smile widened as he turned to shake Sajid's hand. 'Nice Jag, by the way. I guess it's automatic. How do you like it?'

Leaving Saj and Jewksy talking cars for a moment, Nikki sat down in the seat positioned opposite the crime scene photos from earlier and cast her eyes over them. DS Jewkes, Jewksy, seemed amenable to their involvement, and that was always a good thing. Maybe they could work together, divide some of the legwork and help each other out. When Saj and Jewksy joined her, Nikki gestured round the room. 'Operation Sandglass seems quite extensive. Could you brief us on the remit of the task force? That might clarify how we can cooperate on this.'

Jewksy swallowed, his eyes darting over the images on the wall as he got his thoughts in order. 'For the last six months, we've been working on this joint task force because of the dramatic rise in canine-related crime in the region. I don't know if you're aware, but this sort of criminal activity is often the gateway into serious and organised crime like bare-knuckle fighting, money laundering, drug and human trafficking, trading in illegal weapons, and has far-reaching consequences for many vulnerable communities who get dragged into it all.'

Nikki thought about that whilst her eyes charted the evidence of the atrocities pinned to the walls. She hadn't realised that Operation Sandglass had such a broad remit. 'So we're not just talking illegal dog fights then.'

'If only. No, there's a whole range of crimes, from dognapping pedigree dogs, to breeding prohibited fighting dogs, to over-breeding and selling inferior bred pedigrees to unsuspecting dog lovers. It's a sick and dangerous business and because of the high financial return, it appeals to those criminals with an eye on a quick turnaround with a high monetary reward. These fuckers don't give a shit about animal welfare.' He pointed to the CSI images taken from the moors scene earlier. 'This is the tip of the iceberg, but the fact that we caught this scene so fresh is good for us. Till now, we only had circumstantial evidence of this big criminal ring in Bradford – suspicions yes, but nowt concrete. This gives me leverage to get more officers on the case and we want to focus on pursuing evidence that might help us nab this gang. We could do without the added hassle of investigating a body part.'

Nikki got that. She could see investigating the arm would be distracting, especially considering the extent of evidence the CSIs would have uncovered. True, identifying the owner of the arm might be beneficial to Operation Sandglass, but in view of Langley's PM discoveries, it seemed likely that the arm's owner was dead and, judging by the violence demonstrated at the crime scene, Nikki suspected foul play was likely, so that aspect of the investigation fell within her remit. 'We're working on identifying the owner of the arm and the pathologist reckons that it's unlikely that we'll find a live body to match it to. There's clear evidence that a dog bit him multiple times and we're awaiting results to see if we can narrow it down. Although I'm not discounting other avenues, we're going to progress on the assumption of murder until we receive evidence to the contrary. Of course, we'll keep you apprised of our ongoing investigation and …' She looked Jewksy straight in the eye, her tone brooking no argument. 'I expect you'll share your findings with us.'

Jewksy grinned again, his teeth startlingly white against his dark stubble. 'Goes without saying.'

Satisfied, Nikki smiled back. 'So, how will any forensic evidence discovered earlier help you?'

'Well. You said your pathologist was running tests on the dog bites? I'm assuming he might get DNA from saliva and if that's so, it could help identify characteristics of the dog. Operation Sandglass has an active data base where we store all canine DNA taken from dogs we've rescued in the course of our investigations, DNA derived from fluids left at fight scenes and so forth. From this we can ascertain lineage of the dogs if they've been bred solely as fight dogs. We can plot their whereabouts and the movement of dogs from the same litter, which allows us to hone in on the breeder. If we nab the breeder, we can often find out who they sold the dog to and on three occasions so far, we've arrested a handler and shut down some smaller dog-fighting rings. The larger ones are more cautious. They usually bleach the sites, but this morning's site wasn't fully sanitised, because they left the arm. Maybe they were forced to leave quickly. I don't know. But whatever, it'll work in our favour.'

Saj leaned forward. 'Yeah, tread marks might be enough to narrow down the vehicles that transported punters and animals to the sites.' Face flushed, he continued, 'I saw loads of cigarette butts which might match to some con already in the system. This division of labour might work well for both of us.'

Jewkes got to his feet as a group of officers entered the room. 'It's time for my briefing, so you'll have to excuse me. I'll send you all our information over as and when it comes in and I'll await details from your investigation.' Once more his huge paw was thrust towards Nikki, who, glad that Jewkes wasn't one of those men who felt duty bound to show their strength in a handshake, gripped his hand with a smile and said, 'We'll be in touch. Good to be working with you.'

Chapter 14

Freddie Downey was focused on bringing about his daughter's downfall. Rage bubbled like a witch's cauldron just beneath the surface of his skin. It was his ever-present companion – his driving force, and he'd long since stopped trying to smother it by indulging in fleshly desires or other such distractions, Now, every decision he made, every action he completed was to end Nikki Parekh in the most satisfyingly destructive way possible. Which was why he was scoping out his daughter's territory, knowing full well she'd be at work. Something inside him drove him to be near her, to infiltrate the area she thought of as her sanctuary. It calmed him a little to be there, taunting her. Even if she didn't know it yet, it gave him satisfaction to have one up on her.

He laughed and pulled his woolly hat further over his forehead. It was brass monkey weather, which served his purpose well. Huddled up in a huge overcoat, scarf covering his lower face and hat over his head, he doubted even the ghost of his old dead mother would recognise him. In the months since his daughter had last seen him, Downey had changed – become leaner and meaner. Still, there was no way he'd rely only on luck and a big coat to remain anonymous. No, he'd disguised himself properly, using proper professional props and such like. First, he'd invested in heel lifts to make him taller – they'd been awkward to move about in at first, but he'd persevered and now he felt confident that the slight change they'd made to the way he carried himself, combined with the extra two inches in height would put her off track. He'd also purchased cheek implants, which filled out his face and made the mean wrinkles smooth out. Contact lenses gave him dark eyes, and glasses and a wig finished off his disguise. At first glance, she'd never recognise him. Especially since he'd topped off his disguise with a high vis jacket from Yorkshire Water and had parked a van with removable Yorkshire Water decals on the side, just down from her house. Nobody paid attention to workmen, and he doubted the two blokes supposedly guarding her obnoxious scrotes had enough brains between them to think outside the box and scope the place for unlikely threats. They were brawn, not brain, and Downey relied on that.

Her security precautions were adequate, he supposed, but Downey was confident that when the time came, extracting one or even all four of his odious little grandkids and the special needs kid, would be a doddle. But that wasn't part of his current mission. *This* was a fact-finding recce and as he got into the van and started the engine, he thought he'd gathered enough information for now. He'd let those brutes succeed in their security tasks for today at least, but he was certain that soon they'd be wishing they'd kept a better eye out on the periphery. Amateur mistake, if ever he'd seen one!

Thursday

Chapter 15

It's freezing when I wake up. The drips from the holes in the roof are a constant companion when I'm awake and sometimes they lull me into a fitful sleep. I crave the times when I drift off, but it's nice to hear something other than the dogs when I'm awake. Their round plops splatting on the concrete floor, like they're counting out my last life beats, had seemed threatening at first. Now, they're my best friends. With the temperature plummeting through the night, droplets form glittery icicles in the semi-dark. I half-heartedly wonder if I'm delirious. Not that it matters either way. In fact, being delirious might be better. I give a sharp laugh that bounces against the snow-swaddled walls and echoes eerily in the dark, reminding the dogs that I'm here. But even their responses are muted – their yelps half-hearted, their growls less angry; maybe they've accepted me into their little captive canine gang. Not that my membership of *that* particular club would save me when the hounds are let loose with me as bait.

As consciousness seeps over me, I face the truth and leave my delirium behind, I think I'm back in the same building I was in before Calhoun copped it – but I'm not sure. My heart speeds up, and the air pooling around me fills with my steamy breath and I almost hyperventilate. Then, I remember that they returned me to the *other* prison and for some reason, they've given me extra blankets this time. Maybe, they're not going to off me so soon, after all. Still, I shiver, not so much from cold this time, but from fear. I almost wish I hadn't woken up. That instead, during the night, I'd pushed the blankets off my body and allowed the cold to take me. But something, I'm not sure what, made me wrap the blankets over my torso as best as I could. Survivor's instinct? That's a fucking laugh. My whole life's been about survival.

Despite the beatings the other night and what they did to Calhoun, a small flicker of hope still burns deep inside. Every passing minute makes it glow a little dimmer, but I'm clinging to the fact that they haven't beaten me again and my throbbing body hurts less than before. Still, another beating might have been better than last night's nightmares ... Flashes of spurting blood and echoes of tortured screams plagued my dreams. Even with my eyes open, I can't rid my mind of them. I doubt I ever will.

I glance round and for the first time register that dawn has broken, casting pink shadows through the mucky, snow-specked windows. The glow of lights from outside fades, but in the pink hue, I can see my surroundings more clearly. Some cages are empty. I must have slept through the dogs being moved. If I strain my ears, I can hear muffled yelps and snarls from somewhere outside and occasionally the deep tones of men yelling.

My eyes rest on a plate with bread and coagulating beans sitting on the floor, just within reach, next to the bottle of water. Stomach growling at the sight, I realise that despite the disgusting stink of my own waste and the rancid animal odours, I will eat it. God, what have I become? Perhaps I'll morph into one of my caged companions. Maybe my stubble will grow so much, I'll look like a dog. It amuses me to think that if I look like one and act like one, maybe I'll be able to survive this. I pull the plate towards me and using the spoon provided, shovel spoonsful of freezing beans and chunks of bread into my mouth. Prisoners on death row get a better last supper than this. Still, I eat, filling the gnawing ache in my gut, and hoping that the fuel would help me come up with a solution to my current problem. I hold out little hope of that as the door opens and two captors enter, accompanied by two broad-shouldered, snarling hounds. Although they strain against their leashes, thankfully, their trainers keep hold of their chains and, using sticks and guttural orders, the men force the beasts back into their cages.

Before he leaves, one man turns to me and grins. 'Your turn soon, mate. Hope you're up for a fair fight.'

Both men dissolve into stupid laughter and blood runs cold in my veins as the two dogs eye me up. Right now, I'd give anything to see Jacko enter the shack; he was the only one who ever showed me the slightest iota of kindness.

Chapter 16

Charlie took a deep breath and tiptoed downstairs. Her mum would kill her if she knew she was sneaking out like this. Especially after her meltdown earlier this week. On reflection, she shouldn't have done that. Should have kept her frustrations under wraps. Now Marcus and her mum would keep even more of an eye on her and that was the last thing she wanted. All she needed was some breathing space. Everything was too damn intense nowadays and since all that crap last year with her mum freaking out and then her therapist being a lunatic, she'd been boiling up inside with no way to let the steam out. It wasn't her mum and Marcus's fault, but they're so bloody protective. She knew her mum had been through a lot. Still, sometimes she just wanted to shake her and tell her it wasn't *all* about her. It wasn't just Nikki's mum that got murdered, it was also Charlie's Ajima after all. Then Charlie had to put on a brave face for Ruby and Sunni, whilst *she* – the brave and wonderful, Nikki Parekh – had her breakdown. *God*, that was tough! She really thought they were going to lose her. It bothered Charlie that her mum still kept her self-harm kit in the airing cupboard. Every time Charlie went to check she was not using it, her gut clenched and her throat closed up. Sometimes she really thought she'd explode and then who'd be there to hold everything together?

That was why it was so easy with him. He felt the same way as her – the *exact* same way. He knew what it was like to be watched all the time. To have everyone analysing every word you say, every action you take. To have parents checking up on you all the time, making sure you're safe. It was just crap. But what made it worse was that their parents were so worried about their kids being physically hurt that they didn't take the time to look underneath it all – at what was going on inside their minds.

Charlie was certain her mum would freak out big-time if she saw the festering misery inside her daughter. If she could hear her crying all night long, unable to stop herself. All *she* saw was Charlie being strong, because that's how she'd *always* been. That's what Nikki had taught her to be – just like her. *Well, we all fucking know what happened to her last year, don't we? And I'm damned if I'm going to let that happen to me.* Seeing him was the only thing that kept Charlie sane, but there was no way *she'd* approve if she told her. She'd shut it down, lock Charlie up or send her to Ramallah, like she wanted to do in the first place. Then Charlie'd be stuck with nowhere to let out the tension and nobody to talk to. Nobody to confide in, to be herself with.

When Charlie reached the bottom step, she sat down and, with half an ear out for movement upstairs, pulled her trainers on. Thankful her mum didn't have their 'minders' doing the night shift too. She made up her mind to leave through the back door. That way, they'd all be less likely to hear her go out. She glanced at her phone – quarter to five. Just in time. He'd be waiting by the Rec, and they'd have an hour of darkness before she needed to sneak back. Charlie didn't care that it was snowing. When they'd messaged each other earlier, they spoke about making a snowman. *Who does that? Who makes a snowman in the dark?* She smiled – *we do, that's who.* It would keep them warm and Charlie couldn't remember when she last did something fun, something that kids would do. With a final glance upstairs, she held her breath, checking that they were still asleep. Marcus's snores drifted downstairs and for a second, she almost reconsidered going out. Maybe she could just message him? He'd understand, she *knew* he would. She *could* creep back up, crawl under her duvet, just be a good girl and pretend everything was okay. After the row the other day, that's exactly what she should do. But she knew deep inside that she was fed up being the good girl. Fed up always doing the right thing. She hesitated. Then, when Marcus released a humungous snore, she headed down the hall towards the kitchen. No, she wouldn't let him down. They needed to talk, be together, just let off some steam. It's the only thing that helped them feel better. She grabbed a carrot from the veg rack and a tangerine from the fruit bowl. They had a snowman to build.

Chapter 17

Downey was well aware that coming here was risky, especially after he'd been here the previous day, but he couldn't help himself. Something compelled him to be here, to stake out her space. He enjoyed the feeling of power from infringing on her privacy. Watching the recordings of her therapy sessions was great – really gave him a buzz – but being in her locale without her knowing was edgy. Made him feel powerful and in control. He'd seen the security measures she'd taken during the day, and once he'd sussed out that after they were all locked up at home of an evening their external security thugs disappeared, he made it his job to do a tour of the area every so often. Besides, even if she decided to do a middle of the night spot-check, he stuck to the shadows; the snow was heavy enough to hide him.

It amused him that she felt safe with all her brats and that husband of hers all locked up together and her stupid younger sister shacked up with a copper and that docile son of hers next door. Hadn't she ever heard the term sitting ducks before? If he was of a mind to finish her off, he could've done it on any of the nights he drifted ghost-like round the streets she called her own. A petrol bomb through her windows, front and back, a home invasion – short and sharp with a few rounds of ammo and she'd be gone, or a bomb planted under her car and her and all her horrid little sprogs would explode into nothingness. But that wasn't the plan he had for his darling daughter. No, Nikki Parekh had to suffer and he would make sure she did.

He relished the thought that the uncertainty of his whereabouts must be killing her. Not knowing his exact location was an ace up his sleeve. He'd seen her mental breakdown, and this strategy of dropping postcards on her at infrequent intervals would fuel her vulnerabilities. He'd been privileged to see her at her lowest ebb. He'd heard her verbalise her deepest fears through torrents of tears and all the while she twang, twang, twanged that stupid elastic band. His daughter was unstable, and he'd feed that instability. He smiled, shrugging his shoulders deeper into the folds of his donkey jacket. He'd seen first-hand how effective his mind games could be. Soon as she'd seen that postcard he'd sent to the idiot kid, Isaac, she'd reacted and moved him in with her. Like *she'd* be protection for the kid. When Isaac's time was up, Nikki Parekh wouldn't be able to save him. In fact, maybe by then she'd have lost herself completely. Maybe by the time he'd picked off all her friends and family, she'd want to end it herself for real.

Every time he forced her to react, he owned her a little more, controlled her a little bit more. He was the puppeteer, and Nikki Parekh was his Pinocchio. He laughed out loud and pushed himself away from the fence where he was studying the alley that led to the rear yards of both his daughters' houses. Best go home, before he froze and before her bodyguards arrived ... *Oh, hello?*

Movement from further up the street stilled him for a moment. He stood in the shadows, well clear of the streetlights. There was activity from Nikki's back yard. He strained his eyes, then a smile broke out over his lips. The daughter – the oldest one, Charlie. Seemed like little Miss Parekh junior was as reckless as her mother. Perhaps he could use that to his advantage. As he watched, she glanced round, her head moving side to side, taking in her surroundings, then with a final glance at the upstairs windows she was off, heading down the alley in the opposite direction from where Downey hid.

His grin widened. Never one to look a gift horse in the mouth, Downey waited till she reached the end of the alley and turned right towards the Rec, before falling into place behind her, treading in her footprints as the snow continued, offering even more cover. He was unsure what to do with the opportunity. Maybe nothing for now, but at the very least, this departure from Charlie's normal behaviour was a welcome bonus, and he was glad he'd taken the risk of surveying Listerhills twice in the space of a few hours. It had paid off big-time, for if the girl sneaked out of the house before dawn once, then chances were she'd do it again. Of course, it all depended on the purpose of her illicit escape from Fort Parekh.

Downey didn't have long to wait to find out what Charlie was up to. As she crept through the Rec's broken fencing, he spotted a figure break from the shadows and wave to her. She sped up, raising her hand to return the greeting. When she reached the tall figure, he enveloped her in a bear hug and for a moment, in the murky shadows, the two figures were indistinguishable from each other. Downey remained outside the fencing until the figures, hand in hand, moved deeper into the play area. Once certain he could maintain his cover, he squeezed through the fence and followed them, sticking to their prints and keeping a reasonable distance between them. When they stopped, the odd indecipherable word caught in the night air and flew back towards him as he leaned against a tree, his body half hidden by its trunk, and spied on them. They moved far enough into the park to be invisible from the roads and soon the pair began a snowball fight, squealing and chasing each other like kids. Finally, giggling, they settled to making a massive snowball, using the snow that had been pristine until their footsteps had marred its perfect whiteness. In the dark, Downey didn't recognise the lad she was with and, like him, the boy was huddled up in winter clothing. That wasn't an issue, though. He'd find out who he was and why the lovebirds were forced to meet at such unsocial hours.

After pulling a carrot and tangerines from her coat pocket, Charlie stuck them on the snowman's head to make a face before hugging the boy close. They shared a long kiss and then Charlie pulled away from him, her reluctance emphasised by the way she allowed her gloved fingers to linger in his and the long glances between them as she retraced her steps to the fence. Instead of accompanying her, the boy remained where he was, hands stuffed deep in his pockets, back hunched against the icy snow, and when she was out of sight, his shoulders seemed to slump even more. *Poor fucker's got it bad!*

The lad, eyes to the ground, walked through the park in the opposite direction and Downey slid into step a hundred yards behind him. This was his opportunity to identify Charlie Parekh's boyfriend, and after he had that information, he could decide what to do with it.

When the boy reached the other side, he slipped through a similar gap in the fencing to the one Downey had entered by and headed towards the main road. Downey followed him, his footsteps muffled by the snow and the few cars that were braving the icy roads at this early hour. Downey was confused when the boy turned into a residential street. The lad had taken a circuitous route to reach his destination and Downey wondered if perhaps he'd been spotted tailing the boy. However, without glancing in Downey's direction, the lad went through a gate, crept round the house and used the side door to gain access. Downey frowned and glanced round the empty street. His eye caught sight of a vehicle a couple of yards down from the gate, and he grinned. That was a car he recognised and now he had a strong suspicion who the boyfriend might be. He retraced his steps, this new information sending all thoughts of the cold that was permeating his bones flying away. This could be gold. It was up to him to use this to his advantage. With a spring in his step, he took the shortcut back through the Rec, retrieved his car and drove to his temporary residence to warm up and catch a few hours' kip before commencing on the second part of his busy day.

Chapter 18

My mind's playing tricks on me. One minute, I'm dreaming of a picnic with my family. The sun shining, birds tweeting, the smell of fresh baked bread … then I jolt awake and reality sinks in once more. There's something in the air. Undercurrents of excitement. Increased activity, more intensive training sessions for the dogs. Something big is about to happen. When the captors return the animals to their cages, they taunt me, their eyes flashing with the same feral rage I recognise in the animals they train. They kick me, spit at me, get right in my face saying, 'Not long now. You won't know what's hit you.' One of them, the tall lad with the red hair and the Cockney accent, rubs his hands together, his smile revealing rotten nicotine-stained teeth as he laughs like an arse. 'You're going to make us a load of money, you know that? A shed load of the stuff.'

Then the wanker rolls his stick along the bars of the nearest cage, winding the fucking dogs right up. Mouths open, showing their sharp teeth, their saliva drips to the floor, and they barrel against the cage. They've got scars over their faces, barely healed from the last fight and I have no option but to cower in my own filth, my heart hammering so hard and fast I wish it would over-work and just stop.

Then I get a visitor. Not the usual line of thugs, wrapped up in winter coats, their breath steaming the air as they manoeuvre the animals, but the masked man – the one with the balaclava covering all of his face except those eyes, those horrid nasty eyes. The one who beat me and knobbled that young lass on the first night. The one who gave Calhoun to the dogs the other night and laughed when I shat myself. The thugs fear him and don't make eye contact with him. I don't blame them. I've seen what that man is capable of and it petrifies me. My fate is in the masked man's hands, and I know that he has no empathy. Not for me or for the other caged animals. I understand that the animals are victims, just like me. They're held in captivity, forced to train, forced to put themselves at risk, forced to fight for their own survival. No wonder they're feral.

On this visit, the masked man pinches his nose against the overwhelming stench. I almost laugh. Clearly, his balaclava isn't enough to offset the stink. I'm so used to it now that it I don't even smell it and somewhere deep inside, despite my fear, I savour this small token of superiority over the other man. *I* contributed to the foul stench that makes the masked man so uncomfortable and that gives me a little strength.

The boss-man glares at me, lips turned down, nose wrinkled. His eyes rake over me from feet to face. The silence is palpable. Frissons of electricity zap through the freezing building as I wait. Despite the cold, beads of sweat form across my brow. My mouth is dry and, my earlier strength fading, I can't bring myself to meet his gaze. I'm aware of my cowardice as a lump forms in my throat. Hiding behind his mask, he's nothing but a bully who gets off on dominating his victims, so why do I allow him that satisfaction? With little control over my own destiny, I could still take some pleasure away from my tormentors. I could brazen it out, glare at them, disrespect them. The end would be the same, no matter what I do. The only positive outcome of my timidity is that it might wangle me an additional few hours or days on this earth.

But do I want that? Maybe I'd be better off challenging them. Making him angry, forcing him to end my life quicker. After all, sprawling in excrement, freezing and half-delirious, isn't living.

'You really are a scrawny little piece of shit.' The boss's words are flat and disinterested, more like an observation than a question.

I remain silent – waiting.

'You have no idea who I am or what I'm capable of, do you?' He bends over, a taut smile pulling his mask tighter over his mouth. There is no humour in it, no humanity either, as he puts his face in my line of vision, forcing me to make eye contact. When his question gets no response, his eyes flash and before I realise what's coming, his boot connects with my healing ribs.

I yelp, setting off a cacophony of responding snarls from the cages, and when the pain recedes, I look at the masked man again and shake my head. It is a partial lie. I might not recognise my captor, but I know what this man is capable of. I witnessed it with my own eyes. But I understand that *this* is the response he wanted.

The masked man rubs his hand over his nose and snorts before bending over. His anger has been replaced by amusement. 'You might not know who I am, right now, but it won't be long before everyone's talking about *you*'. He snorts a half-laugh, hoarse and cold to match the emptiness that resides in his eyes. 'Mind you, by then it'll be too late, but ...' He prods me as if I'm roadkill. '*You'll* have served your purpose.'

He raises his leg and kicks me again. 'All *you* are is bait.' And with a grunt, he spins round, makes snarling sounds at the captive dogs and when he leaves the building a menacing chill remains.

Chapter 19

From behind the jeep, Jacko, unnoticed, had watched Fugly put on his mask and head into the shack. He was tempted to turn a blind eye and just get into the jeep and sneak home for an early morning cuddle with the missus before the grandkid woke up, but his conscience wouldn't let him. He knew Fugly had plans for the lad, that should keep him safe for at least another twenty-four hours – then again, he also knew how erratic Fugly could be. Last thing he wanted was for Fugly to get carried away and off the kid before Jacko had decided what to do.

Cursing, he flung his half-smoked cig away and headed over to the shack. Even with the extra blankets he'd chucked over him yesterday, the kid would be lucky to have survived the night in these temperatures. A flutter of something very much like relief tickled his innards. If the kid was dead, that would solve his immediate problems, wouldn't it? With the kid gone, he wouldn't have to decide if he was going to save him and the constant gnawing in his gut would go. He placed his gloved thumb and index finger at either side of his mouth and massaged his chin. He was a coward. What sort of man snuck home for a quickie when there was a kid freezing to death in a shed? Unbidden, the image of the skinny beaten lad chained up like a dog was replaced by one of his skinny drug-addled daughter and without warning, the half-digested slice of toast he'd scoffed before heading out from the farmhouse landed at his feet, its acrid stench making him gip again. Bent double, hands on his knees, he shook his head before straightening then, using the toe of his boot, he brushed snow over the rancid pile. Still shaky, he spat a glob of sick onto the ground and walked over to the shack.

The overnight blizzard had half-covered the windows, so rather than risk attracting Fugly's attention, Jacko stood on tiptoe and peered through the mucky glass. He could just about make out the huddled frame of the lad, lumped in a foetal position, shivering in his own filth, under the blankets with Fugly towering over him, his mask tight round his ugly fucking face.

By now, Jacko knew his boss well enough to surmise what he was thinking, but guessing was unnecessary as fragmented sentences drifted through the ill-fitting windows.

'… Weak little tosser …'

'… Cowed …'

'… scared as piss …'

'… no fight left …'

'… self-respect …'

'… no gumption …'

Then, as Fugly began pacing before the broken boy, his voice raised and his words became clearer. 'There's a word. Gumption. I've got plenty of it, but you … you disgusting, snivelling little knobhead … Not a single damn iota of it. Not even a pretence of it. You should be ashamed of yourself.'

Now Fugly bent over the lad, roaring in his face. 'Still, *I* didn't choose you for your brains *or* your bravery.' His laugh verged on maniacal and if it chilled Jacko to the marrow, fuck knows what it did to the lad. Was now the time to interrupt? But he hesitated as curiosity got the better of him. Fugly had commissioned Jacko to recruit that lad specifically, and it intrigued him, for he could see nowt special in the boy. Maybe if he listened for longer, he'd find out more.

Fugly was still ranting. 'I've got plans for you. Big plans. Bigger plans than you know.' He kicked the boy, eliciting nothing more than a muffled grunt. 'Doubt *you'll* put on much of a show, but that won't matter. You'll be dead by the end of it and you'll have served your purpose.'

With another well-aimed kick, he turned on his heel and headed for the door, waiting till he'd exited the shack before pulling his mask from his face.

Jacko, walking round the side of the building as if by coincidence, noted Fugly's heightened colour and the sweat on his forehead and tried for a non-committal tone. 'All right boss?'

Fugly's screwed up lips flattened onto a more normal smile and the furrow across his brow smoothed as he looked up at Jacko. He was still panting, but he seemed more in control of himself. 'Fine, Jacko. Fine.' He set off back towards the farmhouse, indicating that Jacko should join him. 'Had some good news this morning. My sources tell me there's been an increase in online chatter, on the dark web like, but not on the sites normally viewed by casual punters. Seems our speciality provision is drawing some interest in the right quarters.'

Jacko kept his head down, hoping Fugly wouldn't see the shock on his face. Things were getting worse and although he'd become used to Fugly's disregard for human life, he hadn't realised just how much demand there was for the sort of atrocities Fugly revelled in.

'I'm on to a right money maker with this venture.' Fugly nudged him on the arm before adding. 'Best keep on my good side, eh, Jacko?'

A snort of laughter left Fugly's mouth, sending a chill down Jacko's throat when he added, 'Don't want to bag you up in bits and deliver you to your widow now, do I?'

Jacko summoned up a snort of his own and met Fugly's eyes. 'No worries there, boss. I'm loyal.' Hating himself, he jerked his head towards the group of thugs gathered near the barn door for a fag break, 'Which is more than can be said for those tossers.'

Fugly's penetrating gaze rested on the kids, haloed in a fug of smoke. Jacko exhaled, yanked a glove off and lifted his fingers to his crucifix. *Shit, if I don't do something soon, who knows what'll happen?*

'The women are the fucking worst. Maybe one of them will be in line for my next little show. Maybe one of those two lesbos, eh? What do you reckon, Jacko? Shall we pitch one of the lesbos to the dogs, see how tough they are then?'

Fugly's laugh chilled Jacko, who couldn't think of a response, but thankfully none was needed for, still cackling, Fugly turned and strode over to his car, throwing an order over his shoulder. 'You're in charge, Jacko. Get those lazy bastards working. I'll be back soon.'

Chapter 20

Nikki was never at her best first thing in the morning. Even after years of early starts and middle-of-the-night call-outs, she hadn't adapted to early rises and rarely spoke before at least two mugs of coffee and a slice of toast. This morning she didn't have time to fortify herself for the day ahead, for barely had she entered the kitchen, her hair still dripping from her shower, when Marcus approached and whispered in her ear. 'We got a problem, Nik.'

One look at the tension lines pulling his lips into a grimace had Nikki's heart thudding. A quick glance at the table told her Sunni and Ruby were okay, but there was no sign of her eldest daughter. 'Charlie!'

Not waiting for Marcus's response, she spun on her heel and headed back along the hallway ready to pound upstairs to her daughter's room, but Marcus grabbed her arm and stopped her, talking in urgent tones, with the sound of her two younger children squabbling over toast and cereal in the background. 'She's fine – I checked. She's out for the count. Hardly moved when I told her it was time to get up.'

The tension leeched from Nikki's shoulders at the news her children were all safe. The threat of Downey lurking in the background meant she was continually on edge, waiting for the axe to fall. Lack of caffeine making her tetchy, she glared at Marcus, 'So what the hell's all the drama? You almost gave me a heart attack then. What's the damn problem? The sink blocked? Are we out of milk?'

Marcus's lips twitched. 'Nothing as serious as that, still …' He tipped his head towards the kitchen, indicating she should follow him, and headed to the back door.

Dread gathered once more in Nikki's stomach. Had Downey delivered a postcard in person this time? Or was it something worse than that? Marcus unlocked and opened the door letting an icy blast of air into the toasty kitchen.

'Aw Dad, shut the door, it's freezing in here.' Sunni, strawberry jam all round his mouth, shivered, and pulled his bare feet up and under his bum as he tried to keep warm.

Nikki dropped a kiss on the top of his head. 'That's why you have slippers and a dressing gown, Sunni. Go put them on, eh?'

Ruby, dumping her plate and mug in the sink, laughed. 'That'd be being too sensible, Mum, and you know Sunni's just a *boy*.'

'Sooo!' Sunni, face flushing, knelt on his stool. 'Nowt wrong with being a boy, Rubster choobster, better than being a smelly girl.'

Nikki rolled her eyes and walked past her children to join Marcus at the half-open door. 'What is it?'

He opened the door wider, and Nikki poked her head through. She scanned the snow-covered doorstep, taking in the footprints leading down to the back yard and across the path to the gate. 'Shit.'

'My thoughts precisely,' Marcus said, glaring at the rapidly filling prints that trailed from the gate to the back door. 'No urban fox made those, Nik.'

Unsure whether she it was cold or fear that made her shiver, Nikki glared at the prints as if she could obliterate them. Then she swallowed her fear and examined them. The snowfall had made it impossible to get any tread marks from them, so Nikki didn't even consider calling CSIs, and with the yard empty and no obvious threat in sight, there was no point in calling in her colleagues either. She bent down and studied the nearest print – the one on the top doorstep. Marcus was right. Although more like large indents in the snow, a person clearly made them. 'Definitely human prints.' She looked at Marcus. 'Our visitor didn't leave any little surprises?'

Marcus shook his head. 'Not that I could see. Maybe they took something or maybe they just wanted to freak us out.'

Nikki snorted. 'When we say *they*, we mean Downey, don't we?'

Marcus shrugged. 'We can't know for sure, but it seems the logical assumption. Who else would enter our yard in the early hours and traipse up to our back door.'

Nikki kicked the door jamb. 'Bastard! Fucking bastard! How dare he?'

Marcus put his arm round her shoulders, but she pulled away, her brow knit in a tight frown. 'Look, the tosser even retraced his steps. He walked up to our door just because he could and then retraced his steps, taking care to tread in his own footsteps.'

'What's up? What are you two doing with the door open? You're freezing out the house.' Charlie, hair mussed and hopping from foot to foot to keep warm, her arms wrapped round her slender frame, glared at them.

With the memory of Charlie's accusation that they always excluded her, fresh in Nikki's mind, she took a deep breath and opened the door wider, pointing at the footsteps that were disappearing as the snow fell heavier.

Charlie approached, her face pale, blinking rapidly, and Nikki regretted her decision to include Charlie in their discovery. The poor kid looked petrified. Charlie's eyes locked on the indents in the snow that now looked nothing like footprints. 'I … I …'

Nikki wrapped her arms round her daughter's shoulders and hugged her tight. 'Look Charlie, I don't want you worrying, but you said that we excluded you, treated you like a kid, so we wanted to be upfront with you.'

Charlie pulled away from Nikki, her brown eyes wide as her gaze settled first on her mum and then on Marcus. Thank God, some colour had come back to her cheeks, Nikki thought. Charlie opened her mouth to speak, but then closed it again, shaking her head as if denying the incriminating footprints. Nikki understood her daughter's reaction. She'd had a similar one only moments earlier. The impulse to deny the threat that Downey was closing in on them was natural. 'I don't want you to worry, Charlie. This might not be Downey. It could be some kid pranking us, or maybe Zain or Haqib popped over. I'll ask them later.'

But Charlie was now raking her fingers through her hair, the flush on her cheeks growing brighter as she moved to collapse onto a chair by the table. Marcus rushed over and flicked the kettle on. 'I'll make you some tea. You've not to worry about this, Charlie, okay?'

Nikki, taking her cue from Marcus, all thoughts of her own lack of caffeine dissipated, knelt before Charlie and took her daughter's freezing hands in hers. Gently rubbing them, she looked into her daughter's eyes, trying to instil confidence and security in her daughter. 'Don't worry, Charlie. We've got this. I'll get one of Ali's lads to stay overnight. Marcus will put a lock on the yard gate and we'll add extra locks to the doors and windows. We just need to follow the rules and not go anywhere unaccompanied.'

The flush faded from Charlie's cheeks and her hands shook. Nikki flashed a concerned glance at Marcus, who thrust sweetened tea onto the table beside Charlie before placing his arm round his stepdaughter's shoulders. 'Don't you worry, Charlie. This is a good sign. It means he's here, and that means we're close to catching him. This'll all soon be over.'

Nikki smiled at Marcus. He always knew the right thing to say and although his words weren't necessarily one hundred per cent accurate, hopefully they'd reassure Charlie and who knows, maybe this would lead to them catching Downey sooner rather than later. But Charlie jumped to her feet, banging into the table and causing her drink to spill and drip onto the floor. 'You lot are soooo bloody annoying. You're still patronising me. You don't even know if that's Downey's footprints. You're all so bloody het up on having a monster chasing us that you can't even consider that he's still in fucking Thailand or Venezuela or wherever else, and he's just messing with us. You're paranoid – both of you, you're paranoid – living in fear of an old man, when we *should* be living our lives. You all make me sick … SICK!'

And she wrenched herself away from her mum and stormed upstairs, leaving Nikki and Marcus gobsmacked, staring after her. After a few moments, Nikki turned to him, and said, 'Shit, Marcus. I just can't get this parenting malarkey right.'

Slumping into a chair beside her, Marcus pulled her into a hug. 'You and me both, Nik. You and me both.'

Chapter 21

Charlie rushed upstairs and opened her bedroom door before slamming it shut behind her with as much force as possible. It reverberated around the attic space, but they wouldn't hear it downstairs. Her frustration settled like a clenched fist stuffed down her throat. Everything swirled round her brain, from the damn row with her mum to her stupidity at not considering the footsteps she'd left in the snow. *Stupid, stupid, stupid!* She slammed the heel of her hand against her forehead, and beads of sweat smudged across her brow. *Fuck, I feel crap.* Her throat was as dry as a cat's arse and it hurt to swallow. *I can't be ill. Not today. Not right now. Not when all this has just kicked off.*

With a deep breath, she turned, clicked the lock shut and flung herself on top of the bed. What she really wanted to do was crawl under the duvet, pull it over her head and pretend nothing had happened, but she couldn't. It was crazy that because she'd crept out in the middle of the night, her mum now thought Downey was on their doorstep. She couldn't have made things worse if she'd planned it. Tears seeped from her eyes. There was no way out of this without hurting someone. *What the **actual** fuck? Can't believe it. Fucking Marcus smarty pants spotting my footprints in the snow?* Trust those two to jump to the Downey narrative. *Of* *course*, the prints had to belong to Downey. *Of course*, the Downey monster had snooped around their back yard with the foxes and the wheelie bins. *Of course*, they were all under imminent attack from an old geezer in his fucking sixties. *How much damage can a codger like him do?*

Thinking of Downey prompted a mixed reaction and Charlie's mind jumped between when she saw Ajima in hospital all battered and dying, and her funeral. *Fuck's sake, Charlie. You know what Downey's capable of. You've seen it.* But she wouldn't allow herself to dwell on that.

Instead, she rolled onto her back and scrubbed the tears away. Of course, her mum made it all about *her* … again. More restrictions, less freedom. Might as well curl up and die for all the quality of life she'd got. She inhaled and flinched as the cold air prickled her throat, she grabbed her water bottle, and took a tentative sip. As the liquid trickled down, it felt like she was swallowing razor blades and, as if to confirm that she was ill, a shiver engulfed her entire body.

A quiet knock sounded on the bedroom door, and groaning, Charlie stuffed her pillow over her head so she couldn't hear her mum's whinging and pleading. Voice husky, she said as loud as her sore throat would allow, 'Leave me alone. I'm taking a mental health day, all right?'

The words came out in a poisonous snarl, but she couldn't summon up the energy to care. Why should she walk around like she was on thin ice?

Everyone else said and did what they wanted. Telling Charlie to listen to her mum and stressing how dangerous Downey is. After a few seconds, Charlie removed the pillow from her head and strained her ears for sounds of *her* hovering outside, but the house felt empty. As if to confirm her suspicions, the front door slammed shut and when she sneaked over to the window, she saw her mum and Marcus kissing each other goodbye. *God, can't they just get a damn room?* Her mum glanced up at her window and Charlie jerked back, not wanting to be seen spying on them. Her mum half raised her arm in a wave and then seemed to reconsider as she and Marcus separated and headed to their vehicles – him to his work jeep and she to her new car. Ruby and Sunni were already in the backseat, ready to be dropped off at school, Isaac riding shotgun and no doubt singing the song, too. Sunni was bouncing around and the Rubster's head was bent over – *she'll be texting crap to one of her lame friends.* She watched her mum get in and start the engine but didn't she drive off straight away. *What's she faffing about with?* Charlie's phone signalled the arrival of a text and Charlie realised what she'd been doing – texting her. She opened it.

> **Mum: Charlie, you can have the day at home. Maybe you need some alone time. Don't go out. A couple of Ali's guys are coming over to watch the house, to make sure Downey doesn't show up. Please stay safe. Don't go out! Love you xxxx**

Talk about a big brother state. She couldn't even skip school without having her every movement monitored, and no doubt reported back to her mum. Charlie sighed and flopped back down on the bed. Now she'd got the freedom to do nothing all day except stuff her face with chocolate and watch Netflix, the day loomed ahead of her. She'd have been better off at school. At least there she wouldn't have to worry about being spied on. Besides, it was much easier to skip out of school. Ali's guys only turned up at break times and lunchtime. Nobody had caught on yet to the fact that when sixth formers had free periods, they could leave school premises. If she didn't want to stay indoors alone all day, she'd have to swallow her pride. Her fingers flew over her phone.

> **Charlie: Stop worrying. I'm going to school. Ali's guy can drop me off.**

Despite feeling like a cow, Charlie was too pissed off to be nice, so she withheld her usual three kisses and the emoji love heart. She wasn't ready to forgive her mother. It wasn't like Charlie to behave like this and she knew it. She didn't want to be like this, but just didn't know how to stop. It was her fault her mum and Marcus were on even higher alert. If she hadn't sneaked off last night, her mum might have started to relax. All she'd done was feed her mum's paranoia and for no good reason. She smiled. *Well, not for no good reason.* On the contrary, she'd had a great reason to sneak out and Charlie didn't regret it one bit. She just wished her mum would realise that Downey was in the past. There was no way he'd come back to the UK, never mind Bradford. Why would he risk everything, his freedom, to get back at them? He was just toying with them, but her mum couldn't see it and Marcus and all her cronies at Trafalgar House had just conceded to her. Hell, even Sajid and Langley believed her.

The doorbell rang and when she looked out the window, Haris, Ali's cousin, stood, gawping up at her window. Well, at least she wouldn't have to make small talk on the way to school. Haris didn't talk much. Charlie waved and signalled she'd be right down, but before she moved, she sent off a text:

Charlie: Got a free period at 10. Can you meet up?

When his text arrived with a thumbs up, Charlie smiled. Perhaps today wouldn't be so bad after all.

Chapter 22

Despite the upset around the footsteps in the back yard and Charlie's latest meltdown, the prospect of whatever her boss, Archie Hegley, was about to reveal was at the forefront of Nikki's thoughts. She suspected Archie had received confirmation of Downey's presence in Yorkshire. After all, that would fit in with the continued arrival of postcards and the snow prints that had appeared overnight. She'd left Marcus to update Ali and his team, whilst she'd had a hurried conversation with both Sajid and DI Zain Ahad by the drinks machine in the hall before they made their way to Archie's office. She'd tried to prod some information from Ahad as they walked, but he was having none of it. To shake off her annoyance, she lagged behind Ahad and mumbled 'Bloody Dark Knight' to Sajid.

The day had barely started and yet exhaustion weighed down on Nikki. Shoulders slumped, she slurped water from her bottle, wishing it was an extra strong coffee and bemoaning the fact that Marcus's 'lay off the coffee and hydrate' was actually very good advice.

With Ahad already inside the cramped office, DCI Hegley greeted them at the door, his gaze not quite meeting Nikki's, as he ushered them inside with a, 'Come away in the two o' ye.'

Despite the friendly tone of Archie's greeting, Nikki wasn't reassured. His colour was heightened and his arm movements seemed effusive. Whatever Archie had dragged them in to talk about, Nikki's clenched gut told her it wouldn't be good news.

After exchanging another glance with her partner, she and Saj walked over and sank into the seats in front of Archie's desk. Being there was familiar to Nikki. She'd been rollicked whilst sitting right there opposite Archie. She'd also been praised, sent home, told off, given bad news and listened to. Today, though, she couldn't work out which option Archie was going to utilise. His demeanour spoke of nerves, which made Nikki veer towards some trick or other from Downey. If it was information on Downey or his whereabouts, she could work with that. As long as Downey remained at large, her family were at risk, so anything, no matter how obscure, that could point her in his direction would be a bonus. She'd opened her mouth to share her thoughts, when she noticed Archie was standing behind his desk and Ahad was sitting in his chair. *Odd.*

She cast another glance to Saj, whose slight shrug told her he'd noticed the weird set-up on the other side of the desk too.

Archie looked at Sajid. 'I hear congratulations are in order, DS Malik.'

Saj cleared his throat, a slow flush spreading up from his neck to his cheeks. Nikki grinned. Despite drawing attention to himself with his natty designer wear and perfectly matched clothes, Saj hated being the centre of attention and found receiving compliments difficult. He'd once told Nikki that in his house, his parents had frowned upon compliments. Nikki understood that sort of climate in families like her own. Whilst her own mum had been nurturing, Nikki's early years spent avoiding injury, or worse, had left a lasting scar on her ability to trust. She found it harder to understand that lack of nurture in supposedly 'functional' families. Praise was clearly the last thing Saj had expected to come from Archie's mouth as he nodded, offering a garbled thanks. Thankfully, though, Archie was oblivious to the reaction his words had prompted as he continued in his usual bluff way. 'Well, laddie, I've got some proverbials of mah own tae share.' Archie, arms behind his back, rocked from toe to heel, his face awash with colour, his chest puffed out in front of him like a massive robin redbreast whose red had seeped upwards.

He looked round at each of the three of them, although still not making eye contact with Nikki. 'I'm retiring. Had enough of all the crap after …' He waved his hand in the air as if to waft the memory away. 'Ye ken, that stuff before Christmas.'

A smile broke out across his face, making him look younger and somehow more carefree. 'So, we'll be having a double celebration, you and me, Malik.'

Nikki was glad that all the attention was on Saj, because Archie's announcement, coming so soon after Saj's own news, hit her like a double whammy. Losing Saj was bad enough, but to lose Archie too was unbearable. What was he thinking? Retiring from the police? Really? Archie? No way? But there he was, blabbing on and on about his plans to set up a security firm or a Private Investigator business. Waffling on about already having clients and a few potential employees too, courtesy of Ali. Her heart hammered against her chest. Her breath hitched in her throat and stayed there, as she took small gasps to try to clear the lump that stopped her breathing properly. *How the hell can I go on without Archie and Saj by my side?* Their voices rolled over her, discussing details of Archie's plans, offering all the usual platitudes about the place not being the same without them, but she couldn't focus on what they were saying. She needed them: their friendship, their support, their solidity. However, she also knew that she owed them her support, her encouragement, her well wishes. So she swallowed the lump and hoped her smile didn't look too maniacal.

Archie frowned. 'For cluck's sake, Parekh, didn't you hear what I said?'

Nikki blinked, forcing herself back to the present and rather than succumb to tears, she injected a dismissive tone into her reply. 'Course I heard. You practically bellowed it out. In fact, I'd be surprised if anyone in Bailden didn't hear. You're retiring and it's well deserved and I'm happy for you and I hope it all goes well for you.'

Archie shook his head and raked his fingers through his hair – what there was of it. 'You didn't listen. Not properly, Parekh. You need to get your proverbials in order if you're going tae step up to the mark. Do you hear me?'

Now it was Nikki's turn to frown. What the hell was he on about? Step up to the mark? Her eyes moved from Saj's grinning face to Ahad's sardonic smirk as she wondered what she'd missed. It was Sajid who put her out of her misery. 'There's going to be a vacancy now that the boss is retiring.' He paused as if waiting for understanding to dawn on her face, but Nikki was still flummoxed, so Saj, released an elongated, 'give me strength' sort of sigh. 'Which means …?'

Nikki shook her head. Her sluggish mind wouldn't work and the desire to prod Sajid's arm was overwhelming. It wasn't even nine o'clock, and she'd already had too much excitement for one day. She closed her eyes and said 'I've no idea what you're on about. You'll have to spell it out.'

'Clucking hell! *I* bet my *proverbials* on you and you cannae even hold it together for ten minutes.' Archie's face had turned a deep maroon colour as he glared at her. Nikki almost welcomed the familiarity of receiving a rollicking from Archie. That was something she was used to. Something she could relate to, even if she wasn't sure what she'd done this time to merit it.

Archie, slow and steady, growled out an explanation. 'Ahad here is stepping up to DCI.' His frown deepened, and he lasered Nikki with his eyes whilst prodding himself in the chest. 'That's *my* old job. The one I'm stepping down from, yeah? You got that, Parekh?'

The urge to curl her lip and fold her arms across her chest

like Charlie did was strong, but she satisfied herself with a nod as Archie continued in a less growly tone.

'He's experienced enough for it and would have been fast-tracked by the end of the year, anyway. All my retirement means is that he's been fast-tracked a bit sooner.'

Nikki nodded again and slipped her hands under her thighs so she wouldn't be tempted to twang her elastic band. It made sense, she supposed. Still, Ahad was new to the team and although he had the necessary experience … he wasn't Archie, was he? Who knew what sort of changes he'd make? It was all too much for her to absorb right now. So, she elected to pin a smile on her lips and let everything else flow over her until she could escape to the loos and do a bit of meditating.

Archie was still rambling on. '… means the DI job's up for grabs again.'

Shit! Nikki hadn't even thought about that. Saj and Archie going was bad enough, Ahad taking over from Archie might prove challenging, but she wasn't sure she'd be able to cope with yet another change. Why couldn't everybody just slooow the hell down? Why couldn't they all just take a breath and stop hurtling forwards like a runaway train? She zoned Archie out for a few seconds and tried a couple of slow breaths, before zoning in again.

'… well with your track record, especially with all that before Christmas, you're the top runner for it.'

Top runner for what? Were they sacking her? Moving her into admin, demoting her? Nikki turned her gaze to Sajid, hoping he'd come to her rescue and fill in the gaps, but he was standing there grinning at her, like she'd gifted him an upgrade on his Jag. As her eyes scanned his face, his smile faltered and he took a step towards her, speaking in a quiet tone. 'Archie's offering you the DI job, Nik? Didn't you hear?'

The DI job? She wasn't being demoted. They wanted to promote her. If she took the job, she'd have one less change to contend and for a second the weight in her chest lightened. Then, she shook her head. No. She'd still need a new DS and knowing her luck, she'd end up with Springer when she came back from maternity leave. No way could Nikki stomach that situation. She jumped to her feet and ran her fingers through her hair. 'Wait a minute, boss. I tried the DI hat on before and I hated it. And …' She looked at Sajid. With half her team gone there was no way she'd be able to cope. But Archie tutted and took a step forward, leaning in close. He held Nikki's gaze. '*You'll* be DI *and*, instead of sloping off to Cybercrimes, Malik will step up as DS. It'll be great. The best team in the station. And with Ahad at the helm, you'll be frontline investigator so …' He shrugged, threw his hands out before him and grinned. 'That's decided then.'

'But …?'

'Just take the plucking, proverbial job, Parekh.' drowned Nikki's words out.

So, swallowing her misgivings, she did.

Chapter 23

'And you'll never believe what the cheeky cow said.' Nikki didn't give Sajid a chance to guess. 'She said – wait for it – "I'm taking a mental health day." What the hell was I supposed to do with that, eh?'

Sajid sipped his coffee and took a bite of his toasted teacake. They were in Lazy Bites café discussing the morning's briefing, but the events chez Parekh followed by the various bombshells dropped by Archie only half an hour earlier had got in the way. They'd spent the duration of Nikki's first two cups of coffee coming to terms with their new roles and were now discussing Charlie's earlier behaviour. When Nikki's stare turned into a frown, he grinned. 'Oh, you want a response now. Well, all I can say is, she's her mother's daughter. Wish I'd been half as sparky when I was her age.'

Nikki glowered. 'Not helping, Saj. Not helping at all. She's a bloody madam, that's what she is. It's like she thinks *I'm* to blame for all of this Downey crap. She seems to think *we're* all overreacting and every time we put a measure in place to keep everyone safe in case Downey's got something planned, she pushes against it.'

If she was being honest, Nikki would admit that she felt

114

responsible for everything that was happening. Downey was *her* father after all and it was she who had exposed his villainy, making it necessary for him to flee the country. Plus, she'd goaded him. She'd been goading him from when she was a kid and she realised just how evil he was. He blamed her for her mum leaving him, he blamed her for every bad thing that had happened to him and *now* he would stop at nothing to obliterate everything she held dear. He'd already stolen her precious mum from her and *she* would do whatever it took to protect her family – she'd also do whatever it took to destroy him.

Sajid placed his hand on her arm. 'You're not responsible for his behaviour, Nik, so don't go down that rabbit hole. You're better than that.' Correctly interpreting Nikki's wistful glances at his plate, he pushed the second half of his teacake towards her. 'Are you sure that those footprints belonged to Downey? I mean really, really sure?'

Nikki opened her mouth, indignant words on the tip of her tongue, then she closed it again and shrugged, twanging her elastic band twice before pulling her sleeve down to cover it. 'Don't know what to bloody think, Saj. I double checked with Ahad and Haqib and neither of them were roaming about my yard at the crack of dawn. Who else could it have been?'

Now it was Saj's turn to shrug. 'No idea ... it's just ...' His lips tightened.

'Just what? Come on, spit it out, Malik.'

'It's just, Downey does *nothing* without a purpose, does he? I mean why would he wander up to your back door in the middle of the night? Just seems a strange thing to do. I mean, it's not like he left a message. If he'd written something in the snow or pushed another postcard through the door, *then* it would have served a purpose, but just walking about doesn't say Downey to me. I mean, he'd want it to seem like a threat. He knows we've no way to ascertain if he's in Bradford or not. He keeps sending those postcards, but we've had no confirmed sightings of him. His known contacts swear he hasn't been in touch and I'm inclined to believe them. If he wanted to leave a message for you, Nik it would have been clearer and more threatening.'

The same thought had niggled Nikki. Initially, she'd gone down the *Downey's been in my back yard* route, but then, after she'd dropped the kids at school and driven Isaac to work, she'd had second thoughts. Saj was right. Downey was more wrecking ball than tiptoe through the snow. She bit her lip and glowered out the steamed-up windows at the still falling snow outside. 'Then who?'

Sajid ran his hands through his hair. He'd had a thought, but he wasn't sure whether to share it with Nikki or follow it up himself. His gut told him to put out feelers on his own before worrying Nikki, but his head told him that Nikki would be pissed off with him if he didn't share his suspicions. He shrugged. Nikki had been pissed off with him before, and *he* was a grown man. He could handle a little Parekh huffiness. He'd deal with this on his own before sending Nikki into a tailspin. 'Come on. Let's see what the briefing reveals. We might have an ID for our body part. And if not, Jewkes gave us a list a mile long to follow up on.'

Distracted from worrying about the footsteps in the snow, Nikki grabbed her coat, shoved her bobble hat on her head, wound a matching scarf round her neck and yanked her gloves on. Trafalgar House might only be a few yards away from the café, but she'd no intention of becoming an icicle before she got there. 'Yeah, let's go, I'm particularly interested in checking out that list of vets. Can you believe the audacity of these dog owners that they'd have them fight to near death and then have the gall to employ a vet to patch them up again? Sick, sick, sick fuckers! What kind of sick vet would stand by and let all this happen in the first place?'

Chapter 24

Shivering, Charlie bounced up and down on her toes to keep warm. He was late. The problem was that she hadn't had time to dry her coat after their snowball fight in the early hours and now it was a sodden chilly mass against her jeans and jumper. If she'd been smart, instead of falling right into bed, she'd have draped her stuff over the radiator in her room. The shiver came again and combined with her scratchy throat and the slight fever, she felt like crap. By the time Haris, her 'bodyguard', dropped her at school, her bones ached and the persistent pain of broken glass slicing her throat with every swallow could no longer be blamed on her crying fit. She groaned. *I can't be poorly. Not now.* The last thing she needed was to be confined to the house with tonsillitis or flu. She'd never survive. All she lived and breathed for were these moments of freedom and if her mum's reaction this morning was anything to go by, they were soon to be curtailed.

It was lucky Haqib wasn't at school today. No way would Charlie be able to sneak out unnoticed with Haqib on her case. Good job he was on that stupid work experience with Zain Ahad. A smile twitched her lips at the thought of Haqib following DI Ahad around like a puppy. Talk about hero worship. Last time she saw Haqib like that was when he was seeing Fareena – and that didn't last, did it? She frowned and gave herself a mental shake. Haqib had had it tough, so if he could relate to Zain Ahad and end up with a good job, then good luck to him. He deserved it. Besides, looked like Auntie Anika and Zain were getting very cosy. The other day, Charlie caught them hugging in the kitchen – she opted not to share that bit of gossip with her mum though. She'd store that gem up for when she needed a distraction. Mum wouldn't be best pleased that Anika was at it with her boss, though that thought made her grin. Her mum was soooo easy to wind up. If she wasn't so protective of everyone and just chilled a bit and let everyone get on with their lives, everything would be fine.

After dragging her gloves off, she stuffed them in her pocket and texted him.

Charlie: WRU? I'm freezing my ass off here. I'm going to Costa in Broadway for a hot chocolate!

M: Be there soon. Fucking dad's watching me. Get me a HC too – with sprinkles and cream!

His reply made her smile as she wandered away from Bradford Interchange, heading for Broadway shopping mall. He was such a big kid, but even just getting a text from him lifted her mood. Despite the warmth spewing from the huge vents in the roof when she entered Broadway, she was still chittery.

The Costa was quiet, so she snagged a chair at the back, away from prying eyes, and settled down with the hot chocolates. *Got to avoid the spies my mum's got all over the bloody city!* When he arrived, all tall and bouncy, Charlie couldn't help grinning. His new hairstyle suited him – longer than he used to have it, but it worked and he looked handsome. Sometimes she had to pinch herself that he liked her. A warm flutter started in her stomach when he looked at her, his eyes wide and teasing, his big grin declared how happy he was to see her, even though it had only been a few hours since they last met.

He settled down opposite Charlie, pulled his mug over and took a sip. He even looked cute with a frothy cream moustache, which lasted only as long as he took to lick it away. 'So, what's up, babe?'

Charlie let the 'babe' endearment slide, aware at the back of her mind that just a few months ago, if some lad called her babe, she'd have given him a tongue lashing. But he wasn't *some* lad. He was her *sort of* boyfriend and being his 'babe' *sort of* worked for her. He made her feel special and loved. She rolled her eyes and let it all spill out. Marcus finding her footprints in the snow in the back yard, him and her mum jumping to the conclusion that they belonged to Downey and her mum's overreaction in insisting they have additional security. Charlie huddled over her drink, fingers linked round the mug, savouring the warmth. She kept her head down not wanting him to see the frustrated tears that had welled up in her eyes, but it was like he sensed just how distraught she was for he leaned forward, pulled her hand from the mug and held it tight. Charlie looked up and lost herself in the depths of his eyes. *I'm soooo lucky to have him and I don't care that my mum would disapprove. She's not the boss of me.*

'She's just looking out for you, Charlie. My parents are the same. It makes me mad.'

His smile was gentle, and Charlie's tummy flipped once more as his fingers tightened just a little. When he spoke again, the sparkle had left his eyes. 'How I see it is we've got three options. One, we come clean and admit you sneaked out to see me. Two, we keep quiet, put up with the extra hassle and see what happens. Three, we move – leave Bradford altogether – just the two of us. We could move to where nobody knows us – Sheffield or somewhere, maybe even London.' His fingers tightened more as he said option three, and Charlie wasn't sure how to respond. He looked so despondent, so sad now.

'I … I'm not sure …' She hated the way her hesitancy made

his shoulders slump. Hated that he released her fingers and she especially hated how he leaned away from her, his eyes drifting sightlessly over the other customers. When he reconnected with her, his eyes had lost their sparkle. 'Don't know how much more I can take, Charl. I've let my dad down. My mum's a nervous wreck. I hear them whispering about me when they think I'm asleep. When I go out and about everyone's talking about me, giving me dirty looks. Shit, last week someone egged the house and the week before that someone spray-painted "Paki bastard" on the front door.'

He lowered his head, his voice falling to a whisper. 'I'm scared when I'm out and about. This morning when I walked home from the Rec, I took the long route and even then I thought someone was watching me.'

His last words were so quiet that Charlie had to move closer to hear them. 'I can't take much more.'

Charlie inhaled and gripped his hand. She'd been so selfish. Of course it was crap for him. Everything that had happened over the past few months had been worse for him. Apart from the supposed 'Downey threat' – which wasn't real – Charlie didn't fear for her life. She bit her lip.

His eyes lit up, hope shining through them as a hesitant smile tugged at his lips. 'No rush, Charlie. Take your time.' He tilted his head to one side and wiggled his eyebrows, making her laugh. He was such a goof. 'But not too long, eh?'

Chapter 25

The morning briefing consisted of allocating tasks to each of the team and to the uniformed officers assigned to them. The list of known illegal dog breeders and dog fight organisers was divvied up between Operation Sandglass and Nikki's team. The social media appeal for information on the tattoo had thrown up a few leads, but none had provided a positive ID. Dr Campbell had forwarded test results as they'd come in. Although useful evidence for when and if they got a prosecution on this, there was nothing that provided a positive ID. The DNA from the arm came back without a match in the system. However, bloodwork showed that they had dosed He Who Owns The Arm with ketamine.

'Langley was lucky to detect the ketamine. They can only detect these date-rape drugs in the blood for a few hours. He says that indicates that he took the drug no earlier than three a.m., else he would have lost his window to detect it.' Saj flicked through Langley's reports and filtered salient information to the team as he did so. 'Langley, having done further tests on the arm, is confident that the arm belongs to a male between the ages of twenty and thirty who as a child – between the ages of five and ten – broke his wrist and suffered various other bone traumas itemised in his report. These facts may prove useful in identifying the person to whom the arm belongs.'

Nikki looked at the details Anwar had added to their investigation board. 'And let's face it. It looks like we're going to have our work cut out. We really need to find the rest of the body, for I'm pretty sure we can assume this man's dead.'

Williams, flicking through his tablet, stood up and hurried over to Nikki. Some of the CSI tests results were coming in. He grimaced and handed his tablet to Nikki. 'They extracted and typed some blood found in the fighting area. Guess what …?'

Nikki was already reading the blood test results. 'Bloody hell. I hope this doesn't mean what I suspect it does.'

Nikki waited until Anwar and Sajid had located the relevant blood report. The frown on Saj's forehead and Anwar's 'bloody hell' told her they'd reached the same conclusion as she and Williams. Not allowing them to become distracted by the horror of it, she raised her voice. 'The presence of human blood in the fighting area *could* be innocent. However, in the quantities isolated by the CSIs, I think we can dispel that idea. So …' The sentence trailed off as she tried to force the memories of that scene from her mind, but failing to do so, she continued. 'With the blood type matching that of our dismembered arm, it appears that He Who Owns The Arm must have ended up in that arena with at least one fighting dog. We've got the bite marks on his arm to corroborate that, and now his blood found and isolated in that area confirms it. DNA results will come through later today, but I'm sure the swabs from the arena will match that of the arm.'

She shook her head, trying to dislodge the gruesome images from the scene and handing Williams's tablet back to him. She was about to continue when Anwar's, 'You seen this, boss?' distracted her. Her heart thumped as the younger woman's horrified expression told her that whatever Farah had read in the detailed CSI report would not be pleasant. 'Go on, Farah. What've you found?'

'You know the metal loop with blood they found at the scene? Well, we all assumed it was a dog chained up there, but …'

Nikki's heart sank as Farah's frown deepened and her lips tightened.

'Seems the lab has identified human blood on the loop and the chain and human excrement in the vicinity. They've sent the blood off for DNA testing.'

The 'Fuck' left Nikki's lips before she could hold it back. This fresh development corroborated their fears that He Who Owns The Arm had, at some point, been chained up like an animal. What sort of sick bastards would do that sort of thing? This was becoming sicker and sicker by the minute and despite the lack of DNA confirmation, Nikki was convinced they had enough ducks in a row to escalate their investigation to a kidnapping or slavery one and probably a murder one, too. A quick glance round the room informed her that her team was on the same wavelength. Sajid, jaw tight, slight pulse at his temple, Williams sitting upright, eyes on Nikki awaiting instructions and Anwar, pale yet clear-eyed and calm, awaited her lead. It was time for a brainstorming session.

'Soooo, thoughts on these developments?' Nikki sat down. A multitude of unanswered questions filled her head, and she now wanted some input from her team, yet no one responded. Allowing them a little more time to plan their ideas, she continued. 'We must proceed on the assumption that this is a murder investigation or at least a death by misadventure.'

Williams, eyes flashing, bounced in his chair as if to release his pent up anger and was the first to break the heavy silence. 'Got to be a murder investigation, boss. The whole thing reeks of nastiness and intent.' He began counting off points on his fingers as he spoke, and Nikki exchanged a 'that's my boy' look with Sajid. Williams's confidence was increasing daily and today he'd even overcome his fear of committing to an opinion in front of her. '*One*, the arm was wrenched off the body, presumably by a dog. *Two*, the arm's owner was roofied – why do that if killing or torturing him wasn't the intent? *Three*, they had moved the arm from what looks like the kill site. *Four*, the DNA on the loop sort of confirms all the above.' He looked up and met each of their eyes. 'We know this because the CSIs found no traces of human blood anywhere else other than in the cage where the arm was found and in the fighting arena and now on the loop. *Four* ...'

Anwar grinned, her voice filled with grim humour. '*Five*. You've done four already.'

With a weak smile, Williams said, 'Sorry, *five*, the fact that they left the arm, but no other body parts, tells us it wasn't an accident.' He frowned. 'Well, it seems that way to me, anyway. If it had been an accident, wouldn't you either leave all the body *or* remove the lot? Why leave us an arm to find?'

'And that,' said Nikki, 'is the crux of the matter. Why would the organiser of these illegal dog fights leave evidence of another more serious crime?'

Saj nodded. 'DS Jewkes told us these dog fight organising gangs are often very professional. They usually sanitise the area, leaving few blood traces because they're so efficient – using massive tarpaulins covered with sawdust to line the area. He says they remove as much evidence as they can from the fight sites, but yesterday's scene was like a massacre. Never seen such a macabre crime scene. It beggars belief.'

'So, why deviate from the norm?' Nikki looked around the small circle. 'They didn't care if we discovered evidence at the crime scene, *nor* did they care if we found that arm. Having said that ... they removed the fingers.'

'That's it.' Williams blurted out. 'That was my point six. They left the arm with an ornate tattoo sleeve but removed the fingers. Seems odd to me. Why bother? That tattoo is so distinctive that it's inevitable that at some point someone will match it to a family member who is AWOL.'

Nikki grinned. 'Way to go, Williams. You're on a roll today. Yep, taking forensic counter measures like the removal of fingers doesn't correspond with the rest of their actions. Just can't quite get my head round the reasoning behind it.'

She stood up. 'Anwar, Williams, have another look at missing persons reports and do another trail of the morgues. The quicker we catch an ID on that arm, the sooner we'll get to the bottom of this. Also, see if you can find out who called this in. That person might have information we could use. Have the lab expedite the DNA analysis on the blood taken from that metal loop. I want all I's and T's crossed.'

'Erm, Nik?'

She shook her head at Saj. 'Don't give me crap about I's being dotted. This is a capital "I" and it needs to be crossed, okay?' She moved over to grab her coat. 'You and I should check out the vets from the list Jewkes shared with us. Before we head out, I'll contact the Royal College of Veterinary Surgeons. See if they can add any names to this list of dodgy vets. Ahad's not wasting his time in his new DCI role as he got me a warrant to that end this morning – seems that they're keen to root out the dodgy practitioners, so they like their I's crossed too.'

As she winked at him, Saj rolled his eyes. 'You won't convert me to crossing my eyes, you know!'

Nikki looked at him, her gaze blank –and pointed two fingers at her eyes. 'I think you'll find it's my eyes that are crossed …'

Before Saj had the chance to object, she'd swung out of the room, thrusting her arms into her coat as she went, leaving him to share a bemused smile with Anwar and Williams before he followed her.

Chapter 26

It had been sheer chance that he'd spotted her at the Bradford Interchange. He'd been testing out his disguise, tootling out and about his old haunts, deliberately placing himself in view of any old friends and acquaintances, to see if they spotted him. Thankfully, his new look passed the test. He'd not chanced his luck by approaching any of them directly or owt, preferring to hover around, see if when their eyes landed on his face they showed any sign of recognition. For this outing, he'd chosen to dress up. Brand new upmarket suit, long overcoat similar to the one that Malik lad wore and a tie. Even if he said it himself, he scrubbed up well. He laughed. It made him feel like an unstoppable force.

He'd felt so invincible, in fact, that he'd risked a trip to the Lazy Bites café. And he'd been in luck, for Parekh and her side-kick were already ensconced in a booth stuffing their faces whilst that little special needs kid pranced about in the kitchen like he was doing a real job or summat. Mind you, the lad made a good bacon buttie and nice strong builders' tea. Parekh and Malik were so engrossed in themselves that he was brave enough to slip into the booth behind them. With his back to Nikki, the risk of her spotting him and identifying him was low. Still, he kept his head down and his ears open. They were moaning on about Charlie, her daughter. As the conversation continued, they began talking about him too. *Tut tut, tut, Nikki Parekh, you should use your powers of observation. Wouldn't you be pissed off if you realised what you were giving away to your biggest enemy just by being unobservant? So much for all your security.*

He almost laughed when he heard that she thought the footprints leading up to her back door belonged to him. It was good to know something about his granddaughter that her own mother didn't. Seemed like the great and mighty Nikki Parekh had no idea of her daughter's 'other' life. *She isn't so superior now, is she?*

He'd listened to her mouthing off, ranting and raving and bemoaning how crap she was at parenting, and allowed her obvious fear of him to warm his belly and fire him up. Nikki Parekh had no clue what she was in for and she'd just handed him even more ammunition without even realising it. *Life is good!*

Then, not an hour later, he'd spotted Charlie at the bus station and followed her as she strolled towards Broadway. He could tell she was ill by the way she shivered and rubbed her upper arms as she made her way down the side of City Park to Broadway shopping mall. Served her right for choosing romance in the middle of a blizzard over a good night's sleep. Mind you, he couldn't talk. He was a tad shivery himself and could do with a kip, but later. This chance encounter was too good an opportunity to skip. Again, it seemed like all the Parekh women lacked the ability to detect threats in their immediate environment, for Charlie didn't so much as glance his way when he joined her in the queue, nor when he occupied the table next to her. Again, luck was on his side because when the boyfriend arrived, he gleaned information he would never have discovered if he hadn't eavesdropped.

Even now he was back home, and wearing his usual old comfy clothes, disguise removed and his pristine suit hung up in his wardrobe, he was undecided quite how to exploit Charlie Parekh's secret. There was nothing he desired more than to cause Nikki

Parekh as much distress as possible before allowing the final blow to fall. All he had to work out was how to force Charlie's hand and make her leave with the boy. He had a few ideas about that and he'd all night to finesse them. He sifted through the images he'd taken with his phone that day, smiling as he did so. Nikki and Sajid in Lazy Bites, Isaac serving coffee to Nikki's boss, that old Scottish bloke Hegley, Charlie in Costa at the interchange. Any of those would freak Parekh out. He just had to decide which one, and how to deliver it for maximum impact. Today was a good day on many fronts.

Chapter 27

Ahad had emailed the warrant to the Royal College of Veterinary Surgeons, yet Nikki had still received a frosty reception on the phone. Never one to be fazed by a less than enthusiastic welcome though, Nikki had harangued the personnel officer until she'd agreed to consult their records of vets in the Yorkshire region who had been disbarred over the previous five years. She came up with three vets who were already on Nikki's list, one of whom was deceased, and an additional two had been struck off for inhumane practices, both during the last two years and neither on her list. Which made a grand total of five to check out. Nikki thanked the woman and informed her that although they were focusing on vets in the Yorkshire region at the moment, she might need to contact them again if they needed to widen the parameters of their search.

Saj grinned when she hung up. 'Way to go, Nikki. Those poor admin staff will now try to dodge any calls from Yorkshire. You could have just got them to email you the results.'

Nikki snorted. 'You're going soft, Saj. The only way to guarantee that your request is treated with urgency is if you stay on the line. That way, they can't forget or bump you to the bottom of the pile.'

With a cheeky grin, she turned to her computer. Poring over

Google Maps, Nikki wished she could use a proper spread-outable-fold-uppable paper map instead. Not wishing to give Sajid any ammunition to tease her about her lack of computer skills, she persevered trying to pin the five different locations on the map so they could work out a sensible order of travel. Pushing her out of the way, Saj took over, pinned the locations on the map and printed out their itinerary, whilst Nikki hid her relief under a grumpy expression that fooled nobody, least of all Sajid.

Three quarters of an hour later, Sajid pulled into a pot-holed drive of an old farmhouse and Nikki consulted her list of five vets whose dodgy, illegal behaviour had resulted in them losing their licence to practise. 'Gordon James Collins. Lost his licence due to assaulting a client who, as a result, lost his sight in one eye. Jewksy says he has no additional information about him, as he's only recently been added to the list.' A man in a wax jacket exited a dilapidated barn to the side of an equally dilapidated farmhouse. Its only nod to home comforts was the smoke drifting up through the chimney, because the few windows visible were filthy, broken or covered with curtains half falling off their rails.

Nikki and Saj exited the car and walked towards him. 'Gordon James Collins?' Nikki kept her tone affable and extended her arm as she neared. The man, resting on a walking stick, scowled before looking her up and down. 'Police, eh?'

Nikki was impressed. Not everyone picked her and Sajid out as police straight off, mainly she believed because of the difference in their personas. Saj was all elegant and well turned out, whereas Nikki looked more turned over than turned out. 'As it happens, yes, we're police. She flashed her ID at him. 'I'm DS … I mean, DI Nikki Parekh and this is DS Malik. We'd like to ask a few questions about your whereabouts on the evening of 22nd into the early hours of the 23nd of January.'

Gordon Collins looked at her proffered hand, ignored it and sniffed. 'No idea what this is about, but I've been nowhere near that Brian Lewis. Nowhere near him. I learned my lesson.' He pierced Nikki with a bright blue gaze. 'I don't regret what I did to him, you know? He deserved that and more. Ten donkeys he had in that sanctuary. Not *one* of them healthy. Skin and bone they were.'

A braying from the barn startled Nikki, and she glanced towards its door. 'You keep donkeys yourself, do you, Mr Collins?'

'Aye, that I do.' The old man's face broke into a smile that chased his sullenness away, making him lose ten years. 'I tricked the lot of them. When they took his donkeys from him, I intervened. Might have lost my vet's licence for smashing him in the face, but I saved ten animals that day and I don't regret a thing.'

Saj, having avoided each snow-filled pot hole, approached. 'You're saying you lost your veterinary licence because you punched a man for maltreating his donkeys?'

Collins frowned. 'Thought you got that, lad? That's what happened, but I've never set foot near that bugger again. I might get some of my mates to check up on him now and again, to see he's not breaching the terms of his bail, but I don't go there myself. If he says I was there two days ago, then he's talking rubbish.'

Nikki exchanged a glance with Sajid. It seemed unlikely that such an animal advocate would be involved in illegal dog fighting, but Nikki still had to 'cross her eyes'. 'We're not here because of Mr Lewis. It's something completely different, and the sooner you tell us where you were, the sooner we can be on our way.' She took any sting in her words away by smiling. She liked this irascible old man, despite his attitude. What wasn't to like about someone who was prepared to risk his job to protect vulnerable animals? Besides, she was pretty certain that Collins didn't have the physical strength to keep up with angry dogs.

'I was at my daughter's in Whitby. Only got home today. Was just making sure that old bugger Jones down the road took good enough care of my pets.'

'They'll confirm that, will they? Your daughter and Mr Jones.'

'You don't have a lot of trust, do you, lass? Of course, she'll

131

confirm it. Here's her number.' He rattled off a number and repeated it twice to make sure Sajid had noted it down correctly, then rummaged in his pocket. 'Here's my train ticket. I left on the 16th and got back this morning.'

Nikki smiled and took photos of the train tickets with the seats reserved under his name. Just to be doubly sure, she'd speak with his daughter and Northern Rail to verify his statement, but for now it seemed she could score Gordon James Collins from her list. Still, whilst they were here, there was no harm in corroborating his alibi with farmer Jones down the road.

Although it took only an additional fifteen minutes to reach farmer Jones's property, locate him near a large chicken coop and ask him to confirm that Mr Collins had indeed been absent from his property on the dates stated, Nikki would gladly forfeit the pleasure of driving down another pot-holed lane. Didn't these farmers want visitors? As the thought popped into her mind, she grinned. Of course they didn't. Both Jones and Collins were miserable old sods and she would have been hard pressed to work out which of the two was the most curmudgeonly. Still, Jones had confirmed that he'd been 'babysitting those damn hee hawing creatures' since the 16th of December.

'Doesn't let old Collins off the list yet, Nik. Just because he wasn't here doesn't mean he wasn't helping out with those dog fights, does it?'

'No, we'll wait till we get confirmation of his alibi before taking him off the list.' She pulled out her phone, noticed she'd no signal and sighed. 'Bloody middle of nowhere. Branson can travel to the damn moon, but can't make sure we get a signal on the Yorkshire Moors. Picking up the car radio instead, she issued an order for Anwar to organise a uniformed officer to check out the details of Collins's alibi.

By the time they'd interviewed the next two vets on their dodgy vet list, Nikki was flagging. She didn't like to admit it to herself, never mind anyone else, but the events of the last few months had taken their toll on her. Although mentally she was coping, her body sometimes let her down. It had been a lengthy day, and even Saj looked a little drained.

After talking with Michael Dornan, Nikki ached for a long, scalding hot shower to rid herself of the filthy feeling that lingered. He showed no contrition for treating and doctoring pedigrees from illicitly bred dogs, and in Nikki's opinion, he deserved his lifelong ban from practising veterinary medicine. Remembering the conditions these so-called pedigree dogs were subjected to, Nikki was tempted to drag Mr Smooth Dornan down to the nick, just for fun, but that still wouldn't be enough punishment for him. Dornan's whinging about 'making ends meet' when he owned a humungous detached property with a covered swimming pool to the side, even had Sajid ready to floor the bloke. His alibi of 'a small winter break in the Swiss Alps' until his return the previous evening seemed to let him off the hook. However, Nikki, when she called it into Trafalgar House, specified that she wanted his alibi triple-checked. Dornan had seemed just a tad *too* interested in the money-making prospects of the illicit dog fights for her liking. Nikki, whilst she had Wi-Fi, shot off an email to DI Jewkes, telling him her suspicions that Dornan, although possibly not their vet this time, was a likely candidate for being recruited by illegal dog fight organisers in the future.

The third vet on their list was annoyingly effervescent. 'Call me Anji – that's-with- an-i', was one of those vivacious characters that made Nikki feel dull and lifeless at the best of times, but at the end of a long day? Well, that was just too much verve. In impossibly high heels, with lashes that almost swept the floor and impeccable make-up, Nikki wondered if they'd got the wrong Anji Jordan. She couldn't imagine the woman who'd flung open the door to them, with a welcoming smile that seemed to extend to her ears – despite the property being set back from the road and it getting dark – dealing with animals. Yet according to the information Nikki held in her hand, this woman had been a farm vet, employed by a prestigious veterinary practice specialising in cattle and sheep. Even when she confirmed her name, Nikki doubted she'd ever wear wellies and stick her gloved hand up the rear of a cow in labour.

Nikki was tempted to say, 'We've come for your jewellery and expensive electronics', to see if that blinding smile would fade or if it would widen as she let them in and packed all her possessions into bags for them. As if sensing his boss's attitude, Saj summoned up a smile and stepped forward, explaining the purpose of their visit as he did so.

Ms Gushing Anji-with-an-i Jordan ushered them inside, looking appalled, the smile reducing by a mere two centimetres from blinding to irritating. Her hands splayed in front of her, she sighed. 'I made a minor mistake. That's all. And yet I'm still paying for it. Anytime some dodgy vet does something illegal, you lot land up on my doorstep. I've paid for my mistakes. I lost my job.'

Saj, an insincere sympathetic smile on his face, nodded, but before he replied, Nikki, tiredness making her patience even shorter than normal and having had her fill of discredited vets trying to make out they were in the right, butted in. 'Minor mistake? Minor mistake? You took a bribe from a farmer to poison another farmer's cattle. That's not what I'd call a "minor" mistake. More of a major whopping one. What do you reckon, DS Malik?'

Anji-with-an-i's smile disappeared as she looked between the two detectives, a shimmer of tears in her eyes. 'It only made them ill for a short while. Just till Mr Nicholson sold his herd, that's all. I didn't *kill* them.'

Nikki opened her mouth, but Saj broke in over her, nudging her and casting a warning glance her way. Nikki's mouth snapped shut. She was being unnecessarily combative, but the woman pissed her off. How could anyone poison an entire herd of cattle and try to justify it? She stepped away, twanged her band, and let Saj establish that Anji-with-an -i had been in London to see *Phantom of the Opera* with a group of girlfriends. They'd made a week of it, spa-ing and lunching and being self-indulgent. So much for paying for her misdeeds!

Saj took the details of her friends, the places they'd visited and so forth, and bade her goodbye. Nikki, relieved to be away from the woman, was glad to slam the door of Saj's Jag shut behind her, put on the heated seats and exhale. She squeezed her eyes shut and opened them wide before repeating the process a couple of more times. 'I'm shattered, Saj. It's been a long day and I'm letting my temper get the better of me. What say we call it quits for today, have some uniforms to follow up on these alibis and start again tomorrow, eh?'

Sajid studied her for a little longer than Nikki was comfortable with. His dark eyes seeing right through her brave smile to the tension across her shoulders. *What did I do to deserve a mate like him?* She reached over and squeezed his arm. 'Thanks for caring, Saj, but I'm okay. Honestly, I am. There's just been a lot to deal with today. That's why I'm breaking off here. I'm being sensible. Look …' She pointed both index fingers to her chest. 'I'm Ms Nikki-with-an-i Sensible.'

Sajid's snort of laughter loosened the tightness in her shoulders and she settled down for the ride home, glad that she'd listened to her body and her mind for once. Marcus would be so proud of her.

Chapter 28

Charlie didn't *want* to meet up with Saj, but he didn't give her any option. He'd already arranged with Haris that he'd pick her up from school and he'd told Marcus that he and Langley would feed her tonight and drop her home later. Like she was some sort of charity case. Or a kid who had to have after-school activities planned out for her. Charlie wanted to yell *Fuck off Sajid* into the air, but her throat was too damn sore now. So painful she could scarcely talk and every swallow was like a razor blade in her throat. Her chest was tight and sore too now. Each breath made her eyes water, so instead she was taking shallow ones that made her sound like an asthmatic duck. She was tempted to actually type that as her reply to Saj's text, but she couldn't do it. Not to Saj. She just wanted to go home to bed. One minute sweat was pouring off her and the next she was shivering. All Charlie wanted was to go home and have her mum make her some masala chai or, better still, some elchee doodh like Ajima used to make. She blinked the tears away and texted back a reluctant 'OK'.

Charlie was convinced her mum had been going on about her 'behaviour'. Probably told him she was 'acting out', and Saj was so far up her arse he'd do anything for her. Charlie could just catch the bus and go home. Leave Saj stranded there waiting. But the thought of two buses and a wait in the Interchange filled her aching limbs with dread. She wouldn't make it to the bus stop in this condition. Maybe she could convince Saj to just take her home. It's not like she'd made her sore throat up or owt. She felt like crap, she really did. Now she needed to think about what she and her boyfriend had discussed earlier too. Could he and Charlie really just up sticks and leave? Her brain ached thinking about it. She wasn't even eighteen yet so her mum would stop her, which meant if they were going to do it, they'd have to do it in secret. But then her mum would assume Downey had snatched her, so she'd have to leave a note. As Charlie shook her head, a shooting pain zoomed across her skull forcing her to close her eyes till the pain abated. It was too much to think about. Way too much. Besides, now she had to placate Saj too. Her phone pinged. It was Saj telling her he was outside. As she got up, she wobbled a bit and waves of dizziness made her want to vomit. Somehow she made her way out the school entrance. However, as she headed down the concrete stairs, the wobbling intensified and the last thing she remembered was landing on the bottom step. She opened her eyes to see Saj's worried ones frowning as his hands skimmed over her leg and forehead checking for injuries. 'You passed out, Charlie. You not well?'

Charlie struggled to sit up, her head all fuzzy. With Sajid's help, she pulled herself over to lean against the steps. She tried to speak, but nothing came out.

'Fuck's sake, Charlie, you're running a temperature. How long have you been like this? Why didn't you tell your mum?'

Instead of replying, she closed her eyes and rested her head on his shoulder. She couldn't even summon up the strength to protest when he hefted her into his arms and carried her over to the Jag. 'And your clothes are soaking too. What's going on, Charl?'

Sajid slipped Charlie into the heated front seat and her body sunk into the warmth. As he clicked the seatbelt into place, he leaned over and said, 'Look, I know you're not well right now, but as soon as you are, we need to talk.'

Charlie's eyes sprung open and met his determined gaze, but all she could do was shake her head. Sajid knew something, Charlie just wasn't sure exactly what it was and that was just another thing to think about. Before he closed the door, he dropped his bombshell. 'This is what happens when you go out in a snowstorm in the middle of the night to meet a damn lad. I hope he's worth it.'

Charlie's eyes sprung open as she digested his words. *Does he know who I'm seeing? If so, it won't be long before he tells my mum, if he hasn't already. What am I going to do?* Charlie closed her eyes. She didn't even have the energy to fire off a warning text to her boyfriend. All she could do was face the music. But not now. Not. Right. Now. Not till she was better. With that thought in mind, she drifted off to dreams of cosy pyjamas, warm milk and a home with no stress and anxiety, and didn't even wake up when they reached home. When she opened her eyes, it was pitch black and she still felt crap, but she was warm and safe. She sighed and wondered what the morning would bring. Then she saw the thermos flask next to her bed with a Post-it with *elchee milk* scrawled across it. She faced the enormity of knowing now whatever she decided to do, she was going to disappoint someone she loved. She just wasn't sure who yet.

Chapter 29

A pressure which verged on pain had lodged itself in Jacko's chest. His shoulders ached and every so often, he rubbed the area just below his heart. Meanwhile, Fugly sat opposite him in his chair by the fire, humming to himself as he trawled through the messages on his different burner phones. He had loads of them and seemed to change them regularly. To the casual observer, they would look like an old married couple. Jacko, taking advantage of Fugly's preoccupation with his phones, sank deeper into his chair, allowed his chin to dip down till it rested near his chest and closed his eyes. Under the pretence of snoozing, maybe he'd be able to focus on what he should do.

He started by thinking about what he'd ascertained. Over the years, he'd become more and more observant. Fugly had let slip that there was a lot of police scrutiny directed towards these sorts of operations – that's what Operation Sandglass was all about, according to Fugly anyway. The fact that Fugly knew the code name of the secret investigation showed that Fugly had access to police records. Whether that was through his 'dark web' cronies or through some rat on the police force was uncertain. That was the main reason he was wary of contacting the police. If Fugly caught wind of him having spoken to the pigs, he'd feed Jacko to the dogs in the next fight.

The other key piece of information he'd gleaned was that there was a lot of bad blood between Fugly and his competitors. Which was why Fugly was always doubly cautious, and it was why he paid his thugs well over the odds. He wanted to keep them sweet and didn't want to risk them defecting to his competitors' camps. He'd also mentioned that he, Fugly, had rats in the enemy camps too and he often boasted about that. 'Those bastards think they have intel on me, Jacko, but they're just stupid. Every bit of information they think they've gleaned about me was fed to them intentionally. I made sure to keep them off the scent.'

As Fugly worked through his phones, mumbling to himself, Jacko peering through his half-closed eyes, saw him lift a glass to his lips and savour the bite of the neat whisky as it travelled down his throat. Could he add a sedative to the whisky bottle? No, that was a no go, for Fugly was in the habit of sharing his whisky with Jacko. He'd suspect something if Jacko refused a wee dram. He'd have to think of something else to get him out of the way for a bit so he could snoop. Maybe in a mug of tea?

Jacko shelved that idea to consider later on and stirred as he sensed Fugly rise to his feet. A second later the sound of a log being added to the fire and a blanket being tossed over his supine form, relaxed him. Fugly thought he was asleep and seemed happy to let him rest. Now, all he had to do was to come up with a plan.

As the sparks from the log flickered and glinted, Fugly finished his whisky and was just gathering the burner phones together to lock them away in his safe when one rang. Jacko was all ears now as Fugly reached over and picked it up, a faint frown drawing his brows together when he identified the caller. 'Yes?'

Jacko could tell from his tone that the caller was important and so, under the pretence of shifting in his sleep, he rolled his body round in order to watch Fugly's reactions. Hopefully, he wouldn't start pacing round the room like he sometimes did. When the caller replied, Jacko almost grinned. Although he didn't recognise the voice, it was loud enough for him to hear almost every word and when Fugly rolled his eyes at the contraption and moved it a little away from his ear, it served Jacko's purpose even better.

'Got the Dean Mill location sorted, boss. Perfect for our plans. Isolated, yet close enough for us to transport the whole kit and caboodle. Plenty of space to spread out. You know, make it a real event? We're starting the prep from our end. It'll be ready for the big hunt, no probs.'

Fugly slapped his thigh. 'That's mah boy! Think you'll see a bit extra dosh coming your way for that. Now send me images of the site and a detailed report on accessibility, resources and so forth.'

'Will do, boss.' Even from this distance, Jacko heard the pride in the lackey's voice. Another disposable fool brought on board by Fugly. Poor sod better not make any mistakes or he'd suffer the boss's wrath big time. Fugly was a mean player and in Jacko's eyes that made him unpredictable and more dangerous. All those breadcrumbs he kept banging on about were drawing the pigs in closer and closer and Fugly was getting off on it big-time. Jacko had to find a way out of this mess. For his wife and granddaughter's sake, if not for his own. Again, he reached up and touched the crucifix and moving his head, he saw that Fugly's dark eyes were focused on him, an impenetrable expression on his face as his lips moved into the semblance of a grin.

Jacko's heart hammered as he affected a yawn and a stretch. Shit. He had to make his move soon.

Friday

Chapter 30

I'm getting weaker. I can feel it in the heaviness of my head as I try to lift it from the floor and how my wrist barely supports the weight of the chain and handcuff. It won't be long. I didn't stand a chance against the dogs before, but now I'm fucked. No way I can defend myself against them. I've even stopped eating the crappy food they bring. Even a single mouthful of the cold boiled potatoes or the almost frozen baked beans makes me vomit, so I've just stopped eating. My wrists are killing me. The skin where the cuffs rub, is all ulcerated and pus-filled and the stench of my flesh rotting away is stronger than the stink of the animals. This is hell and I just want it to end.

Does anyone at home miss me? Have they noticed I've gone? I doubt my mum's even missed me yet. She's got too much on her own plate to worry about me, and as for my sisters – well, I don't see them much. Before all of this, seeing them reminded me of what I was … Who I was, or rather, *what* I was the product of. When I used to think about that before, my chest would clog up and I'd want to explode. It was like the anger became part of me, part of everything I was and everything I did. Just seeing them made me sick to the gut. They repulsed me so much that I bought a punch bag hoping it would dispel some of my fury,

But despite hours thrashing the bag, sweating like a pig, punching until my knuckles were raw, it didn't relieve the knot of disgust that settled in my belly. I resented *everything* that had happened in the past, things I hadn't known about. Things that made me abnormal – a monster, a freak. I was powerless to change a single thing about it, yet it consumed me. Maybe that's why I'd been so easily duped. I took my fucking eye off the ball because I was so stuck in the past.

Right now though, I'd give anything to see my sisters and my mum. None of what happened to us was their fault and deep down I always knew I needed help to sort out my head. Now, it looks like I won't get the chance. There's no escape from this mess and even if my sisters are looking for me, they won't find me. Hell, even I'm not sure how I ended up here.

The dogs are eyeing me up again. Sometimes I wonder if they pity me, but mostly I'm all too aware that they can smell the blood and gunk from my cut wrist. They look longingly at me, salivating, licking their chops like I'm their next meal. Well, that's not too far from the truth. From the way the rising sun casts shadows across the dully lit shed I can tell it's early morning. How many days have they held me captive? How many days have I been missing?

Even if nobody is looking for me, perhaps they're looking for that bastard friend of mine. I exhale, my breath steaming as it hits the air. Who am I kidding? Nobody would bother about my mate either. Both me and Roddy Calhoun were Mr Unreliables, letting folk down left right and centre. Nobody depends on me, nobody cares about me, because the bottom line is I've always been a total jackass. That says a lot more about me than it does about Mr Unreliable. I was the idiot, putting up with his crap, calling him a friend when all he was, was a hanger-on with an eye on a quick buck and an easy screw.

Why had I been so stupid as to consider Roddy Calhoun a mate? Well, that was easy. I'd been so caught up in my own problems, my own guilt, my own rage that I'd taken the easy way out. The path of least resistance. Instead of keeping in touch with family and my *real* mates from school, I'd opted to spend time with losers because I didn't have to give any of myself to them. I'd buttoned myself up, hid behind a mask and controlled the rage through exercise and drink and cruelty.

I close my eyes, drained and exhausted, just waiting for death, but before I drift off into a feverish dream-filled sleep, I promise myself that if I escape this, I'll address my demons head-on and make up for all the ways I've hurt my family and friends.

Chapter 31

It had been a shock for Nikki to see Charlie so unwell the previous night. She'd been prone to tonsillitis when she was younger but hadn't suffered a bout for a while and although a course of antibiotics and rest would have her on her feet in a couple of days, Nikki berated herself. Some mums had the luxury of being at home with their kids and looking after them, but Nikki hadn't initially had that option and although she could cut back her hours now, she recognised that she still wouldn't be one of those stay-at-home, baking muffins, attending PTAs sort of mums. Besides, she'd just accepted the DI job Archie had dangled in front of her nose. She'd barely had a chance to talk to Marcus about it, never mind discuss her worry that she'd accepted the role only because it would keep her team together. She visualised Marcus saying, 'And is that such a bad reason? You and Saj work well together. And you'll be kickass at being a DI. You smashed it last time, so you can do it again.'

This time, her worry wasn't that she couldn't do the job. It was more that she'd end up spending even longer at work, leaving Marcus to hold the fort. He didn't mind. He wanted her to do what she was good at and between them they provided all the security their family needed. She shrugged. She wouldn't even be having these thoughts if she was a man. Even now, it was a struggle to ditch society's expectation of what a wife – or in her case, partner – and mother, should be. Nikki wasn't conventional in any sense of the word, but her kids were happy and well-adjusted and so she firmly put her negative thoughts to bed and embraced her new DI role.

She tiptoed into Charlie's room, laid a pack of antibiotics next to the bed with a glass of water and replaced the flask of milk she'd left overnight with one of masala chai. As she lifted the flask, she shook it, pleased to see that Charlie had almost finished it. Nikki took a long moment to stare down at her daughter. Some of the feverish flush had left her daughter's cheeks and her breathing was less laboured than it had been during the night when she'd dropped in. Nikki hated to leave her when she was so poorly, but she had to go into work. Thankfully, Marcus's job as a landscape gardener allowed him flexibility and at the moment his main job was clearing snow and gritting roads on the estate on which he was employed, so he could stay with Charlie this morning and then Anika had promised to sit with her this afternoon. Pressing her lips to Charlie's forehead, Nikki smiled at the mumbled protest that left her daughter's lips and then with a last glance at her sleeping child, she headed downstairs to get ready for work.

The temperature had plummeted overnight and Nikki was glad of her warm coat and scarf as she left the house. Her car might not have heated seats like Sajid's but it was a damn sight better than her old one. Still, she wasn't looking forward to scraping the ice from the windscreen. She approached her vehicle, shivering in the cold air and got in, started the engine up and retrieved her ice scraper. She'd asked Ruby to scrape it and received a derisive snort in response, and whilst Sunni was all too eager, he was just not tall enough yet. The inside of the car was no warmer than the ambient outdoor temperature so Nikki wasn't tempted to linger. Instead, she kept the engine running, put the rear and front heaters on and resigned herself to her task. It was only when she was back on the kerb, next to the windscreen that she spotted that someone had already partially scraped it. For a nanosecond she smiled, thinking Marcus had started the job for her, then she saw that only the area around the passenger window was clear and that underneath the wiper was a padded A5 brown envelope.

Despite the cold, sweat formed on her brow, making her forehead itch. Her breath quickened as she cast frantic glances round the deserted street. There was only one person who would put something under her wipers in the middle of winter and there was nothing innocent in his actions. Whatever Freddie Downey had placed in that envelope – and Nikki was in no doubt it was him who'd placed it there – it would be threatening in nature. He was escalating. First postcards from afar, then Europe, then footsteps in her yard and now this. Satisfied that nobody was watching her, that Downey wasn't nearby and that her family was safe, she took out her phone, and marching round to the passenger side of her car, she phoned Marcus. 'Can you come outside? Now, please?'

'Oh Nikki. I love you. You know that, but there's no way I'm scraping your windscreen for you. Just do it.'

Breaking through Marcus's quipping response, she said, her voice as icy as the morning air. 'Downey's been here.'

Marcus hung up and within thirty seconds, he was out the door, boots unfastened, yanking his work coat on, over his sweatshirt. When he reached Nikki, he placed his arm round her shoulder and the two of them stared for a few seconds at the envelope before Nikki said, 'It's got to be from him.'

She shuddered, her eyes homing in on Marcus's, gaining courage from his calm nod as he replied, 'Yep, who else could it be? He clearly knows this is your car.'

Nikki nodded, then scrabbled in her pocket for one of the evidence bags she kept there for moments like this. She paused as she pulled it out. *Not* for moments like this. *Not* for moments when she or her family were threatened. She kept them there for use at crime scenes – for *other* people's problems. This was too close to home. Far too close and once more she wondered if they should have all upped sticks and left.

She opened her mouth, catching Marcus's eye again, but anticipating her words, he shook his head. 'No way Nik. No way is this tosser making us run. We'll get him. This time we'll get him. No way does anybody threaten *my* family and get away with it. This is good. Now we know for certain that he's back and that we're in his sights. Go on, pick it up and open it.'

Nikki rummaged in her other pocket, secured a pair of crime scene gloves and pulled them onto her already freezing hands. She then extracted the envelope from under the wiper. 'There'll be no prints – no trace – you know that, don't you?'

Marcus shrugged. 'Yeah, but might as well follow procedure – just in case. He's only human and one of these days he'll slip up big time.'

With Marcus holding the evidence bag, Nikki inserted the envelope in it, then took another one from her pocket and wafted it open. 'Hold that bag steady and I'll open the envelope and see if I can extract the contents. It's bulkier – as if it's not just a note inside. I'm not waiting till I get to Trafalgar House to find out what the bastard has left us.'

With care, she unsealed the envelope and using her gloved fingers, pulled the contents from within and popped them straight into the second evidence bag. Marcus sealed the first one and Nikki flung it on the passenger seat ready to transport to her work. They turned their attention to the contents that now occupied the second evidence bag. They were photos, but positioned face to face so Nikki couldn't immediately see what the images were. Using the plastic to manoeuvre them, Nikki counted two. She gestured to her car and without speaking they got in, Nikki in the driver's seat, Marcus in the passenger's one. Fumbling in her glove compartment, Nikki took out yet another bag and extracted one of the photos before reinserting it in the empty bag. Now they were able to view both photos without contaminating any potential evidence.

'Fuck!' The blood drained from Nikki's face. The first image was of her and Sajid in Lazy Bites with Isaac placing their breakfast on the table. 'He took this yesterday morning. I know because Sajid was wearing that stupid tie with the pink dots on. How the fuck did he take this without us seeing and why the hell was he so close to Trafalgar House?'

'Might he have got someone else to take the photo? You know, paid them?'

With her heart pounding, Nikki picked up the second bag and studied that image. 'Marcus, I hope you're right because if you're not, then that bastard got close to Charlie too. Look.'

The second photo showed Charlie in a café blowing on what looked to be a hot chocolate with whippy cream on top. Opposite her was a boy with dark hair, who was otherwise unidentifiable. Marcus frowned, 'When was this taken?'

Nikki, eyes wide, head throbbing, pointed to the jumper - 'Charlie wore that yesterday. I'm sure because it was soaking wet after she fell down the stairs at school. Her coat and the jumper were soaked when Sajid brought her home, and I shoved both in the wash. Besides, look – she's flushed and feverish. This was taken yesterday too.'

Marcus exhaled but before he could say a word, Nikki threw the car door open and jumped out. 'That little cow has been dogging school. The bastard could've grabbed her.'

She strode across the icy road only stopping when her feet slipped from under her and she landed with a thud on the road. 'Ouch!'

Tears streamed down her face as Marcus helped her up. 'What the hell is wrong with her? Why is she taking such *stupid* needless risks and …' She pushed Marcus away, turned and glared at him, hands on her hips, her eyes flashing, 'Who the hell is that bloody boy? I'm going to kill her. Tonsillitis or no damn tonsillitis, I'll kill her.'

Chapter 32

Despite the hassle of getting up extra early to travel to Nikki's house, and taking precious time out of his busy day, Freddie Downey had viewed it as a necessary evil. Although not his initial intention, as a result of new information, taunting Nikki with these images had become a significant part of his plan. Ratcheting up the pressure was an enjoyable aspect of his work and using her family was a sure-fire way of eliciting a response. Her rashness would lead to her making mistakes and he counted on her rashness putting a wedge between her and her daughter. He was counting on his daughter overreacting and, from the little he'd discovered about his granddaughter from his surreptitious observations, he suspected her similarity to her mother would result in a major combustion. Charlie Parekh was as wilful and stupid as her mother and if he was able to coax her away from her mother's protection by driving them apart, then that's precisely what he would do. His desire to annihilate his daughter was his driving force, but before that, he wanted to see her crawling about on the floor, tortured and bereft, knowing that everything she loved, everything she held on to, every person she put before herself, would be at his mercy. That would give him satisfaction. That's what would make him happiest. Well, that and the money that his current venture afforded him.

He would have loved to see Nikki's face when she saw the envelope under her wipers – more so when she opened it and saw just how close he could get, how ineffectual her precautions were – but that wasn't an option. It was far too risky. Instead, he contented himself with imagining the chaos that would ensue. He was no stranger to Nikki's hot temper. Even as a child she was a bolshie brat, but those images of her daughter with a boy, flouting all the security measures she'd put in place, might just be enough to push Nikki Parekh over the edge. He'd seen her wallowing in her own vulnerability before. He'd watched the recordings over and over again, savoured her weakness, assessed her vulnerabilities and planned how he would exploit them. Yesterday's little gem landing right in his lap was manna from heaven.

He'd thought hard about what he'd overheard. About how he'd use it to his best advantage. Coming up with his plan had been easy. If he could set mother and daughter against each other, then maybe, just maybe, Charlie would give in to the boyfriend's demands in order to escape her controlling mother's clutches. He'd been careful not to reveal Charlie's mystery boyfriend's identity in the images. If the brat was anything like her mum, she'd not want his identity known and no doubt she was as stubborn as her bitch of a mum. Keeping that little snippet of information back gave him power over both mother and daughter and did they but know it, when he revealed the lad's identity, Nikki Parekh's life would implode. It would set every security blanket she relied on alight, and this time when she fell to pieces, there would be no Dr Helen Mallory around to pick her up.

His thoughts warmed him from the inside out, enveloping him in a sense of invincibility as he plotted and planned and checked up on his other little venture. He was busy, of course he was, but despite the damn cold, he loved it. Humming an old Beatles song to himself he pulled his coat tighter round his body and stepped out into the cold. He had a list a mile long to complete if he was to be on target for his big finale. Mind you, adaptability was his middle name, so whilst he held the broad strokes of his plans in his head, he was secure knowing that should he need to tweak them, he could easily do so. A lot depended on Nikki Parekh and her actions over the next few days and he'd have to be extra sure that he kept on top of monitoring his various sources in that respect. He blew on his hands and strode over to meet his contact. Yes, life was good!

Chapter 33

Before Marcus could stop her, Nikki was out of the car, slamming the door and hot-footing it towards the house. Blood thrummed through her body and electric volts sizzled in her brain. How could Charlie have done this? This wasn't like *her* Charlie. *Her* Charlie was responsible. *Her* Charlie was sensible. *Her* Charlie wouldn't do anything that would expose the rest of the family or herself to risk, so why the hell had she been so reckless? Nikki's foot hit a patch of black ice, sending her legs skittering from beneath her, her arms windmilling for a moment, hands gripping the evidence bags with the photos in them. As she tried to catch herself before she fell, realisation dawned at the exact moment she landed on her backside near the gate. It was that damn boy she was meeting up with. *He* was the bad influence. *He* was the one who was leading Charlie astray. *He* was the one making her behave like an immature little girl. *He* was the one corrupting her little girl and turning her into a monster with no regard from her own or her family's safety.

Two arms grabbed her under her armpits and hoisted her back to her feet. On one side Marcus stood, blue eyes pleading with her to slow down and take a breath, on the other side was Haris, a frown drawing his brows together, his dark eyes amused.

'In a rush, Parekh?'

Nikki tutted and brushed the snow from her coat. Trust bloody Haris to witness her acrobatic fall and graceless landing. She glared at him, her chin jutting out, her fists clenched by her sides. All the anger and confusion and guilt that flooded her body, she now directed at the massive bald man standing in front of her. 'You sleeping on the job or something, Haris? I trust you to keep my kids safe …' She stepped closer to him, his blank expression fueling her anger as she prodded him in the chest. 'You didn't even know Charlie was skipping school, did you?' Another prod. 'You didn't realise she was playing you – my seventeen-year-old daughter getting the drop on a big man like you?'

As she went in for a third prod, Haris, any remaining amusement drained from his eyes, glared at her. '*I'm* not her mother, Parekh.'

And those five words were enough to make Nikki pause. Blinking rapidly, she swallowed hard trying to dislodge the spiky ball of guilt that had taken up residence in her throat. Her hand, prepared to administer yet another sharp prod, fell to her side and her eyes filled with tears as they met Haris's. She tried to speak, but the ball was stuck there. Tried again and managed a shake of the head and a mumbled, 'I'm sorry, Haris. You're right. You're doing us a favour and I'm acting like a dick.'

Haris shrugged and glanced at Marcus, dismissing her apology. 'Kids ready for school?'

With a nod, Marcus headed for the house. 'I'll get them.'

Haris studied Nikki for a moment as she watched Marcus climb the steps to the front door. 'Charlie playing up, I take it?'

'Eh?'

'Charlie pushing the boundaries? I mean, she's had attitude for the past few weeks. She hates the restrictions. Hates having what she calls "bodyguards" escorting her everywhere.' He shrugged. 'It's only natural, Parekh. You need to work out a way to bring this to a head and end it. Once and for all.'

Hearing her earlier thoughts confirmed by Haris made her realise how much of a toll this extended operation was taking on everyone. She exhaled, and handed over the evidence bags containing the photos. 'Maybe that'll happen closer than you think, Haris. This confirms that Downey's in town. He left these on my windscreen this morning.'

Haris took them, studied the images and frowned, uttering an expletive that summed up Nikki's thoughts. 'Shit. He's brave – not afraid to get close to you. This is a threat, if ever I saw one.' He glanced round, breath puffing from his mouth as he exhaled, his eyes piercing every grey shadow and car as his gaze raked over the entire area.

'I already checked. He's not here right now … but he's been here. First the other night and now this! He's threatening us, trying to make us panic, tightening the screws.' Fiery anger flushed her cheeks as frustration made her kick the fence bordering her house. Juddering, it sent a mini avalanche of snow to the ground by her feet. 'He's walking on fucking thin ice though, Haris. No one, especially not Freddie Downey, gets away with threatening my family. No one.'

But Haris, still studying the images, his brows puckered in concentration, didn't respond.

'Haris? You listening?'

'Eh, yeah, yeah. Just thinking.' He glanced once more at the bag containing the photo of Charlie in the Broadway Costa and then replaced it with the one taken in the Lazy Bites café. 'Doesn't Grayson have cameras? Didn't he get them installed because of those lads hassling the kids he has working there?'

A grin spread across Nikki's face. 'You're right. He does *and* they're discreet. Downey is unlikely to have noticed them, so maybe he won't have been too careful.' She frowned, 'Though how Saj and I didn't spot him I don't know. His ugly, arrogant, nasty face is ingrained on my retinas, so …' She lifted her arms and expelled a frustrated gasp. 'Pheeew.'

'He caught you unawares, Nikki, that's all. Besides, everyone's bundled up in winter coats and who knows perhaps he's using some basic disguise or other.'

His use of 'Nikki' rather than his usual 'Parekh' told Nikki how concerned he was. Haris would never verbalise his concern for her family, nor would he indulge in sentimental condolences or platitudes, but that single word told her how invested he was in his quest to keep her family safe.

'Look, I'll speak to Ali, okay? He'll be happy to double the number of people assigned to this. We can make sure we have frequent taxi drive-bys here and at the kids' schools and at Lazy Bites. That's no big deal, just a few detours whilst collecting fares.'

Nikki shook her head. 'No, Haris. Ali has done enough. I can't expect him to do this. He's got a business to run and he can't keep footing the bill for me.' She looked him straight in the eye. 'Besides, you're right. *I'm* their mother. It's *my* job to keep them safe …'

A rare grin spread fleetingly across Haris's face as he handed her back the evidence bags. 'Dun't be a martyr, Parekh. I was only mouthing off. That bastard killed your mum, he's threatening your family. We got this. You've been there for us, with that thing with Mazin before Christmas. You putting in a good word for him helped and Ali dun't forget his friends.'

The front door opened and Sunni tornadoed down the steps, coat flying open despite the freezing cold. He grabbed handfuls of snow which he made into a snowball and with a 'Hey Hari, you all right', he launched it at Haris. The tension broke, sparing Nikki from replying. Haris, laughing, responded by forming a snowball and aiming it straight for Sunni's chest before opening the door and saying, 'Get in you monster, where's the Rubster?'

Opening the gate, Nikki headed indoors, throwing an 'I'll hurry her up' over her shoulder.

Ruby, with Marcus chiding her for her tardiness, rolled her eyes as she thrust her arms into her coat, a slice of buttered toast dangling from her teeth, her 'yeah, yeah, yeah' a barely decipherable mumble. Nikki ruffled Ruby's hair as she passed her on her way up to Charlie's room, then paused before backtracking down the stairs and thrusting the image of Charlie towards her younger daughter. 'Hey Rubes, recognise this lad?'

Ruby, coat now on, bit off some toast, and chewing noisily looked at the photo, before swallowing and turning scornful eyes at her mum. 'For God's sake Mum, you got someone following us – taking photos – stalkerish, much?'

'Don't be an idiot, Rubs. Freddie Downey took these and left them on my windscreen this morning. *Now* do you get why I'm so concerned about them? I repeat, do you recognise the lad?'

Ruby paused, mouth open ready to take another bite of toast, her eyes wide as they flicked down to the photo. She swallowed, then not quite meeting her mum's gaze shrugged. 'No idea who Charlie's with. You should ask her. None of my business.' And before Nikki could insist on Ruby identifying the boy, she'd skipped past her and was down the steps heading for her lift to school.

Marcus shrugged. 'The women in this house have minds of their own.'

With a snort Nikki nodded, 'Yes, and that little so and so knew who Charlie was spending time with, but wasn't prepared to dob her sister in.'

'Well, that's a good thing, isn't it? We've taught them well. They have each other's backs.'

Nikki huffed and puffed, 'Yeah okay, it might be, but I wanted ammo for when I face Charlie with this.'

Marcus laughed. 'Just go easy on her, eh? She's not well and …'

Nikki pinned him with a look designed to freeze. 'Don't go there, Marcus. She put herself at risk. What if …?' Instead of finishing her sentence, she moved forwards, circled her arms round Marcus's waist and took a few moments to savour his strength before she went to confront Charlie.

Moments later, Charlie's muffled grunt when she knocked on the door told her the girl was awake. Mindful of Marcus's instruction to be gentle with Charlie, Nikki took a few deep breaths before pasting a smile on her lips and popping her head in. Ignoring her daughter's exaggerated 'humph', Nikki sat down on the edge of Charlie's bed. Leaning against her pillows, phone in hand, Charlie looked less feverish than the previous night. Still, Nikki placed her hand to her daughter's brow and although she was warm to the touch, Nikki was pleased to note that Charlie had drunk some of the chai she'd left for her earlier.

With the photos face down in her lap, Nikki hesitated before speaking. The last thing she wanted was to distress her poorly daughter, but she was fuming that she'd behaved so recklessly and her instinct was to rant and rave at her. She wished she'd let Marcus deal with this. Marcus was so good at the quiet 'I'm so disappointed in you' look. She exhaled, swallowed and began. 'How's the throat?'

Charlie shrugged and offered a croaky, 'Sore, but not as bad as yesterday.'

'Good! Because I've got something I need to ask you and it's best you're not feeling totally crap when I do.'

Alerted by the seriousness of her mother's tone, Charlie met Nikki's eyes, a small frown furrowing her brow.

'You skipped school yesterday, Charlie.'

A flush rose in Charlie's cheeks and as she opened her mouth to reply, Nikki shook her head. 'Let me finish. I know you were in Costa …'

This time, Charlie wouldn't be silenced and despite her hoarseness, her annoyance tinged every word. 'You're following me? Really, you're following me?'

Mindful of the promise she'd made to Marcus to be sensitive and non-accusatory, Nikki closed her eyes and counted to five before, schooling her tone to be neutral. 'Of course I've not been following you, Charlie. I *trusted* you to stick to the rules we established as a family. The rules we agreed in order to keep you safe ...' She hesitated and channelled Marcus before continuing, hoping she sounded calmer than she felt inside. 'And I'm disappointed you didn't do that.'

Eyes flashing, Charlie glowered, her lips pursed like a petulant child as she spat her response at her mother. 'You didn't need to spy ...'

Nikki held her hand up, her tone sharp, the fragile hold she had on her temper all but obliterated. 'Stop it! Listen to me for a minute. *You* put yourself at risk, Charlie. Look at this.' All thoughts of pussyfooting around her sick child dissipated by the little madam's attitude, she flung the photo of Charlie in the Costa onto the duvet and, breathing heavily, waited for Charlie's response.

For a few seconds, silence reigned as Charlie studied the images. 'One of *your* mates took photos of *me*?' Despite her huskiness, Charlie's anger sliced through every word.

Nikki matching her tone to her daughter's, her own eyes flashing, her lips tight, replied. 'No. Freddie Downey took this. I found it under my wiper a little while ago.'

Charlie, eyes glued to the image of her and the mysterious boy, fiddled with the duvet, her fingers kneading it as if it was a lifeline. 'But ...'

Nikki threw the other photo on the bed, wishing her stomach would unclench itself, but aware that if it did, she might lose her rag totally. 'We're *all* at risk, Charlie. Downey's been at Lazy Bites, he's taken photos of me and Saj. This is *real*. You can't go off on your own. You *can't* put yourself in danger like this.' Her tone hardened on the last few words and when she met her daughter's eyes she saw indignation mingled with worry reflected there.

'I'm not cross, Charlie. I just ...' She shrugged, exhaled. 'Actually, I *am* damn well cross. I'm furious. I just don't *get* it. Why would you do this?' She gestured at the bagged photos that lay scattered across Charlie's knees. 'Meet up with a lad when you

163

know he's out there – it's ridiculous.'

Now she'd started, Nikki was unable to stop. 'Do you know what he's capable of, Charlie? He's a paedophile. A child trafficker. A rapist. A torturer and a murderer. Do. You. Get. That? He's not some innocent old man. He's a …' She twanged her band, hard on her wrist, searching for a word that would describe Downey. 'An animal. No, actually he's not, for most animals wouldn't behave the way he does. Most animals look after their young, most animals only kill for food. He's a devil … you understand?'

Her bottom lip jutting out, Charlie, eyes dull and emotionless, glared at Nikki. 'You don't get it. You never do! Just butt out of my life, will you? I can't breathe with you always trying to control me.'

Never do? Control her? Butt out of her life? Nikki let the words settle with her. Was Charlie's accusation accurate? Did she never 'get it'? Did she never see things from Charlie's point of view? Was she too controlling? Granted over the past weeks she'd been single-minded about things. A lot had happened and with the threat from Downey imminent, she'd focused on keeping everyone safe. Hadn't she been there enough for Charlie? Deep down Nikki was well aware that she relied on Charlie too much. More than she should rely on a seventeen-year-old. More than any teen girl should have to bear. She counted on her to help Marcus keep the other two kids and Isaac safe. Maybe she'd not spent the time she should have in talking through Charlie's feelings. After her angry outburst before, Nikki had intended to make time for Charlie, but then the footprints in the snow in the back yard had driven that thought from her mind and now there was this. She hadn't even noticed Charlie was poorly. *Shit, I'm a crap mum!*

Intending to gather Charlie in her arms she moved forward, but Charlie's head jerked up, her brown eyes now cold and empty as she glared at her mother. 'I'm fed up with this. I want a normal life. I don't want to watch the kids. I don't want to be responsible all the time. I don't want to be the wonderful Nikki Parekh's daughter. I want to be *me*.' Charlie's voice broke on the last word and with it Nikki's heart also broke a little.

'Aw Charlie. It's hard but …' Charlie's snort was derisive, her lip curled up, her eyes betraying deep anger. The sort of anger Nikki had carried with her since childhood and at once Nikki realised she had failed her daughter. That knowledge slammed against her chest, sapping the energy from her. All this while she'd thought she was protecting her, but in reality, all she was doing was smothering her, making her hate her mother, making her conceal things from Nikki, putting her in danger. Struggling to calm herself, Nikki ignored her tight chest, and tried to get a grip of herself. She had to be the parent here. She had to take control. That was her job and even though Charlie was being a teenager – a difficult teenager, Nikki mustn't let her daughter's anger and frustration thwart her from carrying out her parental obligations. Quiet and reasonable, she looked at Charlie. 'Charlie, who is the boy in the photo, the boy you met up with in Costa?'

Now it was Charlie's turn to close her eyes and play for time. Nikki waited for what seemed like eons. Then Charlie opened them, looked straight at Nikki and said, 'None. Of. Your. Business.'

'What?' The word came out on a feeble breath – weak and disbelieving. Where had her Charlie gone and who had replaced her with this monster?

Despite her pallor, Charlie hardened her gaze; her eyes, so like Nikki's, were stone cold as, in the same hoarse voice as before, she said, each word dripping with venom, 'Maybe *I've* had enough of *your* obsessions. *Your* stupid rules, *your* self-absorption. Maybe I *should* just leave. Maybe I'll be better off away from *this*.' She wafted her hands to encompass the entire house. 'Maybe that's what I should do. Leave you all behind and start a new life for *me*.'

The challenge drove a hole through Nikki's chest. Charlie had never, not even in their fiercest disagreements, been so distant, so nasty, so full of hate, and Nikki had no idea what to do or say. Instead, she gave an abrupt nod, gathered the evidence bags and stood up. She had expected Charlie to relent, to apologise, but her daughter remained stubborn. Nikki strode to the door and left, feeling like a piece of her heart remained discarded and fossilised on the floor in her daughter's bedroom, still wondering who her daughter's mysterious coffee-drinking partner was. Pounding down the stairs, chest heaving, Nikki had the good sense to realise that her daughter was just mouthing off, but that didn't stop her words from hurting. Each one had stabbed through her brittle armour. Nikki cursed the fact that she had to go to work, had to have the photos processed, had to make contingency plans to ensure her family's safety. Charlie would be here when she returned from work and they could talk then. Besides, Charlie needed to rest. Perhaps her ire would have died down by this evening and they'd be able to talk calmly then.

Chapter 34

The quiet click as her bedroom door closed behind her mum was followed by footsteps thudding on the stairs, reverberating right up to the attic bedroom as Nikki stomped her anger out on the worn stair carpet. Charlie allowed her head to fall back on the pillow, welcoming the reprieve from the strain of holding it up. Her skull felt like it had a gang of workers hitting each fragile bone with minuscule hammers, each sending shock waves through to her temple and, although her breathing had eased, her throat was raw. She glanced at the flask of chai, still half-full by her bed, and contemplated pouring herself some more. Its fragranced warmth would soothe her aching throat, but instead of indulging herself, her chin rose, and she scowled at it. No way would she drink that, not when that cow had made it. She'd rather suffer than take anything from her mum. From now on, she would not accept any help from her mum and Marcus. From now on, she was on her own.

Sinking further down until she was prone on the bed, she pulled the duvet up to her chin, and closed her eyes. She'd deal with all this crap from her mum when she felt better. Although … seeing those pictures had shaken her. How had neither of them not noticed Downey taking them? She thought back to when she was sipping hot chocolate in Costa the previous day and tried to recollect who had been sitting nearby. But her mind was a blank, so she soon gave up. She'd been too engrossed in their conversation to notice anyone. With a twitch of her lips, she acknowledged that she'd have been unlikely to spot a naked snowman jiving past their table singing 'Let It Snow'. That made her think about his suggestion that they leave Bradford.

Until today, she'd thought her mum was overreacting about the whole Freddie Downey thing. In her most unkind moments, she'd suspected her mum's mental health issues were making her obsessed with Freddie Downey and that she was behaving irrationally. A faint pang of guilt stabbed her. Had she been too harsh on her mum? Then she thrust it aside. This was her mum's battle to fight, not hers. It was her *mum* who had the history with Downey, her *mum* who received the postcards from him – not her. Her hesitation turned to indignation as she thought about the photo of her. And that one of her mum, with Isaac in the background. Those weren't threats *only* to the amazing Nikki Parekh. Those were threats to her and to Isaac. *Shit!* She'd never forgive herself if anything happened to Isaac. She could take care of herself, but Isaac was different. He was too trusting, and that made him vulnerable to Freddie Downey's lies.

And what about Sunni or Ruby? Shit. No! Nothing could happen to them. A peculiar tension radiated across her chest, a heaviness that had her wondering if she was having a heart attack, then she realised it was fear – fear that maybe, just maybe, her mum had been right to be overprotective of them. That maybe her mum's precautions were sensible and not an overreaction. That those she loved *were* at risk from the monster who was Freddie Downey.

Her phone beeped. Reaching over, she ran her finger over the sensor and smiled at the text. It was from 'M'– the name she'd stored her boyfriend's number under.

M: You ok?

Charlie: Hey you, missing me? Got tonsillitis. 😣 If I feel better later, can we meet?

M: Aw no! 😭 Sure we can meet. Let me know when and where. Look after yourself. I'll mask up. 😷

Charlie slipped the phone back onto her bedside table and snuggled in. There were many reasons to say yes. So many reasons to take off with him and leave Bradford. Leaving might make it easier for her mum to look after everyone else. It might be easier for her if she didn't have to worry about Charlie. Maybe she'd be safer away from her family, too. But deep down, she realised those reasons were selfish musings on her part. Her mum would be frantic if she left, and she'd worry about everyone left behind and she'd miss them. Still, she was in love and the thought of not having to creep around to see her boyfriend, of being able to spend as much time as she wanted with him, was so tempting.

Besides, *his* life was crap here in Bradford. He was unhappy and that wouldn't change anytime soon. He was going to leave with or without her, she was certain of that. The only thing was, she wasn't sure she would survive without him. Exhaustion overtook her, and she sank into a fretful sleep filled with dreams of snowmen wielding machetes chasing her and a huge laughing face taunting her, telling her she was a coward, whilst another one, equally manic, equally scary, told her she was going to die.

Chapter 35

'You didn't think to call me over?' DCI Zain Ahad, glared at Nikki, his aquiline nose almost quivering in annoyance as he studied her like she was a dead rat on a biology student's desk.

Nikki, still acclimatising to the new set-up in Archie's old office, studied him. She'd only known him a couple of months, but even in that short time, his appearance had changed. Flashes of grey by his temple made him look older than she'd first thought – maybe early forties? – and despite being well dressed, Ahad's wardrobe didn't stretch to the designer brands that Sajid's did. Where Sajid's rounded face spoke of honesty and reliability, Ahad's sharp features, constant cynical lip curl and permanent brooding frown spoke more of pent-up tension and 'I don't do the namby-pamby feelings stuff.' Not put off by his demeanour, Nikki met his angry stare with one of her own. 'Why? So you'd come swooping in on your Batmobile and do *what,* exactly?'

'Batmobile?' Ahad pursed his lips, his frown deepening as his eyes drifted from Nikki to land on Sajid. Holding the younger man's gaze, he spoke, his tone conversational. 'You mean like Batman? A superhero? The Dark Knight?'

Squirming a little, Sajid smothered a snort, glowered at Nikki and attempted an unconvincing nonchalant shrug, before focusing on some evidence photos on his tablet.

Inwardly cringing, Nikki batted the question away. She didn't want to admit to Sajid that one night over a few beers at Anika's house, she *might* have drunkenly admitted to Ahad that Sajid called him the Dark Knight behind his back. She'd never hear the last of it if she did. Hell, Sajid would be so pissed off with her that he might refuse to use his Jaguar for work … and it was still freezing and his heated seats were soooo comfy. Her voice got even more shirty. 'No, more like Robin, Batman's *much* less super-heroey and not half as interesting sidekick. My point is, there was sod all *you* could do. Downey wasn't there anymore. Marcus was with me and Haris rolled up soon after. Besides which, I don't need a bunch of men jumping to my assistance. I'm able to look after myself.' She cast a glance at Sajid, whose mouth was still scrunched up as he cast small caustic glances her way. Boy, would she have some back-pedaling to do later. But for now, she wanted Ahad off her case and she could only do that by reassuring him she'd followed protocol. 'After photographing them, I uploaded them to Downey's file. Then, as per protocol, I had a uniform take the photos off to be processed. Not that they'll have anything linking them to Downey on them. Now, if you'd stop harking on, likening yourself to a superhero, which you're most definitely *not*, we can crack on with checking out the security cameras from Lazy Bites. Anwar's chasing up cameras from Broadway and the Costa, to see if there's anything on them.' Not giving Ahad a chance to correct her superhero comment, she turned to Malik. 'Saj, do the honours.'

Narrowing his eyes, his lips still a tight line of annoyance, Sajid pointed the remote at the pull-down screen Ahad had installed in his office and grainy footage of Sajid and Nikki entering Lazy Bites the previous day popped up. Allowing it to play at normal speed, the trio of officers watched as Nikki hugged Isaac before she and Saj settled into their booth to await their order. The rest of the café appeared empty. Sajid manoeuvred the remote, and the screen divided in two so that they could see themselves in the booth, alongside footage from another camera directed at the door to the café. Before Grayson delivered Nikki and Saj's order, the door opened and Isaac stepped forward to the counter, smiling at the man who'd just entered the café. Sajid paused the footage and the three of them studied the male figure.

Nikki's heart pounded as her eyes raked over the man they suspected was Freddie Downey. The man responsible for murdering her mother. Her biological father. Her skin itched, and she longed to dig her nails into her flesh and scratch and scratch and scratch until she bled. Instead, she twanged her band until her wrist stung and red ridges circled her wrist. Neither of the men beside her tried to stop her, and she was glad of that, for the band was the only thing that allowed her to keep hold of her emotions. Exhaling, her fingers released the band one last time and made their way to the scar at her throat. Downey was responsible for that, and over the years she'd used its presence on her neck to empower her. A reminder that she'd thwarted him before and she could do so again. All the while, she stared at the still before her. 'Can you make it bigger? I need to be sure.'

Sajid enlarged it as far as he could without distorting it too much and positioned it next to the last captured image they had on file of Freddie Downey – one they'd obtained from CCTV footage around the time he killed her mother. He was thinner than she remembered and taller. More well-dressed and with a beard. His face was fuller, and for a moment she doubted it was him. Could they have got this wrong? Was the man in Lazy Bites some other enemy of hers?

A shudder travelled up her spine as her earlier confrontation with Charlie sprung to mind. Surely, she couldn't have put her family through this for nothing? For some poxy, little stalker who she'd arrested years before? Breath hitched in her throat, then she stepped closer to the screen, eyes narrowed, studying the man now. If it hadn't been for those soulless eyes – eyes that had scoured her childish frame salaciously, eyes that had darkened and scorched her sister, making her cower in a corner, eyes that had sparked and come alive as he thrashed her mother time and time again – she *might* have believed she was mistaken. She couldn't speak, so instead she gave a curt nod.

Downey might disguise his body, change his height, dress up smart, alter his facial profile, but nothing ... *nothing* could erase the memory of those eyes. When she finally tried to speak, only a groan escaped her lips. With her jaw clenched and her back teeth grinding together, it was as if someone had punched her in the gut. Forcibly, she relaxed, feeling the ache leave her jaw as she exhaled. 'That's him – no doubt about it.'

Eyes still fastened on Downey, Nikki was aware of the brief exchange of glances between Ahad and Sajid. She tensed, desperate to seek comfort in twanging her wrist band, but pride wouldn't let her. Her fingers tingled with the effort it took to keep them by her side and not fluttering up to stroke the scar on her throat. Now wasn't the time to show weakness. Now wasn't the time to give Ahad even an inkling that she might be unravelling. She no longer had Archie fighting her corner, watching her back, so she had to hold it together, no matter how much she'd suffer from the effort later on.

To give them their due, despite the obvious discrepancies between the man in the Lazy Bites and the Downey they had on file, neither Ahad nor Sajid challenged her identification. Instead, they averted their gazes, allowing her the space to adjust to the implications of this confirmed sighting until she was ready to move on. 'When the footage from the Costa and Broadway comes in, it'll confirm my identification. It was him in the Costa too. I'm certain of that. The bastard followed my daughter.' Despite the fervour of her words, Nikki delivered them in a matter of fact, low voice, almost as if she was commenting on the weather.

She directed a curt nod in Sajid's direction, who, correctly interpreting her intent, got rid of the file image of Downey and went back to the camera footage from Lazy Bites. Saj pressed play, and the footage sprang into motion once more.

Downey, smiling, walked over to the counter and began conversing with Isaac. Whatever he said made the lad blush and his chest puffed up in an action Nikki recognised as pride. Downey was practised at lulling people into a false sense of security when it suited him. Isaac would remember whatever kindness Downey had shown him in that short interchange and, in his mind, he'd consider Downey a friend, such was his trusting nature. An icy claw grabbed Nikki's heart as the full extent of Downey's threat became apparent. Voice wobbling, she pointed to the screen. 'Rewind a little, Saj. You see, the way he glances towards us? He'd already clocked us before he even entered the café. His gaze went straight to us and lingered for a fraction of a second.'

In silence they watched Downey again, saw him clock them, saw the smirk flash across his lips before he turned his attention to Isaac.

'We need to protect Isaac. He's too close to you, Nikki, for Downey not to consider using him to get to you.' Ahad's tone was matter of fact, but his jaw tightened. 'I'll take care of Anika and Haqib. Are you okay with that bloody Ali and his band of merry men looking out for you?'

It annoyed Ahad that they relied on Ali's contacts for protection. He'd said he didn't like feeling beholden to them, thought it was bad for the police to rely on external sources to protect the public, but he'd also been wise enough to admit that they didn't have the necessary resources. He continued, 'Now that we've identified him, it won't be long till we catch him. I'll issue a BOLO for him and have this new image circulated' He flashed a reassuring smile at Nikki. 'This is positive, Parekh. It means we're closing in on him. He won't escape us.'

Eyes still on Downey, Nikki's response was a nod combined with a half-hearted shrug. They'd underestimated Downey before, and he'd murdered her mum. She didn't share Ahad's confidence in catching him quickly. Downey was tricky, devious and completely amoral. He'd not have shown himself like this if he didn't have a plan in mind. None of the intelligence they'd gained this morning had been without Downey's say-so. He was too damn smart for that. An image of Downey reeling in a huge fish with her features on it accompanied the sinking sensation that he was playing them. She only hoped that Ahad's complacence wouldn't cost any of them dearly.

Ahad cast his eyes down for a moment, fidgeted with some paperwork on his desk, and when his dark gaze rested back on Nikki, his tone brooked no dissent. 'We've got this, Parekh. This is for the Downey task force to pursue, not you.' As Nikki opened her mouth to complain, he shook his head and spoke over her. 'No! I mean it. NO! Archie's not here anymore. I'm in charge now and I don't want you anywhere near this. The Downey investigation is not part of your remit, Parekh. Understood?'

Defiance flashed in Nikki's eyes. How dare he? How bloody *dare* he? Two minutes in Archie's chair and he was acting like a dick. A hot flush spread across her cheeks and she had to force herself not to jump up, toss her warrant card on his desk and storm out of his smarmy new office throwing the words, 'I'll do what I fucking well need to protect my family and if it doesn't suit you, then that's your problem,' over her shoulder as she left.

Ahad sprung to his feet, fists resting on the desk, as he leaned towards her, his voice a whisper. 'Understood?'

It was Sajid's harder than necessary kick to her ankle that made her back down. She gave a curt nod, not meeting Ahad's eyes, but that wasn't enough for the new DCI. 'Say it, Parekh!'

Her eyes narrowed. Why the hell was he pushing her this way? She'd agreed, hadn't she? That's what a nod was, wasn't it – assent – agreement? Maybe she should write it in blood. She took a deep breath, realising she was being irrational. If she stormed off, it would be her and her family who'd suffer. This way, she'd at least have access to everything they uncovered regarding Downey. Her eye twitched as she raised her chin and responded like a churlish schoolkid. 'Understood.'

Ahad sat back down and nodded. 'Good. Now, *you* have your own investigation to pursue. I expect an update on Operation Sandglass after you've given your morning briefing.' And with that he dismissed them.

She straightened, exhaled and addressed Saj. 'Come on, we have tonnes of work to complete on Operation Sandglass and I want to find out if He Who Owns The Arm has been identified yet.'

Downey might be a constant niggle for Nikki, but she knew Ahad was right. She was damned if she'd allow the bastard to compromise an ongoing investigation.

Chapter 36

What's that thing they say about asking a busy person if you want to get things done? Fugly glared at the two idiots he'd entrusted to load up the animals ready for transportation to the site of their next fight and, for a mere nanosecond, Jacko almost felt sorry for them. In their shit-covered wellies, their wind-raw faces chapped and ruddy, they looked like their brain cells had frozen along with their ability to fulfil direct orders as they puffed on their wonky roll ups, huddled together in the barn's shelter whilst the animals shivered outside. *Morons*! Hadn't they learned anything from the dog fight the other night? The way they were behaving made Jacko wonder if the two lasses had a death wish.

Fugly's eyes narrowed – a sure sign that an explosion, accompanied by extreme violence, was about to occur. Jacko watched as his boss's gaze moved from the idiots to the three cages behind them. Inside were shivering, angry dogs, hurling themselves against the bars in their attempts to protest their current conditions. Yes, the boss wanted them angry – that was the whole point, treating them mean made them mean, but he also needed them *healthy* and leaving them a foot deep in the snow-covered yard with wind howling through the bars wasn't ensuring they would be in tip-top condition for the fights later on this evening.

They *should* have been loaded into the van by now with the other dogs. Shielded from the raw weather, preserving their energy. But these two idiots had elected to have a fag break rather than do their damn job. Jacko tried to think of a distraction, but his mind went blank. He couldn't stomach any more violence, any more death. He really couldn't. Especially not when he knew what was on the cards for this evening's entertainment. They were so bloody stupid that when they noticed Fugly glaring at them, their gormless faces broke out into huge smiles, as if he was their long-lost uncle or something. 'Hey boss, we're nearly done.'

Fugly stabbed a finger in their direction, but maintained his distance, his face contorted like the caged dogs. He glared at the girl with the weird ear plug thing that made her ear resemble an arsehole when she took it out, until the gormless grin melted from her lips, leaving her darting anxious glances to her friend with the pink hair, as if asking for support. 'Can't you see the animals are shivering? That's why they're barking so much. Get them into the van, pronto!'

The idiots' grins widened, accompanied by nonchalant shrugs before the taller one, tossing her cig into the snow where it hissed before being extinguished, offered a gleeful response. 'Teaching them not to bark, boss.'

Jacko almost rolled his eyes. The idiots needed to learn how to read the room. They were walking a very thin line, and Jacko couldn't think of a way to save them. Then an idea struck, and he stepped forward, schooling his face to mimic Fugly's anger. 'Shame we need Hoddit and Doddit to drive the dogs to the venue, else I'd bloody sort them out right here and now.'

He turned to Fugly. 'You know, boss, these prats make me think of two humungous watermelons. Imagine if I just …' He took a step closer to the girls and, centimetres from their heads, crashed his bare hands together like a pair of cymbals. '… Smashed their water-fucking-melon heads together. Imagine their gormless bloody brains splattering all over the snow.'

Aiming a kick at Hoddit – the one with the ear plug arsehole – Jacko tried to swallow the guilt he felt when she grasped her shin and let out a yell of pain. He'd had to make it convincing, otherwise his distraction wouldn't work. Shame the lass didn't realise he'd saved her from a much worse beating.

It had worked! When he turned back, Fugly was grinning, his manky teeth sending waves of halitosis through the air as he laughed. Seconds later, he was off, leaving Jacko to sort out the girls. 'Maybe later! Get them sorted out, Jacko, yeah?'

The shorter one, Doddit, picked up on the undercurrents and sidled towards the forklift, ready to lift the cages into the van. Crisis averted. Jacko wrapped his fist round his crucifix and closed his eyes for a moment, allowing the tension to leave his body.

According to Fugly, the grand finale from the other night had upped the stakes. The punters' expectations ran high now and some of his most ferocious punters were baying for a repeat performance. Capitalising on their depravity suited Fugly. He didn't care how he made his money as long as he did. Jacko knew Fugly intended to use his captive to fulfil tonight's thirst for blood. Now he wondered if the two daft lassies had sealed their own fates and given the lad in the shed another reprieve. One or both of these idiots would fit the bill, and neither of them would be a huge loss. But Jacko had had enough. He couldn't stand back and let Fugly kill any of the three kids. He watched as Hoddit, still limping, and Doddit manhandled the cages onto the trucks. Then his gaze drifted to the closed door of the barn. Mulling over all the things he'd learned about Fugly, he realised he should have paid more attention to the lad in the barn. Why had Fugly kept him alive when the other lad Calhoun had been sacrificed? Had Jacko underestimated Fugly? Perhaps using Calhoun at the first fight had been his intention all along. After all, wouldn't the condition of the lad in the barn make feeding him to the dogs an anti-climax? At least Calhoun had tried to escape – put on a show, ran around a bit, yelled and screamed and pleaded for mercy. But that lad, fuck, he was already half dead. They'd be lucky to get a twitch out of him when they threw him in the ring. Now Jacko wished he'd paid more attention to Fugly when he'd sent him to recruit the lad.

As they loaded the last of the dogs and the drivers all set to transport them to Chester where the next fight was scheduled for later that evening, Jacko's gaze once more travelled towards the barn. Should he risk going in and trying to get some details from the lad? Try to figure out something he could use against Fugly? Over the years, he'd realised that getting out whilst you were ahead was a wise tactic. It was too late to escape before tonight's big event, but Jacko swore that this one would be the last. He took a step towards the barn, but the sight of Fugly hurrying towards him made him alter his direction.

'Come, Jacko. Want to run the plans for tonight through with you.'

The familiar sensation of sweat soaking into his vest and jumper accompanied Jacko as he followed Fugly into the farmhouse kitchen. The more he placed himself between Fugly's temper and his employees, the more Fugly trusted and relied on him. It was a double-edged sword. On the one hand, he was saving the kids from the boss's increasingly frequent burst of violence, on the other, he was becoming more embroiled in Fugly's activities and was finding it ever more difficult to get away from Fugly for long enough to put any sort of plan in order.

Resigned to more time spent in discomfort, pretending to be as excited by it all as the boss, Jacko took up his position by the fire and tried to work out which snippets of information Fugly let slip were valuable.

'So, after tonight, we'll finish up the planning for the big hunt – the grand finale. Tonight is merely a warm-up. A means to whet the punters' appetites and draw them in.'

On and on, Fugly droned. Patting himself on the back for being so clever, for finding a gap in the market that only he was warped enough to fill. Sipping tea and nodding as required, Jacko shivered. Even with the fire blasting at him and the sweat drenching his clothes, he was chilled to the marrow. He wondered if he'd ever be warm again.

'My contacts have already set the wheels in motion, advertising this "unique hunting experience".'

Shit, he even used those stupid bunny ears like it was something wonderful, something worthy of being wrapped in inverted commas, something momentous – a fucking brilliant USP. Jacko's chest contracted and a momentary wave of dizziness made the room waver in front of him. He should have eaten the toast Fugly had offered him earlier, but he hadn't been sure he could keep it down, so he'd refused. Now he was paying for that. Fugly was pacing again, all eager excitement and energy.

'What we're offering on the big hunt, Jacko, is a main event involving active participation by the punters. Isn't that great?'

Fugly's eyes were on him, demanding a response, so Jacko obliged. 'Eh, yeah. Inspired. Yeah, but dun't your usual clients prefer to watch from behind the fences, like? Didn't know they wanted to be hunters, like.'

Fugly's grin widened. 'Oh, Jacko. You just don't get how many supposedly normal folk living their day-to-day lives – teachers, bankers, doctors, politicians – crave something that society says is illegal.'

Fugly plopped down opposite Jacko, and leaning forward, rested his arms on his thighs. 'Some of them up till now have satisfied their blood lust vicariously through the dog fights and most of them will never dabble in anything more than that, but …'

As Fugly's fevered eyes met his, a shiver raced up Jacko's spine, for lurking in his boss's eyes was something that he'd never witnessed before – evil. Pure, unadulterated evil. Fugly's jerky hand movements backed this up and salivating speech. 'There are some desperate enough to take a gigantic step into the unknown. Those who are prepared to let their desires rule their mind, who are ready to pay big bucks for a unique experience, the likes of which they'll never experience again.'

Fugly was back on his feet, his body unable to contain the excitement that coursed through it as he circled the room like a lion in its cage. 'Never mind fox and hounds, what I've planned goes further than that – way beyond it.'

Eyes blazing, he stopped abruptly, spun on his heel and collapsed in his chair, staring right into Jacko's eyes. This time, his gaze was glassy, as if he couldn't see Jacko, so wrapped up was he in the prospect of his 'final hunt'.

Already the ether was buzzing with Fugly's depraved plans. The sick fuckers out there were circulating the information for him. The money was pouring in. Fugly's plans were in place both for tonight and for the big hunt in a couple of days' time. Fugly was out of control and Jacko felt helpless to stop it. None of this would end well. None of it.

Just when Jacko wondered if Fugly would ever move again, the other man jumped to his feet. The mad fanaticism disappeared from his eyes as quickly as snuffing out a match.

'Got things to do, Jacko. I'll meet you at the new kill site tonight. You bring the lad. Don't trust those tossers with even the simplest of tasks.' And with a snort, Fugly left. Seconds later, the sound of his engine starting up reached Jacko's ears and for the first time that morning, he gulped in deep breaths of air and allowed his shoulders to relax as he murmured a prayer. Little did Fugly know it, but he'd just given Jacko what he wanted: an excuse to spend time with the captive.

Chapter 37

When Nikki re-entered the incident room, she found it almost empty except for a few officers inputting information into the various systems and DS Jewkes, standing, hands behind his back, studying the crime board images of the dismembered arm. As she went to greet him, a text message arrived. A quick glance told her it was Ali, so she opened it:

Ali: We need to talk, Parekh. Phone me!

After the events of the morning, Ali's casual words took on a more sinister tone, but then, with a shake of her head, Nikki dismissed her maudlin thoughts. He probably just wanted to go over the arrangements to increase security for her. If it was anything more urgent, he'd have rung her instead of texting. So, deciding to deal with it later, she slipped her phone back into her pocket and walked over to Jewkes, wondering why he'd made the trip to Trafalgar House.

As Nikki neared, Jewkes turned and shrugged with an awkward smile. 'Thought I'd come over. See how you operate. We're hearing a bit of chatter on the Dark Web. References to "hunts".'

Nikki frowned. 'Hunts? Like fox hunting?'

Jewkes exhaled and his shoulders slumped. 'No, not foxes. What we're hearing seems to infer something worse than that. They're coded, but the sense we're getting is that the sick bastards are upgrading from using the dogs to fight each other to using them to hunt instead.'

As if his legs wouldn't hold him upright anymore, he fell into a chair. It took Nikki less than two seconds to work out what he wasn't telling her. But it was Saj who asked the question. 'You mean …?'

Face grey, Jewkes pinched the top of his nose with his thumb and forefinger and released a long, slow sigh. 'Yeah, that's right. The fuckers are organising some sort of interactive hunt where the prey is human. Our lot have discovered that there's quite the demand on the dark web for violence by animals against humans. We're still trying to decode it all and get more detailed information. It's all vague at the moment, but it looks like one of these dog fight organisers has gone rogue and upped the stakes. What we're hearing are mixed opinions about this new outfit. The bottom line is that these bastards aren't restricting their barbarism only to animals but have escalated to hunting humans too.'

He paused, and swallowed hard. 'From what we've decoded, there appears to be an underbelly of sickos who've curbed their baser instincts so far by spending huge amounts of bitcoins streaming supposed live kill and torture on the dark web and are now keen to participate in a live hunt themselves. Some of them have, by the looks of it, attended live dog fights before. Our experts say the internet's buzzing with reports of a man being thrust into a ring with a dog and ripped to shreds. It's been hyped up and is gaining traction, but we can't get a handle on where it originates or who is behind it. The most we've got is that some of the other dog fight teams are furious, claiming it's a ruse. We unfortunately have physical evidence to the contrary. Although most of the ones on our radar are distancing themselves from this, none of them are dropping any names. It's like they're too scared to say too much. We're playing a waiting game. And it's so fucking frustrating.' He slammed his palm on the table, and gave his head a shake as if to energise himself, before jerking his thumb toward the images of their tattooed arm. 'Any ID yet?'

Now it was Nikki's turn to exhale as frustration welled up in her chest. This was horrific. Bad enough that people got entertainment from maiming animals, but to extend their barbaric practices to humans too was nauseating. 'We're drawing blanks everywhere we look. Missing Persons has no details of anyone sporting that sort of tattoo on file. The bite marks found on the arm match with those found on the girl in Pinderfields, yet we still don't have an ID on her and she's still not able to speak to us. We've extended the search nationally. Still no hits. Our social media appeal caught no valid information, so we're going to extend that to local, regional and national news. Someone must know who this arm belongs to. If your sources are accurate, the more time that passes, the likelier we'll find another person killed in a similar way and we've got no damn leads to speak of and now you're telling me there's word of a bloody human hunt.'

Pulling up a chair opposite Jewkes, Saj sat down. 'If your information is accurate, and I see no reason to question it, then we're definitely looking at murder here. He Who Owns The Arm is a murder victim.'

On hearing the phrase, Jewkes's eyebrows quirked, 'Eh?'

Nikki wafted her hand. 'Forget it – long story – Harry Potter reference. Gallows' humour and all that.' Nose scrunched up, she looked at Saj. 'If only we had the rest of the body.'

'Or at least an ID on the tattoo that we could work from. Why are we getting nothing back? We've tried every option – morgues, missing persons, social fucking media, for God's sake and even the short bit on Calendar and Look North elicited nothing other than a load of IDs of healthy two-armed people. Where the hell is the rest of the body?'

Nikki shrugged. 'Could be anywhere. Those moors are ideal in winter for delaying anyone finding a body, which makes me ask again – why leave the arm, but take the rest of the body away? Are they toying with us?' She turned to Jewkes. 'What do you reckon? Operation Sandglass knows more about these dog fights and their organisers than us. Why would they do that?'

Hands splayed before him, Jewkes shook his head. 'Never, in all my years investigating animal cruelty, have I come across something like this. Never.' He sniffed. 'Any luck with the vets?'

'Still got two to interview. We'll be heading out soon, but so far, they've all supplied alibis which are currently being checked out. I suspect this is a waste of our time. We don't even know if they had a vet.' She shrugged. 'However, we've not a lot else to go on at the minute, so we might as well follow up on the two we have left on our list.'

As one, their eyes turned to the crime wall and for long moments, Nikki, Sajid and Jewkes studied the images as if willing them to spark some chain reaction that would help them progress their investigation. Then Jewkes stirred. 'Best be off. I'll keep you updated from our end, and I'm sure you'll do the same.'

At the door now, Jewkes waved. Nikki nodded farewell, her thoughts already checking off the investigative processes they'd undertaken and searching for other avenues to pursue. 'Saj, get teams with cadaver dogs to head out to the crime scene. I want them to search the area again, starting about a hundred yards from the old barn and moving in ever-widening circles. Those animals are expert at finding dead bodies regardless of the weather. If they have left the body near the kill site, I'll bet my new car they'll find it.' Head to one side, she grinned. 'Care to match my bet?'

Saj snorted. 'Yeah right, your heap for my baby? Eh that'll be a *no*, Nik.'

As he picked up the phone to execute her orders, Nikki continued her contemplation. Had they narrowed down the list of vets too much? Should she have involved the cadaver dogs earlier – before they had any confirmation of foul play? Inhaling, she shook her head. *Come on Nik. No self-doubt!*

She took a last glance at the crime board, checking off all the 'actions' listed there. No ID on the arm. No additional results back from the lab. They still awaited the prioritised DNA results from the arm, the blood found on the metal hoop and from the floor around it, as well as the other forensic analyses from the scene. Why did everything seem to move at a snail's pace right now? When Saj had finished his phone call, she grabbed her coat. 'Come on, Malik, we've got disgraced vets to interview.'

Chapter 38

Jacko waited a good fifteen minutes after Fugly drove off before moving from his position at the fireside. His heart pounded and a dull throb radiated up his face. It was only when the pain reached his temple and made him wince that he realised he was clenching his jaw. Slowly, he moved his lower jaw in a circle and as the tension left his body, he tried to gather his thoughts. Fugly had gone to the location of the next dog fight, near Chester. Realising he was second guessing himself, Jacko ran through every possible scenario that lay before him. Every conceivable thing that could go wrong. He'd watched Fugly for weeks now – learned his ways, seen how devious the man was – and he'd no intention of falling foul of him. He thought he'd covered up his disgust at Fugly's plans, but had he? Who knew? Fugly would enjoy lulling him into a false sense of security before sweeping in with a tortuous punishment if he had even a whiff of Jacko's treachery. Just thinking about the sort of punishment Fugly would dole out if he caught Jacko betraying him, started him off sweating again. He could smell his rankness and suspected that it smelled extra fetid because of the fear that flooded his body. Maybe Fugly already had him in his sights. Perhaps the bastard would feed Jacko to the dogs later on. Maybe he *was* sitting in his fancy jeep, just up the road, ready to come back and catch Jacko out.

In the end, it was thoughts of his wife and grandchild that spurred him to move. He could hesitate for ever, if he wanted to, but that would do him no good. He had to at least try – for their sakes, he had to give it a go. The window to escape Fugly's tenacious hold was narrowing and his gut told him that the lad they held captive in the barn had a solution for him, even if the lad himself didn't realise it. All Jacko needed to do was to keep it together. If he could stop anyone being killed tonight, he would – although a quick glance at his watch told him that was unlikely. How could an unarmed man protect his family as well as the captive lad in the face of all those fanatical faces? His mind jumped back to the last time. All the men's faces a blur of flashing eyes and snarling mouths baying for blood, the air filled with the stench of animal sweat, human testosterone and blood, so much blood, his ears ringing with their chants and Calhoun's screams.

His orders from Fugly were clear. Make sure the rest of the vehicles carrying the equipment set off at intervals, taking a variety of routes to minimise the risk of detection. Jacko's main job was to transport the captive in the back of his jeep – which he'd already fitted with false number plates – via the M6, which was a much longer route than some of the others, to Chester. He had to arrive in time to collect the vet, who was travelling by bus, and drive all three of them via a series of A- and B-roads to the fight site near Hatton Heath. Jacko neither knew nor cared how Fugly had come up with the location. Fugly got whatever he wanted whenever he wanted it, and Jacko was reluctant to appear too interested in that side of things. The less he knew about operational aspects, the less Fugly would view him as a threat.

Fugly's instructions were detailed and he tolerated no deviation from them, so Jacko knew to stick to the plan. His primary worry was the condition of the captive. When he'd looked in on the lad overnight, he'd been delirious and shivering, so Jacko somehow needed to warm him up, feed him up and tease him into a communicative state, before he could pump him for information. However, he didn't want any of the remaining workers becoming suspicious if they saw him near the barn as they loaded up their vehicles.

Satisfied that Fugly wasn't likely to return unexpectedly, Jacko scoured the farmhouse for blankets. In the upstairs bathroom cabinet, he found a half-used bottle of antibiotics with the name Elsbeth Smith on it. The date was eighteen months ago, but Jacko reckoned that pumping the lad full of them wouldn't do him any harm and they *might* do him some good. He also found co-codamol lurking at the back and bearing in mind the way the lad had winced when he'd covered him with an extra blanket, Jacko reckoned a few strong pain killers wouldn't go amiss either.

After stuffing his things in a black bin liner, he snuck into the yard and headed over to the large bins that lined the side of the wall nearest the barn. Despite the wind that was picking up as the morning moved into afternoon, the sound of the lads traipsing back and forth to their vans carrying fencing, lighting, PA system and the refreshments drifted over the muddy yard. Rolling grey clouds and intermittent flurries of snow offered some cover as he crept past the bins and all but sprinted to the ramshackle barn. Pushing the door open, he gipped as the sewage smell caught in his oesophagus, but he pushed that sensation away and shut the door behind him, standing with his back to it as his eyes became accustomed to the semi-darkness. It was strange being in here without the threatening presence of the dogs, slathering at him, their barks and growls sending shivers down his spine as their eyes followed his movements.

His eyes homed in on the huddled up bundle on the floor. Was the lad moving? Jacko's breath hitched in his throat as the realisation that he might be too late dawned. The boy had been in a right state earlier, he could now be dead. Clutching his crucifix, Jacko edged closer, holding his breath not just against the odours, but because he was scared. Was the boy still alive?

Was that a twitch?

Jacko crouched beside the boy, bin bag by his side, his arm outstretched ready to prod him when the lad's eyes snapped opened and stared at Jacko – right into his soul – as if berating him. No sooner had Jacko recovered from his surprise than they closed again. An audible breath escaped his lips, then all business, Jacko set about emptying the bag. First, he peeled the soiled blankets and raggedy clothes off the boy and, after using them to massage some warmth into his skin and soak up any moisture, he tossed them aside. Next he coaxed on a warm jumper, trousers and socks, before covering him up with three thick blankets. As he worked, Jacko focused on the end goal. He had to get the lad well enough to communicate with him. Every sense told him this boy held some personal significance for Fugly. Why else would Fugly have let him live so far? Fugly must have his reasons and Jacko was sure that if he could only encourage the lad to speak to him, he'd have one up on Fugly. Every slight touch elicited a corresponding whimper from the captive that reminded Jacko of his daughter last time they'd tried to get her clean. Locking her in the back bedroom, hearing her scream, seeing her shiver and vomit and fall apart had been torture for him and his wife, but they'd done it out of love. Jacko had been brought up on a 'cruel to be kind' sort of diet. Their efforts had been in vain, for only a few weeks afterwards, her dealer lured his beautiful daughter away from them. With the boy as warm and comfortable as he could make him, Jacko hefted him up to a sitting position and forced him to drink some water and to swallow the pills he'd brought. His head kept lolling to the side, his eyes fluttering shut, but Jacko persisted. All the while his ears strained to hear if any footsteps approached. After watching the boy take the pills, Jacko opened a flask and tipped lukewarm tomato soup into his mouth. Dribbles rolled down his chin and although Jacko couldn't be certain, he thought the lad had managed a few swallows.

Conscious that he'd been with the lad for a while, Jacko stood up. It was time for him to wave vehicle one, with its equipment, off on its journey to tonight's kill site. Reluctant to leave the boy, yet conscious he'd done all he could for now, Jacko sneaked out the barn, and was pleased to see the workers were too busy locking up their vans to be bothered about him and his activities.

Chapter 39

Nikki had never been in a large racing stables before. The extent of her contact with horses had been on the odd times she'd taken one or other of the kids for horse riding lessons at a local stable. They'd all been part of a working farm, with a lived-in well-used, rustic feel to them. The one Sajid had pulled into, on the outskirts of Harrogate, was as far from her memories as it was possible to be. Disgraced vet Giles Lincroft's stable was pristine and modern with a driveway surfaced with robust clay-coloured tiles that led to well-proportioned buildings separated from the driveway by ornate metal gates, large enough to drive a bus through. Lincroft was the second-to-last vet on their list. He'd lost his licence to practise veterinary medicine by accepting bribes to doctor blood test results on racing horses to hide the fact that illegal drugs enhanced the horses' performances. Unlike the vets Nikki and Sajid had interviewed yesterday, Lincroft was from a moneyed background.

A helpful stable hand directed them to a tall man, leaning against a fence watching two enormous horses being trained. He turned at their approach, looked at Nikki and then directed his 'How may I help you?' to Saj.

Saj raised an eyebrow, took a step back and said nothing,

leaving it for Nikki to do the introductions. Even after that, Lincroft still insisted on ignoring Nikki and directing every response to Saj. 'No, I don't know anything about illegal dog fighting, other than it's a disgrace.'

Better people than Giles Lincroft had ignored Nikki, and she refused to be cowed by his behaviour. She smiled and sharpened her tone. 'So, you'll be able to confirm your whereabouts on the evening of 22nd January until the early hours of the 23rd, then?'

Turning his back to Nikki, Lincroft smiled at Sajid, his too-white teeth, perfectly straight in his supercilious mouth. 'I'm a busy man you understand. I breed thoroughbreds and run my own stables. And as it happens, Midnight was foaling on the 22nd right through to the 23rd. It was a hard labour. You can ask my stable hands – those two over there – and of course my vet, Davy Bond. He'll confirm my whereabouts.'

Enjoying the fact that the supercilious git was under the misapprehension that he was proving some sort of point to her, Nikki smiled. 'Oh, I thought you were a vet, Mr Lincroft?' Then she slapped her palm to her forehead and with her smile widening said, 'Oh, silly me. I forgot. You're not a vet anymore, are you? That's why you need a real vet to come along to look after your thoroughbreds, isn't it? You can't be trusted with them, can you? The owners wouldn't take too kindly to a discredited vet foaling their animals, would they?'

Lincroft's lips tightened, but at least his attention was focused on Nikki now as he glared at her. 'I've answered your question and I've got a busy day ahead, so if you don't mind …'

He made to strut past Nikki, but unsmiling, she moved to block his path, her eyes never leaving the older man's face, and spoke in a mild tone. 'Oh, but I *do* mind. I mind your attitude. I mind your rudeness and *most* of all I mind your sexism. I suggest that if you don't want to take a trip to Bradford with us, then you turn round and answer the rest of my questions …' She paused before adding, 'Of course, that's if you don't mind.'

Nikki wasn't sure what she enjoyed more; Lincroft's crimson cheeks or his indignant huffs and puffs before he snarled at Nikki. 'Get on with it then. I haven't got all day.'

Tempted though she was to drag it out for longer, with the sole intention of annoying the man, Nikki wanted to finish the vet interviews and return to Trafalgar House. She was eager to catch up on developments regarding Downey's whereabouts and she wanted to be in Bradford in time to drive Isaac back home when his shift finished. She nodded to Sajid to check his alibi with the stable hands whilst she finished her questions. 'What do you know about illegal dog fights?'

Spluttering as if she'd asked if Santa Claus was real, Lincroft stared at a spot beyond Nikki's shoulder and snapped his answers out like he was doing her a favour. 'My interests are a lot more upmarket than tawdry dog fights. Waste of good beasts if you ask me for no purpose other than monetary gain. Barbaric!'

The shudder that accompanied his words was so convincing Nikki was inclined to believe his pleas of innocence. However, she wouldn't let him off the hook just yet. 'Oh, but wasn't it "monetary gain" that made you doctor those blood tests?' Her frown was all innocent, but there was no doubt her barb was intentional.

'Don't you get smart with me now, missy …'

'*Missy*?' The word exploded from Nikki's mouth, drawing the attention of all the stable hands and Sajid and making Lincroft jump. He stepped back, but Nikki barely keeping the spark of anger under control, took three steps towards him, crowding him and backing him up against the fence. 'Don't you "Missy" me. I'm Detective Inspector Parekh and *don't* you forget it.' She backed away then, and as he made to follow her, she spun back round. 'I've got my eye on you. I'll make sure your business – accounts, practices, dealings with others – is scrutinised within an inch of its life and if I find you've been lying and you have anything to do with these low lives who organise the dog fights, I'll make sure you're not allowed near another animal again. Got it?'

Lincroft paled and Nikki, satisfied, nodded. 'If you know anything about anyone involved in this sort of crap, now is the time to tell me.' She stared him down and when he shook his head, she whipped a card from her pocket and handed it to him. 'Keep your ears open, Mr Lincroft, and if you get even a whiff of info about illegal dog fighting or breeding, you phone me – remember you're in my crosshairs now.'

Despite his sexist behaviour, and his odious, money grabbing morals, Nikki didn't get any inkling that he had any knowledge of illegal dog fights or illegal breeding of canines. Still, maybe he'd make it his business to find out some information that might help them, even if it was only to get Nikki off his case. When a grinning Sajid joined her, they headed back to the car. 'The stable hands confirmed his alibi although they seemed very amused to see him taken down a peg or two. He's not the most popular of bosses.'

Nikki snorted. 'He's a tosser, that's for sure.' She watched out the window as Lincroft stormed across the driveway to a jeep, glancing at his watch as he went. Someone was in a hurry to get somewhere. Nikki consulted her list and sighed. 'Let's head to the last one. Jon Ross, is it? He lives on a pig farm in Cullingworth so it's on the way home. Seems it was owned by his wife's family and he's inherited it. Hm, some folk land on their damn feet, don't they? He loses his vet's licence, but still gets to run a farm?'

An hour later, Sajid and Nikki pulled into a smooth, if slush-covered drive that led to a parking circle with a huge well-maintained Yorkshire sandstone farmhouse in front of them and a series of buildings of varying sizes dotted around the sides and towards the rear of the property. When they got out of the car, the familiar, if unwelcome smell of pigs greeted them but, looking at the luxurious home, Nikki reckoned that was a small price to pay. 'Definitely doesn't seem like having criminal records and losing their jobs has set any of these idiots back financially, does it?'

Sajid snorted, 'No, the only one who seems to have suffered

at all was Gordon Collins and he didn't harm any animals nor benefit financially from his crime.'

'Exactly, poor old sod. That house of his must be freezing and yet look at the others on this list. Every one of them still seems to be okay financially.'

'So, Nik, what did Jon Ross do to lose his licence?'

Nikki consulted her list. 'Malpractice, overprescribing, unnecessary procedures, dodgy bookkeeping and so forth. His practice was in Leeds but when he took over the pig farm after his wife's parents died, he set up a small practice here in his daughter's name and he employs her as the vet. He has a stake in the business but no longer practises. Which still allows him access to the sort of drugs and suchlike Jewksy told us these dog fighting vets need.'

They got out and approached the well-lit house that belonged to Jon Ross. The doorbell pealed a cheery sound when Nikki pressed it and she waited a full minute before pressing again. It was only after the third ring that movement came from the back of the house. Through the frosted glass, Nikki saw a figure in a bulky coat and hat approach the front door. The door was opened a couple of inches and a young woman peered through the gap in the door chain. 'Yes, can I help?'

Nikki showed her official ID. 'I'm DI Parekh, and this is DS Malik. We'd like to speak with Jon Ross please.'

Even through the limited space, Nikki watched as the young woman's face, pale and drawn, crumpled and her shoulders slumped. Barely coherent, she said, 'Wait a moment.' She closed the door, disengaged the chain and reopening it, invited them into the house.

Once inside, Nikki assessed the woman before her. She was about the same age as Nikki and wore wet wellies and a massive padded coat with a beanie on her head. Thick gloves lay at her feet. The woman stared blankly at them, though her pallor concerned Nikki more than her blankness. 'Are you okay?'

She nodded, Nikki's words apparently bringing her out of

whatever reverie she'd been in. 'Of course, oh I'm so sorry. You must think I'm mad. Look, let me get my coat off and we'll go through to the kitchen. I was out the back feeding the hens and the other livestock. We've got pigs and two goats.'

Now that she'd started to talk, it seemed that the woman would be difficult to shut up. As she spoke her hands fluttered all around her, giving the impression that she was in perpetual motion even when she stood in one place. Kicking off her wellies, careless of the mucky snow melting on the carpet, she shrugged her coat off and led them along a hallway into a spacious kitchen. 'I'm Julie Ross. It's my dad you want to see. But I'm afraid you're too late.'

She sniffed, grabbed a tissue from a box on the work surface and proceeded towards the kettle which she switched on. 'He died. The funeral's next week.'

Nikki bit her lip and exchanged a glance with Sajid. This was such an awkward situation. Jon Ross may well be deceased but they couldn't rule him out of being involved with the dog fighting *unless* he died before the fight. Nikki nodded to Saj, telling him he should take over. Although she sympathised with the woman, who was grieving her dead father, tact was not one of Nikki's skills. Sajid, on the other hand was Mr Smooth in delicate situations and he took over the questioning seamlessly. 'Oh, I'm so sorry to hear that, Julie. No wonder you're upset. When did he die?'

With a tremulous smile Julie smiled at Saj. The sincerity in his eyes seemed to relax her as her shoulders slumped and she hefted herself onto a bar stool. 'It was so sudden. Two days ago. The 23rd. I wasn't expecting it and there's *so* much to sort out.'

Nikki sighed. Mr Ross, the disgraced vet wasn't exonerated from any illegal dog fighting activity on the 22nd of January, but neither were they able to interview him. That seemed to be a dead end. If Ross had been offering his services to the dog fighting ring, then they'd be needing a new one.

Julie Ross sniffed and reached over to grab another tissue but Sajid beat her to it, extracting one of his silk ones from his pocket and placing it in the forlorn woman's hands. 'It's just the two of you then?'

Not wanting to intrude, Nikki sat on a chair by the kitchen table and took in the decor whilst Saj worked his magic. The room was warm and modern. However, evidence of Julie's low mood and distress was evident in the pile of dishes near the sink. Plates filled with food that was barely touched indicated her lack of appetite, whilst empty coffee cups scattered every surface. Droplets of spilled coffee and milk covered the surfaces and there was a faint but unpleasant smell in the air that Nikki was sure originated from the overflowing bin. Next to the bin the recycling was also overflowing and Nikki noticed three empty gin and two wine bottles among the debris. Julie Ross was a mess and who could blame her. Nikki had been a mess when her mum died and she'd had her family for support. Poor Julie didn't appear to have anyone, but she didn't seem drunk right now. Traumatised and in grief, yes … drunk, no.

'Yes, it was just us two. My mum died five years ago. Cancer. Dad's death was unexpected.' She gazed into Sajid's eyes. 'Car crash. Out of the blue. When the police called me to tell me what had happened, it was as if my entire world imploded.'

It looked like Jon Ross was out of the picture in terms of the dog fight on the 22nd, although not necessarily in involvement up until his death, which meant Sajid would have to extricate them from here without causing Julie Ross any more distress than was absolutely necessary, whilst trying to find out more about her dad. Good job it was Saj in charge of things. Nikki was useless at that sort of thing.

'I hate to trouble you at a time like this Julie but …' Saj was all sincerity and concern. 'We need to ask you a couple of questions. Is that okay?'

Julie rubbed Saj's pristine hankie over her eyes, blew her nose and nodded. 'Yes, of course. What's wrong?'

'There's been some illegal dog fights in the area and we're

reaching out to vets to see if they've noticed anything that may help us.'

Nikki appreciated Sajid's white lie. It might elicit information and it wouldn't cause Julie the same distress that admitting they'd come here with the sole purpose of finding out if her father was the vet responsible for treating wounded animals at these dog fights.

'Oh, then it's me you want to speak to. Dad's not …' Her eyes welled up again. 'Wasn't a vet anymore. I run the practice now and I'm sorry, I can't help you. I have a cohort of regular domestic pet patients and a few farmers on my books, but anything like that would catch my attention straight away. You know,' she frowned, 'fighting dogs' injuries are distinctive. I've never come across any here.'

Nikki, keen to continue her practice of crossing eyes, cleared her throat before speaking. 'I know this might seem indelicate, but could you just confirm *your* whereabouts on the evening of 22nd January through to the early hours of the 23rd? '

Something flashed in the other woman's eyes, but it disappeared before Nikki could determine what it was. It may have been grief, frustration, even a dash of anger. All of which were acceptable reactions to the police asking for proof that you weren't at some dodgy illegal dog fight in the middle of nowhere, whilst you were up to your ears in grief and funeral arrangements.

The young vet's lips drooped and her hand drifted up to brush her hair from her forehead as she exhaled. Her eyes flitted around the room as, biting her lip, she tried to focus. After almost half a minute, she snapped her fingers, pleased to have plucked this fragment of memory from her mind. 'That was the night I went on that *disastrous* blind date with Graeme Morrison. Thelma Jones set me up, not that I asked her to. Seems you can't be single around here without someone trying to set you up. It was awful. He was divorced, still in love with his wife *and* allergic to pets.' Her snort and the slight upturn of her lips indicated that the third transgression was by far the worst in Julie's eyes and was the first trace of humour Nikki had seen since they'd entered the farmhouse.

Keen to cling to the memory of her failed date, Julie continued. 'I hadn't had time to change since leaving work, and so *he* spent the entire meal sneezing and peering at me through red-rimmed eyes. I offered him an antihistamine, which he quaffed down with a glass of red wine and that was the end of the evening. He almost conked out over his tiramisu and I ended up paying the bill, hefting him out to my car and driving him home. I felt so crap that I hadn't stopped him mixing the wine with the meds, that I put him to bed and slept downstairs on the sofa, checking on him off and on through the night.'

Julie leaned over and grabbed an envelope from the bundle on the table and scribbled on it. 'That's the restaurant name and Graeme's phone number and address. He'll be able to verify it all, right up until he conked out.'

Saj accepted the note with a smile and slid off the barstool. 'I'm *so* sorry for your loss Julie. Look, I'll leave my card in case you hear about any dog fights or anything that strikes you as odd. Sorry to have bothered you.'

Julie slid from her own seat, hand extended to first Sajid and Nikki. 'To be honest, you're the first people I've spoken to about anything other than funeral arrangements since dad's passing. It's a relief to think about something normal for a change.' She glanced at her watch and muttered an 'Oh crap' under her breath.

'Late for something?' Nikki asked.

'No, not really. Just another appointment about funeral arrangements. I'll follow you out.'

In the car once more, Nikki exhaled. 'Well, today was a bust. Looks like we need to look further afield for leads. Hell, maybe they're not even using a proper vet or maybe the vet they're using is still in practice. One thing's for sure though, there are too many vets in the district to make this a viable line of investigation.

We'll have to shelve that for now and find another line to work on. Take me home, driver.'

Saj had just signalled to re-join the main road, with Julie's car waiting behind them, when Nikki's phone rang. When she saw who was calling, she straightened in her seat and listened to Poppy, the owner and trainer of one of the cadaver dogs she'd had sent up to the moors. When Poppy finished speaking and Nikki hung up, she turned, eyes sparkling, to Sajid. 'We got a body, Malik. We bloody well got a body, and it's a body with only one arm!'

Sajid grinned and did a U-turn. 'Looks like we're heading back to the crime scene then, doesn't it? Did you remember to grab your wellies from your car, Nik?'

Even the realisation that her wellies were in the boot of her car back at Trafalgar House wasn't enough to dampen Nikki's spirits. 'Only a bit of snow, Saj. My DMs will cope. Not sure your suspension will fare so well, though?' and ignoring his pissed off expression, she revelled in the warmth of the seats, glad that for once, they appeared to be making progress.

Chapter 40

By the time Charlie woke up, it was dark outside and she could see the gentle drift of snow as it plopped on the Velux window of her attic room. For a second, she luxuriated in the cosy safety of her bed, then she remembered the earlier confrontation with her mum, the images of her and her boyfriend in Costa and the ones of Isaac and her mum and Saj. Despite her throat being less sore, she had difficulty in swallowing and a weight seemed wedged in her gut, making it impossible for her to settle. *Why is everything so messy? Why is everything so bloody complicated?*

She pulled herself into a sitting position with her duvet tucked up under her chin and her legs crossed as she remembered some of the hurtful things she'd said to her mum. Charlie was never like this. Never so bolshie and stubborn. A slight smile twitched her lips – well, okay, she was stubborn. She got that from her mum, but she wasn't usually so unreasonable and she didn't enjoy feeling this way. Haqib was normally the one to cause conflict, not her. She snuck a glance to her phone that lay, on silent, by her copy of *Invisible Women* by Caroline Criado Perez and sighed. That was the crux of it. Constraints on her freedom because of a man, albeit a very dangerous one, made her feel invisible. As if her thoughts and opinions were irrelevant. As if unseen forces beyond her control dominated her. As if her needs were secondary to keeping the entire damn family safe. A niggle of guilt contracted her heart. That wasn't fair, and she knew it. Her mum had an impossible job to do, and she'd thought her mum had exaggerated the danger. But now, with those photos … She shuddered. It didn't bear thinking about. Downey had been so close to her, and she'd been so wrapped up in her boyfriend that she hadn't noticed. He could've followed her and snatched her on the way back to school, forced her to lure her mum or her brother and sister or Isaac or Marcus or even Haqib to him. This time, the niggle turned into a shudder as the severity of the situation hit her.

Reaching over, she lifted her phone and checked the notifications. Haqib, her mum, her mum again, Haqib, Marcus, Ruby and one, two, three … no … fifteen texts from her boyfriend! They made her head throb, and she wanted to slip under her duvet, pull it over her head and ignore everyone. Being honest with herself, she accepted she was behaving out of character. She'd always slagged Haqib off for getting all love struck, but here she was acting like an idiot and her only excuse was that she'd never felt this way about a lad before. As she opened the most recent text, she thought about her behaviour and about how the lack of privacy made her feel. She wanted an end to the constant questioning. The continued presence of her 'bodyguards' when she left the house, the tension that emanated from her mum and Marcus all the time. It was exhausting, just exhausting, and she'd had enough. Something had to change. She picked up her mobile and, as her fingers flew across the keys, the weight on her shoulders eased a little. Soon … soon.

Chapter 41

Jacko was about to head over to the outbuilding with the things he'd gathered from around the farmhouse when his phone rang. *Fugly!* He hesitated, then decided it was too risky to ignore the call. 'Boss?'

'Thought I'd let you know, our vet had a visit from the plods asking about illegal dog fights.'

For a second, Jacko wondered if Fugly was accusing him of leaking information. He shook himself. Of course he wasn't. If Fugly suspected him of betrayal, he wouldn't call him. 'That's not good boss.'

'Yeah, well. It's no surprise they followed the veterinary lead, is it? After all, it's not rocket science to work out that we'd need an animal medic on hand during the fights. Still, I hadn't expected them to be on it that fast.'

Breathing easier now, Jacko asked, 'Was it plods from Operation Sandglass?'

'Nope. Two from CID; Parekh and Malik were their names.' Fugly laughed. 'The vet described them as a wishy washy poncey bloke and a woman who thought a bit too much of herself. Vet said they gave them nothing. Still, I wanted to give you the heads up. It's even more important you get the vet safely to the location.

Make sure you keep an eye out for trouble.'

Fugly was enjoying this. Jacko could imagine him all flashing eyes and manic grins. He loved the 'hide and seek' of it all almost as much as the actual money-making side. 'Will do, boss.'

After the boss hung up, Jacko held his phone to his chest. He couldn't wait any longer. He couldn't risk the wrath of Fugly if he was late picking up the damn vet. So despite the captive's drowsiness, he slapped his face gently, trying to draw him into consciousness. 'Come on, come on. Wake up!'
Clearly, giving the boy the painkillers earlier had been a mistake, for rather than his previous delirium, he now seemed to be in a restful sleep. So much for getting information from him before taking him to Fugly.

'What the hell am I going to do?' Jacko yelled the words out loud, letting them reverberate around the empty farmyard, and trying to decide how to make his next move, he paced the floor of the barn. Should he pour icy water over the lad? He groaned. He couldn't do that. The lad had been through enough already. He had to work out a more humane way to wake up the lad. After all, he wasn't fucking Fugly, was he?

A faint groaning sound made him turn round. The lad was lying there, eyes half open, watching him warily. His yell must have been loud enough to wake the boy. Smiling, Jacko rushed over and crouched beside him, wrapping the blanket round him and placing his fingers at the boy's brow. He seemed less feverish. 'You'll be all right, lad. You'll be all right. I'll take care of you.'

But the boy's eyes, filled with fear and distrust, were open now. His skinny frame shivered under the blanket and Jacko realised it was terror, not cold, that elicited this reaction.

He offered the boy some water, but he was too weak to take the bottle. Jacko hefted him up till he was half leaning against Jacko's knee and tipped trickles of water between the lad's dry lips. When he'd had a few sips, Jacko placed an antibiotic on the boy's tongue and tipped more liquid into his mouth. 'It's antibiotics. They're good for you. Help you get over the infection in your wounds.'

The boy hesitated for a moment, then met Jacko's eyes. Jacko nodded and tried another smile. 'Go on, now. They'll help.'

The captive's lips trembled, but he swallowed, then gagged as the pill caught in his raw throat, and Jacko tipped more water into his mouth, willing him to swallow the medicine this time.

Pill swallowed, he closed his eyes and sagged against Jacko's knee. Jacko waited till the boy's trembling abated before saying in a low voice. 'I don't know who you are, but whoever you are, the boss seems to have something special planned for you. If you weren't special to him, then he'd have killed you before now. You understand what I'm saying, lad?'

The lad's eyes flickered as he gave a tiny nod.

Jacko exhaled. Thank God for that. The lad was responding to him. 'Truth is, lad, I'm in too deep. I didn't sign up for owt like this. And I want out. I didn't think he'd kill anybody, but he's lost it big time. If you help me, I'll get us both out. Honest I will. I need to know who he is – his real name, not the false one he gives out to us lot. You've got to give me something, lad. Anything.'

But the boy just shook his head. His eyes flickered, and he drifted back into an uneasy sleep. When Jacko glanced at his watch and saw the time, his chest went tight and his breath came in fast pants. Soon he'd have to collect the damn vet and transport the captive to the new fight site. He hoped to hell that both he *and* the lad would survive the night, for it looked like he'd get no more information from the boy tonight. After considering for a moment he decided. Shaking the boy, he forced another two painkillers into his mouth and poured in water until spluttering, the boy swallowed them. If the lad was comatose, then Fugly might forget his plans to throw the captive to the dogs tonight. Jacko shut down the thought that Fugly might be tempted to replace the captive with Jacko. No, no, that couldn't happen. Surely Jacko was too useful to the boss. Surely, if he was going to go ahead with his warped plans for tonight's entertainment, he was more likely to choose one of the clods who'd messed up earlier. Jacko groaned. *What have I become? A monster willing to barter one kid's life off against that of another.*

With his hands gripping his crucifix, he breathed until he was calm. He had to ignore the distractions and think of the bigger picture. All he had left to fight for was his future – the future of his wife and daughter and granddaughter – and that was the only thing that was important and he was sure that this lad had the answers for him. He'd sent his wife and granddaughter off to her sister's in London for a few days. She'd protested, but Jacko had insisted. If it went tits up, she'd be harder to find. He had no doubt Fugly would seek her out if he wanted to, but Jacko was betting on Fugly having other things to worry about if everything went wrong.

He bent down, hefted the lad onto his shoulder as if he weighed nothing, and took him out to his jeep, fastening him into the back seat. If Fugly questioned him about being changed and dressed, Jacko would tell him he couldn't risk transporting him in the state he'd been. He just needed to stay focused, keep his eyes open and stay alive.

Sliding into the driver's seat, palms sweating, he set the sat nav for the station in Chester and headed off to collect the vet. Why he couldn't have picked the vet up more locally, he'd no idea. But Fugly didn't want to take chances. Wanted to minimise interactions between all the players on his team. So Jacko, even if he thought it was overly cautious, would follow the instructions to a T – for now, anyway.

Chapter 42

The evening sky was a tantalising variation of pinks and greys, lit only by the moon as Nikki and Sajid arrived back at the crime scene. Now that the light was fading, it looked creepier than it had when they'd first witnessed it. The CSIs had finished processing the scene, so there was no activity by the barn, although police and CSI vans still filled the pot-holed yard. Two officers battled to secure in place a roll of crime scene tape between the edge of the barn and the rusty chassis of an old Massey Ferguson tractor, which signified the outer cordon. It was a pointless task because access to the dump site was possible from every conceivable direction across the moors, if you were determined enough. Still, it was protocol and allowed access from this point to be recorded, which was always a good sign. Anwar and Williams had arrived before them and had taken charge of the crime scene, so no doubt, they'd have tried to mark a perimeter around the body where possible.

A few hundred yards beyond, powerful lights beamed through the smattering of snow that, although not yet heavy, held the promise to become so. Unidentifiable figures, encapsulated in white suits, moved in the distance like animated snowmen around a ghost white igloo tent: Anwar, Williams, the CSIs and possibly

Poppy and her cadaver dog. Nikki opened the passenger door. For all her bravado about not having the luxury of her wellies and the extra warm hiking socks she'd stuffed inside them, the instant waft of icy air that hit her made her groan. Could it be any colder? As she heaved herself out of the car, pulling her coat, hat, scarf and gloves on, Sajid took his time pulling on extra socks before yanking his wellies on, all the while humming 'Let It Snow' under his breath. Nikki shoved her gloved hands into her pockets and, not waiting for him, marched across the marshland towards the lights, ignoring the squelching sound that met her ears with every step. The body dump site was farther away than it appeared and the uneven terrain, the marshy conditions and lack of visibility made the walk towards it worse. By the time she reached the uniformed officer stationed just where the metal treads placed by the CSIs to preserve any forensic evidence around the scene began, she was panting but apart from her feet which were so numb she couldn't feel them and her cheeks which were ice cold, she felt quite toasty. At the inner cordon, she put on disposable coveralls, nitrile gloves and bootees, cursing the fact that these protective measures necessitated the removal of her thermal gloves. Hearing her approach, Anwar looked up and gave a taut smile. 'We've had TOD confirmed and set the CSIs to process the perimeter. It'll be another half hour before the morgue transportation arrives to take it for post-mortem. Williams contacted Langley and he'll start the PM tonight. I thought you'd like to view the body in situ. Poppy took the dog, Jasper, home cos it was cold and, in her words, "Jasper's done his bit".'

Nikki smiled. Jasper had indeed done his bit, and she'd make sure he got a boxful of healthy doggy treats for his good work. With a single twang of her band to ground herself, Nikki approached the flood-lit tent. She'd no desire to see the body, but the need to glean any possible information presented by the manner in which they dumped the body trumped her reluctance. With a deep breath, she yanked the tent door open and walked through. In the heat from the lights, the snow surrounding the terrain had almost melted. Although the CSIs had worked like dogs to record evidence before it melted, Nikki, bearing in mind the inclement conditions over recent days, doubted they would get much.

Choosing to focus on the area surrounding the body first, Nikki cast her eyes round the tent, scouring the damp, yellowy brown bracken that gathered in pitiful clumps around the body. Whoever had placed He Who Owns The Arm here, had taken little effort to hide him. If they'd set the initial search perimeter a hundred yards wider, they would have found him earlier, but they'd had no guarantee there was a body to look for. Seeing nothing that piqued her interest in the surrounding terrain, Nikki stepped closer to He Who Owns The Arm's body and studied it, starting with the feet and moving her eyes upwards as she absorbed each tiny detail. One tennis-socked foot, dirty and with what might have been blood stains, poked out from tattered sodden jeans. The jeans looked like they'd been mauled, and Nikki shuddered. Judging by the darker stains surrounding puncture marks in the denim, Langley would find evidence of canine bite marks on his lower limbs when he removed the trousers. The other foot still had its trainer in place and was bent so that the unshod leg draped over it just above the ankle. The leg of that jean was equally torn. Sajid joined her. 'Took your time, Malik,' she said, not taking her eyes from the body.

He Who Owns The Arm wore a dark green hoodie, but where his right arm should have been was only bloody raggedy fabric. A CSI stepped forward and showed Nikki an evidence bag containing the lower part of the hoodie's sleeve. 'We found this just here.' The CSI pointed to the plastic crime scene marker with the number seven on it. 'It was folded just like this, so I'd hazard a guess it was placed there, rather than thrown.'

That added up. The only sleeve on the arm they had discovered two days earlier was the intricate tattoo. Although it was understandable that whoever had left the arm for them had removed the remaining fabric in case it could somehow help them identify the body, but it was intriguing that they'd actually folded it and placed it beside him. Definitely strange!

Again, there was evidence of canine bites all over the young man's torso and remaining arm. She continued her perusal of the boy, allowing her gaze to land on his face. It was muddy, and the snow and cold had blanched it of all colour. Bloating made the features difficult to identify and Nikki wasn't sure that they'd get an ID even after Langley had cleaned the body up. For a long moment, she and Sajid looked at the lad whose life had been taken in such a horrific way. Her throat ached, her head throbbed, and all she could think of was what this man had suffered. How petrified he must have been. How desperate to escape. She swallowed hard, then touched Sajid's arm, and with a nod to the CSI, she retraced her steps out of the tent whilst telling herself, 'I'll catch the bastard who did this. I'll catch him, I'll catch him, I'll catch him.'

Chapter 43

The floodlights blinded Jacko as he struggled his way through the baying throng back to his jeep. Every time he tried to swallow, an acrid foulness filled his mouth. His clothes were more drenched with sweat than the persistent sleet. His nightmares for years to come would be filled with anguished human shrieks filling the night air to the accompaniment of frenzied snarls. He shook his head as he pushed against figures bulked out by heavy winter coats, their faces covered with balaclavas and masks, whose blood lust pushed them forwards, fisted hands raised to the skies and their lips, visible even beneath their masks, drawn back, screeching their desire for more … more … MORE …

Determined to distance himself from the violence behind him, Jacko, head down, used his shoulders and elbows to push against the mass of angry, blood-thirsty spectators. Images he knew would never leave him filled his mind … blood … sinew … fear, but worse than any of those images were the feral, glassy eyes of the punters, as they egged the dogs on … demanded more death … more horror … more bloodshed.

As the crowd thinned, snippets of conversations reached his ears.

'That were some other level shit, yeah?'

'The crew came up with the goods. Can't wait for the big hunt, can you?'

'Fucking brilliant show, hope the next poor fucker's just as entertaining.'

So many deviants in such a small area. Jacko kept moving, not too slow and not too fast. *Don't want to draw attention to myself, do I?* His heart thrummed and with each step it was increasingly difficult to keep the disgust from his face as his eyes moved from image to image. Drunken slobs lined up by the side of a rickety shed, vying to see who could piss the highest. Groups chattering, holding champagne flutes like they were at the opera rather than this warped entertainment. Smoking, talking, laughing like they hadn't just seen Hoddit slaughtered before their very eyes. Every one of them more than eager to see it happen all over again. To his left, the vet he'd picked up in Chester leaned against a tree, smoking, head down as if unwilling to take part in the revelry. There'd been no real need for a vet for tonight's entertainment. With the odds stacked in the dogs' favour, no animals were injured. For a moment, Jacko wondered if the vet shared his misgivings, then he dismissed the thought. He couldn't afford to risk finding out. Trusting anyone else would be foolish at this critical stage and Jacko was done being foolish.

Chest tight, he forged his path through the men, determined to reach his vehicle. A quick glance told him Fugly's thugs, hired specially for the evening, patrolled the periphery, rifles held loosely in their arms. Jacko hoped their focus was more on keeping uninvited guests out than on letting the boss's right-hand man through. Tonight had been the final straw for him. The animals weren't the ones constrained in the ring behind the fences. No, these animals roamed freely, hidden behind masks of normality by day, only to hide behind different masks by night as they played out their darkest, most obscene fantasies. His skin itched and the desire to stand under a scalding shower till it all peeled away was overpowering. Risking a glance to either side,

Jacko renewed his efforts to break through the writhing crowd. He had to get back to his car before Fugly saw he was missing. The risk to himself was no longer his utmost concern, it was his soul he was more concerned with. What right did he have to wear his crucifix if he stood back and did nothing when evil things happened? He'd been a coward, but no more. *Now* he would take action. His wife and granddaughter were safe, for now, and he'd do the right thing.

A hand landed on his shoulder, gripping it tight. Fear exploded in Jacko's stomach and his heart fought to escape his chest. Breath streaming from his mouth, Jacko looked into the glacial eyes of the man he least wanted to see. Even with the balaclava, Jacko had no trouble identifying Fugly. Despite the number of evil eyes in this damned place, no one else's expression was so devoid of life.

'Where do you think you're going, Jacko?' Fugly's maniacal smile lifted his face under the mask and chilled Jacko to the core.

Jacko glanced ahead of him. His jeep was close, but with Fugly here, it might as well have been on a different planet. Despite the hammering in his chest and the clawing ache in his gut, Jack cast about for something to say and then, meeting Fugly's gaze, he frowned and reached out to grip Fugly's forearm. 'Thank God, I found you, boss. Fuckers have gone mad back at the barn. They're backing down. After they saw what the dogs did to Hoddit, they're refusing to throw Doddit into the ring. Seems they think it's cruel to do that to girls.' Jacko paused and gestured to the howling men, baying for more. 'Things will get out of hand if …'

Fugly pulled his balaclava off and releasing a piercing yell of his own, threw the mask to the muddy ground and set off through the crowds to the enclosure where the animals were.

Taking a moment to calm himself, Jacko inhaled, then as the crowd swallowed Fugly up, he made the dash back to his jeep, threw himself into the driver's seat, turned the ignition and accelerated away from the other vehicles, uncaring that he bashed a van behind him setting off their car alarm as he did so. As he approached the armed security guards, he lowered his window. 'The boss wants you all in the woods. There's been a breach and our competition is gathering out there. Go find the bastards.'

Heart pounding, he watched as the two guards, speaking into their walkie talkies, jogged towards the woods. Hopefully, that little added distraction would buy him some more time. He'd no clear destination in mind, other than as far away from Hatton Heath, Fugly and his hideous deviance as possible.

A sound from the rear seat made him jump and swerve across the road. He glanced back and gave a taut smile to the boy, who lay sprawled over the back seat. 'It's okay, lad. I'm getting you away from here. Don't you worry. We'll talk later. Rest for now.'

Although he was glad that the lad seemed more with it, Jacko had to focus on driving. Fugly could send vans after him in a matter of minutes, if he caught wind of Jacko's defection. He counted on the noise of the crowds and their focus on seeing more violence to distract Fugly for a while. Fugly might soon realise that Jacko had lied to him, but then on the other hand, Fugly was an act-now-ask-questions-later sort of man. Jacko counted on him going in all guns blazing, yelling at the men to give the audience what they wanted and ordering them to toss Doddit into the ring. Hopefully his subterfuge with the security men might add more chaos to the mix. With luck maybe, just maybe, he'd have enough time to get away. However, first things first, he needed to dump this jeep and find a new ride. He needed to get the lad somewhere safe, get him cleaned up and then they could decide what to do next.

Heart in his mouth and eyes on the rear mirror the entire journey, Jacko breathed a sigh of relief when he reached Chester city centre. Still on the lookout for anyone following them, he dodged into the Market Place multi-storey car park and within minutes had secured a place in a quiet corner of the car park. Leaving the semi-conscious lad in the back seat with a blanket over him, Jacko patted his pocket to ensure he had the equipment he needed and, leaving the car park, ventured into the city centre. Before becoming embroiled in Fugly's business, Jacko had made a reasonable trade by stealing and stripping cars down for parts. Now the small key fob cloning device he used to swipe the cars would come in handy again.

As he walked, he kept an eye out for anyone just leaving their vehicle and when he finally spotted an old man easing himself from a 2016 Audi, Jacko, on the pretence of having a heated phone conversation stomped back and forth further up the road, waiting till the man exited the car and locked it. When the man walked away, Jacko moved closer and pressed the device which cloned the key as the old boy, none the wiser, moved away. Jacko waited till he was out of sight before approaching the car and checking that his cloned key worked. Of course it did. No surprises there, he'd done it before, after all. All he had to do was swipe some number plates from another car, exchange them, and he had a new vehicle. Locking the car once more, Jacko moved to the front of the car, dipped down and within seconds had taken off the front number plate. After a quick glance around him to make sure he was unobserved, he repeated the process on the rear plate, before setting off in search of a suitable vehicle to swap the Audis plates with. On a quiet side street with subdued lighting, Jacko found a Mini, half parked on the curb and just out of line of the cameras from the nearby bistro. Two minutes later he was back at the Audi, replacing the number plates and breathing a sigh of relief that the trickiest part of this process was successfully completed.

Twenty minutes later, Jacko parked the Audi in front of his old jeep and helped the frail, but now conscious lad into the front seat and headed off. By this time, he could barely keep his eyes open. The nervous energy used throughout the day had taken its toll and Jacko wanted nothing more than to sleep for a week. However, he needed to get them somewhere safe, so despite his exhaustion, he persevered, and drove them all the way to Liverpool then phoned around till he found a bed and breakfast that was prepared to take cash for a twin room for one night. Giving a false name, Jacko didn't care that he paid over the odds for the room. First a good night's sleep, then tomorrow, he and the lad would have a talk and he'd decide what to do next.

Saturday

Chapter 44

By the time Nikki got home in the early hours of the morning, she'd no energy left to think about Charlie's behaviour and had contented herself with checking that her daughter's temperature was abating., Then she snuck into bed and woke Marcus up by placing her freezing feet on his legs.

'Ouch, Nik, your feet are like icicles.' But instead of jerking away from her, he turned round and pulled her to him, allowing his body heat to penetrate her bones. That was only one of the many reasons that she loved this man.

Hoping that the warmth and safety of being beside him would ease her into sleep, Nikki closed her eyes, but her thoughts kept drifting back to He Who Owns The Arm. What had he done to earn such a horrific death? It was so barbaric and Nikki couldn't get her head round what had made the dog fighting ring escalate to using human prey. She and her team had spent hours with DI Jewkes and his team scrutinising the evidence, trying to match He Who Owns The Arm with known suspects in the dog fighting world, but had come up with nothing.

'Okay, Nik. Twenty minutes and not a second longer, okay?' Marcus, rubbing his eyes, sat up, yanked her into a sitting position beside him, and put on the small light. He dropped a kiss on her forehead and grinned. 'If you don't talk through this, neither of us will get any sleep, so … talk.'

For a moment, Nikki considered arguing that she hadn't kept him awake, but then she exhaled. Why waste her allotted time on arguing? She was damn lucky he was the sort of guy he was. 'Well, we've still not got an ID. His face was …' She wafted her hand in the air but didn't finish her sentence. 'Well, we couldn't match it. Best bet is that after Langley's cleaned him up, we might have a clearer picture. Although his remaining hand had its fingers intact, that was a no go, for his prints weren't in the system.

She paused, drew her legs up to her chin under the duvet and placed her arms round them, resting her chin on her knees and trying to pinpoint what was bothering her. As usual, Marcus, so attuned to her thought processes, got to the crux of the matter. 'It bothers you that they left the arm behind, doesn't it?'

Nikki exhaled. 'Yes. Yes, it does. Everybody else seems to think it was either an oversight or just for the shock factor – some sort of prank. Jewkes's team seems to believe that it's the sort of dumb trick these men would pull, but …' She shook her head. 'It doesn't sit right with me. The reason they had to establish Operation Sandglass was because these gangs are sooo organised, sooo efficient that they've not been caught. So, why would they risk tossing an arm, minus its fingers, into the middle of the site of an illegal dog fight and then dumping the rest of the body only a stone's throw away? Why not just cover it all up? Not like we've had any corresponding missing persons reports. For all the progress we've made so far, they could have got away with it. They must've realised it would grab the attention of CID. They must've known we'd work out it was murder and that would draw even more unwanted attention their way. More officers scrutinising them, making their illegal activities riskier to conduct. It's too foolhardy a move to be plausible. Unless …'

Marcus's blue eyes met Nikki's. 'Unless it was deliberate.'

Nikki nodded. 'Yes. Unless it was deliberate …' She frowned

and flopped back onto the pillows. 'You mean unless it was left for me.'

Marcus shrugged. 'Maybe. Unlikely, but …'

Nikki exhaled and shook her head. "Nah, we're being paranoid. It's something else. Got to be. All this chatter on the internet – the dark web or whatever – it's creepy, Marcus. Really creepy. I mean, organised hunts using humans as prey? Fuck, it's like that Starving Games crap that Ruby watches.'

Marcus's lips twitched. 'Hunger.'

Nikki shook her head. 'No, I'm full up. I treated the team to kebabs earlier.'

'Eh, no. I mean it's *Hunger Games*, not starving games.'

Nikki looked at him as if he'd gone mad. 'What are you talking about?' She frowned. 'Actually, no, I don't want to know. Just focus on the human hunt thing. That's some other level perversion. How many folk do you think would pay or could even afford to pay thousands of pounds to take part?'

Marcus shook his head, but Nikki kept talking. 'I mean, I know there are sickos out there. But … God, it makes me want to scream. If we can't get a handle on all of this, and if Jewkes's information is accurate, then somewhere in the UK there will be a massive, organised hunt using human prey. We have to get ahead of this, Marcus, but I've no idea how. It's like my hands are tied till Jewkes's cyber team come up with the goods or until we get an ID on the poor sod in Langley's morgue.'

She looked at Marcus and tried out a taut smile. 'I'm exhausted – just shattered.' Then, correctly interpreting his sudden frown, she squeezed his arm. 'Not *that* kind of shattered. Not the take to my bed for a month shattered, or the break out the razor blade shattered. Just tired, you know?'

Marcus studied her face for a long moment, before, seemingly satisfied with whatever he saw there, nodding. 'I know. You've had a lot on. Just … you know? Look after yourself.'

She moved her hand down and linked her fingers through his,

marvelling at the difference in size of their hands. Being here with Marcus grounded her. Kept her solid. Especially now that they had a pact to share their 'wobbles'. That in mind, she looked at him. 'I've got a wobble to share.'

Marcus's lips tightened. 'Downey?'

'Yep, Downey. It was him, Marcus. He tried to disguise himself, but his eyes were a giveaway. Evil.' she sighed. 'The Dark Knight has told me to stay in my lane … Bastard.'

Marcus disguised his smile. 'Your own lane?'

'Yeah. I'm supposed to focus on Operation Sandglass and identifying He Who Owns The Arm and let the Downey task force get on with locating him. Like I can forget all about Downey.'

'I'm sure Zain doesn't expect …'

'Don't you defend him. He's a smug bastard since he took over Archie's role, you know. Who the hell is he to tell me to butt out of the Downey investigation? It's not his family that's at risk, is it?'

'Well, he has …'

'Don't be all reasonable, Marcus. Let me vent a bit, for God's sake. I know he's bent over backwards to keep us safe. I know he's not even objected to Ali's involvement and I know he's not excluded me from accessing the information they dig up, but …'

'I know Nik. You and Saj could do it better.'

'That's right.' Mollified by Marcus's words, some of the fervour left her eyes. 'I feel helpless. They've not caught any more sightings of him. They've done the rounds of his known contacts, but that was a bust. It's like he's a genie in the box, popping up whenever he wants and then popping back out of sight again.'

She caught Marcus's amused look and ran her fingers through her hair, grinning. 'Don't you go telling me I got it wrong. I'm well aware it's a jack-in-the-box, but I'm keeping you on your toes. Besides, I think Downey's sufficiently devious to be both.'

They sat shoulder to shoulder in silence for a few moments, Nikki making a mental 'to do' list for the next day. Then … 'Twenty minutes up yet?'

Marcus grinned and pulled her down into the bed. 'Maybe not quite, but I have another trick up my sleeve to help you get some sleep.' He flicked off the light.

Chapter 45

'Come on, son, wake up. I've got some tea for you. Come *on*.' Jacko, despite the night's rest, felt like a truck had run right over him. He'd tossed and turned most of the night in the hard single bed with its floral pink duvet that smelled of stale smoke mingled with a musty undertone. Periodically, he checked on the lad, whose name he still didn't know. Time was running out, and he had to decide what to do next. They couldn't stay here in this overly feminine, yet tawdry B&B. Fugly's contacts were far-reaching and despite all his diversionary tactics, he couldn't be sure they weren't on his radar. Fugly had gone to a lot of effort to find this lad, and had shown remarkable restraint in keeping him alive, so it was unlikely he'd let his disappearance go unavenged.

No, the boss had no boundaries, and when he received a personal slight, which taking the boy from under his nose certainly was, his idea of self-preservation went out the window. The most Jacko could hope for was that Fugly would be too busy trying to sort out the big hunt to focus on Jacko *or* the boy. *Who am I kidding?* Although Fugly hadn't admitted as much, Jacko believed that the lad, now stretching and blinking up at him, was key to Fugly's plans for the big hunt. He hadn't been able to work out what the boss was up to and Fugly hadn't deigned to share, but Jacko was almost certain of that. Which made it even more imperative that he find out everything he could from the lad. If he was going to turn himself in, he needed to make sure he had enough info on Fugly to use as a bargaining tool. He'd have to do some time, but hopefully, if he could provide enough incriminating, provable information against Fugly, then he'd be out before his granddaughter left high school.

Awareness of the extent and depravity of Fugly's contacts made him break out in a cold sweat. Maybe Fugly could get to him inside a prison? It wouldn't surprise him, but he couldn't think about that right now. He had to be positive.

The lad looked up at him. Fear hovered in his eyes as he tried to back away from Jacko. This was the most coherent he'd seen the lad, so it was time now to convince him to talk.

Plonking himself on the edge of the lad's bed, Jacko smiled his gentlest smile and spoke in a soft voice. 'I got you away from the boss, lad. But now you need to help me, yeah?'

Unblinking eyes stared up at him, so Jacko hefted the lad into a sitting position, resting his skinny shoulders on fluffy pillows and held the mug of tea to his lips. Eyes fluttering around the room, the lad shook his head, but Jacko persisted. 'It's only tea. It'll do you good. Then, when you've had some toast, you can have another antibiotic and some painkillers. I've been looking after you. It's me that got you away from …'

Jacko shrugged and held the mug closer to the lad's lips. This time, he opened his mouth and sipped the lukewarm liquid. When he'd finished, he looked at Jacko with wary eyes. 'It was you who took me to that stinking barn.'

It surprised Jacko how strong the lad's voice sounded. Sure, it was hoarse, yet the words were strong, almost defiant. As if the antibiotics and pain relief had given him a dose of bravado, too. A pang of guilt cut through Jacko's chest. 'Yes, you're right. It was me who brought you to the farmhouse. But I swear I had no idea what he was going to do with you. How he would treat you.'

227

He hung his head. 'I thought it was just dog fighting. Didn't …'

The lad gulped, his eyes wide, a pulse thrumming at his temple. 'Calhoun … fuck Calhoun …'

'That's why I got you out of there. I could see how things were going. But … the boss … you mean summat to him. That's why you're still alive. I *need* to know more about him.' Jacko gripped the boy by the upper arms and allowed his desperation to show as he pleaded. 'Tell me what you know about him. Who he really is. Then we can go to the police.'

For what felt like hours, but was actually only seconds, the boy stared at Jacko, his split lip curling, his bruised, red-rimmed eyes filled with hatred and disbelief. '*You* expect *me* to help you?' He opened his mouth and laughed, a hoarse sound that echoed round the small bedroom. Then, he coughed so much that his frame seemed to rattle and Jacko thought he might never stop. When he finally slipped a bottle of water to him, he noticed the lad's lips were red and some blood specks had sullied his pale pink duvet. *Shit!* This couldn't be good.

Dropping back onto the pillows, his breath coming in wracking wheezes, the ashen-faced boy opened his mouth. At first he made no sound, but he tried again. 'No idea who he is. You've …' He heaved another laboured breath before managing anything else. 'Made … mistake.'

His eyes fluttered, then closed and Jacko's heart thundered against his chest as with frantic fingers he checked the boy's neck for a pulse. Nothing. No pulse. A low keening moan left Jacko's lips as he moved his fingers to the boy's wrist. Still no pulse. What had he done? Why hadn't he taken him straight to the hospital? That's what he should have done. Head bowed over the boy, Jacko gripped his crucifix and prayed like he never had before. Not for forgiveness, not even for leniency, but for the boy. When he next opened his eyes, the boy's chest rose and fell in slight, slow movements.

Weak with relief, Jacko exhaled, then not wanting to jinx his answered prayer, he found strength from somewhere and lifted the boy into his arms and carried him downstairs, out the front door and along the road to the stolen Audi, unaware of the van that had just entered the street from the other end. From the window, the B&B owner watched, a slight smile playing on her lips, as Jacko placed the boy onto the back seat before moving round and slipping into the driver's seat.

She'd earned her money and now she could wash her hands of the whole sorry event. As Jacko pulled into the traffic, the other vehicle fell in behind him, but Jacko was too concerned with finding the nearest hospital to notice.

Chapter 46

Nikki woke up early, if not refreshed, then certainly more relaxed than she'd been for days. She had a busy day ahead of her and not wanting Charlie's reproachful scowl to set her back, she left for Saj's before the kids were even up. A text from Langley had told her he'd completed the PM overnight and if she wanted to drop in and travel into work with Sajid, he'd give her his findings verbally and follow up with a written report after he'd had a couple of hours' kip. Desperate to be on top of things, Nikki jumped at the chance to mix scoffing some of Langley's freshly baked bread, courtesy of their next level bread-making machine, slathered in blueberry compote, with a verbal update. Who cared if heading over to Lister Mill took her a teensy bit out of her way … she'd take the hit in the interests of their investigation.

Nikki had spent most of the drive over trying not to think about the frostiness that still existed between her and Charlie. Marcus telling her that it would all blow over didn't improve her mood much. How the hell would he know? It's not like he'd ever been a teenage girl with hormones flying all over the place, was it? Although Nikki hadn't been as flighty as her sister, memories of her own teenage years reminded her how unreasonable hormones could make you. Apart from that though, she knew the current situation was untenable, and she sympathised with Charlie. There was no way they could keep this up for much longer. Nikki was stir crazy and the restrictions on *her* activities were nothing compared to those she'd placed on her children and Isaac.

When she hammered on their door, it wasn't even 7 a.m. Using the time to scroll through her messages, she spotted another three texts from Ali: 'Call me'. She considered calling him right away whilst she remembered, but then, looking at the time, decided not to. Ali wouldn't thank her for interrupting his breakfast, besides, if it was urgent, he'd have rung her. She brayed on the door again, so desperate for coffee now that she almost bounced on the spot as she waited for either Sajid or Langley to let her in. When it opened, after what Nikki considered an inordinately long period, she all but barged her way past Sajid. Then stopped short. Sajid was still in his dressing gown. His hair, normally so smooth and shiny was all over the place, and he looked flushed. Her heart sank. What would she do if Saj was ill? 'You all right, Malik? You look, sort of red and beetrooty.'

His glare combined with an exaggerated tut, reassured Nikki that he wasn't poorly. Probably knackered. She could sympathise. She'd had very little sleep too. Mind you, Sajid was usually all bunny tails and whiskers even on a couple of hours' kip. She followed the aroma of bread and coffee through to their open-plan sitting room cum kitchen and grinned at Langley. Langley's greeting was less enthusiastic than usual and Nikki sneaked a glance between Sajid and his boyfriend. Was Langley just tired or was something up that the two of them weren't sharing? As Langley pushed a mug of coffee and some still steaming bread towards her, she thrust her worst assumptions to the back of her mind. Langley had been up half the night doing a rush job at her behest, so no wonder he looked wan. As for Sajid, he too had been up most of the night and was entitled to some time to gather his thoughts before the start of the day. Spreading jam over her bread and attempting not to salivate too much, Nikki watched as Sajid stood looking uncertain near the breakfast bar, before shrugging and heading off to the bedroom with a mumbled, 'I'll get ready then.'

Nikki chewed for a moment, savouring the fresh bread topped with, not blueberry, but gooseberry jam, before biting the bullet. She could just let her misgivings lie, but over the years working with Sajid they'd become friends, and she was constantly learning that friends looked out for each other. Saj always looked out for her, and now, no matter how much it went against the grain, Nikki had to reassure herself that all was right between her friends. 'You okay, Langley. You and Saj, I mean?'

Busying himself at the sink, Langley, shoulders taut, shrugged. 'Yeah, we're fine. Just tired.'

Old Nikki would have accepted this reply, even if she suspected it was a lie. New Nikki, however, couldn't just leave it. Not when her two friends were concerned. Okay, it might not be her business. It might be something private that they didn't want her nosing into, but she just had to push a little but more. 'I'm your friend too, Langley. I mean, I know he's an annoying git sometimes, but you know I'm here for both of you, not just him.'

Langley turned, dried his hands on a tea towel and pulled out a seat opposite her. 'Best you ask him, Nik. Now finish your breakfast and I'll fill you in on the initial PM results.'

His words sent shivers down her spine. Why was it best that she ask Saj what was up? Was he ill? Was the little toad still moving jobs, despite being promoted to DS? She sighed, rammed the last of her bread into her mouth, washed it down with a glug of coffee and tried to focus on the PM results.

'Well, our arm belongs to the body I post-mortemed overnight – but that's no surprise. Not many one-armed corpses flying around Bradford.' Langley flinched as if realising his words were in poor taste and cleared his throat. 'I know you've already run the remaining fingerprints through the system and came up blank, but I can add a few other things that might help as identifiers.'

Nikki took out her phone and after gaining Langley's permission set it to record as Langley shared his findings. 'Cause of death is a heart attack, I suspect brought on by the shock of having his arm ripped off and the subsequent continued and ferocious canine attack. I counted over fifty bite marks all over his remaining torso, limbs and face. We should, as mentioned when I examined the arm, be able to match some of the canine bites with the dog which inflicted them. The same holds true for DNA. Although the canine DNA from the body may be corrupted, I hope the lab might extract sufficient amounts to match the DNA found on the body with that found on the arm. Judging by the few bite casts we got, at least three dogs were involved in the attack. Of course, animal activity – you know, nibbling and so forth, half his ear is missing, probably rats at this time of year – around some of the wound sites have made that more difficult.'

Refilling her cup, Nikki bit her lip. 'So far the DNA we got from the arm didn't match to anyone on DI Jewkes's Operation Sandcastle list. Perhaps with the additional samples we'll be lucky and get a hit.'

'That would be good.' Langley paused, collected his thoughts and then dove back into report mode. 'This is the body of a young Caucasian male likely between the ages of twenty and twenty-six years old. He suffered a series of historic injuries which will be detailed in my written report, but basically, these injuries include multiple broken and subsequently healed ribs, broken right wrist, dislocated shoulder ...' He looked at her. 'It's quite a substantial list, but our victim had a pretty crappy childhood, I'd say. Although I'd need to obtain specialist confirmation, my initial exam indicates long-term systematic abuse spanning from birth to around the age of sixteen.'

Nikki allowed this information to sit with her for a moment. Their victim appeared to have had a harrowing childhood and then suffered a traumatic death.

Langley continued, 'My dental examination shows that he

had poor dental hygiene and judging by the number of cavities latterly at least, he didn't attend a dentist regularly. However, there is some dental work which could be useful if we need to match dental records down the line.'

This was all solid evidence that would serve them well when they apprehended their villain, but so far, none of it was any help in pointing them in the right direction. 'Any human DNA, fibres or anything like that?'

With a shrug, Langley smiled. 'I've sent numerous samples to the lab. Hair strands, a variety of blood samples, skin samples from under his nails – I expedited that one in case they come from the perpetrator, all his clothes. I'm hoping that in due course they will prove useful to the investigation, but for now it's a waiting game.'

Releasing a whoof of air, Nikki tried to not be too deflated. Perhaps the additional information provided by Langley would help ID their victim. Nikki would get the team circulating what little they had. If they got a name, then that might be enough to link everything else to their victim and from there they would be on the trail of the perp.

Sajid, dressed, hair still damp from his shower, walked into the room. 'You up to date, Nik?'

Nikki stood up and nodded. 'Thanks for your time, Langley. It's given us a few things to work on. Now, go grab some sleep before you kip over into your coffee cup.'

Conscious of Saj's lacklustre goodbye to Langley, Nikki followed her partner out of the flat. Somehow, she kept quiet until they were in the car and heading to the briefing at Trafalgar House. Her head was filled with the things Langley had told her as well as her list of 'to dos' that needed sharing at the briefing. Still, until she'd dealt with the niggle about her friend and his boyfriend, she wouldn't be able to focus on the day ahead. 'So, what's up?'

Saj flicked the wipers on to clear away the snow which was

now turning into a blizzard. 'Don't know what you mean.'

Nikki's snort was inelegant, but she didn't care. She took her glove off and using her proddy finger poked Sajid's arm. 'Don't give me that crap, Malik. Something's up with you and Langley and I want to know what it is.'

Seeing Sajid's face darken into a scowl, Nikki smiled and back tracked. 'Okay, okay. I know it's none of my business, but … for God's sake the atmosphere in your flat was – phew – *tense*.' She gripped his forearm and gave it a gentle squeeze and when she continued, all frivolity had left her voice. 'I'm worried, Saj. I'm worried about you and Langley. You know what I'm like, I'm imagining all sorts, so …'

A low exhalation left Sajid's lips as he glanced her way with narrowed eyes and glared at her. 'You know, Nikita Parekh, you're one of the most manipulative people I know.'

Nikki pointed both thumbs to her chest and widened her eyes. 'Moi?'

'Yes, toi. Manipulative, devious, nosey, overbearing, bossy …'

'I hate to tell you, Saj, but as a diversionary tactic, this isn't working. Just tell me what's up. Who knows, I might be able to help.'

Whilst he mumbled something that sounded very like Archie's 'ducking proverbials' under his breath, Nikki waited. She'd worn him down. She knew she had. He'd tell her and then she'd be able to help.

'He went and proposed.'

The four words exploded from his mouth like rapid gunfire and Nikki took a moment to make sense of the meaning of the words through his angry delivery. 'He …'

'Yeah, that's right. He proposed. Last night. Well, technically in the early hours of the morning.'

Nikki was confused. Langley and Saj loved each other. They lived together. Neither had eyes for anyone else so … what was the problem? She didn't have to ask, for the words spilled out as

235

though Sajid had kept them bundled up in a festering heap in his chest for a long time. 'Imagine it. A fucking wedding with all of Langley's wonderful family on one side, supportive and loving and then on my side – nobody. Not a sodding person there to celebrate with *me*. To support *me*, to care for *me*. It'd be a farce – a fucking farce.'

Nikki wanted to tell him to park up so she could hug him, but had the sense to realise that a hug was the last thing Saj needed right then. All of his anxiety, his anger, his fear came from his conflicted feelings about letting his family down and being true to himself. It was unlikely that many of Sajid's family would attend his wedding to another man, but Nikki knew some would. More, possibly, than Sajid realised. His entire family didn't hate him. True his parents had disowned their Muslim son for being gay, but some of his family had reached out to him and Langley since Saj had been outed.

'You know we'd all be there – on your side, I mean. We'd all be there to celebrate with you, to support you, to be happy for you. But that's irrelevant, because yours and Langley's wedding wouldn't be about us. It would be about *you* two. You need to talk to him. For one, you need to decide if you'll be DS Sajid Malik-Campbell or DS Sajid Campbell-Malik. Personally, I'd go for Malik-Campbell or MC for short. Got a sort of ring to it and I always had you down for a closet rapper – but hey, your choice.'

As if the matter was decided she looked out the window humming Bruno Mars 'Marry You', under her breath.

Saj shook his head. 'Good one, Parekh. Can always rely on you to get to the heart of the matter … not.'

Chapter 47

'Come on, come on. Move out of the way, you dozy bastard.'
Flecks of sweat flew from Jacko's brow, foot to the floor. He
peered ahead for gaps in the traffic. He had a rough idea where
Royal Liverpool University Hospital was, because he'd seen signs
for it the previous night as he'd driven from Chester. It couldn't
be far and as he swung from Everton Road onto the A5049, he
saw the sign.

He glanced behind him. 'Stay with me, boy. You gotta stay
with me. We're nearly there. Not long now.'

He faced forward again, mumbling to himself, as he kept
driving, 'I'll tell them all about that big hunt. I'll tell them everything. Every damn thing. Just let the lad live. Fugly dun't realise I
know so much, but I heard him talking to the vet. Got the location
for the big one: off A675 Dean Mill Reservoir north of Bolton.
I know that area. Middle o' nowhere, that is. No buildings. That
Fugly's a wise bastard, using that area for his big hunt.'

Palms slipping across the steering wheel, breath coming in
laboured gasps, Jacko slammed the brakes on with a curse as
the car in front of him dawdled, deciding whether to turn off.
Glancing in the rear-view mirror, Jacko's face paled. The jeep
behind him had nearly rear-ended him, but it wasn't that that

had caused the colour to drain from his face. It was the identity of the man in the passenger seat. A huge grin covering his face, Fugly leaned on his horn, causing Jacko to jump and eliciting a groan from the back seat of the Audi. Fuck! Fuck! Fuck! How had he found him? How the hell had Fugly located him? He could've sworn they hadn't followed him.

Yanking the wheel to the right, Jacko glanced to make sure he was clear before pulling out and overtaking the loitering vehicle that had almost caused the accident. Once past him, he pressed his foot down again, but his phone slid across the dashboard and crashed into the windscreen. Jacko let out a yowl. Idiot. Stupid bloody idiot. Of course, Fugly was tracing his phone. *Why didn't I think of that?* He was tempted to hurl the thing out the window, but there was no point. It was too late. A quick glance in his rear-view mirror told him that a jeep separated him from Fugly. He only needed to get to the hospital. He just had to get the boy to safety.

As his driving became even more erratic, earning enraged toots and ferocious fists from other drivers, he remembered the landlady's changed behaviour at breakfast from her abrasive behaviour the previous evening. The way she'd fawned over him, tried to detain him with more tea and pointless conversation. She'd taken a phone call just as he'd come downstairs and it was after *that* call that her behaviour had changed. Even as he carried the lad downstairs, the old witch was in his face, telling him she'd get a doctor. Fugly had seen he was there and paid her off. Promised her money to delay him till he got there. Jacko was certain of it. Fugly was a devious git.

Just ahead, the turnoff to the hospital loomed. If he could only get there in time. He didn't care what happened to him. Not anymore. It was *all* about the boy now. That was all that was left. His fingers cradled the crucifix, and he raised it to his mouth and in a fond farewell to his wife, daughter and grand-daughter, he kissed it.

Swerving into the drive leading to the hospital, he once more jammed his foot to the floor, ignored all no entry signs and road markings and headed straight for A&E. He drove right up to the ambulance ramp and flung his door open. Not even looking to see where Fugly was, he lifted the lad out, ran to the door, with two paramedics running after him, stopped, spun on his heel and thrust the boy at the paramedics, forcing both of them to take the weight of the boy in their arms. This gave Jacko enough time to dodge round them, and back to his still running car, before they could stop him. Once back in the Audi, he flung it into gear and took off, with the image of Fugly's jeep in his peripheral vision. 'Come on Fugly, Come on! Follow me. Leave the boy behind'

He made it to the end of the road before Fugly's jeep pulled up level on his right. He glanced over and saw Fugly's sneering face and the gun. Then nothing.

Chapter 48

M: Feeling Better? 😊

Charlie: A bit 😄. You ok?

M: Yeah. Need to talk. You up for it?

Charlie: Not today. Too many eyes on me. Tomorrow, usual place, usual time?

M: Suits me. Miss you!

Chapter 49

Conscious that she still hadn't followed up on Ali's texts, Nikki gestured for Saj to enter the incident room whilst she made the call, but it rang out. Before thrusting her phone back into her pocket, Nikki typed out a quick text:

Nikki: Got your texts. Urgent? If not, can it wait? Up to my ears in dead guys.

She'd just got to her feet to address her team when Ali's reply came in:

Ali: It can wait, but we need to talk!!!

Not sure what to make of the exclamation marks, Nikki frowned, then dismissed it. If Ali said it wasn't urgent, then it wasn't urgent. If it was something to do with Downey or her family's safety, Ali would have insisted they talk immediately. Thrusting all thoughts of Ali and his effusive use of exclamation marks aside, Nikki took a deep breath and began by summarising the post-mortem results learned from Langley earlier that day, ending with, 'We'll get Langley's written report and some of the lab reports later on today.'

She paused and looked round the room. Saj sat in his usual spot, scrolling through reports that had come in overnight on his tablet. Anwar and Williams, regardless of the dark bruises under their eyes, focused on her every word. Williams was adding notes to his tablet with fingers that sped across the keyboard at a rate of knots. His dedication to multi-tasking was inspiring. The uniformed officers were scattered over the remaining desks and chairs, awaiting her instruction. Before she continued, Nikki did a mental inventory of the points she wanted to cover. Satisfied she had everything in hand, she began. 'Right. Who's been checking out the vet's alibis?'

Like a shot, Williams's hand was in the air. 'Me, boss.'

Nikki was on the point of telling him to continue, but he cut her off by diving straight into his report. 'Of the five vets you and DS Malik interviewed, all but two of their alibis seem watertight.'

Nikki was sure that the uncorroborated alibis would belong to Anji-with-an-I Jordan and Giles Lincroft, so was rendered speechless when Williams said, 'Gordon James Collins's alibi initially stood up to scrutiny, but then I got chatting to his daughter on the phone.'

He flushed. 'She seems nice.'

Despite being disappointed that Collins's alibi was questionable, Nikki was a realist. The reason they checked alibis so thoroughly was because they *could* be broken. Even innocent people got flustered when asked to provide proof of their whereabouts. Nikki hoped this was the case because she'd liked the curmudgeonly old bloke. Puzzled by the flush that had risen in Williams's cheeks, Nikki frowned, then smiled. The lad had liked Collins's daughter, and that's why he'd extended the phone call.

Clearing his throat, Williams ploughed on. 'Turns out old Collins borrowed her car a few times over the course of his visit. Told her he wanted to check out some donkeys that were being maltreated. Reading between the lines, it seemed like she was glad to see the back of him for a few hours, so she gave up her keys. So … he wasn't completely truthful with his alibi. He could have travelled back to our crime scene if he wanted to.'

He glanced up at Nikki and, seeing her mouth open to interrupt, he raised his hand. 'So, when she gave me the dates on which he borrowed her car, I cross-referenced them with the dates of known illegal dog fights provided by Operation Sandglass and …'

His flush was deeper – more beetrooty now, but not from embarrassment. This time, it was excitement and Nikki, pleased to see her protégé coming into his own, gave him his moment of glory.

'They matched.' Williams, all but bouncing in his chair, was on a roll. 'So … I got ANPR to track the daughter's car and—'

Sajid's drawl broke through Williams's excitement. 'For God's sake, Williams spit it out, eh?'

Nikki flung a frown in Saj's direction. He didn't need to take it out on Williams because he was in a mood. '*Malik!*'

Sajid snorted and buried his head in his tablet again as Nikki, wondering when she and Sajid had swapped roles, smiled at Williams, encouraging him to continue.

'Not got all the ANPR results back, but it looks like he was back in Yorkshire on the 22nd January. Trouble is, a lot of the B-roads don't have any footage, so the nearest we can get him to the crime scene is on the A65, A59, A61 and A646. Any of those are close enough to the dog fight location. But he could have been checking out farms for donkey maltreatment like he told his daughter … or he could have swapped cars. Daughter said he didn't come back till the early hours of the morning.'

Williams had been thorough, and Nikki grinned at him. 'Have you …?'

'Yes, yes. I've sent two uniforms to question him about it.' His eager smile morphed into a worried frown. 'Was that okay, boss?'

Nikki would have preferred to interview Collins herself, but for the sake of expediency she appreciated that Williams had made the right choice. Her efforts would be better employed elsewhere. 'Good job, Williams. Now, what about the other alibi?'

Williams flicked a finger across the screen of his tablet, cleared his throat and began. 'Julie Ross. We always said her alibi was weak. I mean it was obvious she could have nipped out whilst her blind date was in bed, so we got ANPR to check out if she left his house at all overnight and …' Again with the eager look, Williams grinned round at the room, eliciting another snort from mardy arse Malik. 'She didn't, but …'

With Williams's melodramatics irking, Nikki satisfied herself with sending a warning frown in Sajid's direction whilst rolling her hand in front of her to hurry Williams along.

'When I spoke to her blind date, he told me something interesting. He told me that his home security ran on a continuous loop and recorded all comings and goings, so …'

Nikki closed her eyes, muttered 'give me strength' and when she opened them again a moment later, Williams projected the CCTV footage onto the large screen. Moving over to sit beside Anwar, Nikki looked in fascination at the grainy image of Julie Ross's car, pulled into Graeme Morrison's drive and parked beside his two-car drive at 9.03 p.m., followed seconds later by her skirting the car and helping him from the passenger seat into the house. It was clear he was worse the wear, still Julie manhandled him with ease into the house. Williams fast-forwarded to 9.50 p.m. and everyone leaned forward as a hooded figure appeared from the front door, bypassed Julie's car and instead got into Graeme Morrison's Toyota Land Cruiser. The lights went on and the car backed out of the drive before heading towards the exit.

'Please tell me you got ANPR to track Graeme Morrison's car?'

Beaming, and chest puffed out, Williams nodded. 'Course I did.'

The tension in the incident room was palpable as Anwar punched him on the arm. 'And? Tell us what you found out, you idiot!'

With a tut, Williams rubbed his arm and said, 'Turns out, Julie

Ross headed towards the moors and then of course got lost in the B-roads, where ...'

'Yeah, we know there are hardly any cameras.' Lips turned down, Anwar finished his sentence, then brightened up as a thought occurred to her. 'Still, we could track her phone. See if we get any pings from the tower nearest the dog site location.'

'Did that. Did that already!' Williams bounced on his chair. 'Got a ping from the cell tower nearest to the location at 10.39 p.m. But it also pinged for Collins's phone at 11.05 p.m. in the same locality.'

'Bring her in. Bring them both in.' Nikki gestured to two of the officers nearest the door. 'Read them their rights if you have to, but I want to speak with them today.'

As the two officers left, DI Jewkes burst into the incident room, his coat flapping behind him as he strode down to the front of the room. 'Just got a report in. There's been another body found at an improvised dog fight location. A woman this time.'

A collective gasp went round the room as Nikki stepped forward, offering Jewkes a seat. 'Where?'

'Fucking Hatton Heath.'

'Eh?' Nikki had never heard of the place.

'Near Chester – secluded. Outside our jurisdiction, but the Chester police are happy to liaise with Operation Sandglass and a team from Sheffield is going over as we speak. Best I stay here and try to push forward with our local knowledge. I've got my team scouring the dark web and social media. My undercover officers have nothing but rumours to offer, but are trying to dig deeper. They reckon the operations they've infiltrated are pissed off with this organiser — pissed off and scared. Seems they too think whoever's organising this crap is a psycho.'

He thumped the heel of his hand on his forehead. 'If something doesn't break soon, we're going to lose more lives. The chatter is strong about this "big hunt", but we still can't break the codes. They're operating in some sort of Red Room or other. My team wasted valuable hours following links all over the place, only to meet a dead end. Seems like they've worked out a way to issue passwords to select invitees and we can't get a handle on it. And, to make it worse, the bastards have posted a video of the most recent death on social media sites, with the caption "join the big hunt now". We've had them taken down, but they keep popping up again. It's sickening that people keep sharing them.'

Nikki sat beside him. 'It's getting near the end-game, isn't it? This organiser, whoever he or she is, is gearing up for a big climax with a real live hunt and we've no idea where it is.'

Jewkes nodded, 'My bet is the fucker will disappear into thin air, hundreds of thousands of pounds richer, only to surface again months or years down the line with an equally warped money-making enterprise. If we don't catch him, he's just gonna keep on reinventing himself.'

They sat in silence for a moment, each wracking their brains for inspiration, then Nikki stood up. 'Right. First up, I want up-to-date tracking records for those vets' phones and get ANPR to check their vehicle movements too. The current warrant should suffice, but we need them ASAP. I want to know if either Collins or Ross were anywhere near this Hatton Heath.'

She explained to Jewkes what they'd discovered and smiled when his face perked up at the news that they had some sort of lead to follow. 'We need to revisit every lead we have. Anwar, put out an appeal through any tattooist networks for information on that tattoo. Contact the Tattoo Artists Guild for that. We need to identify He Who Owns The Arm, but there's no guarantee he got it done locally.'

Jewkes sighed. 'I'll interview the vets if you don't mind, Parekh. I reckon my knowledge of these sickos might help me shake something loose from them.'

Much as Nikki would have liked to interview them herself, she saw the wisdom of Jewkes's suggestion. His expertise might be the difference between a successful interview and a failed one.

She nodded. 'My team will focus on crossing the I's and the T's.'
If Jewkes noticed her strange choice of words, he didn't comment
as he made his way out the door.

Chapter 50

Nikki craved coffee as she directed operations in Trafalgar House. Jewkes and one of his DCs had just begun the interview with Gordon Collins, having agreed with Nikki's suggestion that Ross still seemed like the most likely candidate of the two and that keeping her stewing in a holding cell might loosen her tongue. Although tempted to watch via the remote viewing facility, she left that job to Sajid, who was more than capable of picking up on the interviewee's body language and using his observations to guide Jewkes through earphones.

All around her, her team were hard at it, sifting through reports, checking witness statements, following up on loose ends, and Nikki was filtering and checking all the incoming data from the Sheffield branch of Operation Sandglass who currently liaised with the Chester police force. The body was that of an unidentified female, whose fingerprints were also not on the system, causing Nikki to curse. When would they get a break on this case? The post-mortem on the body was underway and Nikki awaited the findings so she could pass them on to Langley for comparison with He Who Owns The Arm's body. She was desperate to see if DNA from the young woman's body matched any they'd found at their crime scene – but of course they'd have to wait for that.

As she worked, DCI Zain Ahad entered the shared office space, with his shadow Haqib close on his heels. He spoke in an 'I'm ever so important' tone, as if Nikki was wasting his time. 'Parekh, visitor for you. I left them in the kids' interview room to give you some privacy.'

Frowning at Ahad's retreating figure, Nikki sensed that this barking information disguised as 'ultra-efficiency' was how things would be in their office now that Archie had retired and she resented it. She missed Archie, and she wasn't good at dealing with change. Not much of a people person herself, she at least had the sense to realise that barking information at colleagues only made them nervous and when you're nervous, you make mistakes. She made a mental note to have a quiet word with Ahad later on – maybe over a beer at Anika's house. And that was another thing. Nikki wasn't sure how she felt about Ahad and her sister getting closer. Not that they'd confided in her, but even Nikki wondered about their relationship. Of course, Anika had denied it – told Nikki they were 'just friends' and that Nikki should 'butt out'. Maybe she should have left it to Marcus to suss out what was going on. After all, he got on better with Anika than she did.

Whilst she wanted her sister to be happy, and she saw the benefits of Ahad's influence over her nephew, Nikki still had reservations. Ahad was grieving and the last thing either Anika or Zain needed was a rebound relationship – especially not with Nikki in the middle. But that was a problem for another day – she had more than enough problems to deal with right now.

As she got to her feet, Nikki took the time to study her nephew, Haqib. Work placement from school had allowed him the chance to stalk his superhero, Zain Ahad, whilst learning more about the career he himself was determined to follow. With pleasure, she observed that he positively glowed. His handsome face had transformed from carrying a surly teenage sulk to having an almost constant grin on it. His jawline was firmer, his cheek-bones more defined, and Nikki put his leaner body mass down

249

to the exercise regime he and his mentor followed. He'd bulked up and most of his teen plumpness had turned to muscle. Nikki was proud of the lad, and seeing him bubbling with enthusiasm confirmed the wisdom of their decision to ride out the Downey storm here in Bradford. Haqib was putting all the history with his dad, his youthful misdemeanours and his unsuitable girlfriends behind him at last.

Haqib paused beside her desk, his face all serious professionalism as he spoke. 'It's Josie that's here, Auntie Nik. You know our cousin from Manchester – well your niece Josie Flynn – you remember?'

Resisting the temptation to reach up and smooth down his hair, Nikki took refuge in her usual brusqueness and frowned at him. 'I'm not bloody senile, Haq, course I remember her.'

Whilst always pleased to hear from her recently discovered relatives in Manchester, the knowledge that Josie had sought her out at work with no prior appointment, filled her with a sense of foreboding which was exacerbated by the knowledge that Freddie Downey, Josie's grandad and Nikki's biological father lurked nearby waiting for the right moment to annihilate them. Had she taken her eye off the ball in not including her Manchester relatives in her considerations? When she'd discussed it with Marcus and Sajid, they'd agreed that Downey's likely focus would be on Nikki and her immediate family. Although she'd given Josie and her other Manchester relatives a heads up to be on the lookout for Downey, Nikki hadn't thought it necessary to put them on high alert or to offer them any protection. Now she wondered if that had been a wise decision. 'She seem all right to you, Haq?'

Haqib, wide-eyed, soaked up the images of the dog fighting arena on the wall and gave a distracted shrug. 'Eh? Yeah, yeah. She looked great. Got a new tattoo on her wrist – looks brill, but …' The lad directed his sombre eyes to Nikki, and his eyebrows pulled together as if to emphasise the seriousness of his next statement. He shook his head from side to side, like a morose funeral director at a wake. 'I know that getting a tatt isn't an option for me. Not with my career choice.'

Smothering a smile, Nikki patted him on the arm. Haqib had gone through a phase of designing a range of tattoos for when his mum *eventually* caved and allowed him to have one. Thankfully, he'd been too young, or no doubt he'd already have two sleeves of dubious quality tattoos that he'd now be regretting. No way was Nikki about to tell him that a concealed tattoo would be all right. She'd kept her own recent tattoo on her lower back a secret from most people. She'd needed to immortalise her mum, so she'd had a lotus flower tattooed in the small of her back with her mum's name underneath. It made her feel close to her and had somehow helped with the grieving process.

She'd initially struggled with the fact that it had been one of Helen Mallory's ideas, but in the end, she'd overcome her unease. If Mallory was unaware that she'd gone ahead with her suggestion, then the woman had *no* control over Nikki. None whatsoever! Still, the occasional niggle that accompanied any memories of how Mallory had deceived her, abused her power and betrayed Nikki's confidences in the worst possible way, still rankled.

As she got to her feet and headed to the room where Josie waited, Nikki realised she hadn't clapped eyes on Josie since her mum's funeral. That side of the family was coping with their own trauma, so they'd scarcely spoken even then because everyone was too overwhelmed with their own grief. Freddie Downey had a lot to answer for. Although Nikki didn't know them that well, she'd attempted to periodically check in with them, hoping when things were more settled and everything they'd all suffered wasn't so raw, they'd be able to connect in a meaningful way. Apart from Anika and her mum's extended family, they were the only blood relatives Nikki had left, and she would eventually like to get to know them better.

When she entered the room, Josie jumped up from the couch, rushed towards Nikki, a relieved smile on her lips as she smothered her in a hug. Not used to this level of intimacy with people she hardly knew, Nikki stiffened for a second before loosening into the embrace. She liked Josie. The other woman had been through a lot, but she displayed an inner strength and outward benevolence that Nikki envied. She was the rock keeping the Manchester side of the family together, in the same way Nikki kept her small family in Bradford safe and well. Despite their different personalities, Nikki suspected that in the long run, she and Josie would be good friends.

'Been in the wars again, Auntie Nikki?' Josie pointed to Nikki's latest scar, the one she'd got during a fight at a peaceful vigil before Christmas. With it paling to a slim white line down her cheek, Nikki had opted not to have surgery to reduce its visibility. Instead, she wore it as another badge of honour, like the gnarled rope scar across her throat. A symbol of her inner strength. Occasionally it made interviewees a little off kilter – sometimes looking like she spent her time brawling had its benefits.

Nikki rolled her eyes, grinned and placed her fingers over the scar. 'You should see the other guy. Let's just say he's still pissing blood and his sperm production is at risk.'

She studied her niece for a few seconds before continuing. Nikki didn't remember the trail of lines spreading from the corner of Josie's eyes. She noted how her niece held her shoulders taut as if allowing them to relax would make her melt into a puddle at Nikki's feet. Nikki's misgivings about Josie's visit seemed well founded, so, never one to make small talk, Nikki dove straight in. 'Good to see you Josie, but I take it this isn't only a social visit. Sit down and tell me how I can help.'

Although Josie's shoulders relaxed just a fraction as she turned to reclaim her seat, her lips tightened. Once settled, with Nikki sitting opposite her, Josie picked up a large envelope from the chair arm and, her eyes never leaving Nikki's face, she upended it on the small coffee table. A bundle of envelopes and post-cards landed on top. 'Mum's had three postcards over the last few weeks. I brought the envelopes they were delivered in, too. They're from Downey.'

A tense band spread across Nikki's chest and she berated herself again. She *should* have considered the threat to her extended family more seriously. She'd warned Josie that Downey was back, but because Josie had told her they'd received no postcards and because Nikki had been arrogant enough to assume that *she* was Downey's main target, Nikki had assumed Josie and the rest of her family weren't in his crosshairs. She *should* have known better. Should have remembered that Downey was a master at keeping his options open. With the increased security around Nikki and her family restricting his access to them, of course, he'd consider turning his attentions to the other side of his family. That was pr*ecisely* what he'd do, and she'd been too damn blind to see that!

The band squeezed tighter, constricting her airways and for a second a wave of cotton wool filled her vision, making her feel lightheaded. Glad that she was sitting, Nikki focused on the scattered cards, willing the tension to ease and the dizziness to pass, allowing her to concentrate. Blinking to clear the fuzz in her head, Nikki leaned forward and studied the cards without touching them. Though it was unlikely they'd get any usable forensic evidence from them, she'd have them processed. None of the postcards she'd received had ever elicited anything incriminating Downey. Nor indeed had they offered any clues. No DNA from a licked envelope or stamp (damn self-adhesives were some police investigator's worst nightmare). No random hair caught in the envelope – or rather, none belonging to Downey. They'd wasted time analysing a few hairs only to discover that they either had no DNA or that they belonged to some random person not in their database.

No identifiable prints to any known contacts of Downey's that they could have followed up on. No postmark with a huge 'Here I Am' arrow pointing to his current whereabouts. Nothing that led them in a direction that they could follow through on with an investigation. Nikki knew these cards would be the same. The cards themselves were similar to those she'd received. Random tourist scenes. One was of the Louvre, another Blackpool Tower, the third was of Media City in Salford. The address on the envelopes was written in the same sloping writing she now recognised as belonging to Downey. Using the end of a pen, she flipped the cards over one by one. Having done so, she discovered that the major difference was the content. The scrawled message on the back comprised the same three words written on each card.

'Blame Nikki Parekh.'

Her name seemed to pulse up at her as an icy chill blossomed in Nikki's stomach and worked its way up to her throat. She swallowed a few times before she was able to speak and her breath hitched in her throat. There was no doubt in her mind; these cards *were* a direct threat to Josie's family and *she* was the one responsible for putting them in Freddie Downey's scope. Playing for time before speaking, Nikki scuffled through the envelopes, moving them around on the table as she attempted to decipher the postmarks on each one. They were blurred, but she saw the end letters on two of them: 'dham'. Oldham? Possibly. It made perfect sense because Nikki's half-sister, Josie's mum, Candice, lived in Oldham with her son, and Nikki's nephew, Johnny. Downey had either visited Oldham or a town with the same ending to post them, or got one of his dodgy contacts to do it for him. She needed no more evidence to prove that her nemesis was in the area, but this brought a whole new dimension to her thinking. It widened the threat level and a shard of ice lodged in Nikki's chest.

Oldham was near Manchester and was only a stone's throw, or an hour's drive from Bradford. Downey could operate easily in both areas. Keeping a lid on her anger so as not to frighten Josie any more than she already was, Nikki kept her tone bland. 'When did the first one arrive?'

Josie tutted and shrugged. A frown had crawled across her forehead upon witnessing Nikki's worry. 'A couple of weeks ago, but …'

Nikki's head jerked up, and she met the other woman's gaze. 'What? A couple of weeks and you're only contacting me *now*? I *warned* you he was back.'

Josie extended her arms, her head shaking from side to side as she did. 'She didn't tell me about them at first, Nik. You know what my mum's like. She's not been herself since we lost our brother and the whole Downey thing, you know?' Her hands flopped back onto her lap, her fingers clenched tight. 'She's not coping. Not functioning and Johnny's been no better. It's all been too much for her … you know with Da … well, *him*, you know?' At the last words, Josie's lips tightened. Her eyes flashing in anger.

Nikki sympathised. She knew all about having a deviant as a dad and although she'd had years to process things, Josie and her siblings were still in the early days of trying to come to terms with the previous year's revelations. As for her half-sister, Candice? Well, her struggles were ongoing. Nikki remembered how her own mum had been in the early days after escaping Downey. Vacant, dissociated, anxious, wary. It took years before her mum had been able to function again. To enjoy life again and much of that was achieved not through any formal therapy – there was none in those days – but through the love of her family and her children. Then, just when she'd put that behind her and relaxed enough to enjoy her life, the bastard had returned and stole that from her again. Yes, Nikki understood only too well that when Candice faced something unpalatable or unsettling, she'd struggle to cope and was likely to not only ignore it, but to bury it and pretend it wasn't happening. Hell, Nikki had been there and done that herself. Josie glanced away, but not before Nikki caught the shimmer in her eyes and the way she clenched and unclenched her fists. Nikki's stomach lurched, and the words spewed from her lips like rapid gunfire. 'Something else has happened, hasn't it?'

Josie released a whoosh of air and collapsed back into the chair, a single tear trailing down her cheek, the anxiety she'd tried so hard to control overwhelming her now she was with Nikki. 'Johnny's missing. He left for a building job on the moors a few days ago. Hasn't been back home since. Mum's climbing the walls. She doesn't like being on her own and she relies on Johnny to do the shopping for her because she won't leave the house.'

When she looked at her aunt, her eyes pleaded with Nikki not to judge. 'And then she showed me these, so …'

Again, Josie shrugged. Words were unnecessary. She'd come to Nikki because if anyone knew the sort of evil Downey was capable of, it was Nikki. With an effort, Nikki kept her tone level. 'You've tried to contact Johnny?'

'Yep. He's not answering and his friends haven't seen him either. Nobody knows where he is.' More tears trickled from Josie's eyes, as if the act of sharing her concerns with Nikki had released a dam.

It was what Nikki had expected. Everything pointed that way. The postcards with their 'Blame Nikki Parekh', Johnny's disappearance and the taunting photographs on Nikki's windscreen all pointed that way. Although she hoped otherwise, she was certain that her nephew was now in the hands of Freddie Downey. 'I'll get a trace on his phone. Did you all activate your GPS like I asked?'

That was the one thing Nikki had insisted they all do, but at the time, it had been a precautionary measure. One Nikki had assumed would never be necessary to access.

Josie nodded. 'Yeah, course we did. We know what he's capable of so we did everything we could. But it looks like Johnny's phone's off, or else he deactivated the app, for it's not showing up.'

'Tell me what you can about this job Johnny was going to do.'

'Well, it was Mu … Mum I spoke to about it. She's …' Josie bit her lip, uncertain how to describe her mum's health, but Nikki didn't need it spelling out.

She reached over and squeezed Josie's hand. 'I know it's been hard for Candice. I know she's struggling, but I need to know everything she told you. If Downey's got Johnny …' This time it was Nikki's turn to shrug, but there was no need for her to finish her sentence, because Josie inhaled and began to speak.

'That's just it. Business has been slow for Johnny. You know; Covid and all? So, he took this job on word of mouth from someone he met in the pub.'

Eyes wide with worry, Josie's right foot tapped a rhythm on the floor. 'None of his mates know anything about it. They were pissed when Johnny was talking to the bloke and their descriptions were vague.'

'What about his van? We could track that on ANPR. What's the reg?'

But Josie shook her head. 'They must have picked him up cause his van's still parked up in front of Mum's house.'

The chances of getting a lead on Johnny's current whereabouts were decreasing with each new piece of information. 'Don't suppose the neighbours ...?'

But Josie was already shaking her head. 'Nobody. Not one of them saw Johnny that day.'

Nikki pressed her fingers to her temples and massaged the slight throb that was developing there. She needed to gather her wits and think things through. After a few minutes she lifted her mobile and first phoned DC Anwar, to get her to take over from Sajid in the observation suite, and then Saj, asking him to organise a warrant to put a trace on Johnny's phone before joining her and Josie. 'Say it's part of the ongoing Operation Sandglass investigation. That way we can expedite it.'

Whilst waiting for Saj to appear, Nikki went over everything with Josie again. She should at the very least notify the Downey task force, but she couldn't bring herself to. This was *her* responsibility. If anything had happened to Johnny, then it was down to her and she would do everything she could to make things right.

After Saj arrived and had greeted Josie, offered her a drink – something that Nikki had forgotten to do – and been brought up to speed, they brainstormed their options.

'CCTV from the pub Johnny was in with his mates when he met the bloke?' said Saj.

A sceptical look made its way into Josie's eyes. 'I doubt they'd have any security cameras in the Dog and Bone. It's a right dive – spit and sawdust.' She shuddered, and Nikki understood why. In her well-coordinated, smart, but not too expensive clothes, Josie was more likely to frequent a wine bar than a pub like that.

'There're loads of illegal stuff going on in there – not sure what exactly, but I've told Johnny not to go there. Trouble is, some of his mates like to do a bit of illegal gambling on dog fights and that's where they make their bids.'

At the words 'dog fights', Nikki and Sajid exchanged a glance. Was this too much of a coincidence? Nikki was wary of coincidences. Too often they proved to be linked and, in this case, with Manchester, Chester and Bradford all being close to each other, the coincidence was too strong to be ignored. Nikki had never got her head round dog fighting rings. It wasn't the purview of her team, but her team's involvement in Operation Sandglass had given her insight into the criminal activity linked to dog fighting and with the two incidents involving humans as prey at dog fights and the amount of information being scoured by Operation Sandglass's cyber experts, Nikki's throat closed over. Could Downey somehow be involved in the warped dog fights and the big hunt that they were trying to track down? She'd always considered him all brawn, nastiness and violence, but now she thought about it, she wondered if Downey could organise something so vile.

Reluctant to share her fears with Josie, she kept her tone calm. 'We'll speak to colleagues in Manchester Met, and we'll make a trip to this pub – see what we can find out. If you give us a list of his friends with their contact numbers, we'll see if police interest in their activities might loosen their tongues a bit.'

All of Nikki's instincts told her they had no time for dilly dallying, and because of the ongoing threat Downey presented to her and her family, she knew DCI Ahad would sanction their focus on finding Johnny and might even get help from Manchester police. But even if he withheld his support, Nikki was in no mood to negotiate. This was her nephew and she would do everything in her power to help him. After all, Johnny's disappearance was out of West Yorkshire police's jurisdiction and, all things being equal, would not arouse any suspicion in the normal run of things. A young man disappearing off grid for a few days with no other suspicious circumstances, wasn't enough to warrant an investigation. It was the wider picture that demonstrated the urgency of investigating Johnny's disappearance. The postcards linked Downey's threats to Nikki with Johnny's disappearance. Hopefully Manchester police would realise the significance of that link and act accordingly.

She was on the point of wrapping up her meeting with Josie when Williams hammered on the door. Not waiting for a reply, he burst through, coming to a halt just in front of Nikki, his breath coming in short pants. 'You have to see the latest lab reports, boss.' He glanced at Josie and added, 'Outside.'

The euphoric expression he'd worn since the briefing a few hours ago was gone. Now Williams's tight lips and the pulse at his temple told Nikki something significant had come in. Throwing procedure out the window, Nikki grabbed the tablet from him and peered at the screen. 'I don't get this.'

Sajid's peered over her shoulder, his only response a 'Fuck!'

Nikki studied the tablet and then jerked her head to the door. 'In the corridor, Now!'

With the door closed behind them, Nikki twanged her wrist band a couple of times before putting into words what the report implied.

'According to these results, the DNA found in the blood taken from the metal hoop in the floor at the crime scene doesn't match *our* victim's DNA and we got no hits in the DNA database – so, no ID.'

Sajid nodded. 'So, there was someone else chained up at the site. The woman they found in Chester, perhaps?'

Williams, shuffling from foot to foot, grabbed the tablet back and scrolled down. 'Here! Read this bit.' He handed the tablet back to Nikki, but his finger prodded a section mid-screen.

The section was sub-headed, *Familial match to DNA records held on file*. She read it, then read it again, 'But ...'

Saj, still peering over her shoulder, issued another, 'Fuck!' before adding, 'Nikki, the blood on the hoop is a 6.95 per cent match to you. That means ...'

Nikki nodded and slammed her palm against the wall. But it was Williams who finished Sajid's sentence. 'Whoever this blood belongs to, they're related to you. You and this person share nearly seven per cent of your DNA.'

For a moment, Nikki hesitated. Should she share this information with Josie or not? She pulled on her ponytail, welcoming the slight pain. It seemed to sharpen her mind, making it easier to decide. Glancing at Sajid, she nodded to the door and the pair of them re-entered, Williams trailing behind.

After explaining the rudiments of the report to Josie, Nikki waited for the other woman's response. Although not aware of the wider context of Nikki's ongoing investigation, Josie realised the significance of the DNA report and pale-faced, she sank to the chair beside Nikki. 'That's Johnny's blood on that metal hoop, isn't it?'

Nikki reached over and gripped her arm. 'We don't know that for sure ...'

Wide-eyed, Josie glared at her. 'Don't patronise me. You've had blood from a metal hoop at some crime scene or other analysed and it's come back as a familial match to you. Is that right?'

All Nikki could do was nod. 'Well, unless you have any other family member unaccounted for at the moment, then the likelihood is that it belongs to Johnny, right?'

'Yes.'

'Then you better get moving, Auntie Nik. My mum couldn't stand losing him. Not now!'

Nikki groaned and looked at Sajid. This was a nightmare, and she was numb. She reached for her band and twanged it and twanged it again, then again and again, whilst Sajid, Williams and Josie looked away, allowing her to do what she needed to get herself back in the game. When she was done, she stood up, turned to Sajid and said, 'Thoughts?'

'Nothing definite, but if we have a rough idea of when Johnny left home that day, maybe we can pick him up through CCTV. You know, monitor vehicles on cameras nearest to Johnny's house and see if we can narrow down the possible vehicles.'

It was a long shot and time-consuming, but Nikki reckoned it might be worth the effort. They needed a lead to follow and if Downey had already had Johnny in his clutches for four days, then time was against them. She gave an abrupt nod to Williams. 'Do it.'

As he scurried from the room, she turned to Josie. 'Can you convince Candice to move in with either you or Maria? Just till this is over. If Downey has Johnny, he'd like nothing more than to snatch another one of us. We need to keep our families safe. We need your mum to move.'

Candice had become agoraphobic since her youngest child was murdered the previous year and all the startling events that had further traumatised her afterwards. It wouldn't be easy to convince the woman to leave her home, but unless her daughters moved in with her, Nikki couldn't guarantee her safety there. Even with her daughters in situ, there was no guarantee Downey wouldn't get to them. He was devious and determined and he wasn't afraid to take risks to get what he wanted. He understood Nikki, because there was no surer way of getting to her than an attack against her family. Freddie Downey was slowly but surely drawing her out and everybody close to her was at risk. They needed to find him and the sooner the better.

'Maria and I already forced her. It wasn't pleasant, but she and Maria have moved in with me, we feel safer that way and I've had additional security fitted. We'll manage. You just focus on finding Johnny.'

With barely a tremor to betray her emotions, Josie stood and pulled her coat on ready to go. A dart of anger sharpened by hurt made Nikki go to her. 'This is my fault, Josie. It's me he's after. I'm sorry your family has become involved in all of this.'

Josie smiled. 'Don't you go taking all of this on your own shoulders, Nikki. That's a bad habit you and I both have … *You're* not to blame for this. The only one to blame is Freddie Downey. He's an animal and I have faith in you. You'll find him. I know you will. But you've got to absolve yourself of guilt. It'll smother you otherwise and you shouldn't give that bastard the satisfaction of seeing you falter.'

After kissing Nikki's cheek, the younger woman left, leaving Nikki in a turmoil of emotions as she watched Josie walk out of the door. If only Josie knew. Freddie Downey, courtesy of Dr Helen Mallory's duplicity last autumn, had already witnessed Nikki falter. He'd seen her at her lowest, at her weakest. He'd seen Nikki confess things that should never have left the confidentiality of the psychiatrist's room; he'd seen the extent of her breakdown. It angered Nikki that he would gain vicarious pleasure from witnessing her splintering, again and again. The only consolation, as Marcus had pointed out to her, was that seeing her at her lowest might make Downey misjudge her. He had no idea that Nikki, phoenix-like, had risen from the ashes of her breakdown, stronger, meaner and more determined than ever to make her father pay for every wrong he'd ever inflicted on her and her family.

Although Josie's words were intended to be supportive, it left Nikki feeling hollowed, her stomach raw and in spasm. Thanks to the recordings made and sent to Downey by her psychiatrist, the woman she'd trusted with her darkest secrets, Downey's evil sadism had been fuelled. He'd gained strength and hubris by witnessing Nikki at her lowest ebb.

However, she didn't have the time to ponder Downey; her most pressing thought was that they were already too late to rescue Johnny. It felt as if Downey had them playing catch-up. He held all the cards and Nikki was running around trying to keep her family safe, whilst trying to track him down at the same time. She wondered which of them would win this fight.

Chapter 51

Downey glared at Jacko lying there in his own crap, where that stupid grandson of his had once lain. The old bastard had caused a lot of inconvenience and his gut instinct had been to make Jacko pay the ultimate price, but something had held him back. Instead of shooting him like he'd planned, he ordered his driver to nudge Jacko's car into the pillar by the exit. With a gun to his head, they'd hauled the old bastard from the stolen Audi and flung him in the boot of their vehicle. It did not bother Downey about being caught on CCTV as they had false number plates and as for the nearby witnesses, a little wave of the pistol in their direction, had them shitting their pants. Then they'd sped off, turned into a nearby multi-storey and repeated Jacko's trick of stealing a car. It was all over before anyone could even dial 999.

Back home, Downey needed to work out what to do. His plan had been to lure Parekh out with her stupid half-baked nephew Johnny Flynn but now this old fucker had put the kybosh on that. He swung his leg and landed his steel-capped boot in the old fucker's groin, knocking his balls right into his throat. The scream of pain was nowhere near as satisfying as he'd have liked. Still it was better than nothing and would have to do for now.

He wasn't sure why he'd spared Jacko's life. Hell, maybe he'd still kill him, but something had made him hesitate. He grinned. He wasn't going soft – that wasn't in his make-up – but he'd grown to enjoy having the old bastard around. He hadn't thought Jacko would betray him. Assumed the old guy was too scared to do that. After all, Downey knew where his daughter was and Jacko's wife and grandkid. For now, the wife and grandkid were AWOL, but he'd be able to find them – when the time was right.

Jacko looked up at him, his eyes crusty slits after the beating he'd endured. His nose was broken and blood smeared his face. Two of his fingers were twisted to one side. Downey grinned. He'd enjoyed doing that. Enjoyed the widening of Jacko's pupils as he exerted slow pressure on the bones until with a final screech of pure delight, he'd bent them so far they broke. Mind you, Jacko's screech had been equally loud, if less full of joy. With the boy in hospital in Liverpool, things had become complicated for Downey. He'd left two of his people there – the tall scraggly bint and her lesbo partner with the bird tattoo across her neck – to monitor him. So far, the lad remained unconscious and for now, that was fine.

However, the pressure was on. He'd counted on luring Parekh to the big hunt, had counted on her coming to rescue Johnny. Now he'd have to reconsider. He needed human prey and as he looked around at the bunch of idiots hanging around in the barn, salivating for more blood to be spilled, he couldn't decide. Of course, he could use Jacko as the warm-up act – you know, to get the paying guests in the mood. Or of course, Jacko's junkie kid. He'd sent two of the boys off to pick her up. That wouldn't be hard, she hung out at Forster Square arches most nights.

Neither of them were fit enough to be the main act, though. Too slow, too out of it to last for any length of time against the dogs and hunters. But maybe both together would whet his guests' appetites enough to keep them engaged. After all, they'd paid exorbitant amounts of money for these unique experiences and he didn't want to disappoint them. Last thing he needed was the hunters baying for his blood as he made his graceful exit. No, he wanted to keep them sweet until he'd gone. He'd have enough people after him if he pulled off his biggest coup.

Lighting up a cigarette, he inhaled the smoke, then grinned. What was he talking about? There was no 'if' about it. It was a definite when. He walked over the slush-covered yard back to his jeep. He had to make this work, and he had only twenty-four hours in which to work out his new strategy. Time to look at other options. He smiled as he slid behind the wheel. He hadn't paid his granddaughter any attention for a while. How remiss of him. There was something that would definitely lure his whore of a daughter out.

Chapter 52

The rest of the day had been taken up with convincing Ahad that she and Sajid were the best people to investigate Johnny's disappearance and organising her team. This was supported by Jewkes, who, like Sajid and Nikki, was convinced that Downey was involved in Operation Sandglass, *and* the fact that the Downey task force was seriously short-staffed because of Covid. In the end, Ahad had given in only because his police contacts in Manchester Met had promised significant back-up.

Because of Jewkes's expert interrogation skills, both of the suspected vets had spilled the beans. The old farmer Collins, as he'd told his daughter, had been checking out reports of maltreatment of donkeys on a farm near Hebden Bridge. What he *hadn't* told his daughter was that he'd also arranged a booty call with his on-again, off-again girlfriend in Cullingworth. Collins's girlfriend's sullen son had corroborated his statement, and complained about the disgusting noise made by the love birds. The Hebden Bridge farmer who complained about Collins's aggressive questions regarding the welfare of his donkeys had also corroborated the statement. Mr Collins pleaded with Jewkes not to tell his daughter about his girlfriend. Keen to get rid of the old boy now he was in the clear, Jewkes promised, with the proviso that if he ever misled the police again, he'd see that his daughter found out about his sex life.

Julie Ross, softened by being left to stew, gave up her right to a solicitor. Threatened by imprisonment, she capitulated when offered a non-custodial sentence and a promise not to inform the Royal College of Veterinary Surgeons of the malpractice, if she revealed what she knew about the dog fights. Of course, that was a lie. Jewkes had every intention of going for the maximum penalty not just for cruelty to animals, but also for aiding and abetting criminal activity and, as an accessory to murder and making sure she wasn't allowed anywhere near an animal for the rest of her life. That would be up to the Crown Prosecution Service though. Now he had her co-operation, he began the taped interview under caution and teased out everything he needed to incriminate the vet. Turned out she had been the on-call vet for the illegal fights and had tended to the dogs. The only names she gave that were also on Jewkes's extensive files, belonged to low-level felons on the periphery of Operation Sandglass. The identities of the rest, including the main man, known only as 'the boss', and a man called 'Jacko' remained anonymous. Ross admitted to being the vet in attendance at the fight in Chester and that something bad had happened. When all hell had let loose, one of the hired security guards had dropped her back in Chester. The only information she could give was that it appeared to surround a man called Jacko who had picked her up from Chester railway station. It seemed that this Jacko had made off in the middle of the fights with something belonging to the boss. Despite Jewkes's persistence, she could offer nothing other than that. Jewkes had left her under the supervision of his colleague, poring over photos of known dog fight owners, breeders and organisers. When the DNA evidence linking the Yorkshire moor crime scene to Nikki arose, Jewkes showed Ross a photo of Downey, which she confirmed as belonging to the boss. Now, with the depleted Downey task force and the Bradford contingent of Operation Sandglass working the various leads brought about by this new information, it was all systems go.

Nikki had spent the rest of the day organising her team so that she and Saj were free to follow up on the only lead they had regarding Johnny Flynn's movements – the pub he'd visited with his friends. With everything else in place, Nikki used the drive from Bradford to Manchester in Saj's car to relax and clear her mind ready for the trials that lay ahead. Her body longed for sleep, and the heated seats didn't help, so she switched hers off. The last thing she needed, knowing where they were heading, was to be drowsy on arrival at their destination.

The Dog and Bone pub was in a small village called Bloxham, on the outskirts of Oldham and as Saj pulled into the car park, Nikki groaned. It was worse than she'd imagined. From where they now sat in Sajid's car in the pot-holed car park, it looked dire. Racist graffiti and National Front symbols were sprayed over the sandstone walls with little attention to detail and with no indication that they had made any attempts to remove them. The graffiti looked like it had been layered on, with fresh spray paint barely concealing the racist sentiments of previous graffitists. Banksy, the artists were not. Nikki shuddered at the thought of entering the joint and gave her wrist band a couple of reassuring twangs. *I got this. I've faced worse than this in my life!*

Underneath the creaking sign with its illustration of a feral-looking snarling Rottweiler, jaws wide open, flecks of saliva dripping from its mouth and with a massive blood-stained bone at its feet, floated a ragged NF flag. As if the message wasn't clear enough, attached to the wall, at eye level beside the door was a hand painted sign proclaiming:

No Blacks

No Migrents

No Jypos

If it wasn't so sickening, Nikki might have laughed at the misspellings, but here in this isolated car park, two police officers of Asian descent waiting to confront what lay within those walls was anything but funny. In principle, she found these sorts of uninformed racists less threatening than those who covered up their prejudice. They were the ones who held actual power and could cause real damage. However, in their current situation, ill-informed racists were the most immediate threat to their safety.

Saj turned to Nikki, his brown eyes shadowed, a frown spreading across his forehead. 'You know Nik, I'm not sure I should have brought my Jag. No *way* it'll still be here when we come out.' He hesitated and then added. 'I'm not convinced either of us will make it back out …'

Nikki nodded, her eyes on the vehicle to their right that took up two parking spaces. The carcass of that car was also liberally graffitied, all but masking its original bilious green paint. The registration plates, side mirrors, the rear left passenger door and all four wheels were missing. Precarious piles of concrete, breeze-block or old bricks propped each corner of the vehicle up, making it slump to one side like a defeated participant in the grand prix, hobbling home three days after the spectators had left. She injected a positive tone to her voice. 'I get what you mean, but when the local uniforms turn up, we'll leave them to stand guard out here. You'll see, no one will touch your car.' She didn't add any reassurances about the state of their persons.

Sajid's snort exploded in the air between them and Nikki couldn't blame him when he said, 'That doesn't reassure me, Nik. How the hell do you expect us to get out of that shit hole in one piece, law enforcement or not?'

He was right. Their skin colour would incite the same violent anger that waving a red flag did to a bull. Still, it was their job and although nervous, Nikki was long past allowing racism and prejudice to stand in the way of her doing what she had to do. Besides, they had no option. If they wanted to stand even a remote chance of discovering the identity and/or whereabouts of the man Johnny Flynn had spoken to in this pub, they'd just have to bite the bullet and brazen it out. It wouldn't be the first time. At least Ahad had had the foresight to request back-up from contacts at Manchester Met.

As they waited for their promised back-up to arrive, the wind increased, sending thrashing sleet against the windscreen, causing the pub sign to creak and groan. Nikki watched it sway back and forth, back and forth as prickles of unease ran up and down her spine. The movement gave the illusion that the dog was about to launch itself out of the sign and hare after them, hackles up and saliva speckling from its frothing mouth. Nikki tried to dismiss the thought that this was not a good omen ... *not* a good omen at all.

Relief flooded through her when not one, not two, but three patrol cars, drove into the car park and bumped and ground their way towards Sajid's Jag. The additional presence of six officers would make their chances of escaping alive, if not uninjured, much more likely.

She and Saj got out and met the six officers in a huddle near the door. As they discussed their strategy, the bar door opened, releasing a not unpleasant odour of hops. The hop smell was followed by an undernote of vomit and a small man, unlit fag in his mouth and a peaked cap on his head, lurched out. Not glancing at the officers as he nudged his way past them, he made it to the edge of the footpath and vomited on the floor, before straightening and heading off on his way, humming what sounded like 'Sweet Caroline', under his breath.

'Lovely.' Nikki screwed up her nose and tried not to gag as the sickly alcoholic fumes reached her nostrils.

All six of the officers were familiar with the pub and all of them looked as if they'd drawn the short straw in being directed to give back-up to the Bradford officers. One of them, a tall woman, with blonde hair and a serious expression, her baton already drawn, took the lead. 'They're unpredictable. Depends who's inside. On the whole, you can expect a load of racist and sexist abuse. Doubt you'll get any information from them, but …' She shrugged her shoulders, her eyes clouded with doubt. 'I s'pose you need to try.'

'They're a right bunch of racist, sexist gits in there. They won't like either of you two.' This unnecessary intel was offered by a massive man with muscles that made even Marcus's hench body look flabby. Nikki, grateful that he was one of the officers entering the premises with her and Sajid, was convinced that he would be a tremendous asset if it came to blows. The Manchester officers had their batons out and Nikki was glad she and Sajid had had the foresight to bring theirs from the car too.

They decided that four officers remain in the car park, phones at the ready, in case things got tricky inside. Reluctant to go in all guns blazing, Nikki decided that two uniformed officers were sufficient back-up and would prove enough of a deterrent to limit any violent overtones. Nikki straightened her back, put her game face on and smiled as Sajid did the same. No one would suspect from their demeanour that they had any qualms about entering this pub in this lawless area outside of Oldham.

With a couple of twangs on the elastic band round her wrist to steady her nerves, Nikki was ready. She pushed the door open and was engulfed in a cacophony of masculine grunts and aggressive-sounding conversations. Allowing their eyes to become used to the dim light, Nikki and Saj, with their back-up behind them stood in the doorway unobserved for a moment. Nikki used the time to study the pub's inhabitants. Josie's description of it as a 'spit and sawdust' dive was more than accurate. There were only about fifteen men in the room. Five propped up the bar, pint glasses filled to differing levels, in front of them. Others sat in groups of twos and threes around the periphery of the room. All sported tattoos of some description either meandering up their necks, or in full or half sleeves on their arms. Most had shaved heads or a number one cut and most were under forty years old. Dust motes floated in the dull light that tried to penetrate the filthy windows.

The barman, a man well into his sixties judging by the wrinkles creasing his forehead, was the first to spot Nikki and the others. He quirked an eyebrow in their direction. As well as his head, his torso was completely hair-free as revealed by the baggy dirty white vest he wore and a bar towel was slung over a skinny shoulder. He looked hardly strong enough to pull a pint never mind keep control over the bar's occupants. When the barman's eyes fastened on Nikki, his mouth opened revealing a gummy orifice, from which 'Pig Alert!' was spat in a surprisingly deep tone.

Nikki smiled and stepped up to the bar, aware of all eyes following her progress and trying not to wonder if they saw a bull's eye marked on her back. Keeping her tone firm and level, she pushed a photo of Johnny across the sticky bar and asked, 'Recognise this lad?'

The barman's gappy smile widened, but he didn't even look at the photo, before picking up a glass and drying it, using the less than clean tea towel from his shoulder. 'Nope!'

Nikki pushed it closer. 'You didn't look.'

Holding her gaze, the barman's expression didn't falter. 'Noooope!'

Nikki wanted to thrust the photo under his nose, but knew that wouldn't help matters. Instead, she hefted herself onto a bar stool. 'Two pints of Carling … and the answer to my question.'

She'd no intention of drinking the beer. Not only because she was on duty, but because she'd seen the scum marks on the displayed glasses. Although she sensed the men around the bar standing up and forming a semi-circle around her, Nikki was confident that Sajid and the Manchester officers had her back. Besides, she wasn't useless in a fight herself. Eyes fastened on the old man, she pushed the image even closer to him. His eyes flicked to someone who stood just over her right shoulder – a shadowy figure who she couldn't identify when she cast a glance in his direction – then the scrawny barman looked back at her, before finally resting his gaze on the image of Johnny. She'd find out later from Saj which punter it was.

His shoulders relaxed, and a smile came on his face, which puzzled Nikki. The man had expected the police to be here about someone else and Nikki wondered just who that might be. He picked up the photo and snorted. 'That skinny little toad. He was here the other night with some mates. Only had a pint of shandy – pussy! – then he left.'

He flicked the image back over the bar towards Nikki, aiming to her side so that it flicked past her and landed on the floor. As Sajid, bent to pick it up, one of the other men moved in and stamped on it, catching Sajid's fingers as he did so. 'Oops, sorry, Paki boy. Did I catch your little brown fingers there?'

Sajid left the photo on the floor, and still in his semi-prone position raised his head, and met the man's smirking look. Then, with unexpected speed he stood upright, catching the man in the groin with his shoulder as he did so. 'Ooops, sorry, *white* boy. Did I catch your little white goolies, there?'

As the crowd surged forwards, the back-up officers inserted themselves, batons drawn between Sajid and Nikki and the punters. Nikki climbed from the stool onto the bar. 'Look you all need to back off. We want one poxy piece of information, that's all and then we'll be on our way. However, if this all kicks off, we'll close the bar down and make sure we have everyone from health and safety to the taxman and CID crawling over the premises – and, by extension, all of your lives – for the next fortnight. We'll hound you until we find something that will put you away for a long time.' She splayed her hands in front of her palms up. 'On the other hand, you tell us who this lad was speaking to that night and where we can find him and we'll be on our way … your choice.'

All eyes left hers and went to a tall man, the oldest of the group who stood apart from the proceedings. Nikki was willing to bet that he was the one who'd silently directed the barman to answer her question. Taking another image of Johnny from her pocket, she held the man's gaze and offered it to him. The crowd parted, and he stepped forward, yanked the photo from her hand and studied it for a second. He sniffed from deep in his throat, hoiked up a gob of phlegm and rolled it around in his mouth as if savouring a culinary delicacy, his eyes never leaving Nikki's face. Rising to his unspoken challenge, Nikki held his gaze, ignoring the acid that filled her throat as evidence of the contents of his mouth were visible as his tongue moved. *Grotty bastard!*

After a long moment, he jerked his head to a booth by the window that already had a near empty pint sitting on the table. 'Bring the lady's drink over, Little John, and I'll have another. The rest of you piss off and mind your own business.'

Amused that the toothless barman was called Little John, Nikki's lips twitched. She moved to join the man who appeared to be the boss of the group. With the man whom Sajid had injured still glaring at him, Sajid wandered over to join Nikki and the big man in his booth, leaving the other two officers to stand guard near the bar.

Instead of offering a hand, the large man introduced himself with a nod first at Nikki and then at Saj. 'Name's Hoody, Robin Hood.'

Still recovering from 'Little John', Nikki couldn't resist studying the bar occupants before asking, 'Which of them is Maid Marion, then?' She winked at her partner. 'My money's on the one you castrated, Saj.'

Robin Hood rewarded her with a snort and a twitch of his lips, before all trace of humour left his face. 'Look lass. You come in here, where you know your kind aren't welcome, attack one of my men and then try to cause trouble. It's not on. Not on at all.'

He shifted in his seat, and said nothing as Little John deposited the drinks on the table, spilling some of Saj's on his trousers. Nikki grinned. She'd told him to dress down and avoid his posh rags, but he wouldn't be told. Served him right!

'But?' Nikki sipped her beer, still with her eye on Hoody. She sensed he was weighing something up. He wasn't the sort to cooperate with the police, so something must have made him at least consider it or they'd have found themselves on their arses in the car park rather than ensconced in a booth with him. She assumed it was something to do with the fact that they'd expected the police to be enquiring after someone else entirely.

Hoody took a long gulp of his beer, his throat muscles working, making the snake that covered his neck look like it was slithering upwards as he did so. Nikki was intrigued by it and recognised that to create that movement in a tattoo took skill and precision. 'That lad.' He pointed at the photo. 'Was a bit of a dick, like. He didn't bother to hide that he didn't like our … shall we say … ideology?'

He could say 'ideology' all he liked, Nikki preferred to call it 'racist crap', but she'd save that little gem for later.

'He was with a couple of other lads, but this bloke – a stranger, like – well a stranger to us, that is, not part of our firm, if you get my drift – were chatting to him.'

Nikki got his 'drift' in more ways than one. Every time Hoody moved or waved his arm, a waft of BO drifted to Nikki's nostrils, making her want to wiggle them to get rid of the stink. Nikki smiled, trying to ignore Sajid's frantic attempts to wipe the beer stain from his pants. He'd regret doing that, because when he stood up to leave the pub it'd look like he'd pissed himself. 'Yeah, got ya.'

'This older bloke was chatting to your lad, like. I mean he wasn't one of our lot, but he fitted in here. Both of them did. They weren't Pakis like him.' He lifted his chin towards Sajid. 'Or half-castes like you or anything.' He smiled, looked straight at Nikki and said, 'They looked normal like.'

Nikki's gut clenched against the casual racism and she wanted to lambast him with a *Fuck off, Hoody! Normal isn't being white, you tosser. Normal is having a brain cell, compassion, empathy, humanity.* Instead she contented herself with a narrow-eyed glare.

'You know, he'd a couple of the usual tats – swastikas and that – but nothing too extreme.'

Nikki exchanged a look with Sajid in response to the 'nothing too extreme' comment but remained silent.

'Anyway, he chatted with your bloke here.' Again, he pointed to the image of Johnny that was now soaking up the spillage from their slopped beers.

'They shook hands at the end before they left. Like they'd made a deal or something.'

'A deal?'

He shrugged. 'Looked that way to me.'

That gelled with what Josie had told her. 'You get a name for this bloke? Or a description?'

This time Hoody's smile was wide. 'No name. As for description, take a look round here, eh? Any of them could match this bloke's description, like. Skinhead, baseball cap, five-ten, sixties. He was trying to blend in, I think.'

A twinge of disappointment niggled Nikki. She'd expected more when Hoody took them to his booth, but that sort of generic description would get them nowhere. Still, Nikki was curious. 'Why are you telling us this, Hoody? Your kind don't usually cooperate with us.'

'No, that's true. Don't cooperate with pigs or blacks, but this fucker – he was casing the joint out. Since he's been here, my business has decreased, if you get my drift. A lot of my regulars aren't so loyal anymore ...' He winked.

Nikki understood he was referring to his illegal activities, which included dog fights and that's why he was okay talking about the man who'd spoken to Johnny – he was Hoody's competition. Nikki made a mental note to pass this information on to Operation Sandglass. She was there to find out about Johnny, Jewkes's team would delve deeper into the activities around Hoody and the Dog and Bone pub. 'You've got something else, don't you?'

'I do that. If you hadn't asked, I wasn't going to tell you, but

277

since you're so smart, here goes. After they left, one of your lad's mates came back in. The one they call Roadrunner. Well, he came back in and this bloke, well he handed him a bundle of readies – couple of hundred big ones I reckon.'

And there it was. They'd got more than they'd expected and Nikki knew from the list Josie had supplied, which of Johnny's mates went by the name Roadrunner: Robbie Calhoun, a long-distance lorry driver. Plus, they'd got out with the only mark on either of them being the piss-like stain on Sajid's trousers.

Sunday

Chapter 53

Downey rubbed his hands together. He'd spent a long time deciding what action to take. His priority had to be making sure he had enough viable candidates for tonight's big hunt and with Jacko's daughter, Jacko, a couple of dispensable slags from his own team and the surprise he hoped to secure before then, he was confident of the hunt's success.

He should be nervous. After all, tonight was the big finale he'd spent months planning. Months of detailed organisation, scoping out his victims, building up his reputation using all the contacts Mallory had supplied, advertising his services and creating his niche product – and all with the sole aim of getting the ultimate, the most delicious revenge on Nikki Parekh. Well, that and making a shed-load of dosh along the way. No point in getting his dream ending if he couldn't enjoy it on a deckchair in the tropics or somewhere, was there? But all that coursed through him was a buzzing energy that kept his momentum up. He wasn't nervous. Why should he be? Everything was going to go to plan and when it was over, he'd slip off into the sunset, leaving the Parekh world in turmoil.

He paced the farmhouse, wishing it was time to go. Time to put the final pieces into play, but he knew better than to rush things.

Being hasty risked things going wrong and Freddie Downey had been stung that way a few times – not anymore though. This time, success would be his.

He had eyes on everyone and all he waited for now was the call from his stooges, telling him it was time. For now, though, maybe some Jacko baiting would take the edge off his surplus adrenalin …

Chapter 54

Ali: Been meaning to talk to you about this. Maz has gone AWOL. Ask Charlie what she knows.

Nikki stared at the text. What the hell was Ali on about? Why would Charlie know anything about Maz or his whereabouts?

She and Saj were driving towards Oldham having pulled an overnighter at Trafalgar House trying to draw things together. Jewkes was on the Dog and Bone angle and her team were trying to locate Robbie Roadrunner Calhoun. The wider Operation Sandglass team were narrowing in on likely locations for tonight's Big Hunt and everyone hoped that they'd identify the location in time. They had five possible sites at the minute, all of them quite distantly spaced from the others ranging from Yorkshire, to Lancashire and Liverpool areas. Jewkes reckoned that if his team could narrow it down to two locations, then Operation Sandglass, supported by local teams on the ground, could cover both. Any more than that and their resources, skills and numbers would be spread too thinly, decreasing the odds of a successful operation. For now, time and technological expertise appeared to be on their side. Nikki was still determined to make every second count, which was the reason for their current trip.

Whilst the rest of them were trying to pinpoint the location, she was determined to use every lead to find her nephew and – she shuddered at the thought – possibly Downey too. Both she and Saj were running on a combination of caffeine and adrenalin and whilst that offered only a temporary reprieve from their inevitable slump, Nikki was determined to maximise this period. After all, people's lives were at stake. Her nephew's life was at stake and if her hunch about Downey's involvement was correct, there was no way she would allow him to kill another member of her family. She suspected that if he won, something deep inside of her would crack and after her experience before Christmas, she wasn't sure she'd recover from another wound like that.

'You see this, Saj.' She held out her phone so Sajid could read Ali's text and then pulled it back again. 'Oops, sorry you're driving.'

Instead, she read it aloud and then laughed. 'Ali's clutching at straws if he thinks Charlie knows anything about Maz's whereabouts. She's only ever spoken a couple of words to him at most.'

'Eh Nik. About that. Well, I've been meaning to talk to you …'

A cloud scuttled over Nikki's eyes as Sajid's tone told her she would not like whatever he was about to tell her. Her heart rate increased and without thinking about it, she twanged her wrist band.

Saj's eyes flicked from the road to her wrist and then back again. 'Aw, Nik. I would have said something earlier, but I wanted to speak with Charlie first. Then she was ill and so I couldn't.'

Twang, twang, twang! But Nikki kept her eyes on the road ahead and remained silent.

Saj cleared his throat. 'I suspected something was going on between them. They just seemed too …' He shrugged. 'Too busy ignoring each other on the occasions we were all together, you know. Like they were trying too hard to look like they didn't even know each other. Then, well Langley spotted them in Broadway just before Christmas. He thought it was nothing. That they'd just bumped into each other. But …' Again with the stupid shrug.

If he hadn't been driving, Nikki might have been tempted to thump him one. Instead, without looking at him, she prodded his arm and in a voice like ice said, 'But, what …?'

Sajid flinched, but didn't complain. 'Then both me and Langley spotted a few surreptitious glances and that. You know. Young love. We thought it was harmless until you said about the footsteps in the snow.'

A strangled sound left Nikki's lips. She'd thought there was something strange about those. Wondered why Downey would go to the trouble of scoping out her back yard, yet not leave any indication that he'd been there. That wasn't Downey's style and she should have trusted her instincts. When she'd found the photos on her windscreen all doubts about the footsteps had vanished. Bitter anger settled in her gut, and her hands clenched into fists. 'That little bloody cow! She risked her safety – everyone's safety – to muck around with Ali's boy? I'll kill her.'

Again, Sajid flinched. But Nikki was too angry to notice that he'd opened his mouth to say something. 'She's grounded. Definitely grounded. Wait till I see her. That's who she was with in Costa – bloody Maz.' She prodded Saj again, this time harder than before. 'You should have told me, Saj. What the hell were you thinking?'

A rare flash of anger flickered in Saj's eyes and his lips tightened. 'What I'm thinking, Parekh is that if you don't stop fucking prodding me, I'll bloody move to Cybercrimes. I'm done being your whipping boy. I'm a detective sergeant, not your fucking little yes-boy-DC and you better treat me like one.'

Nikki's mouth opened, then closed, her eyes wide as the enormity of Sajid dropping the 'F- Bomb' not once but twice struck her. He was mad – no, *more* than mad, he was furious – and feeling Sajid's wrath directed against her churned up her stomach like a Gatling gun had let loose in there. She closed her eyes and willed herself to calm down, but the mix of caffeine and Red Bull drinks had her too wired. She forced herself to sit on her hands because the temptation to twang her wrist band was so strong she thought that if she started doing that she might never stop.

When Sajid next spoke, his tone was calmer. 'Look Nik …'

But she interrupted him and placed her hand on his arm, rubbing the spot she'd previously prodded. 'I'm sorry, Saj. Really sorry. I take our friendship for granted, but that's because you're the first real friend I've ever had.'

As the frown on Sajid's forehead faded, she bowed her head. 'I'm not making excuses and I don't want sympathy. This friendship carry-on is something I need to get my head round, I'm working on it, honest I am.'

If she'd looked up, she would have noticed the slight smile flit across Sajid's lips, but she was too intent on her apology. 'I don't want to take you for granted, Saj. I couldn't have a better DS. I really couldn't and I'll work on being a better friend and colleague, I prom—'

Sajid tutted. 'Just shut up, Parekh. I think you're missing the point here.'

Nikki frowned casting her mind over everything he'd said and then sighed. 'What?'

'You need to find out if Charlie's okay. Check that she's at home. Do it now, then you can continue with your abject apology.' The twinkle in his eye took the sting out of his words and Nikki slapped her hand to her brow. 'Fuck, yes. What the hell am I thinking.'

Within moments she was on the phone to Marcus, explaining the situation.

Call ended, she looked at Saj. 'Marcus says she's not come down for breakfast yet but he's going to check on her and report back.' An uneasy silence reigned for a few seconds, then Nikki spoke. 'You were only looking out for her – Charlie, I mean. She trusts you. You would have got through to her better than I could've. I just can't believe I missed it – her and Maz?'

'I thought I'd have time to speak with her, Nik. I'm sorry.'

Sajid smiled and just like that the tension between them dissipated. As Sajid continued to drive, Nikki wished Marcus would hurry and get back to her, telling her Charlie was safe. When two minutes passed and he still hadn't called her, the Gatling gun in her stomach took off again. What if she'd gone off somewhere with Maz? What if they were in trouble? What if Downey had got to her? Why the hell wasn't Marcus calling her back?

When her phone rang, Nikki almost dropped it in her haste to accept the call, but Marcus's first words made her sag back in her seat in relief. 'She's upstairs. I had stern words with her. She says she broke it off with Maz after the Costa photos. Says it was nothing serious.'

Tuned into Marcus's moods, Nikki could sense the waves of anxiety rolling off him. He'd been worried that he'd find Charlie's bed empty. 'You believe her?'

She could visualise Marcus glaring upstairs towards Charlie's bedroom as he replied. 'No idea. If you'd asked me that a couple of months ago, I would've said hell yes, but some practical joker's made off with our daughter and left a hormonal ghoul in her place. Your guess is as good as anybody's, but I'll be monitoring her, that's for sure.'

At the words 'our daughter' a lump formed in Nikki's throat. Marcus was more than a dad to Charlie. Although she wasn't his daughter by blood, he was her dad in all things that mattered. Maybe it was time to formalise that arrangement, but that was a topic for another day. For now, her friend's son was still AWOL and Ali was worried. 'Did she have any idea where Maz might be?'

'Nah. She says not, but who knows? I'm going to quiz Ruby, see if she knows anything.'

Nikki hung up and sent a text off to Ali telling him what Charlie had said. Now his previous texts about wanting to talk made perfect sense. He'd learned about Maz and Charlie and wanted to talk to Nikki about it, but Ali being Ali, he didn't want to pile on any pressure whilst she was involved in such an extensive investigation. It was then Nikki realised she had more friends than she realised.

Chapter 55

Charlie glowered at the window, oblivious to the driving sleet hammering against it. Marcus had sooo pissed her off. Marching upstairs, not waiting for her to say he could come in before he barged through the door. It's not like he was even her dad or anything. *How bloody dare he?*

She turned her mobile phone over and over in her hand, not knowing what to do. She'd been worried Marcus would demand to see her phone and so when she'd seen his flashing blue eyes and that stern 'you're in for a rollicking' look she'd tucked it down the side of the bed. Now she wasn't sure if she should contact Maz or not. Their arrangement was in place and she'd see him later on as planned, but should she risk sending him a text to let him know his dad knew he'd left home?

She'd told him not to pack anything, told him his parents would notice that straight away, but Maz being Maz hadn't listened to her. She grinned. Idiot hadn't wanted to leave his laptop or some of his favourite clothes behind. He was so predictable. Thing was, if she didn't warn him, Maz might not be so careful. On the other hand, Marcus might come up the stairs at any moment and demand to see her phone or worse, confiscate it. They should have got a couple of burner phones. Maz had told her that's how the Eyes had kept in touch with the idiots who did their bidding before Christmas.

She didn't want Marcus to see the texts she'd sent Maz. They were private. Then an idea came to her. She'd message Maz to give him the heads up and then she'd hide her phone, just in case Marcus tried to confiscate it. If he couldn't find it, then he couldn't see she was still in touch with Maz, could he?

She fired off a text

Charlie: Ali knows you've gone. Parents all over me. See you later!

Then, without even a pang of guilt that she was deceiving her parents and betraying the trust they had in her, Charlie slid her phone into a plastic sleeve, inserted it into a plastic bag and, opening her bedroom window, she hung it from the handle, wrapping a couple of rubber bands around it to ensure it stayed in place.

There, job done. Now all she had to do was work out how she could get out from under Marcus's nose later on. She'd have to bribe Ruby to help her with that one, she decided.

Chapter 56

'So, the last time you saw Calhoun was?'

Nikki could almost see the steam coming from Sajid's ears as he tried to pin down an answer from Calhoun's boss. It wasn't that he was being obstructive – well, not exactly. It was more that he was too busy venting over his own grievances against Robbie Calhoun to focus on Saj's questions. What made this amusing for Nikki was that Calhoun's boss, 'Ziggy – Zig-for-short', was one of those characters who couldn't keep still for even a second. He darted from truck to truck, checking paperwork, yelling orders to his truckers and puffing on a huge cigar as he did so, and Saj struggled to keep up with the man. One minute he veered left, then a quick heel spin, and he was heading right, with Saj dodging round, struggling to keep up.

When she could no longer bear to see such uncoordinated, breathless questioning, Nikki stepped in. Voice firm, hands on hips, she jumped neatly in front of him, causing him to brake and, ignoring the odious cigar smoke, she stared him down. 'Ziggy. This is important. So, let's go to your office for five minutes and then you can get back to your job.'

When he opened his mouth, cigar clenched between his teeth, set to protest, Nikki held up a hand and shook her head. 'Believe me, Zig, this is your best option. Otherwise, it'll be all the way back to Bradford, a few hours whilst we process the paperwork, a little longer whilst we get the details from you, and then the ride back to Oldham. Or, as I said, five minutes in your office should suffice, for now. Your choice.'

Blowing smoke in her face, Ziggy flicked his cigar through the air, waited till it fizzled out in a nearby puddle and stomped off towards an old caravan that was balanced on breeze blocks with a set of wobbly wooden steps leading to the door. Nikki dreaded entering the office because she was sure it would stink of cigar smoke and be as in need of a clean as its owner. However, when she and Saj followed Ziggy inside she was surprised to discover that the office was pristine clean with a citrusy lemon smell lingering in the air, a line of filing cabinets against the back wall and a shiny wooden desk with a laptop on top, pens and papers organised around it.

Apart from Ziggy's comfy office chair, the only other available seating was two plastic chairs, one of which wobbled when Nikki touched it. With a wink at Sajid, which received an exaggerated eye roll in response, Nikki bypassed the wobbly seat and plonked herself down on the less rickety one. With one leg crossed over the other, she nodded at Saj, indicating he should take over once more.

Sajid cleared his throat and repeated his earlier question. 'So, when did you last see Calhoun?'

A flush bloomed across Ziggy's cheeks and, as he opened his mouth, Saj interjected. 'Look, Ziggy. I don't want a diatribe about the number of times he's let you down, or the number of ways his irresponsibility has left you in the crap, or the number of favours you had to call in to get his work done or …'

Sajid wafted his hand in the air as he tried to think of a last example to ground his argument.

'Five days ago.' Ziggy opened a tub of chewing gum, popped a small rectangle in his mouth and began chewing, his teeth and lips making a sloppy, slappy sound as he did so.

Nikki almost laughed out loud at the distaste that had Sajid's lips turning down at the corners. But he overcame his discomfort and recommenced his questioning. 'You saw him five days ago? What time would that be?'

'Half-six.'

If it hadn't been so annoying, Nikki would once more have laughed at the turnaround in attitude. From loquacious to near monosyllabic, in one fell swoop. Instead, she got to her feet, leaving Saj to conclude his questioning, and wandered over to a cork board in the corner of the room. Several photos were pinned haphazardly all over the board. Most, judging from the paper hats and Christmas crackers, were from the firm's recent Christmas party. She studied them, wondering why the hell people would elect to wear vest tops in the middle of winter. Of course, she realised it was to show off their biceps or triceps or quads or whatever bulging chunks of meat men thought were attractive on their upper arms … 'Saaaaj?'

'A minute, Nik. I'm just finishing …'

'Saj!'

As she snapped the word out, she reached over, unpinned one image from the wall and strode towards Ziggy. Placing it on the desk in front of him, she leaned over and prodded the photo. 'That Robbie Calhoun?'

Ziggy put a pair of wire-rimmed specs on and peered down at the image, whilst Sajid, alerted by the way Nikki bounced on her toes, got up and joined her at the other side of the desk.

'Yep. That's Calhoun. Tosser! He tried to get off with my niece that night. I gave him a verbal warning and a less subtle physi …'

'Not now, Zig. I'm taking this image. Thanks for your help. We'll send a couple of officers to interview the rest of your staff. Come on, Saj.'

Not waiting for Saj to catch up, Nikki was off out of the office, leaving a dumbfounded Ziggy frowning after them.

'Shit, Nik, how did you know that was Calhoun, and why are we in such a hurry?'

Shaking her head, Nikki glared at him. 'For God's sake, Saj. Didn't you see it?'

'See what?'

'The fucking tattoo. Look!'

And sure enough, there was Robbie Calhoun, all bulging muscles and tattoos. 'Shit! He's definitely He Who Owns The Arm, isn't he?'

'Looks that way to me. We need to get this info to Langley with some familial DNA and suchlike, but it looks like we've identified our body.'

With a glance at Nikki, Saj unlocked his Jag and waited for her to get in next to him before asking the question that burned in his mind. 'What does that mean for Johnny though, Nik?'

Nikki bit her lip and exhaled. Although she wasn't sure what it meant for her nephew, she was certain it meant nothing good. 'I think we need to get our butts in gear and crack on. It looks like someone is cleaning up their mess as they go and my money's on Freddie Downey.'

Chapter 57

In the fading mid-afternoon light, the tall scraggly girl with the tattoo across her neck walked through the automatic doors of the Royal Liverpool University Hospital and marched up to the reception desk and, without preamble, made her rehearsed statement. 'I've been told you've got my cousin here. My mate says they dumped him at A&E.'

From somewhere, the girl summoned up a tear and a distressed sniff, making the receptionist smile at her. 'It's okay dear. If you give me his name, I'll find out what ward he's on.'

The girl, glancing around her, allowed her bottom lip to tremble. 'That's just it. My mate says he was unconscious and the guy who dropped him here ran off.' She swallowed hard and, eyes wide, gazed at the grey-haired woman behind the desk. 'I'm scared he'll die before his sister, Nikki, gets a chance to see him. I don't think the doctors even know his name. None of us have been contacted, like.'

Understanding cleared the frown from the receptionist's face and her fingers flew across her keyboard as, with a reassuring smile, she said, 'There, there, dear, we'll get it sorted. But I'll need his name?

'Johnny, Johnny Flynn.'

'Now, did this happen yesterday?'

Tattoo-girl closed her eyes and nodded, her stomach unclenching as she realised this woman, Sylvia, according to her name tag, was going to help her.

'And can I have a description of Johnny, dear?'

Forcing a tear to trickle down her cheek, the tattooed girl nodded, her lip still trembling. 'I'm so worried about Johnny. He got in with a bad crowd and with his mam gone … well … it's only the two of them … him and his sister. He came to Liverpool to see me and we got split up the other night and he didn't come back to my flat …'

Sylvia nodded, her smile brimming with sympathy, then tentatively. 'Your cousin's description, dear …?'

Thankful that she'd prepared for this question, Tattoo-girl launched into another rehearsed speech. 'He's twenty-seven with mucky brown hair – shortish. About five foot eight, maybe. Brown eyes, a Celtic knot tattoo on his right arm …'

Whilst she'd been speaking, the receptionist scribbled on a scrap of paper and began scanning the screen before her, her lips moving in silence as she studied the information. After what seemed like an age, she looked up at Tattoo-girl, her reassuring smile fading into a frown as she held her finger in the air, indicating that the girl should wait another minute. Then she picked up a phone and pressed three numbers, before turning her back to Tattoo-girl and whispering into it.

This didn't look good. It didn't look good at all. Tattoo-girl shuffled her feet as she waited, fingers crossed behind her back. The last thing she needed was to hear that the lad – Johnny Flynn had died. The boss would blame her if he had. He was a mean bastard and what he'd done to her mate only two nights ago was still fresh in her mind. Realising she was holding her breath, she inhaled. Now he'd got that old codger Jacko locked up and the last thing she needed was to get in his bad books.

The receptionist turned round and Tattoo-girl almost fainted when she registered the smile on the older woman's face. 'He's in the ICU, but if you go up, they'll talk to you. There are forms to be filled in.'

Tattoo-girl scarcely allowed the woman to finish before rushing towards the lifts with 'Thank you' over her shoulder as she ran. As she jogged along the hospital corridor, the turmoil of contradictory emotions upset her belly, causing her to stop and bend over double, hugging her midriff as she thought through her options. The boss had told her she had to identify Flynn and give them Nikki Parekh's contact details as next of kin. However, she'd been talking to her girlfriend about that, and the pair of them had wondered if that course of action was safe. What if they had police officers up there guarding Johnny? In the end though, they'd considered the police a safer option than the boss, so although it went against every streak of self-preservation pulsing through her, Tattoo-girl had no option. If she didn't complete the boss's instructions to the letter, he'd hunt her down and punish her.

Pulling herself together, she straightened and punched at the lift button to take her up to the ICU. On arrival, she pressed the buzzer and waited for a nurse who seemed far too smiley to be working in the ICU to speak to her through the intercom.

Tattoo-girl explained her reason for being there and the nurse let her in. 'We can't allow you into his room because you're not his next of kin, but,' She frowned and patted Tattoo-girl's arm. 'We have a photo and if you could ID him and give us his next of kin details, we have a visitors' room you can wait in.'

'Is he …?' Tattoo-girl, still reeling with relief that things were going to be so simple, wasn't sure how to end the sentence.

The nurse, however, interpreted her question and nodded. 'He's alive, love, but I can't go into details about his condition. As you're not …'

'Yeah. I get it. I'm not his next of kin.'

The nurse guided her to the visitors' room and settled her in a chair before disappearing, only to return a minute later with a mug of sugary tea. It was only then that Tattoo-girl realised that she was trembling. A momentary pang of shame at gaining the nurse's kindness on false pretences hit her, but she swallowed her guilt and focused on the job in hand.

'Now, before I show you this photo, you need to be aware that the machines you'll see are all there to help him. He's in no pain.'

Tattoo-girl nodded. She just wanted it over with so she could get away from the clinical, medicinal smell and work out how she and her girlfriend were going to escape the boss's clutches. Despite the nurse's pep talk, Tattoo-girl reeled when she saw the photo. Johnny Flynn was a mess. She remembered how he'd been when Jacko first brought him to the farmhouse – cocky, funny, sarcastic. Now, he was skinny with hollowed-out cheeks, his face covered in bruises. If she hadn't already known who he was, she wouldn't recognise him. Her fingers flickered to her lips. She couldn't take her eyes off the shadow of the boy she'd met mere days earlier. This was the boss's work and seeing him like this made her only more determined to get out of it. But first she had to buy them some time. She swallowed hard, trying to dislodge the sharp-edged lump in her throat. 'Yes. That's Johnny.'

Desperate to escape the claustrophobic visitors' room, she pulled the paper with Nikki Parekh's phone number on it and thrust it into the nurse's hand. 'That's his sister's number. She's his next of kin. You need to tell her. I can't …' And jumping to her feet, Tattoo-girl ran from the visitors' room, down the ICU corridor and into the belly of the hospital.

Chapter 58

By the time Nikki and Sajid arrived back at Trafalgar House, the weather had taken a turn for the worse and sleet had battered the windscreen as they drove back to Bradford. Weariness slumped Nikki's shoulders as she headed into the loos to splash water on her face. Her bed called to her, but things were at a crucial stage with various strands in their investigation pulling together. Savouring the privacy of her time alone in the women's toilets, Nikki took a moment to consider what Johnny's fate might be. Her instincts told her he was dead already, but she couldn't quite extinguish that small glimmer of hope in her heart. For her half-sister Candice's sake, she couldn't let go of that – not yet. It would kill Candice to lose another son, and that was something she couldn't dwell on. If there was even the slightest chance Johnny was alive, then she'd find him.

As she patted her face dry with a paper towel, Nikki studied her reflection in the mirror. The bags beneath her eyes testified to her lack of sleep. Her prominent cheekbones, her hollowed cheeks and the frown lines snaking from her lips and across her forehead showed the toll the past few months had taken on her. She tossed the soiled towel in the bin, and raising fingers to her temples, she massaged them lightly. *Come on Nik! You can do* *this. You've **got** to do this!*

Although she'd never admit it to anyone – well, maybe Marcus, but nobody else – Nikki realised her weariness wasn't just a result of lack of sleep. It resulted from a constant grinding, wearing down of her sense of self. A culmination of being on constant alert. Everything about her body was wound as taut as a ballet dancer's tights. Her sagging shoulders, the slight tremble in her hands, the haunted look in her eyes … all of it told her she was a mess, but she couldn't fall apart. Not yet. Too many people relied on her.

She hooked her finger through her wrist band and pulled it a couple of inches from her skin. If she released it now, it would give her a satisfying rush. But her skin was already raw and smarting. She'd relied on the band crutch too much over the last few days, and the boost it gave her was only ever temporary. Perhaps she needed to develop a new coping strategy, one that didn't involve hurting herself. She released the band, flinching as it pinged against her wrist. *When this is over, Nik. When this is over!*

As soon as she re-entered the incident room, she sensed that something had broken. The atmosphere frizzled with excitement. Her team was involved in deep discussion, but instead of the wilting flowers she'd left not ten minutes earlier, they were now in full bloom. William's face was alight as his fingers flew across his keyboard. Jewkes and Malik pored over a large map on the interactive white board and Anwar was working the phones like a pro.

As she approached the two men, Sajid turned to her, eyes sparkling, the only sign that they'd been at it since the previous day was his ever-so-slightly crumpled shirt, his loosened tie and the overwhelming smell of recently applied aftershave. 'Jewkes's team has narrowed the location down to these two sites.' His excitement was reflected in the speed at which he delivered the news.

As Nikki scanned the two pinned sites on the large map, she noted that both were in the middle of a sizeable area of remote countryside: one to the north of Clough Pike mountain peak near Lancaster, the other near Trout Sike to the west of Sheffield. 'They've chosen well, haven't they? How reliable is this information?'

Jewkes, lips taut, traced a line between the two sites with his fingers. 'The cyber team are good at their job. The chatter they've intercepted indicates that this "big hunt" will take place on one of these two sites and the other sites mentioned have been discounted as being venues for smaller dog-fighting locations happening over the next few days.' His lips tightened even more. 'We'll scoop those bastards up too, but for now, we need to focus on these two locations.'

Nikki pulled up a chair and sat down, gratefully accepting the mug of coffee Saj placed in her hands. 'Do we have a definite time?'

An explosive tut left Jewkes's lips. 'No, they've not got a specific time yet. We're lucky to have narrowed it down to a date and these two areas.'

A niggle wormed its way into Nikki's head and she couldn't shake it. 'Could they be playing us? You know, yanking our chains. I mean, it's all quite convenient, don't you think? Almost like …'

'A trap?' Sajid nodded. He'd been thinking the same thing as Nikki.

'That thought had passed through my mind.' Jewkes exhaled and made a 'tut tut tut' sound through his teeth. 'But we've no option, have we? We've got to follow up on it. Lives are at stake.'

That was true. They had no option but to follow up on the leads that had presented themselves, yet a prickle of unease settled in Nikki's stomach. Things were never straightforward with Downey, so why would this time be any different? Realising it was futile to think that way, Nikki gave an abrupt nod and jumped to her feet, spilling her drink as she did so. 'Right, how are we dividing this up?'

'I FaceTimed the Operation Sandglass leads and we've worked out a provisional strategy between us. Of course, we're prepared to be adaptable depending on incoming information, but …' he pointed to the Sheffield site. 'The Bradford and Sheffield teams are working together on this one, with me leading the operation. I've got a team of armed response officers heading to a rendezvous point in Sheffield and have a team of officers ready to surround the area if we spot suspicious activity. Undercover police vehicles, drones and cameras will monitor activity in the vicinity. Now let's get moving. We can fine-tune the plans en route via channel nine on our comms, okay?'

All tiredness gone, Nikki placed a quick call, updating Marcus and checking that Charlie was behaving before grabbing her coat and heading for the door. She and Sajid were waiting for the lift when her phone rang. *Unknown Number*. She almost sent it to voicemail, but something made her answer instead. Maybe it was one of the kids phoning her from a friend's mobile. Restricting her greeting to, 'Hello?', she waited for the caller to identify themselves. When they did, she grabbed Sajid's arm and gestured for him to let the lift go without them and flipped her phone to speaker.

'I'm Dr Matilda Brookes from the Royal Liverpool University Hospital. Your cousin has just identified your brother, Johnny Flynn, for us. He's in a serious condition in our ICU and as next of kin, I think it would be best if you got here as quickly as possible.'

In a split second, her sense of relief was replaced by suspicion. *Brother?* Johnny was her nephew, and she was *not* his next of kin. Candice was. 'I'm sorry, but I'm going to have to confirm your identity before I can speak with you anymore. In the meantime, I suggest you confirm my identity too. I'm Detective Inspector Nikki Parekh with Bradford CID. If you hang up now, check out the number for Trafalgar House police station in Bradford and phone the reception in five minutes and ask for me. They'll redirect you to my desk. Meanwhile, I'll confirm your ID and status with the hospital and await your call.'

'O-kay … this seems all very … strange, but okay, I'll call back.' Without waiting for Sajid to follow her, Nikki retraced her steps to the incident room, brushing past colleagues who were making their way down to vehicles to be part of the Operation Sandglass sting. Her heart was pounding, but she was reluctant to put any faith in Johnny being alive until she'd corroborated the doctor's identity. 'Saj, if this is all legit, I'm going to go to Liverpool. I have to follow up on this lead with Johnny and if this doctor pans out, it looks like he's in a bad way. Time is of the essence, but you need to go with Jewkes. He's struggling with numbers as it is.'

Sajid nodded. 'I thought that myself, Nik. I'll hang on till we know what the situation is and then you need to get to Johnny. He might have information for us.'

Nikki wasn't convinced of that, but they had to try. Seeing her hands trembling, Sajid nudged her out of the way and put in a call to the Liverpool hospital for her. Once they had confirmation from Matilda Brookes's superior that she was a doctor at the hospital and was indeed working in the ICU that day and that she had made the call to Nikki regarding her patient, Johnny Flynn, Nikki relaxed. 'You need to go, Saj. I'll speak with her and then head to Liverpool. You update Jewkes and I'll keep in touch.'

Before she'd even finished her sentence, Saj was out the door and Nikki had her phone out, sending a text to Marcus to update him on what had transpired. Within the allotted five minutes, Nikki's desk phone rang, and she lifted the receiver to hear the same voice. 'Hello, Dr Brookes? Sorry for all the cloak and dagger stuff, but we're in the middle of an active investigation that Johnny Flynn might be able to assist us with.'

'So, he's not your brother?'

Nikki could hear the doctor's frustration rolling down the line. 'No, but he is my nephew, and we suspect he has been the victim of a crime. I don't have a lot of time, so can you just answer a few questions and then I'll leave you to it.'

In a brisk voice, Dr Brookes said, 'Go ahead, shoot.'

'How did Johnny end up in ICU?'

'He was dropped at the A&E entrance two days ago with critical internal injuries. He's been drifting in and out of consciousness since. Earlier, a young woman came in and identified him as your brother Johnny Flynn. She left abruptly. As per hospital protocol in such incidences, security have been instructed to access camera footage of the reception area and the entrance to ICU in case that might help the police.'

Nikki smiled. She liked this level-headed doctor already. 'Is he going to make it?'

When the doctor hesitated, Nikki sighed. 'Okay. I'm on my way. Expect me in an hour and a half. Keep him alive till then and if he comes round and says anything, make sure it gets written down. It could be important.'

After hanging up, Nikki settled herself by inhaling, then set off at a jog. She'd put her foot down and have the sirens on, for she was determined to get to Liverpool well ahead of time.

Chapter 59

It felt like every part of Jacko's body throbbed. Fugly had been careful not to kill him, but still he'd been brutal, making sure he suffered for his betrayal. Even the kids looked unsettled, but Fugly didn't seem to notice. The worst thing was that his crucifix had been ripped from his neck and flung to the side. It had comforted him having it there close to his chest, but now it was lost and with it, so was Jacko's hope.

Like a wounded animal, he shivered against the cold and his pain. He wasn't long for this earth, but he held out hope for his wife and granddaughter … and for the lad. He didn't even know his name, but he hoped he'd got him to the hospital in time. Nobody deserved to die like that, nobody.

The door opened, but Jacko was too fatigued to even open his eyes. What was coming was coming and there was nowt he could do about it. If Fugly didn't kill him off here, then the dogs would later on. He'd already decided that he would not run. Would not put on a show. He was going to curl up in a ball and let the dogs have him. He was too weak and too old for any of this and he'd no fight left. Fugly had won. A foot caught him in the kidney and an explosion of pain radiated from the spot right over Jacko's body.

'Open your fucking eyes, you old bastard.'

Jacko didn't need to open his eyes to recognise Fugly's voice, so he kept them shut. Maybe if he refused to obey him, Fugly would lose control and put him out of his misery for good. Waiting for the next kick to land, Jacko relaxed his body. He wanted it to do maximum damage. Wanted this over with, so there was no point in bracing himself against it. This one landed in his belly and sent him flying a few inches over the stinking floor. Despite his best intentions, his eyes flew open as the air left his lungs. It was then he knew he was in hell, for there, cowering next to Fugly, was his daughter. Sores by her lips, her pupils dilated, crusty scabs up and down her arms, she shivered in her mini skirt and boob tube and looked down at her father with no sign of recognition.

'Brought you a visitor, Jacko, my old friend.' Fugly leaned close to his one-time employee. His cold eyes pierced through Jacko, right to his heart. 'She's on your team. All we have to do is draw straws to see which one of you goes first. You two are the warm-up act.'

He turned and gestured to the two kids hovering by the door. 'Pack the two of them up. It's almost time to set off.'

Chapter 60

Charlie couldn't believe it worked! The Rubster came up trumps and distracted Marcus till she made her escape. Little cow wanted twenty quid for it, though. Greedy little bitch! Mind you, it would be worth it. It had been ages since she'd seen Maz.

Charlie: Got out of Fort Knox! ☺ See You Soon.

M: Already here. Get a move on!

As she looked at his text, her heart broke a little. No matter how hard she tried, someone always seemed to get hurt.

Chapter 61

Thank God for sirens!

Nikki was making good time, despite the weather. Still, she pushed the unmarked police car she'd borrowed faster. She didn't know how much time Johnny had left and she needed to get there. The doctor had said he was drifting in and out of consciousness, so maybe he'd be able to speak to her. Maybe he could confirm it was Downey who'd taken him. She'd spoken to Marcus, and he'd agreed to let Josie know what had happened, which left Nikki free to focus on her driving and working out what else she could do on her arrival at the hospital.

The only thing that made sense about Johnny being dumped in a Liverpool hospital was that either at or after the Chester dog fight, he'd been injured and so Downey or one of his men had dumped him. Perhaps he was proving to be a liability. It made some sort of sense that rather than dump him in Chester, Downey had opted to distance him from the scene of his last crime. However, what made little sense to Nikki was that someone had ID'd Johnny and given her name as next of kin. Was she one of Downey's gang who felt bad about what had happened to Johnny? Or … the more she thought about it, the more she sensed Downey's hand behind it all. Nothing ever happened without good reason in Downey-land.

The ringing of her phone interrupted her thoughts: Marcus. Using the hands free, she answered. 'How did Josie take it, Marcus?'

But Marcus's worried voice broke through the static of the line, sending a chill up Nikki's spine. 'Charlie's snuck out again. Little cow bribed Ruby to distract me, and she's gone out.'

The words hung in the air, and Nikki eased her foot a little off the accelerator. She was almost at the hospital. The turn-off was just up ahead. She was too close to Johnny to turn round and head back to Bradford.

A thought barrelled into her brain. 'He's behind this, Marcus. Downey. He's set me off on a wild goose chase and then lured Charlie out. You *need* to get Archie on this. Archie isn't a copper anymore, so he'll work under the radar with you. He'll get whatever needs doing, done. Also we need Ali and his team for this one. You lot need to get out looking for Charlie, before it's …'

'Nik, I put a track on the kids' phones. I can see where she is right now. Don't worry. I got this.'

Nikki's breath hitched in her throat. Marcus's calmness grounded her. 'Take Archie and Ali with you all the same, Marcus. Downey's behind this, I'm sure of it … and keep me informed. I'll make sure I pick up. I need to know she's safe.'

'I got this Nik. You focus on Johnny.' He paused. 'I'll keep Ahad in the loop too, Nik. He needs to know what we're thinking.'

'Okay …' Nikki paused, before adding, 'I love you, Marcus.'

The smile in his voice as he replied warmed her heart. 'You too, Nik. Don't worry.' Then he hung up just as Nikki entered the grounds of the Royal Liverpool University Hospital. Slowly driving round the car park, she spotted a space that she reckoned she could just about get into. Ignoring the car behind her that was right up her arse, making it more difficult to manoeuvre, she edged forward and reversed into the space, mumbling to herself about inconsiderate drivers.

Shoving her personal phone into the waistband of her jeans so she'd feel it vibrate, she flung the car door open and got out into the freezing Liverpool air. She was zipping up her jacket when she sensed movement behind her. A flash of panic fluttered through her and was instantly dismissed as her training kicked in. Rather than step away from the person, she took a large step towards them, crowding their space, making it harder for them to attack. It was a tall girl with a tattoo on her neck and behind her was another girl – a teenager, with turquoise hair and eyebrow piercings. Raising her arm across her body in a defensive move, Nikki stopped the knife from slashing her chest, but felt the sting of it slicing her arm through her new jacket. Because of Nikki narrowing the distance between them, the thrust was less powerful than it might have been. Nikki was incensed and raised the heel of her hand up in a sharp jab, hitting the scraggly woman on the nose, causing a gush of blood to splatter all over the ground.

She moved forward, stepping past the woman to take on the one standing behind her, when she heard a familiar voice. 'Now, now, Parekh. Temper, temper. I think you get that from your poor deceased mama, don't you?'

Heart thundering, her stomach coiled in anger, Nikki spun round, fists raised, but they outnumbered her. Two lads moved in front of Downey, grinning at him like the useless sycophants they were, desperate for any morsel of praise he might give, whilst the two girls yanked her arms behind her back and zip-tied them together.

'How did she get the drop on you, you useless piece of shit?' Downey sneered at the girl with the bloody nose and then back-handed her, before turning to the other girl, 'Finish it, now!'

Nikki struggled, but a sharp prick in her neck made the world before her flicker and the last thing she saw was Downey's leering face as he dipped his hand into her pocket and grabbed her phone. 'Night, night, Nikki. Boy, do *you* have a night ahead of you.'

Chapter 62

When Nikki came round, she didn't know how much time had passed, but the movement told her she was in some sort of vehicle. A dull buzzing filled her head like someone had let loose a beehive in there. Her mouth was dry and her arm throbbed where she'd been knifed. Every time she moved it she felt blood oozing from it. The bitch had ruined the coat Marcus had given her. *I'll make her pay for that*. With her eyes still shut, she listened for clues of her whereabouts. An Ed Sheeran song drifted from the front of the vehicle, but it was faint, so Nikki assumed she was in the back of an enclosed van, with a cabin at the front.

Straining to decipher any other sounds, she moved her head to the side. Was that the faint sound of breathing? She frowned. Now *that* was definitely a moan. Reluctant to assume that her companions might be friends, Nikki, inch by inch, uncurled her numb legs, hoping her action wouldn't alert anyone to her wakefulness.

Now that the prickly sensation was leaving her lower limbs, Nikki considered her situation. She was in Downey's clutches, but who were the other people? Then a dreadful thought struck her. What if he had Charlie in here? A wave of panic surged to her throat from her gut, bringing with it searing acid. She had no idea how long she'd been out. No idea of the time or where they were. Had they had time to get to Bradford and snatch her child?

Realising she was losing control of herself, she inhaled slowly through her nose and out through her mouth. *Think, Nikki, think!* The slow breathing helped her gather her thoughts. She knew that DI Jewkes's cyber team had pinpointed two viable locations. If they were right, then the chances were that she was heading to one or other of those locations and she knew something Downey didn't. She would have back-up there. Things didn't seem quite so bad now, so maybe it was time to work out who else was in the van with her.

Opening her eyes, she peered around the dark van, the interior lit only by the occasional headlights of vehicles on the road behind them and the streetlights. She didn't think they'd reached the inevitable B roads and mud tracks that they would need to take to get far enough away from public scrutiny for their barbaric hunt, which was a good thing. It meant she had time to work out a plan of action. To her right were two bodies, both lying in the foetal position. She studied them and ascertained that one looked to be an emaciated girl who was under-dressed for the weather. She twitched occasionally, but other than that didn't move. The other person was larger and appeared to be male and much older. As Nikki peered through the gloom, she realised he was watching her through swollen eyes.

Nikki kept her voice to a whisper. 'Who are you?'

The man opened his mouth to speak, but no words came out. He swallowed and tried again. 'Jacko. Name's Jacko.' He rolled over, so he was more clearly in her line of vision, wincing with every movement. 'We need to get you out of here. They'll kill you otherwise. Me? I'm already a goner, as is she. Poor kid's a junkie. She'll not survive the night. He's got a big hunt planned for tonight, has Fugly.'

Nikki frowned. She'd seen Downey back at the hospital, so who the hell was this other man. 'Fugly?'

With a wheezing chuckle that made him cough, Jacko winced and took a minute to catch his breath before replying. 'Fucking Ugly ... get it? That's why I call him Fugly. Disgusting psychopath. Saw a passport once at the back of a drawer. Had the name Downey on it, but we just called him boss.'

Nikki relaxed. Downey was in charge, which would make it even more satisfying when Operation Sandglass brought him down. Using her tied-up hands for leverage, she shuffled towards him so they could converse more easily. The poor old sod's face was a mass of angry bruises, blood-smeared lips and nose, and a weeping cut across his eyebrow in desperate need of stitches. Injecting as much confidence into her tone as she could muster, Nikki smiled. 'We're all going to get out of here in one piece, okay? The police have identified two locations. They've sent armed teams to each one. We'll catch this Fugly guy and we'll be okay.'

A smile flitted across Jacko's face. 'Dean Mill Reservoir near Bolton?'

A flicker of uncertainty fluttered in Nikki's chest. 'No, no, the locations we've identified are Clough Pike mountain peak near Lancaster and Trout Sike near Sheffield.'

The old man rolled onto his back, his whole body convulsing as waves of hysterical laughter overtook him. When his laughter ground to a halt, he looked at her. 'Nobody's coming to help you, lass. You're on your own.'

For a moment, Nikki almost allowed panic to engulf her, then she shook her head. She had three kids and Marcus to live for ... and her sister and Haqib ... and Saj and Langley ... and her new family from Oldham. She would not die on them. No fucking way was she about to let Freddie Downey win. 'I'm not on my own. I'm with you. We'll do this together.'

She thought for a moment, then remembered something. Edging closer to Jacko, using all her energy to propel herself so she lay right in front of him, her head parallel to his, she said with a voice a whisper of urgency, 'Jacko. You need to unzip my jacket and pull up my jumper. I've got a phone in the waistband of my jeans. They took my work one, but this is my personal one. We need to get it out and hope we get a phone signal before we go out of range.'

Jacko didn't appear to be tied up, but he was weak and any movements he managed were cumbersome and made him sweat as pain wracked his body. 'I can't do it, lass.'

Nikki glared at him. She'd no time for this. If Sajid was here, he'd be able to cajole the old guy into cooperating, but that wasn't one of Nikki's skills. Instead, she growled at him. 'Just fucking do it. I'm not asking you, I'm telling you.'

Her anger worked, for Jacko gave a slight nod. His fingers on one hand were broken, but he persevered. It took forever, but finally, her zip was down and Jacko could yank her jumper up a little to reveal the phone. Extracting it from her waistband took another eternity, and Nikki was sure that at any moment the van would bounce off the main road and onto a deserted mud track with no phone signal. Jacko had the phone on the floor in front of him. 'I got it, lass. I got your phone.'

Scarcely daring to hope this would work, Nikki kept her voice calm, although inside her gut was squirming. 'My security code is a large N. Can you do that?'

Jacko focused completely on the task in hand, with his left hand drew an 'N' on the security screen, to unlock the phone. 'There's no signal lass. It's hopeless.'

But Nikki wasn't to be defeated. 'Look. Open up the contacts and find Marcus.'

Ham-fisted, he struggled with that, whilst Nikki held her breath and willed him to succeed. 'Got it? Open up a text message to him'

'Done.'

'Okay, keep touching the screen to keep it active and type in: "Big Hunt Dean Mill Reservoir Bolton. Help. Nik." Then keep an eye on the signal and if it comes live send the damn text, okay?'

As he typed with one of his unbroken fingers, Nikki slid her

313

way over to the drugged-up girl. Her breathing was shallow, her chest hardly lifting with each breath. But at least she was alive. Nikki allowed her gaze to travel down the girl, hoping for something that might prove useful – earrings, a necklace with a sharp point, but there was nothing … until Nikki noticed the belt on her mini skirt. Knowing that she had to take advantage of any opportunity no matter how slim, Nikki turned her back to the girl and used her bound hands to locate the belt. If she could unbuckle it, maybe Jacko could use the metal bit to cut her ties.

Seeing what she was trying to do, Jacko said, 'Psst, over here girl.'

Nikki looked over and saw he was attempting to get something from his jacket pocket. 'Picked it up off the floor in the barn. Thought it might come in handy. Was going to use it on myself.'

Nikki looked at the broken shard of mirror in Jacko's hands. *Why didn't you remember this earlier?* But now wasn't the time for admonitions. Crawling back towards him, she rolled onto her side and said, 'Cut.'

His aim was poor and Nikki's wrists were raw and bloody by the time the plastic ties slit apart. She didn't care though; she was used to smarting wrists. Pulling her hands to the front, she flexed her fingers. The old man offered her the mirror. 'If anybody's got a chance of getting away from them, it's you, lass. I'll keep an eye on the phone signal, you see what else you can find to help you before it's too late.'

Nikki got to her feet, ignoring the wobble in her knees. Careful not to alert the people in the cabin, she moved round the trailer, but there was nothing. Not a thing. Then—

'Done it. Bloody done it, lass.'

Nikki hardly dared to think he'd managed to send the text to Marcus, but when she retrieved the phone from him, she saw it had indeed gone through. But that was the end of their good luck, for the signal had disappeared and the ride became bumpier. They were nearing their destination, getting further and further from civilisation, in more ways than one.

As they bumped their way across hostile terrain, Nikki wrapped an old rag round the shard of mirror, whilst making sure she kept her arms and legs moving. Last thing she wanted was for her to be numb and unable to move when they opened the back doors.

She couldn't tell how much time had passed till the vehicle slowed down. Without the sound of the engine in her ears, Nikki could hear the wind whipping around the van and the ominous snarls and barks of dogs getting closer by the second. She positioned herself to the middle of the door. It opened upwards, and she hoped to aim for under the armpit of the person who opened the doors, whilst thrusting herself out.

A knock on the van's tailgate made her jump. Then the taunting sing-song voice of Freddie Downey filled her ears. '*Nikki Parekh come out to play. Today's the day, I'll make you pay.*'

The door opened and Nikki lunged, but hit fresh air. Instead, the same two lads she'd seen earlier pushed her back into the van. Downey grinned. 'Nikki, Nikki, Nikki, did you *really* think I wouldn't keep my beady eye on you?'

He turned his phone towards her, showing an image of the interior of the van from the direction of the cabin. Nikki glanced behind her and sure enough, nearly undetectable on the divide between the trailer and the cabin was a small camera. How had she not noticed that? But Downey was still talking, taunting her. 'As for that phone. Well, that message is easily dealt with.'

He signalled for the lads to take the phone from Jacko, who valiantly but ineffectually tried to fend them off. When they brought the phone back to Downey, he grabbed Nikki's finger to open it and started a fresh text to Marcus. 'False alarm, babe. Johnny got it wrong.' He looked at her, 'Smiley face or kissy face with a love heart? Kissy face, I think.'

Nikki didn't care how he ended the text. She hoped that Downey's use of 'babe' and the accompanying emojis would be enough to alert Marcus that things weren't as they should be.

He slipped her phone into his pocket and signalled for Nikki to be brought from the vehicle. It was only then, that she noticed the hordes of people watching with gleeful expressions, but in silence. They seemed to be grouped in fives or sixes with the leader of each group holding a dog on an extended leash. Nikki's heart sank. To her left was a group of kids, some male, some female, their heads bowed and their hands zip-tied before them, shivering in the frosty night air. Floodlights lit up this area – a clearing large enough to hold at least twenty vans and minibuses, but beyond that into the velvety night there was only moonlight illuminating the terrain.

Downey looked at her, his grin widening. 'Well, since you're so keen, perhaps you can be the opening act for tonight's entertainment.' The whoops of the crowd were deafening and Nikki wondered what had happened to these people to make them behave this way. As if the human reaction was a catalyst, the dogs began snarling and straining at their leads, their broad shoulders telling Nikki that these dogs were the illegally bred American pit-bulls Jewkes had told her about. Their fangs glowed in the light, saliva and canine sweat filled the air, and Nikki's blood iced over. The death Downey had planned for her was an abomination, but she lifted her chin and glared at him, showing no fear.

He walked over, licked his finger and then ran it over the scar on her throat. Still defiant, Nikki refused to flinch. If he won this battle, then it would be on her terms, not his. He might want to see her grovel but she never would. His win would always be tainted by the knowledge that although he might have killed her, he hadn't managed to break her.

Face dark, lips curled up in a ferocious snarl he leaned close to her. 'Bitch – I'll gut you like I did your whore of a mother.'

Then he turned and waved to a man who carried a flag similar to the ones used in motor racing. 'Give her a two-minute lead. It's more than she deserves, but we're not animals, are we?'

The crowd clapped and jeered at his words, champing at the

bit to set off after her and Nikki had no option but to comply. When the raised flag fell to the ground, she took off running because the hounds of hell were after her.

Chapter 63

Marcus wanted to scream. He'd held it together when talking to Nikki on the phone. She had enough to worry about without panicking about Charlie's welfare. Every muscle in his body quivered when he thought about how their normally so sensible, eldest daughter had deliberately involved her younger sister in a deception that could lead to Charlie being hurt or worse. Ali was already out with a group of his friends scouring the streets for sightings of his son, but Marcus had contacted Archie, Nikki's ex-boss and new gaffer of his own private security company, as back-up. Archie was older, but with decades of police experience and Marcus trusted him with his life. Archie wouldn't hold back, especially now he wasn't restricted by being in the police, when it came to putting an end to Freddie Downey. Besides, Ruby had come up trumps by telling him where her sister had gone. But more than that, she'd slipped her own phone into her sister's backpack because she knew Charlie was leaving hers behind. Thank God that Ruby had finally realised that dobbing her sister in was necessary or he'd have had no idea where Charlie was. By tracking Ruby's phone, he could keep tabs on Charlie's movements providing she still had it on her person. It had led him to the Rec.

Now it was dark, the Rec was locked up for the night, so

Marcus headed straight for the broken fence. As he got to the alley behind the row of shops, Archie's large frame pulled away from the shadows and began walking in a sprightly fashion to the fence. Just having the older man's solid presence there, settled Marcus and the weight in his chest eased. Archie reached the broken fence first and with a hefty pull, yanked it back, creating a space big enough for even his substantial form to squeeze through. Once inside the moonlit park, Marcus, phone in one hand, tracked the dot that signified Charlie's position. Breath billowing in huge clouds before him, Marcus ran ahead, soon leaving Archie dawdling behind, but it wasn't far now. Just round the corner.

As he got closer to the bend, voices drifted towards him on the night air, and he paused, catching his breath, in case he needed to act fast. He couldn't make out the words, but he was sure one of them was Charlie. Creeping, he edged over to the hedge and poked his head round. There, sitting on a bench were Charlie and Maz. Marcus exhaled and then moved round the hedge towards the couple. 'Just taking a little walk, are you, kids?'

Maz jumped to his feet, his eyes darting all around as if he expected to be attacked from all directions. A momentary twinge of guilt made Marcus raise his hand palm outwards in a reassuring gesture. Course the kid was on edge. It was only a few months earlier that he'd been attacked nearby. 'It's okay, Maz. It's only me and Archie.'

By now, Archie too had skirted the hedge and stood behind Marcus, panting and glaring at the teenagers. Maz licked his lips, his eyes doing a second scan of the area and Marcus was sure he was going to run. However, Charlie, throwing a tight-lipped scowl at Marcus, placed her arm on his arm. 'Game's up, Maz. You can't run. You never could run away.'

Run away? The words echoed in Marcus's head. Was Charlie thinking of running away with Maz? Was that what all this was about? He met Charlie's scorching glare, batted it away and took a step forward, trying to swallow the hurt that pricked at the back of his eyes. 'You were going to run away, Charl. With *him*?'

She rolled her eyes and snorted. Her eyes flashing with impatience and … was that disappointment? Disappointment in him? 'Don't be an idiot, Marcus. What do you take me for? Course I wasn't going to run away with Maz. I just wanted to stop *him* from running.' She turned to Maz. 'That would be the single most stupid thing you could do. You'd kill your mum. I know it'd kill mine if I left. I've been thinking about this, Maz. We both need to grow up a bit, and prove that we're not kids anymore. We've got plenty of time. That's all. They nearly lost you and …'

Marcus's phone rang and seeing it was Williams, he sighed. The lad probably wanted to speak to Nikki, but no doubt she'd be in the middle of things. He declined the call and was just about to reprimand Charlie some more, when his phone rang again. Williams was being persistent. 'What's up, Williams? I'm busy.'

'The boss didn't arrive at the hospital, Marcus, and she's not picking up.'

Marcus felt like he'd been sucker punched. When he'd spoken to her less than an hour earlier, she'd been entering the car park She should have been there. Signalling for Archie to listen in, he flicked the call to speaker. 'Go on, Williams, what else?'

The lad's voice wavered, but he didn't hesitate. 'Someone reported a fight in the car park and when the police arrived at the scene, they found blood and an unlocked vehicle. They ran the plates. That was the car the boss signed out. They sent me the CCTV footage of the fight and although it's grainy, it's her. It's definitely the boss.' His voice lowered. 'There were five of them and …'

He didn't need to finish for Marcus had got there first, 'One of them is Downey.'

For long seconds the little quartet in the park were silent. Then Archie stamped his foot. 'Ducking Downey. If I get my proverbials on …'

But Charlie interrupted. 'What are you waiting for?' The girl inhaled, her flashing eyes trained on Marcus, her face pale. 'Go! Go and get my mum. I'll look after the kids.'

Marcus and Archie turned, but Williams's next words stilled them. 'Johnny Flynn died.'

Marcus paused, then thrust the thought aside. He had to think of Nikki now. He'd worry about Johnny's family later, when she was safe. 'The doctor told me he said something before he died.'

'Dinnae mess about, lad. Tell us …' Archie's accent was more pronounced now, signifying his distress.

'So … sorry sir … it's just he … Look … he said, 'tell Nikki, Dean Mill Reservoir'. I checked, it's near Bolton.'

Marcus frowned. Operation Sandglass were focusing on two different locations and neither of them was near Bolton. 'Have you tracked her work phone? I've tracked her personal one but it's gone dead.'

'Yep. No hits. It looks like it's been disabled. Last known location was by the Mersey.'

Marcus scratched his chin. 'Right, get me GPS location for this Dean Mill Reservoir, Williams, pronto. Me and Archie are heading there. You need to contact Malik and Jewkes. They've got the location wrong. I'm certain of it.'

He turned to Charlie and Maz. 'You two back to the house. You …' He glared at the boy, who looked ready to faint. 'Tell your dad to get himself and as many of his team over there now. Tell him to bring whatever weapons he can get his hands on.' And without waiting for a reply, he and Archie ran back to Archie's car.

As Archie drove, Marcus accessed the tracking app for Nikki's personal phone. He doubted he'd be lucky, but he got a hit. It was tracking her movements, and it looked like she, or at least her phone, was travelling along the A675 towards Bolton.

'Ye dinnae think he's pulling a proverbial on us, dae ye lad?' Archie, breaking the speed limit as he drove, glanced at Marcus.

Marcus shrugged. The thought had crossed his mind. Downey

was tricksy. He only hoped that the other two locations were the tricks and that this one was the real deal. He didn't know what he'd do if he lost her. It just didn't bear thinking about. There had been a time the previous year when he'd thought she'd never come back to him, but she had. She'd fought her way back, and it was that knowledge that gave him hope. Nikki was a fighter. She'd not let Freddie Downey win easily.

His phone vibrated and he glance at the screen. Then his heart leapt. A text had just come in from Nikki. It was misspelt and strange:

Big hunt deen mill resrvire Bolton help Nick

Although the location was the same as the one Johnny had given, Marcus worried about the misspellings, and especially the one with her name. Was Downey leading him and Archie down a rabbit hole? He'd no idea, but he also had no options. Jewkes's teams were covering the other sites, all he could go on was his gut.

He pressed the phone to his heart as if forging an invisible link between himself and Nikki through the text message and he remained like that till he got another text.

Ali: on our way twenty minutes out.

Marcus looked at the sat nav. He and Archie were ten minutes out. Archie pressed his foot to the floor, narrowing the distance between him and Nikki. Fuck, he hoped they'd be in time.

Chapter 64

With her heart hammering against her chest, her feet pounded the uneven ground. Snow fell in thick horizontal lines, drenching her as it soaked into her inadequate clothing. But she was thankful for it, as in this stark unfamiliar wilderness, it was only the snow and darkness that concealed her. Her jeans, heavy with moisture, wrapped her thighs like icy tentacles. Her hair dripped glacial droplets which unerringly found their way down the gap between her soaked scarf and the back of her sodden coat. Shivers rocked her body; still, she continued, slipping and sliding forwards over the rugged ground, aiming for a small grouping of trees in the distance that might offer cover. She muttered words of encouragement to herself under her breath as she ran. Whistles and whoops echoed eerily through the murky night as she tried to get her bearings, but with only the moon casting light over the unfamiliar terrain and her vision obscured by the sleet, she was lost. Erratic flashes of activity far in front of her and to the side drew her attention as she strained to make sense of them. Torches flickered, indistinguishable shadows flitted, restless shapes inexorably moved towards her, surrounding her – and not one of them was friendly. Deep in her gut she knew she was on her own, with her pursuers catching up. She glanced behind, seeking out the menacing looming figures drawing closer with every second. Then, the taunt pierced the night air.

'Little girl come out to play. Today's the day, I'll make you pay.'

Icy shudders racked her spine as the realisation hit that nobody was coming to help her. She paused to catch her breath, her eyes flitting around hoping to see an escape route, then a rustling sound to her right jolted her into action. *The dogs?* No, too small. *Foxes? Squirrels? Rats?* The mere thought of their swishy tails and beady eyes unfroze her, and she scrambled away from the sound, all her senses on high alert, uncaring that her agitated clambering might pinpoint her location for the hunters. In her haste she stumbled and her foot caught in a tree root, pitching her forward as her forehead crashed onto a tree trunk, grazing the skin and momentarily stunning her. She blinked, willing herself to remain conscious, determined not to be discovered lying here like a rag doll with no fight left. She attempted to roll onto her back, muffling a yelp as excruciating pain stabbed through her leg. Never mind her head injury, it was her ankle that was of most concern. It was wedged tight in the knotty root. With a whimper, she tried to tease it out, but it wouldn't loosen and the pain made her eyes water. Conscious of the ever-nearing sounds of her pursuers, she reached down and with frozen clumsy fingers finally undid the laces of her Doc Martens.

Ignoring the stiffness in her joints, she persevered until she loosened the boot enough to ease her injured foot out. At last it popped free of its leather casing. Agonising shockwaves ripped through her, causing her to bite her lip to stop the yelps that sprung up from her throat. With closed eyes, she counted to three, grounding herself, allowing the pain to recede before she retrieved her boot from the gnarly hole. Her ankle was starting to swell, so she slackened her boot as far as possible and, once more biting against the pain, she shoved her foot back in, ignoring the nausea that rose in her throat. With short steadying breaths, she pulled the laces tight and struggled upright, ignoring the insistent jeers that reverberated through the night.

'*Nikki Parekh come out to play. Today's the day, I'll make you pay.*'

Her fingers savoured the raspy texture of the tree bark. Its solidity made her feel safer, and whilst its hugeness dwarfed her, she enjoyed the sensation of such a large solid structure casting its leafless branches over her. For a moment she basked in its refuge. She couldn't stay here though, not with her enemies thrashing through the undergrowth. Their animals were leashed at present, but their growling and panting terrified her – she knew she couldn't outrun a dog. She could tell by the guttural straining grunts of the men that they were yanking them back, fuelling the creatures' anger so that when they were released, they would be ruthless in their pursuit of their prey. It had been a long time coming and now she had no option but to accept her fate. What else could she do? No one was going to sweep in and rescue her, she was on her own. Alone except for her aggressors. Alone except for the men who had lost all grasp of humanity and the pets they had groomed for this sort of sport. With no other option, she tested her ankle, wincing as pain shot up her leg. *Come on, you can do this. Mind over matter and all that crap. You've got to get away. You can't let him win!*

For a moment, she considered which direction to follow. Some of her assailants had driven to the opposite side of the moors and now approached from that direction. They'd fanned out to the sides, so no matter which track she took, they'd find her. The whistles and cat calls closed in on her, the muffled effect of the snow making them creepier and more threatening. Gruff male voices calling obscenities into the night accompanied by the feral barking and growling of dogs made her heart hammer louder and faster.

'*Nikki Parekh come out to play. Today's the day, I'll make you pay.*'

Sweat poured down her face despite the ice-cold air and she spun round. The voices approached from all directions. It was like being trapped in the middle of a mosh pit with banging thumping music assaulting her ears. The abrasive sounds engulfed her, getting nearer and nearer. They were so close she could almost smell their animal odour, feel their feral eyes scorching her skin. Whatever move she made now would alert them to her position.

'Nikki Parekh come out to play. Today's the day, I'll make you pay.'

She hirpled on for fifty yards, a few steps forward, a few to her right, a few to her left, attempting to disguise her position. Each step damaged her ankle further, each step brought the risk of her falling, each step increased the likelihood that they'd spot her. What was she doing? Whichever direction she turned, they were there, in front of her, ready to set their animals on her. Eager to watch them ripping her limb from limb. Desperate to hear her panicked cries and pleas as the dogs tore her body apart for their enjoyment. She had nowhere to go. The hounds would sniff her out, sensing her fear, they'd hunt her down, and she'd be at their mercy. Before long they'd release the rabid beasts from their leashes and she'd be finished.

'Nikki Parekh come out to play. Today's the day, I'll make you pay.'

With her back to a tree, her feverish eyes scanned the shadows, as they all blurred into amorphous unidentifiable shapes by the continued sleet. They were alive with activity, blending in and out of form, swaying before her, threatening to engulf her. As sweat and snow dripped into her eyes, the images blurred becoming increasingly menacing. Her fingers grappled around for a weapon, anything she could use to protect herself – a branch, a rock – but they came up empty. She sank down, drawing her knees in, arms wrapped round them as, in a gesture of utter defeat, she dropped her head to rest her brow on her sodden jeans. She waited for the inevitable.

'Nikki Parekh come out to play. Today's the day, I'll make you pay.'

Sharp finger-whistles pierced the air, followed by guffaws and jeers. They had no need for stealth, no need to creep after her, no need to use the age-old skills of actual hunters. Instead, their brute force was sufficient to capture her. Nikki's fingers found her scars. First the one on her neck – rough and long – then the one on her cheek – a mere indent in her skin, yet symbolic of everything she'd been through at the hands of inhumane men. Despite the gnawing in her stomach, she pulled herself to her feet and ignored the flash of pain that shot up her leg from her wrenched ankle and the dull throb where the knife had caught her arm earlier. She ran her hands up the bark, reaching as far and wide as she could, searching for a ridge she could use for a foothold. She was delaying the inevitable, but her anger wouldn't allow her to give up – not yet. Why should she make it easy for them? Let *them* struggle a bit. Make them work for it. When her fingers touched a knot in the trunk, she almost fainted with relief. Bracing her unhurt foot on the ground, she placed her damaged one on the tree and as if shards of glass sliced through her leg, she grabbed the knot and pushed herself up. Balancing two feet from the ground, a hysterical giggle rose to her lips. What was she thinking? She couldn't climb a damn tree. Not with her damaged ankle. Exhaling, she forced the pain to leave her body with her breath. She had time – not a lot of time – but some. She *could* do this. Again, using her fingers, she plotted out the next part of her climb and dragged herself up another two feet. There was a branch above her head. It was spindly and Nikki was unsure if it would hold her weight. If it broke, she'd crash to the sodden ground, no doubt killing herself in the process, but at least she would be unaware of glistening canine fangs ripping her apart.

'Nikki Parekh come out to play. Today's the day, I'll make you pay.'

She hefted herself up and onto the branch. It creaked and groaned before settling into her weight. From her position ten feet from the ground, she was visible to anybody who bothered to glance upwards through the snow. But that wasn't her worry. The dogs would smell her presence and within moments she expected their massive torsos to lunge against the tree, making it shudder and moan in repugnance at their aggression. It would take no time to drag her from her perch and allow the dogs their pleasure.

She hated that those brutes weaponised innocent animals. She hated that they were prepared to escalate their immorality from setting dog against dog, to setting dog against human. Most of all, she hated that they had set her up to die like this at the hands of her own father, Freddie Downey.

Chapter 65

The taunts were louder now. Louder and much more aggressive and Downey's voice was louder than the rest.

'*Nikki Parekh come out to play. Today's the day, I'll make you pay.*'

They wanted blood – her blood. It wouldn't be long now. They were within sight of the tree. The dogs seemed to have scented her, for they were straining on their leashes, pulling their masters towards her refuge. Downey was ahead of the others. He had no dog, but his mouth was curled into a feral snarl as his eyes darted around. The tension around them buzzed as he took another step closer, before executing a slow 360-degree rotation, his eyes peering through the darkness.

'*Nikki Parekh come out to play. Today's the day, I'll make you pay.*'

He paused for a second, then his gimlet eyes bored a path right to her. 'Ah, there you are. Come to Daddy.'

All around him the air erupted with a cacophony of whoops and yelps as the hunters surged towards the tree. Then they were shaking it, the dogs, jumping up at it, their teeth scraping down the bark, their jaws wide, their incisors gleaming in the moonlight. Nikki could hardly hold on. Each time a dog barrelled against the trunk, her tenuous grip loosened. Every face below her was wild and furious. Their mouths spread in dark mimicry of their canine friends – like a less abstract Munch painting.

When her hands finally slipped from their hold and she fell down into the abyss of depravity, she thought of her kids. Her sassy Charlie, arty Ruby and beautiful, funny Sunni. Then she thought of Marcus. She smiled. As she landed, sending dogs scuttling to the side as her weight hit them, she could hear his voice. Distant, yet it sounded like Marcus and that made her happy. If she could just keep hold of his voice whilst they mauled her to death, then it wouldn't be so bad.

Then a thurrump, thurrump, thurrump sound rent through their victorious cries and a forceful gust of wind hit them, making Nikki roll onto her side. As a blinding light illuminated the mossy area, Nikki folded herself into the foetal position. Then arms were gripping at her, pulling her, dragging her … and the animals were still barking, still howling. She fought. Punching and kicking and hitting out until the voice came again, low and calming.

'It's over Nik. I've got you.' She hadn't realised she was sobbing until she opened her eyes and felt Marcus brush her tears away with a gentle finger. He was there, right there and Nikki didn't know if she was dreaming, but she didn't care.

As Marcus pulled her to her feet, she saw a helicopter hovering above her, with officers in full riot gear swinging from ropes as they jumped into the area. All around her other officers – ones she didn't recognise and a few she did – rounded up the hunters. Trained officers had subdued the dogs and managed to lure them into cages using meat. Then Archie was there, his smile making him look like a scary pumpkin, and cars were screeching up with Ali and his mates spilling out almost before they'd ground to a halt. It was like a dream, but she'd take this dream any day after the nightmare she'd just been in. 'Where did you come from?'

Marcus's lopsided grin made her heart skip a beat. We followed your signal till it went dead, but we were so close we made it here at the same time as the helicopter. Thankfully the racket it created made the dogs run away from you and nothing was going to stop me reaching you.'

Nikki slumped against him, her heart still hammering, as she tried to take in the sight before her. She was safe. She'd truly believed that she'd never see Marcus or her kids again. Her hold on him tightened. As her thoughts turned to her daughter. 'Charlie? Is she okay?'

'Relax, Nik. She's fine. Charlie's fine. I'll leave it to you to punish her for all her nonsense.'

Then her eyes swept the periphery. 'Downey?'

Marcus shook his head. 'Not yet.'

'We have to get him.' Nikki's tone was frantic as her hands raked Marcus's arms. 'We can't let him escape. Not this time.'

Marcus smiled and pulled the Swiss army knife he always carried, from his pocket. 'No chance of that, Nik. I'm not letting him leave here alive.'

Then with a last hug, he pushed her towards Archie and was off, running over the marshy ground as if it was a race track.

'No, Marcus'. The words were torn from her throat and, her heart pounding, she tried to pull away from Archie and go after Marcus. But Archie's grip was firm and she couldn't put weight on her foot. 'You've got to stop him, Archie. You've got to stop him. He can't do this. He just can't.' Tears streaked down her filthy face, but she didn't care who saw them as her eyes homed in on the figure running and dodging through the police officers. Was this how it was going to end? Was Downey going to take Marcus from her?

Ali approached. 'You ever going to settle for a quiet life, Parekh?'

But Nikki was too focused on tracking Marcus's progress. He was speeding, gaining on a man who was moving less fluently and who kept looking behind him. With every fibre of her being, Nikki wanted Downey dead, but she'd always envisioned she'd be the one to do it, not Marcus. If he killed Downey she'd lose him.

She wrung her hands together, her head craning to keep track of what was happening, but Ali stood in front of her, his burly frame shielding her from whatever was about to happen.

'It needs to be done, Parekh. You know that and it's best if there're no witnesses.'

Chapter 66

Marcus had never experienced such anger. It was as if his entire body was afire with it and the only thing that could dowse it was doing what he intended to do right now. As soon as he knew Nikki was fine, he'd taken off after Downey. This time, he would end it, once and for all, because if he didn't, then Nikki might try to and he couldn't have that. She had enough baggage without carrying that burden too.

He scarcely noted the uneven ground – one of the benefits of being a landscape gardener: he was used to a variety of terrains, and he was fit. Fitter than the depraved old man who was running ahead of him. With his eye on Downey, he kept going, pushing himself, not noticing the wind whipping his face or the sleet that pelted his cheeks. Downey was making a mistake – a big one! Instead of sticking to the hunt area, where the helicopter hovered, he'd taken the chance to escape into the darkness. This was what Marcus wanted. In the dark, away from everyone else, there would be no witnesses.

He pushed his legs to pump faster and when he was within grabbing distance of Downey, he jumped and tackled the old man to the ground. Marcus's muscled body pinned Downey like a rag doll on the sodded ground and slammed the monster's wrist against the undergrowth until he released the knife he held. Marcus didn't want to end it like this, though, he *had* to give Downey a fighting chance. He wasn't a cold-blooded killer, that was Downey's remit. The old man's halitosis breath hit him as he pulled him to his feet.

'She's got you cock-whipped.' Downey laughed like he'd cracked the best joke ever.

But Marcus just shook him once, before letting go of his lapels. Now Downey was before him, he wavered. He and Nikki had agreed it had to end. That Downey had to be ended, but it wasn't as easy as that.

As if sensing Marcus's indecision, Downey's lips broke into a grin. 'You can't do it, can you?'

Using his foot, Marcus, edged the knife towards Downey. 'Take it. This time you'll not be terrorising an old woman or a vulnerable kid. Nor will you be using your minions to do your dirty work. This time you'll face *me*. Take the fucking knife.' Marcus moved closer and spat the last four words into Downey's face.

'Tt, tt, tt, tt.' Downey shook his head in time with each sound, his dark eyes blazing. 'Why should I make it easy for you?'

Marcus held Downey's gaze but remained silent until Downey bent down and picked up the knife. Before he was upright, he lunged at Marcus, but Marcus was ready for him and dodged it, landing a slice across Downey's forearm as he drew his arm back.

The two men circled each other, sweat pooling at the base of Marcus's spine. Downey jolted forward and Marcus stepped back, his foot wobbling on the uneven ground allowing Downey to nick his abdomen. Marcus ignored the slice of pain and dived forward, his knife plunging into Downey's fleshy belly. He yanked it out and closed in ready for the final thrust. The one that would end it forever.

A shot rang out, loud and clear, even over the helicopter thrum, the dogs and the police activity. Time stood still. A screech of pain tore through the dark and Nikki was running, regardless of her mangled foot towards Marcus. 'No, no, no!'

Ali and Archie kept pace with her, helping her up when she stumbled and all but dragging her onwards. At last they reached Marcus and Downey.

Marcus turned to her, blood pouring down his arm, the knife still in his arm, his eyes wide. 'He's dead.'

Downey lay on the ground at his feet, a bullet hole in his back and beyond them a man stood, gun held loosely in his hand. Nikki hobbled to him. 'Jacko?'

Jacko handed her the gun and collapsed on the floor. 'He had to die, sweetheart. He was too evil to live.'

Nikki handed the gun to Archie who had now reached them and knelt beside Jacko. 'Where did you …?'

He snorted. 'One of those kids left it behind when they went off chasing you. I took my chance. When I saw you falling out of that tree I was going to take as many of them out as possible. But your friends got there first.' He coughed and a bubble of blood appeared at the corner of his mouth. 'Look after the girl in the van, she's my daughter.'

And as the paramedics, alerted by Archie, arrived and loaded him onto a stretcher, Jacko smiled at Nikki. 'Thank you.'

Chapter 67

It felt like Nikki had been in too many hospitals recently. As she lay with her leg elevated in the nearest A&E to where she'd been found, Nikki was still trying to process what had happened. The news that her nephew, Johnny, had died, rocked her to the core. Johnny's last days had been as tormented as the rest of his life had been. Downey's legacy had left Johnny conflicted, but to Nikki, the final indignities he'd suffered at the hands of his own grandfather tortured her. If only she'd connected the illegal dog fights with Downey's activities sooner, perhaps Johnny would still be alive. She'd been blinkered and had taken her eye off the ball, assuming that Downey would focus only on her for his revenge. It had been difficult to bear the grief in Josie's voice during their tearful phone conversation, but what had been harder to bear was the generous way in which Josie absolved Nikki of all responsibility for Johnny's death. If only Nikki could absolve herself so easily.

On the way to the hospital, despite his injuries, Jacko had insisted on sharing everything he knew about Downey's – or Fugly as he called him – activities. The biggest revelation from Jacko was that he'd compiled images and reports of many of Downey's co-conspirators and emailed them to his wife. Officers were currently sifting through the data and Nikki knew that the old man's information would bring a lot of closure for a lot of people. One of Jacko's biggest regrets was not stopping the beating taken by the girl currently recovering in Pinderfields hospital. Whilst they'd whisked Jacko off to surgery Nikki had phoned Pinderfields for an update and couldn't wait to share the news with Jacko that the girl he'd rescued – Amy Brady – was recovering well with her family at her side.

Nikki had a lot to thank Jacko for. Her biggest debt of gratitude was that Jacko's actions had prevented Marcus from killing Downey. Nobody was going to scrutinise Marcus, Archie and Ali's actions too closely. They were all heroes and had provided extra bodies to scoop up the 'hunters' who tried to escape. She gripped Marcus's hand tightly. Despite her throbbing ankle, she smiled at him. No, she wouldn't ever let him go. Marcus was her man. She opened her mouth to tell him so when Archie, grim-faced, swished the curtain aside. 'Got some bad news, Nikki, hen.'

Nikki closed her eyes. *Haven't we had enough?*

'It's Jacko …'

He didn't need to continue for his face said it all. Brave, flawed, Jacko hadn't survived surgery. Yet another victim of Downey. Archie squeezed her arm and with a nod at Marcus, left them alone to cope with even more fallout.

For long minutes, an exhausted Marcus and Nikki, fingers entwined, sat in silence, mulling over everything that had happened. Neither felt ready to put into words what they'd been through, though they both knew that they'd have to make statements soon. Once more the curtain was swished open and this time it was Ahad, followed by Saj who entered. Ahad's eyes raked from Nikki's face to her swollen foot and grimaced. 'You look like crap, Parekh.'

Nikki rolled her eyes. She could cope with his brusque words. If he'd shown one iota of sympathy, Nikki might have cried and for that she would never have forgiven him. She nodded. 'Never felt better, though, boss.'

Sajid pushed past Ahad and engulfed her in a hug. 'You know you're the most annoying, most irritating, most frustrating woman on the planet.'

Nikki summoned a grin and repeated her earlier eye roll. 'That might be true, but I'm still going to be best man at your wedding, Saj, so watch what you're saying. After all, I have my best man's speech to prepare.'

She sank back against the pillow and closed her eyes. All at once her throbbing leg, the adrenalin overload and the memories of just how close she'd been to losing her life made her feel dizzy. As the dizziness took hold, her churned up stomach finally betrayed her and she wrenched forward and vomited into the cardboard bowl one of the nurses had supplied. When her stomach was empty, she looked up at Marcus who held her hair back from her face. They were alone, the curtain closed around them, the lights subdued. 'Fuck, talk about embarrassing myself. If any of them recorded that or ever speaks about what they just witnessed, I'll kill them.'

Marcus removed the bowl and placed it on a chair. He leaned over and kissed her forehead and when he spoke his voice was hoarse and the words came out just a little shakily. 'We're all just glad you made it, Nik. We're all just glad you're still here. Now go to sleep.'

For once, Nikki needed no further telling.

Epilogue

Three Weeks Later

At last, Nikki had time to draw breath. The time since Downey's death had passed in a blur of activity and she'd yet to find time to assess her feelings on the matter. As Operation Sandglass continued to untangle Downey's involvement in criminal activity around dog fighting, breeding and its escalation into human hunt activities, the Downey task force worked on filling in the gaps in their knowledge of Downey's activities. Although he was dead and beyond prosecution, the intelligence that accrued by examining Downey's farmhouse and electronics had opened up several new lines of enquiry. Some led to Dr Helen Mallory and her contacts, some to criminal activity in the dark web and others to gun running, prostitution and drug dealing practised by the criminal gangs also involved in the illegal dog fights. Every day the arrest count increased making everybody involved in both investigations happy, despite being overworked trying to pull it all together.

The vet, Julie Ross, and most of Downey's minions had been arrested and charged with aiding and abetting murder and an assortment of other charges. None of them would see the outside of a prison cell anytime soon. Jacko had died, but Nikki had made good on her promise to check on his daughter and had reunited her with Jacko's wife and her own daughter. Nikki had her doubts whether she'd remain clean – but everyone had to start somewhere.

What had shocked Nikki the most though, had been the number of people who subscribed to the human hunt. Over eighty arrests were made on the night and that was set to increase as more information came to light. What angered Nikki was that many of those whooping and baying for blood as they closed in on her were guardians of society: magistrates, doctors, councillors, lawyers, politicians. Those who spent their daytime hours protecting and upholding the law under a façade of respectability. They'd come from all over the country to take part in the hunting and killing of human prey and it was their privilege that enabled them to do so. It would be a while before Nikki would trust the so-called pillars of society. She and ordinary people like her had been betrayed and hurt by their kind too many times before.

The habit of looking over her shoulder, triple checking her locks, doing a mental inventory of her loved ones' whereabouts was a hard one to kick. She'd lived under the oppressive threat of Downey for so long, that sometimes she forgot he was gone and that they were free from him. Sometimes, at night she'd wake up, heart hammering from a dream where she was falling through the air into the jaws of a snarling dog with faceless people jostling for a better view of her demise. In those times, Marcus, without fully wakening, would put an arm round her and pull her close to him till their heartbeats synchronised.

Johnny's funeral had been a small affair with only his immediate family from Oldham and Nikki's family from Bradford present. Nikki had dreaded it because she felt she'd failed Johnny and as she said her farewells to the nephew she hardly knew, she promised him she'd stay in touch with her extended family.

Nikki looked down first at her half-empty suitcase and then at Marcus's overflowing one. 'Are you sure you need to take your flip flops?'

When he grinned at her, Nikki tried not to wonder if his grin was less bright than before. He'd intended to kill Downey, and she was sure that if Jacko hadn't intervened, then he would have succeeded. That was the one thing she was grateful for in all of this – that Marcus hadn't had to kill a little bit of himself to make them all safe. As for Nikki, well, her burden was lessened. No more Downey to worry about and that had brought an air of relief to the last three weeks.

'We're going to the beach, Nik. Course I'll need my flip flops.'

'Erm …' Nikki nodded towards the window where rain hammered against the panes making the rivulets of water merge into one large slurry. 'You seen the weather, Marcus? It's February, in the north of England. You won't need your flip flops in Filey.'

As Marcus took the flip flops out, and tried to close his suitcase Nikki allowed this feeling of normality to warm her. Ordinary, everyday interactions, without the gloom of Downey darkening the horizon were new to all of them, and they needed time to adjust to their new normality. That was why Marcus had insisted on all of them, including Isaac, Anika and Haqib, taking a winter break away from Bradford. Besides which, Ahad was going to use the time Haqib and Anika were away to move his stuff into his new flat in Bingley. He'd confided to Nikki that he couldn't bear to see Haqib's disappointed face every time he took a box out to his car, and would rather make the move when they were away. Nikki had been relieved to discover that Ahad and her sister were only friends. She'd been worried her sister would be hurt again but, in a rare moment of sibling honesty, Anika had told her she and Ahad had come together as friends over their grief.

Leaving Marcus to carry their suitcases downstairs, Nikki yelled upstairs to Charlie's attic room. 'Come on Charlie. We're nearly ready.'

'At *last*, only two hours later than you said.'

Nikki grinned, for Charlie's voice had come from downstairs. When Nikki poked her head over the banister, Charlie, sitting on her suitcase, beside Marcus, grinned up at her. 'We've been waiting for you.'

At which point Ruby, Sunni and Isaac appeared and stood beside their respective luggage.

'Coooome on Mum, me and Isaac want to have fish and chips when we get there.'

Nikki took a moment to savour the tableau before her. Her relationship with Charlie had improved since Downey's death and although she drew the line at including Maz in their family holiday plans, Nikki had accepted that Charlie needed to spread her wings. Humming a song about holidays under her breath, Nikki jogged downstairs to join them. This was how things should be. These people were her everything.

A Letter from Liz Mistry

Thank you so much for choosing to read *Dying Breath*. I hope you enjoyed it! If you did and would like to be the first to know about my new releases, click below to sign up to my mailing list.

Sign up here: http://bit.ly/LizMistrySignUp

I hope you loved *Dying Breath* and if you did I would be so grateful if you would leave a review. I always love to hear what readers thought, and it helps new readers discover my books too.

Thanks,
Liz

Twitter: https://twitter.com/LizMistryAuthor
Website: https://www.lizmistry.com/

Last Request

When human remains are discovered under Bradford's derelict Odeon car park, DS Nikita Parekh and her team are immediately called to the scene.

Distracted by keeping her young nephew out of trouble, Nikki is relieved when the investigation is transferred to the Cold Case Unit, and she can finally focus on her family.

But after the identity of the victim is revealed, she's soon drawn back into the case. The dead man is a direct link to her painful past.

As the body count begins to rise, Nikki must do everything she can to stop the killer in their tracks before anyone else gets hurt – even if it means digging up secrets she had long kept hidden …

For readers of Angela Marsons and LJ Ross comes a gritty new crime series featuring bold, brave and ferocious D.S. Nikki Parekh! This rip-roaring thriller will have you reading long into the night!

Broken Silence

When Detective Felicity Springer is reported missing, the countdown to find her begins ...

On her way home from a police training conference, **Felicity** notices something odd about the white van in front of her. A hand has punched through the car's rear light and is frantically waving, trying to catch her attention.

Felicity dials 999 and calls it in. But whilst on the phone, she loses control of the car on the icy road, crashing straight into the vehicle ahead.

Pinned in the seat and unable to move, cold air suddenly hits her face. Someone has opened the passenger door ... and they have a gun.

With Felicity missing and no knowledge of whether she is dead or alive, **DS Nikki Parekh** and **DC Sajid Malik** race to find their friend and colleague.

But Felicity was harbouring a terrible secret, and with her life now hanging in the balance, Nikki can only hope that someone will come forward and break the silence ...

The next gripping crime thriller in the D.S. Nikki Parekh series, for fans of Angela Marsons and L.J. Ross!

Dark Memories

**THREE LETTERS. THREE MURDERS.
THE CLOCK IS TICKING …**

When the body of a homeless woman is found under
Bradford's railway arches, **DS Nikki Parekh** and her trusty
partner **DC Sajid Malik** are on the case.

With little evidence, it's impossible to make a breakthrough,
and when Nikki receives a newspaper clipping taunting her
about her lack of progress in catching the killer, she
wonders if she has a personal link to the case.

When another seemingly unrelated body is discovered,
Nikki receives another note. Someone is clearly trying
to send her clues … but who?

And then a third body is found.

This time on Nikki's old street, opposite the house she used
to live in as a child. And there's another message …
underneath the victim's body.

With nothing but the notes to connect the murders, Nikki
must revisit the traumatic events of her childhood to
work out her connection to the investigation.

But some memories are best left forgotten, and it's going to take all Nikki's inner strength to catch the killer …

Before they strike again.

The heart-stopping and totally addictive new crime thriller from Liz Mistry will keep you reading long into the night! Fans of Angela Marsons, Val McDermid and Rachel Abbott will love *Dark Memories*.

Acknowledgements

It never ceases to amaze me how much work goes into getting a book onto the shelves and so many people help along the way. So, I'm going to kick off with giving a mega shout-out to my editor Belinda Toor. Her attention to detail, her insightful comments, suggestions and patience made *Dying Breath* an infinitely better read. Alongside Belinda, the incredible team at HQ work tirelessly behind the scenes from Audrey Linton who is always there moving the process along, to Anna Sikorska who designed such a brilliant cover I was in tears when I saw it, to my fantastic copy editor, Dushi Horti and proof reader Loma Slater who catch all the mistakes I've inevitably missed. HQ is such a lovely family to be part of and I'm just hoping I haven't missed anyone out. Before I send the manuscript I have a couple of trusted ARC readers who tell me if the story should 'leave the room'. Thanks so much Carrie Wakelin and Maureen Webb, for your honesty, support, encouragement and above all your humour and integrity.

My family always play an important part in the process and it goes without saying that I couldn't do it without Nilesh and the kids (although none of them are kids anymore).

One of the most engaging and supportive Facebook book groups is UKCBC (UK Crime Book Club). This group is a source of great joy to me, both as a reader and as a writer, and the positivity and love generated through the group are lifeblood to an author, so huge thanks to all the admin who keep us in check, but especially Carline Maston, David Gilchrist, and Samantha Brownley who are so supportive of my writing.

However, as always, the most important shout-out has to go to you, the reader because your support, commitment to Nikki and the team and the love and joy you share when you shout about Nikki and the books at every opportunity, make my heart sing on a daily basis.

Dear Reader,

We hope you enjoyed reading this book. If you did, we'd be so appreciative if you left a review. It really helps us and the author to bring more books like this to you.

Here at HQ Digital we are dedicated to publishing fiction that will keep you turning the pages into the early hours. Don't want to miss a thing? To find out more about our books, promotions, discover exclusive content and enter competitions you can keep in touch in the following ways:

JOIN OUR COMMUNITY:

Sign up to our new email newsletter:
http://smarturl.it/SignUpHQ

Read our new blog www.hqstories.co.uk

 https://twitter.com/HQStories

www.facebook.com/HQStories

BUDDING WRITER?

We're also looking for authors to join the HQ Digital family!
Find out more here:

https://www.hqstories.co.uk/want-to-write-for-us/

Thanks for reading, from the HQ Digital team